THE SUB

Supernatural Minnesota

The Sub

A STUDY IN WITCHCRAFT

THOMAS M. DISCH

FOREWORD BY ELIZABETH HAND

Supernatural Minnesota 4

University of Minnesota Press
Minneapolis

Originally published in 1999 by Alfred A. Knopf

First University of Minnesota Press edition, 2010

Published by the University of Minnesota Press
111 Third Avenue South, Suite 290
Minneapolis, MN 55401-2520
http://www.upress.umn.edu

Library of Congress Cataloging-in-Publication Data

Disch, Thomas M.
The sub : a study in witchcraft / Thomas M. Disch ; foreword by
Elizabeth Hand. — 1st University of Minnesota Press ed.
p. cm. — (Supernatural Minnesota ; 4)
Originally published: New York : Alfred A. Knopf, 1999.
ISBN 978-0-8166-7220-2 (pb : alk. paper)
I. Hand, Elizabeth. II. Title.
PS3554.I8S8 2010
813'.54—dc22
2010031489

Printed in the United States of America on acid-free paper

The University of Minnesota is an equal-opportunity
educator and employer.

16 15 14 13 12 11 10   10 9 8 7 6 5 4 3 2 1

*To Latasha Pulliam, Mary Ellen Samuels, and
the 37 other ladies on Death Row.*

I would like to thank Matthew Hummingbird, Geraldine Dublin, and Kurt Hagemann for letting me share their knowledge and expertise.

The origin of the pig is shrouded in mystery.

—*Encyclopaedia Britannica*

"I used to be a very good person at one time."

—Dorothy Puente,
age 64, after her arrest for the murders
of nine tenants so that she might
collect their welfare checks

FOREWORD

Elizabeth Hand

Thomas M. Disch's *The Sub*, a bracingly vitriolic dose of Northern Gothic, suggests what might happen to Lake Wobegon if David Lynch came to stay. The fourth in Disch's Supernatural Minnesota novels, it's the only one to feature a female protagonist, the seemingly innocuous Diana Turney, substitute teacher and dowdy vegetarian. Despite her unprepossessing appearance, Diana has a knack for gleeful and rather sadistic subversion. As the novel opens, she's leading her second-graders in a chorus of "Old MacDonald Had a Farm," making certain they make the connection between the song and a younger McDonald. There's no doubt just where all those moo-moos and baa-baas and cluck-clucks will end up—at the working end of a knife and fork. "Hamburgers come from cows. You know that. The cows that you can see off to the side of the highway, browsing on the lovely green grass."

Diana also notes (to herself) how much the children resemble animals: "Surely chubby little Cheryl Sondergard was destined to be a hen, and there were at least two blue-ribbon contestants in the bovine category." And she kindly shares her own childhood experiences of Nature red in tooth and claw and yolk:

> "I grew up on a farm. . . . In the morning I used to go out to the chicken coop and get the eggs the hens had laid. They were there in the straw, still warm. Not like the eggs that come out of your mothers' refrigerators. Sometimes there were little drops of red blood *inside* the egg, which meant it might have become another chicken if we hadn't taken it out of the chicken's nest and fried it."

In *The Sub*, a thin veil separates barnyard life from the rest of the world. Humans are merely another animal species, subject to the same mindless hungers—for food, for sex, for warmth and satiety—as sheep and pigs and snakes and bugs. Diana Turney's gift lies in a newly discovered ability to dissolve that veil: she can discern a person's true, animal nature and, Circe-like, change him or her into whatever creature she or he embodies. Her punning last name signals both her gift and her fate: Diana is a supernatural turner who, at the novel's end, becomes a turnee.

But not before she wastes a number of the inhabitants of Leech Lake, Minnesota (a name I foolishly believed Disch had invented: to paraphrase Dave Barry, he's not making this up). A self-proclaimed witch, Diana comes into her powers after a visit to an astrologer friend named Brenda, who functions as a homespun psychotherapist to clients

> whose tears came like clockwork. She would do their charts, then they'd sit down for a cup of tea and . . . the tears would well up. They'd have their cry, snuffle an apology, and make their good-byes.
>
> But Diana wasn't like that. Her feelings were sealed up like wine in a corked bottle.

Accusations of ritual Satanic abuse have been hurled at some local elementary teachers, and this news finally uncorks Diana. It's a testament to Disch's powers as a satirist that he makes Diana's confession of her own abuse at the hands of her father at once awful and funny, as is Brenda's hilariously restrained excitement at the revelation— "You don't have to tell me any more now if you don't want to. But you might feel better if you do. Sometimes it helps if the pain can be shared."

Sharing the pain turns out to be what Diana is really, really good at—that, and lying. Diana's account of her recovered memories becomes a "strange kind of empowerment . . . So real, so heart-wrenching, so painful, that by the time Diana fell silent, she had begun to believe every word of it herself."

There's little doubt that her father, Wes, is a monstrous figure who sheds moral corruption like fungal spores. Yet it's Diana's re-imagining of whatever happened between them that is the source of her power, a form of spell-casting, of *glamour* in the most ancient sense of the word, deriving from the Icelandic *glamra:* to rattle, to create a public outcry, to defame. "It had happened to her, in the way that poems are said to happen to poets: by an inspiration, a kind of wind filling the sails of speech and sweeping her away."

And so Diana's words are made flesh, and her recovered memories of her father awaken his undying essence—his "potentiality for evil"—which remains in the smokehouse that was the site of both his sexual predations and his death when, after he is injured, Diana refuses to run for help, and he bleeds to death. Years later, after Brenda's confession, Wes's toxic spirit begins to spread like an infernal, unstoppable oil spill:

> If it could have been mapped, it would have resembled layer upon layer of delicate dark lace billowing about the smokehouse, swelling and shrinking like the translucent membranes of a sea anemone, rising sometimes above the small building like a plume of smoke from the chimney, at other times spreading through the underbrush like cilia, searching for the sustenance it was always denied: revenge, recompense, release.
>
> And tonight, as Diana Turney whispered the tale she'd never told before, it was as though a spear had been thrust through the pulsing layers of invisible lace. The cilia of the unseen anemone convulsed and thrashed about until the snake curled up for its wintry sleep beneath the floor of the smokehouse woke and flicked its tail, stiff with the cold, and felt a brief intense spasm of hunger.
>
> And in that spasm the unquiet soul of Wes Turney found, briefly, the breath of a new life.

This reincarnated Wes is an exemplar of raw desire and vengeance: he feeds on the living in a futile effort to fill the black hole that is, or was, his immortal soul. In Tibetan Buddhism, such beings are called *pretas*, hungry ghosts, and inhabit one of the six liminal realms known as *bardos* where living creatures can be reborn. Lama Khenpo Karthar Rinpoche describes them thus:

> The hell realm was in the depths of the earth. Higher up, encompassing places in the earth and water, is the animal realm. The hungry ghost realm is between the hell and animal realms. The human realm is on the surface of the earth. The jealous god realm is above

that of the humans and below that of the gods. The god realms are up in the sky like the stars, and they could also be on the earth.

Alas, the inhabitants of Leech Lake, living, dead, and in-between, are all far from the god realms, earthly or elsewhere, and Diana's return to her roots isn't a normal homecoming, even by Disch's generally loose definition of the word "normal." Her sister, Janet, botched the murder of her philandering husband, Carl, and is now in prison for a year. Diana takes a leave of absence from teaching to care for her brother-in-law and his four-year-old daughter until Janet's release.

What Paris is to romance, Leech Lake is to dysfunctionality— a redneck Riviera that deserves its own page in a white trash Book of the Dead. Against this seedy backdrop of strip malls, tract housing, and defunct farms, not to mention a prison, the nearby Wabasha reservation, and TacoNite Casino, Diana's peculiar gift for sowing mayhem like dragon's teeth is barely noticed. Her transformation into a modern-day Circe is as down-to-earth as the beauty parlor visit that leaves her newly blonde and glamorous, irresistible to the men (and women) she enslaves. She falls off the vegan wagon and rediscovers the "pleasures of protein," acquires some dried mandrake root, used by the local Native Americans in their sweat-lodge rituals, and soon learns that the noxious herb gives her the ability not just to perceive a human's animal form but to transform men to beasts after she has sex with them.

Her first assay is a reenactment of the fate of Actaeon—in Ovid's account an unfortunate hunter who, as punishment for glimpsing the naked Artemis (the Roman Diana), is turned into a stag by the goddess and then torn apart by his own hounds. "They say Diana the Quiver-bearer's anger was not appeased, until his life had ended in innumerable wounds," Anthony S. Kline writes in his translation of the *Metamorphosis*. Disch's version is just as succinct:

> "He's yours," she told the dog, with a savagery now fully conscious and triumphant. "Finish him."

The dog devours his master, and thereafter Diana's power hunger is as unslakable as her father's.

Diana had become a force like the black whirlpool labeled "Drugs" in the videocassette that the Christian Coalition for Family Values had sent. . . . She was evil in the same contagious way as drugs. It didn't make any difference if you were good or bad. If you were bad, the whirlpool would get you in one big slurp. . . . But if you were good, it would get you, too. You might circle around for a while, like a leaf in an eddy, but each circle was a little tighter than the last until it was too late and you were pulled down to wherever whirlpools took you.

She seduces a teenage boy, Alan, who perversely manages to retain his virginity and thereby escapes being transformed. Her slovenly brother-in-law Carl is not so fortunate. While his innate decency (along with a fair measure of authorial oversight) saves him from becoming Sunday dinner, Carl experiences a drastic, permanent alteration (Disch coolly suggests it might be an improvement) that remains with him even after he reassumes his human form.

Throughout *The Sub*, Disch's plotting is marvelously intricate. His web of interwoven characters, while small, is equally complex and sometimes confusing. In the early chapters, one has the feeling of a newcomer being driven around a small town by a loquacious host who cheerfully points out the homes of the town drunk, slut, wife beater, and so on. But soon they all sort themselves out, and *The Sub* becomes a genuine page-turner.

Disch revels in being an equal opportunity misanthrope: the wicked are punished, but so are the sort-of-good. In its final pages, *The Sub* takes on the dark, timeless quality of a fairy tale like "The Juniper Tree" or "Hansel and Gretel," the kind of story that keeps you awake at night even as it enthralls you with its brutally detached descriptions of bloodletting and incest, metamorphoses and murder avenged. It also makes you wonder about the number of roadkills you see in rural counties.

Diana finally meets her match when she picks up the wrong guy at the casino, a low-rent shaman who also happens to be a serial killer and who enslaves Diana as easily as she has enslaved others. No one is innocent in this world, where the original sin isn't thirst for knowledge, or even good old-fashioned lust.

It is commonly believed, wrongly, that Eden was lost by the sexual transgression of Adam and Eve, that the apple they ate was a euphemism for sex. In fact, they had often had sex before they fell from grace, but like animals, they didn't remember what they'd done. After their fall and exile from Eden they remembered everything and regretted everything, for once we are aware that there is an ethical dimension to the universe, evil becomes intrinsic to our existence. We live by eating other living things, and all our heirs are born to follow us (if not precede us) to death. That is the meaning of original sin.

Disch was raised Catholic. Much of his late fiction, and works such as the verse play *The Cardinal Detoxes*, attacked the Church with the cruel, occasionally sadistic obsessiveness of inquisitors buckling an intransigent witness into a Judas Cradle. Unlike John Waters, another midcentury Catholic artist and gay man who specializes in the satirical grotesque, Disch has little use for the notion of redemption. His art is often punitive—*The Brave Little Toaster* is a notable exception—and much of his life as well as his writing was an engagement with the abyss, a pas de deux with despair. "It had been years since the possibility of suicide had crossed Diana's mind," Disch writes in *The Sub*.

> She'd come to think she'd put all that behind her. Now the blackness had returned like an unwelcome lover, someone you hated but at the same time could not resist. Come in, you tell him, come in, and there he is, a permanent guest, with his suitcase in your closet and his shoes under your bed.
>
> It was there like the moon, noticed only at intervals, but always present, even when you couldn't see it, pulling at her. Telling her, you're mine, you've always been mine.

There was an almost ten-year gap between *The Sub* and *The Word of God*, Disch's last novel, published within weeks of his suicide in July 2008. His partner's protracted and terminal illness, the destruction of their country refuge in upstate New York, a fire in their New York City apartment, and Disch's own deeply melancholic temperament ultimately formed a black whirlpool that he could not escape. The unwelcome lover—I imagine the Man in the Bright Nightgown, as W. C. Fields named Death—had arrived. He never left.

THE SUB

1

"And what sound do pigs make, class?" Diana demanded of her children.

There was only a scattering of giggles in reply. No one raised a hand. They seemed, to Diana's practiced eye, unnaturally shy. Little wonder, in view of the media circus that the school had become in the last few weeks. The Goddess only knew what must be going through their minds. To carry on as though nothing had changed scarcely seemed possible, but Diana Turney was not one to be daunted by that. Impossible deeds could be done if you summoned the determination.

"Lloyd." She looked down at the Brandt boy in the front row of desks, where she put potential troublemakers. "Can you tell us?"

Lloyd Brandt scowled up at her with a resentment that was pure instinct, as a small rodent might regard an object in nature that happened to have the shape of an owl or a fox. Diana intended him no harm, and yet there was a kind of wisdom in his scowl, for they were, at some primordial level, enemies. She knew the sort of man he'd become in the fullness of time. His fate was written in his face—in the set of his jaw and the squint of his eyes, in the bristling buzz-cut blond hair and rosy cheeks that would someday sprout whiskers and droop into jowls. Yes, he did well to fear her—or any woman who had her wits about her.

"Well, Lloyd: a pig, what sound does it make? Does it go cluck-cluck?"

The class giggled, which Lloyd took to be an act of communal betrayal, and he scowled all the fiercer.

"Does it go moo?"

"No."

"Well, then: tell us."

"Oink," said Lloyd inexpressively, as though it were a word on the blackboard.

"Oink," she repeated, just as flatly, but pinning him down with her eyes. "Thank you, Lloyd. Now we all know what noise a pig makes. Now we can continue singing. Class." She lifted her ruler, demanding silence.

And then they sang, at the ruler's bidding, the rest of the song—with an oink-oink here and an oink-oink there; here an oink, there an oink, everywhere an oink-oink. And so on with the clucks, the moos, the quacks, the baas.

As they sang, she couldn't keep from matching the various children with the animals in the song. Surely chubby little Cheryl Sondergard was destined to be a hen, and there were at least two blue-ribbon contestants in the bovine category. But the lambs were the great majority. When it came to a baa-baa here and a baa-baa there, some of the lambs could really get into it. Method acting in the second grade.

Logically, that made her their shepherd—not a role she entirely rejoiced in, despite its venerable tradition. Jesus was *the* Good Shepherd, but what did He have for dinner on Passover? Not just bread and wine, in all likelihood.

"That's a fun song, isn't it?" she said, setting the ruler down on her desk.

They nodded warily—cowed (or chickened or pigged, as the case might be) by the automatic transmission of her confidence. That was the whole secret of teaching, whether one had to deal with second graders or seventh graders (and those were the worst). Even in the movies you could tell a good teacher by the way he (and they were usually he's in the movies) took charge right off the bat. Okay, class, let me show you what I know about karate!

"Okay, class," she said brightly. "Have any of you ever been to a *real* farm?"

Not a single hand went up.

Amazing. Here they were in Minnesota, in a suburb, Willowville, that was bordered, at least on its northern edge, by working dairy farms, and none of these children had ever been on a farm. It was altogether possible that their parents hadn't either. She might as well have asked them if they'd ever been to Rome or to Jerusalem. A farm to them was only an illustration in a picture book. If she'd been teaching in one of the inner-city schools, their ignorance might have been still more profound. Oink and moo and baa and cluck no longer related, for most children, to any observable reality. Farm animals were mythical entities, like dragons and fairies and wizards and witches, that belonged to a world that used to be and was no more.

Diana Turney meant to correct that. "I grew up on a farm," she told them. "A real farm, with all the animals that there are in the song. Cows and sheep and pigs and chickens. No ducks, except in the hunting season, when there were wild ducks. In the morning I used to go out to the chicken coop and get the eggs the hens had laid. They were there in the straw, still warm. Not like the eggs that come out of your mothers' refrigerators. Sometimes there were little drops of red blood *inside* the egg, which meant it might have become another chicken if we hadn't taken it out of the chicken's nest and fried it."

Cheryl Sondergard turned sideways to her friend and cousin Gerry Kruger and made a face expressive of disgust.

Diana smiled. "That's where chickens come from, you know. They come from eggs. *Did* you know that, Cheryl?"

"Yes, Ms. Turney," said Cheryl, dismayed at having been singled out.

"Yes indeed, every egg we eat might have grown up to be a chicken if it had been given the chance to do that." This was not true, of course, for not every egg is fertilized, but children in second grade were not aware of such niceties, and the concept of fertilization was not in the assigned curriculum for second graders in Willowville's public schools. Diana knew the boundaries of her position and took care not to overstep them.

"And where do hamburgers come from? Does anyone know?"

"From McDonald's!" crowed the smallest and youngest of her children, little Earl Wagner, who knew perfectly well where hamburgers came from. He was teasing her, and showing off.

"Quite true," Diana replied, unruffled. "But of course you mean the McDonald's in the Willowville mall, not Old MacDonald's farm. I often wonder if there might be a connection. Maybe the McDonald's in the mall gave itself that name to remind us of the song. Because the song is much, much older than the restaurant. I learned to sing it when I was the age that you children are now, and before that my mother and father sang it when *they* went to school. And *that* was a time when everyone, even the smallest children, would have known what a farm was like. Because Minnesota was filled with farms then. If you didn't live on a farm yourself, you would certainly have relatives who did, and you'd visit them on the holidays. And so you would know where hamburgers come from. They come from cows. Surely you all knew that, didn't you?"

The children stared at her, in fear. Not of her but of what they sensed was coming next. Children know so many things that they would rather not know, and it is a teacher's special vocation to make that knowledge tolerable. Were it otherwise, were she here only to din into their heads the simple mechanics of the three R's, teaching the early grades would be pure purgatory. A computer could teach children arithmetic quite as well as she could. But no computer could unveil the mysteries that are the foundations not of knowledge but of understanding, of wisdom, of human existence.

"Hamburgers come from cows. You know that. The cows that you can see off to the side of the highway, browsing on the lovely green grass. The cows that are milked every morning so that there will be cartons of milk the next day in the grocery stores. Of course, not all *cattle* are cows. Cows are women, and bulls are men, and there are also *steers*, and they're men, too, but of a different sort. And when the steers and the cows are old enough, they're sent away from the farms they lived on, and they're cut apart and sliced up, and that's where roast beef comes from and steaks and hamburgers. They're all different parts of the cows. And it's just the same with pigs, and chickens, and sheep. They all are slaughtered, which is another way of saying that they're killed."

She let that sink in for a while, and then she smiled and said, "So, when we sing about Old MacDonald's farm, with an oink-oink here and an oink-oink there, that's what we're really singing about. The dinner on our table."

Earl Wagner raised his hand.

"Yes, Earl?"

"Ms. Turney, are you a vegetarian?"

The little devil: she should have guessed he'd be the one to bring *that* up. But of course, he had an older sister, Joan, who was in the fifth grade now, and he'd probably heard all kinds of stories about the legendary Ms. Turney from her.

"A vegetarian? What do you mean by that, Earl? Someone who only eats broccoli and potatoes?"

Earl shook his wise little head. "No. I mean someone who doesn't ever eat meat."

"Well, as a matter of fact, Earl, I *don't* eat meat. Nor do I eat fish or poultry, which is to say, the flesh of any kind of bird, be it chicken or turkey or *pheasant*. I mention pheasant in particular, because this is the season now for hunting pheasant, and my father was a great hunter of pheasants. Oh my, yes. He would spend the whole weekend marching about through the corn stubble with his shotgun, and then he would bring home the poor dead, bleeding birds in a *sack*. And my mother would have to take off their feathers, such beautiful feathers, and chop off their heads, and take out their gizzards, which is another word for stomach, and cook them for our Sunday dinner. And that's how I became a vegetarian. I could not eat a *bite* of those pheasants. I was twelve then, and I'd never had any problem with hamburgers, or steaks (though we didn't often have steaks in *our* family), or chicken, or . . . whatever. But I could not eat pheasant."

"Didn't your dad *make* you?" Lloyd Brandt asked, without raising his hand. "*I* gotta eat anything they put on my plate. Even if it makes me sick."

"Yes." Diana nodded her head judiciously. "Yes, my father told me I had to eat it. And I did chew it up and swallow it. And I was sick, as I knew I would be. And then I was sent to bed. And the same thing happened the next time we had pheasant. I can still remember the taste of it. Have any of you children ever eaten pheasant?"

Almost all the children shook their heads no.

"Well, I hope you never have to. For Lloyd is quite right. We must all eat what is put on our plates. Because our parents have gone to a great deal of trouble to put it there, and we must be grateful to them."

"You mean," said Earl Wagner, "that kids can't be vegetarians? It's like smoking."

Despite herself, she laughed. The incongruity of the comparison was simply too droll to resist.

"Yes, you might well say that, Earl. Vegetarianism is like smoking. In the sense that it's a choice that you can make once you're a grown-up and in charge of your own life."

At the very back of the classroom, Sue Wong raised her hand. She was Chinese, the only Chinese student in the entire school, and her command of English was imperfect. She'd never raised her hand before in Diana's class.

"Yes, Sue?" she asked, with a special solicitude.

"Can I leave the class, Ms. Turney?"

"Leave the class, Sue? Why do you want to do that?"

In reply, Sue Wong regurgitated her cafeteria lunch of chicken chow mein, three-bean salad, and a Milky Way candy bar across her desk.

2

Janet Kellog's trial for first-degree assault had been going on for three days when the prosecution called Dana Quigley to the witness stand, but practically speaking, it was just getting started, because Janet's husband had refused to testify against his wife, and Dana, who'd been there at the Leech Lake Motel when Janet had put the bullet through him, was the only other person who knew just what had happened that night. She didn't exactly appreciate being in the spotlight like this, since the part she'd played in the story was nothing to be very proud of, but there was a certain grim satisfaction to be had in seeing that Janet got put behind bars. She'd heard that Carl was hoping his wife would get off with probation and that was why he wouldn't get on the witness stand himself. He didn't have to testify, being her husband. But Carl must have been wondering who, if Janet went to jail, was going to cook his meals and take care of the kid and, most of all, who'd haul his ashes. That had to be why Carl was keeping mum, not out of Christian charity and turning the other cheek, because Carl was not particularly bighearted. He probably figured he could make Janet's life more miserable if she stayed at home than if she was sent to Mankato state prison. And he probably could have. He was professionally qualified to do so, having been a prison guard for most of his adult life.

But Dana didn't give a shit about Carl's convenience. He could eat canned corned-beef hash and chili for the rest of his life for all she cared. On the night Carl was shot in the arm, Dana herself could have been killed. That had been the intention of the first five shots Carl's wife had let off into the motel bathroom where Dana had taken refuge, and Dana had no intention of turning *her* other cheek, even though she considered herself a good Christian. The Bible didn't say nothing about testifying in court, unless it came under the heading of Thou shalt not bear false witness, and she wasn't about to. She'd just tell the god-damned truth.

They went through the whole rigmarole that the district attorney for Leech Lake County had rehearsed with her. Yes, she was Dana Quigley, and yes, she could identify the defendant, Janet Kellog, who was sitting there at the table beside her yuppie lawyer, crying crocodile tears. Dana knew better than to make any comment about Janet's knack for tears. Janet was the queen of self-pity, but if the jury hadn't already figured that out, then the prosecution might as well call it a day. Because the only thing that Janet had going for her, as far as Dana could see, was Carl's silence and her own blond pathos and good looks.

But those assets weren't going to get her very far with this jury, if Dana was any judge. The ones who weren't ready to go to Florida and die were sinfully homely. The D.A. said they were an ideal panel for this particular case. Now Dana could see why. They'd identify with Dana, who was not all that good-looking.

Finally the D.A. got around to what had happened on the night of October 13, and Dana, in her own words (interrupted at regular intervals by Janet's yuppie attorney, Ms. Tryon), explained what had happened:

She had attended a Friday the 13th party at the home of the accused, having been invited by the accused, whom she had known in high school some years earlier. There she had unwisely had too much of the punch provided by her hosts, and at either ten-thirty or a quarter to eleven, feeling unable to meet the challenge of night-driving on Route 97, she had asked her hosts if one of them might drive her home. Carl Kellog had agreed to drive her home, and yes, it was true that she had not gone home directly. She had asked Carl to pull over at the Leech Lake Motel because, firstly, she was feeling queasy, and, secondly, she had wanted to phone her baby-sitter, Elizabeth Lifton, to explain that she would be home later than she'd said.

Yes, they had rented a room at the motel, she didn't know if it was in Carl's name or hers, and the reason for that was, as she'd stated, that she had not been feeling well and had wanted to have the option of crashing at the motel. It was then—she couldn't be sure of the time, somewhere toward midnight—that the accused had come busting into their room—or, rather, *her* room—with a loaded pistol—no, Dana could not be more specific, she was not a gun expert—and threatened both Dana and her own husband, Carl. Dana showed the jury how, as she best remembered, Janet had waved her gun about.

There were objections. The D.A. and Janet's lawyer approached the bench. Dana just sat there in the witness chair and fixed her eyes on Janet Kellog until, gradually, Janet got the message and looked up at her. And Janet knew, without a wink or a nod, what Dana wanted her to know, that she was fucked. When she knew that Janet knew, Dana allowed herself a small, triumphant smile, and then, when the judge said for her to go ahead with her story, she went ahead and told how she had locked herself in the bathroom, to allow Mr. and Mrs.

Kellog to have a chance to talk together. How bullets had then ripped through the door of the bathroom, bullets that might well have killed Dana if she had not had the foresight to hide within the bathtub provided by the Leech Lake Motel. The door of the bathroom had been splintered, the mirror shattered, and Dana declared that she was grateful to be alive.

And then, yes, there had been a final shot, and when, after hearing Mr. Kellog cry aloud, Dana had gathered the courage to come out of the bathroom, she had found him, Mr. Kellog, lying on the motel room's bed, bleeding profusely. Mrs. Kellog had disappeared. That was when Dana had called the motel's night manager and told him to phone the police.

There were many more questions, and objections, both sustained and denied, and then there was the cross-examination. Ms. Tryon tried as hard as she could to convince the jury that Dana was some kind of slut or nymphomaniac, but Dana stuck to her guns. She knew the jury wouldn't buy her story that she'd stopped at the motel so she could call her baby-sitter, but the truth of the matter was that she hadn't *ever* had sex with Carl Kellog. Maybe everyone else in Leech Lake County had, but that Friday the 13th would have been Dana's first shot—and Janet had got there first.

And for that she should have been gunned down by the guy's jealous wife?

Basically, that was the question the jury had to ask itself, and when they answered it, their answer was no. No, Janet Kellog didn't have any business shooting anyone, including her husband, who'd taken the last bullet from her handgun in his right shoulder. No, the citizenry of Leech Lake County decided, that was not allowable behavior, even for a wife with a history (most of which was not admitted into evidence) of having been repeatedly wronged, physically, mentally, and spiritually.

The jury's verdict got headlines in the *Leech Lake Sentinel-Courier*, but only three inches in the *Minneapolis Star-Tribune*, which was the only paper Dana's family read. So *they* never found out about the whole miserable mess, which was an unexpected plus.

Janet, when it came time, late in January, for her sentencing, got sent to Mankato for a year. Dana could have wished it was for life, but the bullet, after all, had hit Carl, so she couldn't really feel as though there'd been a miscarriage of justice.

A year was enough.

3

"I see a journey," said Brenda Zweig, touching the Six of Wands and tilting her head back as she narrowed her eyes to slits.

Even dramatized by the candlelight, Diana Turney's face did not show any sign of heightened interest, much less excitement. And Diana was no sphinx. Her least desires were as visible to Brenda's practiced eye as acne. Clearly, a journey was not something Diana cared to see in her cards tonight. "It could be a physical journey *or* a spiritual journey," Brenda equivocated. "In either case, it is associated with a gift. Something very rare and precious, but dangerous at the same time. It might be better not to accept it, but I don't know if that's possible. Gifts are hard to refuse."

Diana could not help but take such bait as this, but even when she asked, "What kind of gift?" Brenda could sense that her anxieties had another, more urgent focus, still undiscovered.

Brenda leaned forward and tapped the wreath on the horseman's staff with her fingernail. "A wreath like this indicates some unusual mental or psychic power. Poets are crowned with laurel wreaths. But the card is reversed, so there may be some kind of treachery involved. Gifts are not always blessings. Think of the Trojan horse. And there's a horse right there on the card."

Brenda rarely dwelt on themes of apprehension and distrust when she read the tarot for a regular client, unless the cards left her absolutely no choice, and that had certainly not been the case tonight. Some imp of the perverse had got hold of her tongue. Already she'd warned Diana to avoid the sexual advances of any strange, fair-haired man during the next six months. Not a very imminent danger in Diana's case, one might think, and so all the more reason to have left well enough alone. Then, when Diana had chosen the Five of Pentacles—reversed!—from the fanned-out deck, what *could* Brenda say? The most innocent Querent could tell by a glance at that card—two beggars on a snowy night passing before a church window—that it boded ill. And Waite's pronouncement, in his "Key to the Tarot," was memorably dire: "Disorder, chaos, ruin, discord, profligacy." Brenda had limited herself to "You seem to be going through a period of great stress," and left it at that.

"Another card," said Brenda. "And this will be the last."

Diana stretched her hand toward the cards spread out before Brenda, hesitated, trembling, like the planchet of a Ouija board, and chose . . . the Queen of Swords, reversed.

"Oh, Lord," said Diana.

"She's your problem," said Brenda decisively, for this was another card that allowed little leeway for a benign interpretation. "It's a woman you know. I think it's someone you work with. And she has behaved very treacherously toward you. Or she's about to. It explains all those other cards. It's as though this woman has cast a shadow across your whole life. I can't say more than that. But you can. You know who it is, don't you?"

Diana nodded.

"Do you want to tell me about it?" Brenda swept up the cards decisively. "I'll make some tea. And there's two slices left of a gooseberry tart. There won't be any more gooseberries this year. The freezer's empty, and I don't know any stores that sell even canned gooseberries. Of course, frozen can't compare to fresh."

Diana seemed relieved by the conversational shift of gears. She smiled a teacherly smile. "You grow your own gooseberries?"

"I know where to find them. I think they're feral gooseberries. Tame once, wild now. They grow around behind that marshy area where I showed you my ruins."

"That tumbledown shack?"

"Someone lived there once. Lord knows when. I did my own little archeological dig and came up with all sorts of rusty cans and broken bottles."

"No arrowheads?"

"No, but it *might* have been Indians living there. It has that feel. Or Native Americans, as you schoolmarms call them nowadays."

"Educators, Brenda—not schoolmarms. And yes, I'd like some of the tart. And why do you say"—Diana followed Brenda into her kitchen, which was homey and rustic in a carefully considered way—"it has 'that feel'? Did Indians dispose of their cans and bottles differently than you or me?"

"I guess what I meant was that whoever lived there had to be even poorer than the people who lived in *this* house. Two rooms, three windows, one stove—pretty minimal. And there were children, 'cause some of the cans were for infant formula."

"Isn't there anyone around here you could ask who lived there?"

"Nobody along the road goes back more than twenty years. This is the oldest house in the area, and it was standing empty for years before I got in. Just in time, too. If I hadn't shored up the beams in the basement, it would be just another hole in the ground. There was a whole *culture* that's just vanished."

"Not quite. There's still a few kids at my school whose parents are subsistence farmers. They live on the edge of a big marshy area where they stopped developing when swamps became wetlands and had to be preserved. Their folks do roadwork for the county, poach deer, and make do somehow. Ma and Pa Kettle types. The only difference is that nowadays one of the Kettles, or both, are strung out on drugs."

Brenda pursed her lips disapprovingly. Her own views on the matter of drug abuse were complicated, and she was not inclined to share them with anyone outside a small circle of intimate friends. Basically, while disapproving of using drugs for recreational or mood-altering purposes, she thought there was a place for them as part of a program of spiritual development. Shamans and sorcerers had to operate outside the dos and don'ts of everyday life. They transcended ordinary morality. Transcendence was, in fact, their special calling.

She busied herself making tea. If she'd been by herself she'd have dunked a teabag in a cup of water and zapped it in the microwave. But paying customers expected more ceremony, and especially this customer, who had made the very pot and the two misshapen cups in which the tea was to be served. Brenda had no less than four such hand-thrown tea services, each one of a distinctive and characteristic ungainliness, each one reserved for the visits of the potter who'd given them to Brenda. At other times such misbegotten pottery was kept out of sight in a cupboard devoted to these and other pariah gifts.

Of them all, Diana's was the most thorough botch—the spout and handle of the pot both visibly out of true, the lid ill-fitting, the colors sickly with a glaze that had blistered into the ceramic equivalent of eczema when it was fired. The cups were just as ugly and tended to scald the tongue and burn the fingers.

"Such beautiful cups," Brenda said, setting the tea tray in the circle of light beneath the faux-Tiffany lampshade that hung over the kitchen table. "The beauty of simplicity. Form follows function. Excuse me a moment, will you? I've something in my eye."

In the little hallway connecting the bathroom to the kitchen, Brenda stooped down and pushed aside a stack of paperbacks to get at the switch that turned on the tape recorder. The microphone was tucked up inside the lampshade over the kitchen table. Nine times out of ten the tapes she made at the kitchen table were of no practical value, but she didn't enjoy the luxury of a professional therapist, who can sit there with pen and notepad in plain sight. And you never knew in advance what little details might prove handy at some later date. The names of old friends or distant relatives, anecdotes from work, childhood memories—all were grist for her mill.

Back in the kitchen, after the first nibble at the gooseberry tart and the first sip of the sarsaparilla-root tea, Brenda finally couldn't resist asking Diana about the situation at the Rudy Perpich Elementary School in Willowville. The story had been in the newspapers for almost a year now, sometimes on the front page. Diana hadn't been involved in any of the fuss, since she'd only been assigned there at the start of the current school year, but she did have a grandstand seat.

"So whose side are you on?" Brenda insisted, after Diana had at first claimed to be an innocent and uncomprehending bystander who knew no more than she read in the papers and saw on TV. "I don't mean like in a law court. Emotionally."

"Oh, emotionally, I'm on the teacher's side, of course—though I've never met her. Miss Armour's suspended from teaching until the trial is over. But I've talked to the other teachers who knew her, and they're all convinced that she sensed *something*. The child had been abused, in some way or other—no one doubts that."

"But the satanic element . . . ?"

Diana furrowed her brow. "That may have been exaggerated. Children that age aren't always clear about the difference between fantasy and reality. The Blair child was in the first grade when the abuse was discovered. Lord knows when it began."

"Her name is Blair? The papers don't give her name or any details about her."

Diana nodded her head. "Vanessa Blair. She's not at our school anymore, of course. Since the school itself is one of the codefendants. Ten million dollars is a lot of money, and if they were only suing Miss Armour and Professor Hutchinson—"

"That's the psychologist who testified at the first trial?"

Diana nodded. "But she's not much better off than Miss Armour. But if the school's a codefendant, *then* the parents stand to end up with a bundle. The county has deep pockets."

"What I've heard is that some of the other teachers at the school have testified against Armour. *And* against the principal."

"Oh, it's become a regular witch-hunt, all right. They're claiming that Mrs. Burroughs, the principal, tried to get Vanessa and another girl to make charges against one of the teachers, Jack Oelker, who testified for the defense at the first trial. He's been transferred out of the school at his own request, and in fact it's his second-grade class that I'm subbing for."

"Was the idea that he'd abused them, too?"

Diana nodded. "The Blairs had had him to dinner at their house several times. They were close. It was natural to wonder. But at the trial the other girl gave the impression that Mrs. Burroughs had tried to get her to make up stories against Jack Oelker. Not satanic abuse, but fondling, suggestive remarks. And that's all part of the official record now. And it's true that Mrs. Burroughs probably did get more involved than she should have. But it's hard to blame her. She's concerned for the children's welfare."

"And now they're trying to get rid of her?"

"The school board is divided on the issue. So is the school. Not just the teachers. In the upper grades it's like the Civil War. The students have very strong feelings, pro and con. There's been vandalism. Some of the PTA members are circulating a petition to have the school shut down permanently. Just bus the children somewhere else. But the county won't consider that, because it would be tantamount to admitting the school was responsible."

"And if they admit that, it'll cost ten million?"

"Well, that's what the Blairs are asking. They might not get as much as that, but they'll probably get a big settlement."

Brenda shook her head with an all-purpose disapproval that said "What a world!" without placing the blame anywhere in particular. She'd had the feeling, other times she'd talked with Diana, that she'd been more upset by the situation at the school than she was admitting to now. That there was some kind of personal involvement. She was holding something back, but what?

As though in answer to the unasked question, Diana began to cry. She had just lifted the last forkful of the gooseberry tart to her lips when the tears started—quiet, incapacitating tears that Brenda encouraged by fetching the box of Kleenex from the top of the refrigerator.

Brenda took a professional satisfaction in any such outburst on the part of a client. An astrologer—which she chiefly was; the tarot readings were just a sideline—is a kind of psychotherapist. The goal is the same, to help people get in touch with the feelings they've stuffed away out of reach. An astrologer just uses different tools to make that connection. Brenda had clients whose tears came like clockwork. She would do their charts, then they'd sit down for a cup of tea and chat for five or ten minutes, and the tears would well up. They'd have their cry, snuffle an apology, and make their good-byes.

But Diana wasn't like that. Her feelings were sealed up like wine in a corked bottle. She would talk about the anger she was feeling, or the pain, even the love. She knew she should be feeling *something*, so she invented emotions appropriate to the occasion. But it had always been, till now, just talk.

Brenda waited until Diana had had a sufficiently good cry, and then asked, "What is it, Diana? Tell me, that's what I'm here for."

"The thing that's happening at the school," she began, wiping the tears away with a tissue from the box. "It brought back . . . memories. Of my own childhood."

"Memories . . ." Brenda prompted.

"What happened to Vanessa Blair . . . it happened to me, too. I'd forgotten the whole thing, but then the memories started coming back." She blew her nose in the damp Kleenex. "Terrible memories." She took another Kleenex and dabbed at her eyes. Blinked. And forced a brave smile.

Brenda was not about to leave it at that. "You were abused?"

Diana nodded. "In the smokehouse, which was up the hill behind our house near Leech Lake. Where I grew up. I was twelve." She closed her eyes and furrowed her brow. "And it must have been about this time of year. I can remember there was snow inside the smokehouse. The roof had caved in, but otherwise it was still solid. The door could be closed, and locked."

"Who was it that abused you, Diana? Was it someone . . . close to you?"

"It was my father."

I should have known, Brenda thought to herself. It all fit together now. Diana was, in fact, a classic case.

"You don't have to tell me any more now if you don't want to. But you might feel better if you do. Sometimes it helps if the pain can be shared."

4

The smokehouse was still there on the hill behind the farmhouse. It was the Kellog farmhouse now, and had been for many years, but the name on the mailbox still said TURNEY. The Kellogs got their mail in a box at the post office, since Carl didn't trust the neighbors' kids or, for that matter, the neighbors.

Carl had always meant to get the smokehouse back in working order, but like a lot of other good intentions, that had been put on a back shelf. Janet had wanted to have the thing torn down and the whole area around it plowed up and turned into a vegetable garden, but she was as much of a procrastinator as he was. So it stayed as it was, the busted roof mended with a five-dollar sheet of plastic, the hinges and the latch on the door dark with rust, the paint peeled away except in a few patches.

In the summer it provided a home for bats, and a large garter snake lived under the stone floor. Generations of wasps had built their nests inside the flue of the chimney, and seen them fall to ruin and built again.

And always Wes was there. Not in the flesh, of course. His flesh had long since rotted away in its coffin in the small cemetery beside the Methodist church in Leech Lake. Not even in the spirit, if that is taken to mean that there was some conscious entity that haunted the smokehouse and knew itself, once, to have been the man Wes Turney. A spirit that might manifest itself, in the right circumstances, to the senses of the living. He had no shape or smell. Nor could he whisper, as ghosts are sometimes thought to whisper, "Remember me."

But he was there, and his presence could be felt, for it was that which drew the bats to congregate beneath the broken two-by-fours of the roof and bid the snake inhabit its dark labyrinth under the flagstone floor and made the wasps welcome within the chimney flue. It was his presence that made the vagrant deer hesitate as they approached the stand of birches before the padlocked door, and snort, and turn away.

He was there because he had no choice. A crime had been committed, years ago, inside its four narrow walls, and until the crime had been atoned for, some undying essence of what had been Wes Turney must remain where the blood of that crime had darkened the wood and stone. He was rooted to the spot like a tree, and like a tree he had grown. Not visibly, for he was not visible. What had grown was a potentiality for evil. If it could have been mapped, it would have resembled layer upon layer of delicate dark lace billowing about the smokehouse, swelling and shrinking like the translucent membranes of a sea anemone, rising sometimes above the small building like a plume of smoke from the chimney, at other times spreading through the underbrush like cilia, searching for the sustenance it was always denied: revenge, recompense, release.

And tonight, as Diana Turney whispered the tale she'd never told before, it was as though a spear had been thrust through the pulsing layers of invisible lace. The cilia of the unseen anemone convulsed and thrashed about until the snake curled up for its wintry sleep beneath the floor of the smokehouse woke and flicked its tail, stiff with the cold, and felt a brief intense spasm of hunger.

And in that spasm the unquiet soul of Wes Turney found, briefly, the breath of a new life.

5

She was still half asleep when he moved up against her, a welcome warmth even under the extra blankets. They nestled like spoons, his paunch in the small of her back, his thighs pressing against hers. Then, as his arms curled round her and he tugged her nightgown up over her knees, the anger she'd been living with every waking hour for the past few weeks lighted up inside her, as though he'd triggered some kind of alarm. She tried to pull away, but already he'd raised his higher thigh over her legs and pulled her over onto her back and was on top of her, his knees nudging her legs apart, his hands on her shoulders, his full weight bearing down, and there was no point now in struggling, no possibility really.

She let him have his 5 a.m. fuck just as though it was still business as usual between them. There'd been enough other times when she'd let him use her the same way, yielding without desire, but without resisting him either. His cunt.

She let it happen, and when he'd shot his load and rolled off her, she got out of bed and went into the bathroom, where she wiped herself off with a towel, then threw the towel in the laundry basket. Instead of washing the towel, she should burn it. And anything else with his sperm in it. The sheets. Her nightgowns. His underwear.

His cock.

But that was as far as her anger would take her. She wasn't another Lorena Bobbitt. She'd shot him, that was a fact. And she hated his guts in a dozen different ways. They hadn't spoken for three days, and she didn't care if they ever spoke to each other again, and if he thought what had just happened was going to change anything, he was sadly mistaken. He'd raped her just now, is what he'd done. He was an animal, except that animals didn't have to do it twice a day like clockwork. They had seasons.

He seemed to think her being sent to jail was all a big joke. He'd been secretly smirking ever since the word had come, through her lawyer, that the judge meant to put her away for a year. The actual sentence wouldn't be handed down till she went back to the courthouse on January 4, but Nancy, her fucking lawyer, said she had it on good authority (meaning, probably, the judge himself) that that was what the sentence would be. "And," Nancy'd added, "you should consider yourself lucky. You could have been sent away for a lot longer." Talk about rubbing salt in the wound.

She got dressed by the glow of the nightlight that had to be left on in the bathroom for Kelly's sake ever since Kelly had taken it into her head that she was afraid of the dark. There was something comforting in how the nightlight lit things up just enough so you could get around but not so much it sliced into you, the way the kitchen light did, especially when you had a headache.

Which she did. With just the nightlight on, she could look at herself in the mirror without flinching. Without thinking, What's happened, where's it all gone? The face she could see in this softer light was pretty near the same face she'd had thirty pounds ago in high school.

God, she hated growing old. She was barely thirty and she already looked more like her mother than Diana did. The way her hips had spread out. The way her breasts sagged if she didn't wear an industrial-strength bra. The way her feet hurt inside any pair of shoes except her bedroom slippers. She could almost forgive Carl for his fooling around.

Almost.

Men got old, too, but it wasn't the same. Carl still qualified as good-looking, even though he'd put on as much weight around his middle as she had. Until the incident at the motel, he'd still dressed the same as when they were in high school, in Levi's and cowboy shirts that were tapered at the waist. Never mind that he popped the buttons on the shirts when he sat down. In his own mind he was still Elvis.

Now he wore his uniform around the clock, and she hated it. It was as though he were saying to her, "This is prison. I'm the guard, you're the prisoner—get used to it." What was even worse, he'd gone and got his hair cut so he looked like a damned skinhead. She'd always cut his hair before. It saved money. And it looked better than any haircut he could have got locally. She had a natural talent that way. But right before the trial he'd got his hair buzzed down to next to nothing, and every couple weeks afterward he got it done the same again. To spite her, just to spite her.

And now she was going to go downstairs and cook his breakfast?

Yes, she was. Because if she didn't act like his obedient fucking wife, he could have her sent back to the fucking county jail to wait for her sentencing there. She was under his fucking thumb, and he knew it. It wasn't probation, but it amounted to the same thing. Nancy had told her to grin and bear it.

She didn't grin, but she bore it. She saw the bastard off to work in the uniform he lived in, and then, because this was Tuesday and on Tuesday Carl left her the car and carpooled with his asshole buddy Clyde, she got Kelly dressed up in her secondhand snowsuit from the last garage sale at the Methodist church and strapped her into the car seat in the back of the Chevy and drove to her mother's place outside Leech Lake.

The snow from two days earlier had melted off the road, and the radio was singing songs she could agree with more or less. She tried not to think about Carl. That had been the minister's advice, Reverend Dubie's: try not to think about him. She'd tried, but when you're married to the bastard, it's not that easy.

Every day the same thoughts went round and round in her head, like a gerbil spinning an exercise wheel: I hate this situation, I've got to get away, there's nowhere to go, what about Kelly? She'd thought of taking Kelly and putting her in the car and just taking off. But where would that get her? She didn't know anyone beyond a radius of fifty miles. She had no money, and no one owed her any big favors. She had zero resources, not even a valid credit card, because Carl, the last time she'd gone on a shopping spree, had canceled their Visa card.

And with Carl being part of the system, even if he was only a prison guard, she had the feeling that if she did try and exit the situation, the whole country would be on red alert looking for her.

She was going to go to jail. A month ago she'd just refused to believe that could happen. But it was. So she had to ask herself: what about Kelly? Carl's answer was a shrug. And when she'd insisted on talking about it, he'd told her that as far as he could see, the only answer was putting her into a foster home for the whole time Janet was doing her stretch.

He'd like that. He'd have the place to himself. His lady friends could come visiting any time he asked them over. Mentally he was still eighteen years old. He could let rip. Poker nights. Beer blasts. Open house.

But if Kelly were there, that wouldn't happen. He couldn't act up that much if his four-year-old daughter was around to remind him he was still her daddy and had to behave accordingly. But for Kelly to be there, there had to be someone looking after her, someone living right in the house.

The big wooden sign planted in the front yard identified her mother's place as NAVAHO HOUSE, AN ADULT RESIDENCE. The sign, which one of Carl's convict friends had made at the prison shop, was probably the classiest thing about the operation. Except that, as Mrs. Boise, one of the old biddies in the home, had pointed out, Navaho was misspelled, and there had never been any Navahos, or Navajos, in Minnesota. But Madge said an Indian was an Indian, and she liked the sound of Navaho House a whole lot better than Chippewa House or Hiawatha Hall, which Mrs. Boise had suggested as alternatives.

Her mother liked to call the place a nursing home, but could it be a nursing home if it didn't have a single nurse working there? Her mother had put in a few years working as a nurse's aide in the late '70s when Janet was in junior high and things had got kind of rocky, and that, along with knowing Larry Haagman, the county clerk, had qualified her to open the place up. Basically, it was a warehouse for old folks from the area who couldn't afford anywhere better to wait to die. They signed over their Social Security and county assistance payments to Madge, and Madge kept them alive as best she could.

Madge insisted that there were other nursing homes in the area a whole lot worse than Navaho House, but if there were, Janet didn't want to know about them. From the start she'd considered the whole idea a big mistake on her mother's part, and she couldn't believe it was paying off. Madge insisted it was, but she wouldn't go into the dollars-and-cents side of it. By the look of the place, a little more dilapidated every year inside and out, Janet figured that Navaho House, like its tenants, was on its last legs. The bank would probably foreclose just about the time her mother was ready to become one of the residents instead of the managing director, which was what she called herself on the letterhead stationery she'd had printed up: MARGARET TURNEY, MANAGING DIRECTOR. Warden would have been more like it.

Janet parked the Chevy on the street, because as usual the driveway hadn't been plowed. Then she woke up Kelly, who started whining right away, and led her round to the back door along the sidewalk, now just one snow shovel wide. All through the winter the front door was kept sealed tight to save on heating bills, and the sidewalk up to the porch never got shoveled at all.

There was no one in the kitchen but Louise, the old half-breed who did all the real work around the place in exchange for room and board and $50 a week. Janet left Kelly with Louise and went looking for her mother.

The dining room table still hadn't been cleared of the breakfast dishes, and from what was left in the different dirty dishes you could see just what the Navaho House inmates had had for breakfast, this morning and every morning—orange juice (canned, because that was supplied free by the county's assistance program), oatmeal, scrambled eggs (regenerated from powder, also courtesy of Leech Lake County), and coffee. There was also a bowl full of apples that came from the Kellogs' apple trees (*not* for free), which served as a table decoration. Truth to tell, they weren't very good eating apples, but they had almost the same staying power as if they were made of wax.

Janet lifted the lid of the coffee urn to see if there was anything left beyond the bitter dregs. Still two inches left at the bottom, so she drew herself a cup from the spigot and stirred in some of the powdered milk from the tin beside the urn.

"I thought you was supposed to be in prison," Madge said, entering from the hallway that connected to the stairs and the TV room. She was wearing an institutional-looking, khaki-colored pantsuit cinched round the waist by a wide patent-leather belt with an enamel buckle in the shape of a big daisy. It made her look more than usually bulgy. Janet hated seeing her mother get a little fatter every year, because she had the same basic body type, and she knew she was going to end up looking just the same.

"I don't get sent off till after the holidays," Janet said. "I told you that before."

"So, to what do I owe this unexpected pleasure?"

"I had the car today, so I thought I'd bring Kelly over for a visit. She's in the kitchen with Louise."

"Louise has got enough to do without acting as your baby-sitter. Today's laundry day."

"Then I can help out by taking Louise there in the Chevy. Kelly loves to go to the Laundromat and put the quarters in the slot."

Madge dug a pack of Virginia Slims from the jacket pocket of her pantsuit and lighted one up. She repocketed the pack without offering it to Janet. After exhaling a meaningful spume of smoke, she said, "Well, aren't you Miss Congeniality today. What is it you want?"

"Just a chance to have a talk. We haven't had a serious talk for a long time. And soon enough we won't be able to."

"Have we *ever* had a serious talk, sweetheart? No, forget that. I'm just in a lousy mood. I've had diarrhea for two days running. No pun intended. And one of the old ladies is too sick to get out of bed. Plus Louise's room has got a leak where the ice has built up under the shingles again. So you didn't pick a very good day to be sociable. But if you want to help me clear up these dishes, and if you don't mind running Louise over to the Laundromat, then, sure, we can have a serious talk."

6

From where he hung above the prison and its grounds, riding the air in a long, down-winding spiral that was anchored, at its base, to his entranced human form, Jim Cottonwood could see all the way north to Leech Lake, where geese still congregated in the unfrozen middle-water. To the east lay the scrub timber and marshes of the "tribal lands" to which the Wabashas, Jim's people, had been consigned for almost a century now, a cheaper prison by far than the twenty-four-story tower below him now.

Westward stood the village of New Ravensburg, for which the prison was named—a rural tenement that once had served the farmers of the area. Now the houses that still stood were mainly given over to the prison personnel and a few local merchants. It was, as much as the lands of the Wabashas, another kind of prison, one that pent in those sentenced there without recourse to walls or guards or barbed wire. The local school, six taverns, and the New Ravensburg Lutheran church accomplished the same purpose for a fraction of the cost.

To the south, beyond some four hundred acres of wasteland set aside for the future expansion of the state facility, the land wrinkled into hills—the timber cleared, the soil untillable—marked to be landfill.

In every direction, then, a different kind of desolation, yet from this height Jim could look down on it as an angel might, with a vision ice could not chill nor poverty taint. This was the first taste of freedom he'd known in twenty years as a convict at New Ravensburg, and it made him giddy with delight. Had he surveyed the pit of hell he would have felt the same exhilaration—simply to have been so high above it, to be released.

He had flown before this, but only in dreams or in visions of the sweat lodge—never as a shaman, in borrowed flesh. The crow had alighted before him, where he'd been resting at the far curve of the oval rooftop track, his chest heaving, lungs seared by the winter air. Their eyes had met, and it was as though the crow had come to him aware of her mission—like a handmaiden entering the darkened chamber and dropping her robes to the floor and whispering that her flesh was, for a little while, his, to use as he pleased.

So he had entered her in that instant, without a nod of recognition. His arms became wings, and as he rose, stroke by stroke, into the upholding element, a cry burst from his throat—his own name: Crow.

By some law that his new muscles—but not his mind—could understand, his crow nature remained constrained by the limits imposed on the human body he had exited. Though he could rise above the prison tower of New Ravensburg in an ever-widening spiral, riding the updraft, he could not break through the invisible boundary that rose over the prison like the funnel of a tornado. He would beat the air with his wings, trying to fly to the east, but the walls of the funnel deflected his flight upward and to the north. He felt like a swimmer caught in the eddies of a powerful river, whose most strenuous efforts never bring him nearer the shore.

So he ceased to fight the current and let it carry him where it would. The sense of elation returned, diminished but still precious. If he could not escape the joint, he could transcend it. These wings were another kind of music. A gift, like music, briefly given but, while it lasted, all the soul needed.

It was not to last long. He could feel the force of the updraft lessening, and his spiraling course along the funnel wall was now all downward, back to the roof of the prison, back—all too quickly—to the familiar flesh of Jim Cottonwood, stale with its prison sweat, rank with the smell of the cellblock.

An eyeblink and he was himself again. The crow that had alighted on the gravel of the track gave a shocked caw of protest at this violation of the natural order of the crow universe, spread her wings in a gesture that said "Back off!" and then, when Jim's response was only a smile—of gratitude and of chagrin—took to the air, clearing the razor-wired ledge beyond the track and dropping from sight.

Jim got to his feet and approached the ledge so that he could see her further flight, over the sere lawn, still visible through the first dustings of snow, until she reached the one bare maple that had been left standing just beside the prison gate. There, braking with a decisive tilt of her wings, she alighted on a high, bare branch and lifted her head to give Jim one last look of flustered reproach. "No more of that, mister! Not with me." Jim felt what he supposed a rapist must feel just afterward—that glow of supreme satiation that is willing to accept the trade-off of a life behind bars for just this fleeting instant of thirst perfectly quenched.

Then, as the glow slowly faded, he could ask himself if it had really happened. Had he flown in that crow's flesh or only in his own imagination?

He smiled, because he knew there was no knowing, and because the answer didn't matter. Either way he remained where he was and what he was, meat in the freezer. And either way he had to be grateful. His human body still tingled with the crow's strength. His deltoid and trapezius muscles felt as though he'd just left the weight bench. His triceps and lats were gorged with blood.

He knew he must be wary. The gifts of the spirit had their own loopy logic. There would be an upwelling of irrational, heaven-sent happiness one day because of the blow that the next day held in reserve. And this new strength that he could feel like a cinching of all the cords of his upper body had not been given unless he was soon to have need of new strength.

And here it came already, his own personal ill wind, in the form of Carl Kellog. Of all the C.O.'s at New Ravensburg, Carl was the one Jim got on with best. Not that he ever made the mistake of thinking of Carl as his there-but-for-the-grace-of-God brother in a blue uniform. No screw is the brother of any con. They are another species, and right now the species distinction was more than usually clear, because Jim had still not exited his shaman frame of mind, and so he could see Carl in his animal aspect.

Carl was a pig.

This was not necessarily, to Jim's mind, a bad thing. We are all of us animals in one way or another, sharing the growl of the wolf, the snarl of the cat, the chipmunk's chatter. And in most people there is a piggish component as well that grunts with satisfaction at the trough and is happy to veg out afterward. In most people but, as a matter of fact, not in Jim's people, since the pig is not an animal native to North America. It had come over with the white men, and it remained a white man's totem pretty much.

Carl Kellog was about as purely pig as anyone that Jim Cottonwood knew on a first-name basis. It was there in the face, with its jowly cheeks, on their way to getting jowlier, and its wide-nostriled, uptilted snout of a nose. It was also there in the intelligence and good humor of the eyes; in the slouch of the shoulders, the sag of the gut, the thickness of the thighs; in the lazy ambling way he moved that could, when the right hormones were triggered, shift to sudden sledgehammer aggression. If you had to pick a totem animal exactly suited to the job description of corrections officer, you couldn't do much better than pig. In that way Carl was a round peg in a round hole, which is always admirable.

Jim himself was—what else?—a crow. He'd known that even before his first dream visions as a shaman. A crow, like a pig, is an animal that has not got a good PR profile. What are crows known for? For having an appetite that doesn't balk at carrion. For being too smart for their own good. For talking too much. They're not accounted downright bad, like rats or buzzards, but they're pariahs just like pigs, the main difference being that crows live free while pigs are meat. They serve a system that means to use them for sausage, but they never know that till it's too late. Very sad, if you thought about it, but then if you thought a little more, kind of appropriate, too. If you breed animals on purpose to eat them, some of their karma is going to rub off on you, whether or not you live with them on a day-to-day basis. It's the other side of the white man's burden, the side that only shows up, disguised, in nightmares and bedtime stories. Hansel and Gretel, Abraham and Isaac, the Gingerbread Man. It was one more good reason, and maybe at bottom the best, for not envying the sons of bitches. Or, strictly speaking, sons of sows.

"Enjoying the view from the penthouse?" Carl asked when he'd come close enough to be heard without raising his voice.

"Yeah, and thinking how this is the perfect spot for hang-gliding."

Carl acknowledged the joke with a smile. In one form or another he'd probably heard it a few hundred times. "You got a visitor," he announced.

"Tell me another." Jim rarely had visitors anymore, except twice a year when his mother would come by to share an awkward, dutiful silence and give him a tin of home-baked cookies.

"No shit. You don't think I'd come up those stairs for the sake of my health, do you? And you'll never guess who it is."

"I won't try. Who is it?"

"Your son. Alan Cottonwood."

"I don't have a son, Carl."

"According to him you do. He's tried to see you before, you know."

"I know. I want no part of him."

"I don't know what you may have heard about the first time he showed up, last summer. He was still a minor, and without permission from his legal guardian he couldn't be put on the visitor's list, so we weren't supposed to tell you about his wanting to see you. Anyhow he's eighteen now, and it's up to you whether or not he can finally meet you. Come on, you've got to be *curious*. Don't you want to know what he looks like?"

Jim sighed. He knew he was going to see the kid, so what was the point in playing hard to get with Carl?

He didn't even have to say okay. Carl understood his sigh and led the way down the stairs and along the Y-block corridor to get a pink pass from the block officer. Then to the bank of elevators in the utility core of the tower, where Carl gave him a pat-frisk before summoning an elevator.

Inside the elevator, the fluorescent light vibrated on Carl's buzzed and brightly pink scalp. Jim couldn't understand why anyone would deliberately get such an ugly haircut. Unless, of course, you *wanted* to look ugly. Maybe from a pig's perspective ugly registered as good-looking. Clearly, the new haircut had something to do with Carl's situation at home—the shooting, and the trial, and now his wife's being sent off to prison. But all that was territory Jim could not ask him about or comment on, even indirectly. The screws might choose to tell you about their personal lives, but unless they broached the subject, there was a strict NO TRESPASSING sign posted on their uniforms.

They rode down to 8, the barrier floor between the cellblocks above and the administration areas below. The visiting room was one floor farther down, but to get there you had to use a ramp. Outside the visiting room Jim was frisked again by the guard who took his pink pass.

The guard directed Jim to take a seat at one of the tables ranged beneath a mural, a bland, badly painted forest scene of a family of deer and assorted smaller animals beside a brook. Jim hated the mural's kindergarten-level, Disneyfied view of the wilderness as a theme park where every animal was some kind of kewpie doll, sexless and huggable, but while he waited he couldn't keep his eyes off the damned thing. The mural and the Formica furniture gave the visiting room the feel of a school cafeteria. They seemed to promise the prisoners that they could expect to spend their whole lives confined to essentially the same institution. School, prison, hospital, and probably even the funeral home you got buried from—everywhere you were sent, the same bleary deer would be there beside the same cobalt-blue brook with the same smeary pines behind them.

Aside from two black cons and their old ladies discreetly making out on the other side of the visiting room, which was furnished with sofas, Jim had the place pretty much to himself, but that was actually less conducive to privacy than if there had been a crowd, as there would be on any weekend. It meant that the guards monitoring him on the remote videos could pick up every word he or his visitor spoke. And given this visit's potential for soap opera, they would probably save the tape and pass it around, as they were known to do with some of the more X-rated make-out sessions on the sofas. Jim was determined not to provide them with a memorable performance, but it wasn't all up to him. Today it was his visitor who would have the starring role.

And there he was, entering at the visitors' door ahead of the C.O. who'd processed him. Even at this distance Jim began to heat up and shrivel with embarrassment. The kid looked like a tubby fourth grader inflated to adult size, with nothing changed except for the addition of a peach-fuzz mustache and a lank mop of blond hair meant to evoke Jon Bon Jovi. He was wearing a cowboy shirt a couple sizes too tight, with a bolo tie and a turquoise and silver belt buckle that matched the clasp of the tie. Boots, too? No: what was even more Native American than cowboy boots? Beaded moccasins.

Where was the war bonnet?

But no, that was not the right attitude. Maybe if there'd been some chance that the kid had taken some of his genes from the Cottonwood family tree, Jim might have some cause to feel a certain dismay at first sight. But that was not the case. As far as Jim was concerned, the kid could have been any eighteen-year-old imitation redskin with a case of mistaken identity—his own. So when the kid offered his hand to be shaken and said, "Hi, Dad," Jim didn't cringe.

He took the boy's pudgy hand in his own, smiled a sociable sort of smile, and said, "I don't believe we've met."

"I'm Alan." Then, in a tone half defensive, half reproachful, "Alan Cottonwood."

"And you've got the idea that I'm your dad. I guess you're Judy Johnson's son."

"Uh-huh. But my name really is Cottonwood now. I had it changed legally. It cost me three hundred dollars."

"You can have any name you like, kid, it's all the same to me. But that isn't going to make us relatives, 'cause we're not. I don't know what your mother may have told you about her and me."

"She never would say anything at all."

"But I guess she let you assume what the jury assumed when they sent me here."

"Uh-huh."

"It's not like I've got anything against you."

"Uh-huh."

The kid looked like he'd been kicked in the balls. Despite himself, Jim couldn't help feeling sorry for him. It was obvious the guy had problems, or he wouldn't have come visiting like this, what with all the red tape that was involved. And changing his name to Cottonwood. That had to mean he wasn't on good terms with Judy, which at his age might be par for the course. Or it might be something serious. Judy had been a handful back then, and time wouldn't have changed that.

Admit it: he was curious.

"So, tell me, Alan—that's your name, right?—Alan?"

The kid responded with a gratitude that was canine in its abjection. "Yeah," he said, wagging an invisible tail, "Alan."

"Okay, Alan, fill me in. Why'd you decide to look me up? I don't suppose your folks suggested it. Your mom is married now, isn't she?"

"She was, but they broke up a while back. She's back in Leech Lake again, living with her dad. And me with her, although I don't know how long that is going to last. We really don't get along, the old man and me. But he's not really up to taking care of the church anymore, and he's not going to find a janitor that'll work for just his board and room like I do. It's a lousy situation, but jobs just aren't that easy to find. Around here. And I didn't want to leave the area until I could—" He attempted eye contact, but it was like someone trying to press more weight than he can handle. His gaze settled back on his own fingernails. "—Until I was able to see you."

"Judy told you lots of stuff about me, is that it?"

"No, sir. Not anything, ever. I found out about the whole thing when I was in fourth grade, from a buddy of mine, who heard it from his older sister. Probably half the kids in the school knew about it before I did. I asked my mom about it then, but she refused to discuss it. In fact, she got really angry. Later on it was always the same. Finally, I went to the library in St. Cloud and dug up what I could from old newspapers. That's how I found out your name. Then later, two years ago, I tracked down your mom. She works at this nursing home, Navaho House. At first she didn't want to have anything to do with me. But then, I don't know, I guess she felt sorry for me or something. She told me some stuff that wasn't in the newspapers I'd read. Like how you were both teenagers at the time, and it wasn't rape at all. It was statutory. And it was only because you were Native American that you got sent to jail. And because Mr. Johnson was a minister. He's also mean as a snake."

"Yeah. I know that."

"I tried to talk to him, after I'd seen your mom, to ask him about it. I mean, you can't say it's none of my business! But he got really pissed off. He'd always been mean to me, but when I was just a kid, I didn't understand why. Anyhow, that was when I first tried to get in touch with you, but there were all these regulations about who can see the people here and who can't. I think they think everyone wants to smuggle in drugs. Anyhow, they wouldn't even let me write a letter to you, never mind visiting. And when they contacted my mom about it, she flipped out. So I've had to bide my time. But I did start to take an interest in my Native American heritage at that point. I've been to some powwows. And I've read a lot. I realize I'm what you'd call a half-breed. But I've met some guys who are only one-sixteenth Cherokee, and for them it's their whole life. So I don't feel it's phony, like my mom says. I guess she just wants to *repress* the whole thing. Anyhow, that's the situation."

The kid, who'd been staring at his fingernails through most of his account, looked up at Jim, begging for approval.

"I don't know what to tell you, Alan. I can see you've been through some hard times over this. But the fact is, though I was very much in love with your mother, we didn't ever . . . make love. At the trial it was her word against mine, and the jury believed her. What can I say? You seem like a nice kid, and I guess you've got a kind of investment in this Native American thing, which is funny, because when I was your age I didn't want to have anything to do with any of that. I just wanted to eat Wonder Bread. But while you were talking I had a thought. You're in a position to do me a big favor. In fact, you might even be able to get me out of here."

"Hey, just tell me how."

"The thing of it is, Alan, if you do what I ask, you'll end up proving that I'm *not* your father. And I've got the idea that you might not want to do that."

The kid studied his fingernails again. "I see what you mean. But the truth is what's important, I know that. In fact, I think I know what you've got in mind, because I had the same idea. A DNA test."

"That's right. If you're my son, the test would confirm it. And if you're not, the test would be a proof of that. When I was sent away, they didn't have DNA testing. But now it's been established in the courts. You could get me out of here, kid."

"And what if it shows you *are* my dad?"

"If it could, would I ask you to waste your time? Think about it."

"Uh-huh. Yeah. Jesus."

"Jesus has nothing to do with it."

The kid smiled.

7

They were shutting down the school. It wasn't the county that had caved in, but the State Board of Education. There had been a bomb threat. More than a threat: the police found a real bomb in a cardboard carton in the school lunchroom's kitchen. That was on Tuesday. For the first time in her teaching career, Diana had conducted a fire drill that wasn't pretending. She'd marched her students out to the playground in just the clothes they were wearing, at which point, with TV cameras watching the mob of shivering children, it had started to snow. Parents started to show up to rescue their kids, and a shouting match had developed between those who blamed Satan and the Armour-Oelker contingent for the bomb scare and those who blamed the principal herself, Mrs. Burroughs, which was, on the face of it, preposterous. The choicest moments of the wrangling were broadcast on the evening news.

Because she was a sub, Diana found herself facing unemployment. Thanks to their contracts, the regular teachers at the Rudy Perpich school would continue drawing their salaries right to the end of the school year whether or not they worked, but Diana would see her last paycheck on January 4, after which, according to Mr. Delany at the Board of Ed office, she could go on unemployment. Or she might continue subbing on a day-to-day basis, as needed, which was something she'd sworn she'd never do again. When you factored in the cost of commuting, unemployment was probably a better idea.

She'd managed to keep her composure talking to Delany on the phone, but afterward she'd completely fallen to pieces. Wednesday night she'd binged. She'd gone to Gum Joy, intending to get just a takeout order of vegetarian fried rice, but once she was there and could smell the food around her, she couldn't resist the temptation. She'd had an order of shrimp toast while she waited for her takeout, and then she'd flipped out totally and ordered moo shu pork.

She had not eaten pig flesh since she decided to be a vegetarian back in seventh grade. She'd had her falls from grace—chicken, fish, and even once, drunk and thinking she was in love, a rib-eye steak. But never pork. Pork, somehow, seemed the ultimate no-no, the wickedest of meats. Was it because it was mentioned in the Bible? She didn't in any other way identify with Jews. More likely because once, on TV, she had seen a documentary about a slaughterhouse where pigs had been showcased. She could still remember the long procession of flayed carcasses that would be tomorrow's pork chops. Who could, seeing that spectacle, ever eat pork again?

She had. She could still remember the taste on her tongue. She would wake in the night, feeling shreds of the moo shu pork between her teeth, and go into the bathroom and floss. But the next night those shreds were there again—unflossable, irremovable, a permanent guilt. And so tasty. Whipped cream didn't compare. Cheese couldn't compete. The grease in the pork did something primal. She hated it even as the memory lingered on, like the memory of her first kiss, which, in the same way, she wished she could forget.

She craved that taste again. Last night she had dreamed of a pork roast, baked with slices of onions and drenched with gravy: sinfully delicious, although in the dream she had not had a chance to taste it. She'd woken just as the platter was brought to the table.

When Saturday came, she managed to keep busy during the day doing all those chores that don't otherwise get done. Cleaning nooks and crannies. Mending old clothes that probably wouldn't be worn again. The hunger was still there in back of the busywork. She went through an entire box of Little Debbie Coffee Cakes. She cleaned the windows inside and out, though they didn't really need it.

Then Jack called. She'd told him not to, but as soon as she heard his voice she became a slut. Even without the excuse of liquor. Having agreed to see him, she went out and bought a jug of Gallo Chablis, and by the time he came over she was already sloshed. They fucked, and within fifteen minutes he did his usual disappearing act. Which suited her just fine. The whole time he'd been on top of her, it was the pork roast she'd been thinking of.

Once he was gone, she continued with the jug wine. And she ate. Because once she got going, once the hunger took control, it was a greased slide, there was no stopping. Only this time it wasn't Sara Lee and Häagen-Dazs. It was meat. She phoned Domino's Pizza and had them deliver an entire garbage pizza—pepperoni, meatballs, anchovies, whatever.

She ate the whole thing and threw it up—as much as she hadn't actually digested. Then, after gargling with the last of the Gallo, she phoned Gum Joy to have them deliver an order of pork lo mein and sweet-and-sour pork. While she waited for the delivery to arrive, she sat in front of the blank TV crying, utterly wretched and ravenous with hunger.

The phone rang. It was her mother.

Her mother never called unless there was a reason. But even so she felt a throb of gratitude. "Mom," she said. "Hey, it's been ages. What's happening?"

"I've got someone who wants to talk to you. Here, honey, take the phone."

"Guess what?" It was Kelly's voice. A tremulous baby alto that connected like an electric wire to everything that was still sweet and wholesome. It was as if Diana had wiped the fog from a pair of steamed eyeglasses and was able to see the world clean.

"Kelly, is that you?"

"Aunty Di?"

"Yeah, it's me."

"Guess what?"

"I don't know, sweetheart. What?"

"You're coming here for Christmas!"

"Oh, sweetheart, I wish I could."

"Mommy's going away."

"I know that, honey."

"But she says you'll be my mommy while she's away."

Why hadn't she seen it coming? Why had she even picked up the phone?

"Oh, Kelly, that would be wonderful. If I could, but . . ."

"Diana?" Her mother had repossessed the phone.

"Mother, it's impossible," she protested.

But even as she said it, she realized it wasn't so. Now, with no job, it was possible. An internal calculating machine started the figures. If she left the apartment she was in in Willowville, where she was having problems with the neighbors upstairs *and* with the landlord . . . And if she was still entitled to unemployment . . . And Kelly *was* such a sweetie.

On the other hand, Carl was unbearable.

"Diana," her mother said, in that tone she had, when she knew she'd already won an argument before a word had been said. "Your sister's here. She just wants to have a few words. Don't get on your high horse with her. This was all my idea, you can blame me. Maybe it isn't possible. I know you've got your job. Although by the sound of it, what we see on TV, it doesn't sound like a nice place to be, that school of yours. But that's none of my business. Here's Janet."

"Hello?" said Janet.

"I can't do what you're asking," said Diana. "It's completely out of line. You know I can't be in the room five minutes with Carl without an argument. I'm sorry you're going to jail, and I don't blame you one bit for what you did. He's a lousy bastard, but *you* married him, not me."

"Hey," said Janet, in the grown-up version of Kelly's voice, "all I said was hello."

The doorbell rang. It was the deliveryman from Gum Joy.

Even through the closed door, Diana could smell the pork.

"Janet," she said, "there's someone at the door. I'll call you later."

8

On the day after Christmas Kelly was feeling the letdown that follows any holiday with too many promises attached. It wasn't that Santa hadn't been good to her. He'd brought the three things she'd most wanted: a tricycle, a dollhouse, and, to live in the dollhouse, two new Trolls, for her ever-growing Troll family. One of them, with pink hair, had been christened Aunty Pinky and had immediately taken charge of all the younger Trolls, including the other new family member, a boy by the name of Orangey, who had shown himself to be a great troublemaker right from the start.

She'd also got a lot of presents besides the ones she'd asked for from Santa, most of them not that exciting, like the snowsuit with matching pink mittens. Some presents she even wished she hadn't got, like the shoes from Grandma Turney that were made of leather and hurt her feet. Her Aunty Di had given her a golden necklace with red jewels, and a book about forest animals that Aunty Di promised to read to Kelly a little at a time, which meant having to sit still and just listen. Her Aunty Di was a schoolteacher, so you had to expect to get books from her.

The really big present that Santa had left beside the Christmas tree had been for the whole family—a video camera that let you make your own television programs. They'd already made one tape, and Kelly had seen herself on TV singing "Jingle Bells" with her grandma and another where she was riding piggyback on her father's shoulders. Her mom said she didn't want to have anyone make another TV program of her, she'd had enough of that already, but then they decided they'd go sledding on the hill in back of the house. So her mom got on the sled with Kelly, and her dad aimed the camera, but there wasn't enough snow for the sled to go down the hill, so it turned out to be a kind of funny TV show, because the sled just sat there with the two of them on it. Even when her mom got off the sled to make it lighter it wouldn't move, so there was a TV show of

Kelly sitting on the sled in her new pink snowsuit and mittens, waving at the camera, and her dad laughing, though you couldn't see him on the TV, just his shadow in the snow. Her grandma said they should send the tape to *America's Funniest Home Videos*, and her mom said, "Yeah, and we'll send them another of the car parked in the driveway." Everyone laughed at that, even Kelly, though she didn't know why it was funny. But it was nice when everyone laughed together.

Today her dad was at work, and after breakfast her mom had had to drive Grandma Turney back to Navaho House, so Kelly was left alone with Aunty Di, who spent a lot of time talking on the phone while Kelly played with her Trolls or rode her new tricycle in the basement—around the washer and dryer and over to the furnace and then, ducking her head, under the Ping-Pong table and back to the washer and dryer.

After that there was nothing to do, so she asked to watch TV, but Aunty Di looked at the *TV Guide* and decided there was nothing suitable.

"Why don't we go outside!" Aunty Di suggested.

Kelly would rather have stayed indoors, because it had got a lot colder today, but she knew if they were outdoors Aunty Di would have to pay more attention to her than if they were in the house. So she said, "Okay, let's!"

"Almost everything's the same," said Aunty Di, after they'd got bundled up and were climbing the hill in back of the house on the path up to the woodshed. "It's amazing. I feel like the princess in the fairy tale who's been asleep for a hundred years and wakes up and finds nothing has changed. I mean, even the old chicken house is still there, and it must be twenty years or more since there were any chickens in it. Your grandma didn't like looking after chickens."

"Mom says we may have chickens again, when I'm older and I can look after them myself."

"And what will you do with all the eggs?"

Kelly looked up, puzzled. "We'll eat them. Won't we?"

Aunty Di laughed in her peculiar, quiet way, puckering her lips and snorting softly through her nose. "Just a few chickens will lay more eggs than one family can eat by themselves, even if you each ate an egg for breakfast every day. Which is not a good thing to do, as we've come to learn."

"Mom says we'll sell the eggs to grandma. For the old ladies in Navaho House. They eat lots of eggs there."

"Well, they're old enough, it probably doesn't make any difference how many eggs they eat."

"You didn't eat any of the turkey," Kelly pointed out.

Kelly waited for her to explain all over again how she was a vegetarian, but Aunty Di just nodded.

They'd come to the top of the hill and could see the outbuildings on the other side, which weren't visible from the house or from the road.

"It's like a little village, isn't it?" Aunty Di commented. "A little village in its own little valley that's been abandoned but hasn't yet fallen into ruin. I'd forgotten how much Grandpa Iverson, who was *my* mother's father, liked to build. He built all these things—the buildings, the stone walls, the wooden fences—and then when they were all built, poor old Grandma Iverson, who was Grandma Turney's mom, she had to look after the animals, because Grandpa Iverson was killed in Germany during the war."

"What kind of animals?" Kelly said, who was interested only in that part of the story, not in all the dead grown-ups she couldn't sort out.

"Well, the chickens were in the chicken house. And there were turkeys, too. My mom, your Grandma Turney, says she can remember there was a horse and cows here when she was growing up. They lived in the barn, which is gone now, and what Grandpa Iverson built where it used to be is that building over there, beside the willow tree. The barn was much bigger, of course. Pigs don't need the same kind of space that cows do."

"There were *pigs* in there?" Kelly marveled.

"Yes, a great many. Even when I was a girl, we had pigs. And they had to be slopped every day. They'd eat *all* our leftovers, and buckets and buckets of mash besides. With pigs you don't have to bother with compost heaps."

"What are compost heaps?"

"That's where you put your garbage."

"We put the garbage in the garbage *can*," Kelly said.

Aunty Di produced another pucker-and-snort. "Well, some things don't change, and some things do."

She turned to the right, following the path along the top of the hill to where there were more trees. Kelly followed along as far as to the first apple tree. There she stopped short. Aunty Di didn't notice at first. Then she turned around and said, "Kelly?"

"Are you going to the smokehouse?" Kelly demanded.

"Yes, I was curious to see if it's still there."

"It's there. And I don't like it."

"Oh?" Aunty Di said, interested. "Why is that?"

"I don't know. Let's get the sled, huh?"

"There's not enough snow on the ground for sledding. You know that from yesterday. Why don't you like the smokehouse? Have you ever been *inside* the smokehouse?"

"No!"

"The way you say that, Kelly . . . My goodness. You sound as though you were afraid of it. If you're afraid of it, you can hold my hand." Aunty Di stretched out her hand.

Kelly shook her head. She could see her aunt's eyes narrow and get a stubborn look. "There's a snake there," Kelly explained. It wasn't the real reason, but it wasn't a lie either. There was a snake.

"Snakes are all asleep during the winter," Aunty Di said in her schoolteacher, book-reading voice. "So you don't have to worry about the snake. Come along." She wiggled the gloved fingers of her extended hand.

Kelly surrendered. She let Aunty Di take her hand, and they walked a zigzag path between the trunks of the trees on the frozen grass and the dead leaves, which made a crackling sound at each footstep. Ahead of them the smokehouse became visible, its paint all flaky, shreds of white on old gray boards. A tall, thin house without windows.

"Someone has repaired the roof," said Aunty Di. "When I was your age, or a little older, the roof had lost most of its shingles, and there were just the old rotted rafters. But it looks like it's been fixed. Did your daddy fix it?"

"Yes," said Kelly. Then, reconsidering, "I don't know."

When they came to the sagging barbed-wire fence, Aunty Di insisted on lifting Kelly up and setting her down on the other side of the rusty wires. Then she pushed down the wires with her gloved hand and stepped over them herself. They walked around to the far side, where the door was.

"And look at this. The door's back on its hinges, and there's a padlock on it. I wonder why that is."

"Let's go back home," said Kelly. "I have to go to the bathroom."

"No, you don't. You're just saying that. Why don't you like the smokehouse, Kelly? Have you ever been inside it?"

"No, never. But mom was. She told me."

"Oh?" Aunty Di's voice changed the way it did when she was interested in what you might say. "She did? What did she tell you?"

"She said when she was a little girl, you put her inside of it. To scare her."

"Oh, for goodness sake, I wouldn't have done anything like that."

"She said you did. She said you would take a flashlight and shine it on your face to look scary. She showed me how you did it. You put it under your chin."

"Well, I may have done that. I don't remember it, but I suppose it's possible. Maybe she confused the two things. If anyone put her in the smokehouse, it would have been her daddy, but I doubt that. She was just a little girl, no older than you, when he had his heart attack."

"Did he put *you* in the smokehouse?" Kelly asked, with a sudden, shrewd intuition.

"Yes. Yes, he did. When I'd done something wrong, and he wanted to punish me."

"Because he knew you were afraid of it?"

"That must have been the reason."

"Why were you afraid?"

"I don't know. People are sometimes afraid of things for no good reason."

"Did you ever see anyone here?"

"See anyone?"

"A man?"

Aunty Di shook her head, but Kelly didn't believe her. She knew that her aunt had seen the same thing she had, and that that's why she was afraid of the smokehouse, and why she wanted to look at it now, with Kelly with her. Because (Kelly knew) the man wouldn't be there if you had someone else with you.

"What kind of man?" Aunty Di wanted to know. "A man like . . . your daddy?"

The man Kelly had seen, and she still recalled him very clearly, didn't have any clothes on. You could see everything, but it didn't seem to matter to him. He was sitting on the big stone beside the door, and when he saw Kelly staring at him, at the big cut along his leg, and the blood coming out of it, he just looked up and smiled and winked one eye and then he wasn't there. The stone he'd been sitting on was still there, and maybe the blood was, too, but Kelly wasn't going to tell Aunty Di anything about him. She'd never told anyone, not her mom, not her dad, not even the Trolls.

"I don't know," said Kelly. "Some man. Maybe he was *your* dad."

Aunty Di didn't say a thing. She just gave Kelly a funny look and then agreed to take her back to the house so she could go to the bathroom.

9

Carl had sized her up at Christmas dinner and decided that his sister-in-law was a pig. She wasn't that fat, though he bet she must spend a lot of her time dieting. No, the piggish thing about her was her basic assumption that whatever she wanted *belonged* to her. The way she tucked into her dinner without waiting for Janet to finish cutting up Kelly's drumstick. Carl had always been amazed at the bad manners of all three Turney women, his wife included. His own family, though they hadn't been any better off, came off as aristocrats by comparison. Somehow bad manners are more noticeable in women. Janet was a confirmed nose-picker, the kind who takes an interest in the result, and her mother was an encyclopedia of bad habits and negative personal hygiene, including B.O.

Di wasn't piggy in those ways. Being a schoolteacher, she had to be more aware of appearances. But once she sat down in front of a plate of food, it was trough time. Carl had been brought up to believe you didn't start eating till your host gave the signal, but she had the manners of someone brought up in a cafeteria, or the joint.

On the other hand, he'd been relieved to see her bolt down the turkey and stuffing the way she did, because on her few earlier visits Di had made a fuss about being a strict vegetarian. That had been one of the main reasons, aside from plain gut-level disliking her, for his having been against the idea of her moving in while Janet served her time. As it turned out, Di's vegetarianism was the relaxed kind that allowed poultry and fish. She was even willing to cook dinners involving beef and lamb, but pork, for some reason, she wouldn't deal with at all. Which suited Carl just fine. He wasn't that crazy about pork himself. Too greasy.

One of the brighter cons in the joint, Jim Cottonwood, had a theory about the kinds of things people would and wouldn't eat. Cottonwood was an Indian, and he claimed that every Indian has his own totem, which isn't the same as a tribe. It's a group of people who all identify in some way with a particular animal, and if you belong to the totem of that animal, you never eat its meat, except, sometimes, on a ritual occasion. So it made sense that Diana, being a pig, wouldn't touch pork. He would have to remember to tell Cottonwood about this proof of his totem theory.

Tonight, their first night together since Janet had finally been hauled away, Carl had put Kelly to bed at her regular bedtime, just before nine, and when he came downstairs he discovered that Di had commandeered his recliner and tuned the TV to a show on channel 13 with Luciano Pavarotti singing his favorite arias.

"Hey," he pointed out, trying to sound amiable, "you're in Papa Bear's chair. Do you mind?"

"Excuse me?" Di said, looking up, but not otherwise stirring a limb. Her thighs had got really big. She was going to be one of those old ladies who spread out from the waist down and grow a big butt and thick legs.

"I said you're sitting in my chair."

"Oh, I thought I was just sitting in *a* chair. I didn't realize it was one of the prerogatives of home ownership."

Carl had learned, from working at the joint, that it was bad strategy to snap back at someone when they wised off or wanted to pick a quarrel. Usually a significant silence is the most effective way to dampen the urge to aggression. The aggressor realizes he's going to have to do all the work. So Carl just stood there to one side of the recliner and waited for Di to vacate.

She got up from the recliner and moved over to the couch, taking the corner that Janet usually occupied.

Carl took the remote from the coffee table beside him, aimed it at the TV, and switched to channel 4, where *Roseanne* had just got started.

"You don't *ask*, you just *take?*" Di wanted to know.

"It's *Roseanne*. I always see *Roseanne* if I'm home on Thursday night. If you really want to watch the Pavarotti thing, you can tape it on the VCR."

"Thanks."

"There's a blank tape beside the VCR that you can use. You know how to do it? It's tricky with the cable. Sometimes you think you're taping, and when you're done there's nothing on the tape. Want me to do it for you?"

"No, don't bother. I'll watch *Roseanne*."

"Suit yourself."

Carl tilted the chair back and watched the show in a lazy way. Most of the time he didn't bother trying to follow the story on the shows he saw. He just looked at the people come and go, listened to them mouth off, in the same state of alert drift as when he pulled duty on the yard. Often enough, even though he wasn't keeping track of the plot, he knew how things would wind up, sometimes from just the first five minutes. On Sundays, when he was home for *Murder, She Wrote*, he could usually tell way ahead of time who the killer was, just by looking at his face. It amazed Janet, who was faked out by even the most simpleminded mystery.

At the first break, Carl took a quick trip into the bathroom and then returned with a beer from the icebox and a clean ashtray from the top of the cupboard. Once the show had started back up, he unpeeled the cellophane from a Dutch Masters and lighted it. He could feel the pressure of Di's disapproval, but she had the good sense not to say anything while the show was on. Carl drank his beer and smoked his stogey and watched *Roseanne*, knowing all the while that he was staking out his territory as much as any dog marking a tree trunk with his piss. Di had been doing just the same thing, and just as consciously, when she'd settled down in his recliner. It was Goldilocks and the three bears all over again, except that Mama Bear was missing and Goldilocks had come for the duration.

"Well," she said when the program was over, "I liked that more than I expected to. I can understand why the woman is so popular. There's something there."

"Oh, yeah, a whole lot of something. Now, if you want to switch it back to the other great fatso, that's okay with me."

Diana smiled one of her less priggish smiles. "We're none of us as thin as we used to be, Carl."

He liked the way she included herself in the observation, as though to say, I may be a pot myself, but you certainly are a black kettle.

"Ain't it the truth," he agreed equably. He took a puff on his Dutch Masters and released a slow, thoughtful plume of smoke. Her eyes focused on the plume of smoke, interpreting it, as she was meant to, as another territorial claim.

"You do know, don't you, about secondhand smoke?"

"Yeah, it's getting to be a big issue, even at the joint. Which is a laugh, when you consider that cigarettes are the main currency there. Which gives the guys who don't smoke a weird kind of edge. But even so, there's some of them who are making a stink about having to be locked up with smokers."

"Stink is the operative word."

Carl removed the cigar from his mouth and contemplated the ashy tip. "Pricey cigars do smell better, I'll give you that. If I was a rich man, as the saying goes, I'd smoke a classier kind of cigar. Though maybe I wouldn't. I've sampled some of them, and they tend to pack more of a wallop than I really care for. It's like beer and wine. Beer is blue-collar, but if I had the money, would I really rather drink wines that cost twenty bucks a bottle, and some a lot more than that? I don't think so. Wine wipes me out. I get sleepy. Beer, on the other hand, just gets me mellow."

"All that is neither here nor there," Di said with an impatient wave of her hand at an encroaching streamer of smoke. "The *point* is that secondhand smoke is harmful to those who have to breathe the same polluted air as the smoker. Including, especially, *children*."

"That's true, I've read that. I've even pointed it out to Janet, who's the cigarette smoker in the house. My daily smoke output couldn't compare to hers."

"Even if that were so, she's not here now."

"That's a silver lining I hadn't thought of before. But I know that's not what you're driving at. You're trying to tell me I should stop smoking. And that's true. And I shouldn't eat so much either. And neither should you—we're both sinners there. But I'm not about to start dieting, or give up the stogeys. Or the beer, if that was the next thing you had in mind, though I don't suppose it is, because from what I've observed you are not exactly a teetotaler yourself. My philosophy is live and let live. Have you got another?"

"You always were a good debater, Carl. I'll give you that."

"And you've always had the idea, because I've got the job I do, and because you're a schoolteacher, that I should be some kind of Archie Bunker, lowbrow asshole. The fact is, Diana, that I was in college nearly as long as you. And I got better grades. And I'm moving up through the ranks faster than you did, *if* you're moving up at all. I mean, all these years as a sub can't look that good on your C.V., whatever your reasons—or your excuses—are. None of which is any of my business, I agree. But how I choose to live in my own house *is* my business. And if you don't approve, then you've got two choices. Lump it or leave it, simple as that. I didn't invite you here, but for Kelly's sake I'm willing to make an effort to get along. But getting along doesn't mean you're in charge."

"Because it's your house?"

"I guess that's what it comes down to. And the fact that I'm Kelly's dad."

"I grew up in this house."

"So you did. And you left it. And your mother *sold* it to me. And now it's mine."

"For a pittance."

"I understand that's been a grievance for you. But that's a bone you've got to pick with your mother, not with me. I paid good money when she needed it to start up her Navaho House. And I'm support-ing her daughter and bringing up her grandkid, with possibly others on the way. So it shouldn't be surprising if she wanted to help us out."

"Oh, you're so *reasonable*," she said, as though reasonable were a sin.

"I try to be. Why don't you?"

To which Diana just glared. Then, when her glare didn't accom-plish anything, she reached for the remote and switched on Pavarotti.

Carl sat and watched the program right to the end, partly to spite his sister-in-law and partly because he genuinely enjoyed hearing the big fat fool sing his beautiful heart out. "Nessun dorma." Or "No One Can Sleep." Not while he was singing, that's for sure. Then a great duet with a black soprano as fat as he was. Unbeatable. Then the all-time favorite, "La donna e mobile," which the an-nouncer explained meant that women are fickle, but which also meant, according to one of the other C.O.'s that Carl worked with, "Women are furniture." And the guy was an Italian, so he should know.

Halfway through the aria, the particular piece of furniture Carl had to deal with tonight levered herself up from the couch and said, "I'll see you in the morning."

He'd won.

For the present.

10

For the first few weeks as a substitute mother, Diana felt like a twentieth-century resident of the Little House on the Prairie. Bus-tle, bustle, bustle. But without the drudgery. She'd always envied the lives of ordinary housewives. The laundry was a breeze when you didn't have to drive miles away to a Laundromat and wait in line for a dryer. No more teaching, no more books, no more *children* with dirty looks.

Her main responsibility was the cooking, and that was a genuine pleasure, especially now, having fallen from grace and being able to enjoy, in moderation, the pleasures of protein. Even such a simple pleasure as a tuna noodle casserole. She explored her sister's paperback edition of Fannie Farmer's cookbook (which was in pristine condition; Janet must *never* have used it) with the enthusiasm of a newlywed bride. Chicken pot pie. Pineapple upside-down cake. Cole slaw, from scratch. And sundry other culinary wonders as the whim took her.

Having depended so long on takeout from salad bars and microwaved Lean Cuisine (there had been no restaurants within striking distance of Willowville), this was culinary heaven. And she knew she wasn't the only one to appreciate her efforts. Carl, who never before had had a kind word to say for her, was almost lavish with his compliments. Once, after a second helping of the chicken pot pie, he actually said, "That was delicious." Clearly, he was not used to much more in the way of home cooking than meat and potatoes, and the potatoes probably came from a box.

Kelly was less happy with the new dispensation. From the evidence of the pantry when Diana had arrived, Kelly had been subsisting on a diet of sugar-coated cereals, Noodle-O's, and whatever other ersatz gluey starches lazy mothers know how to fob off on guileless toddlers. It was no easy task weaning her from such bad habits. She would not eat oatmeal. She would not eat salads or fresh vegetables. She would not eat any bread that wasn't snow-white and pumped full of air. She would not eat fish or rice or drink orange juice that didn't come out of a Tropicana carton. The one time Diana had taken her along to the supermarket in Leech Lake, the child had thrown a fit when Diana had refused to load the cart with Little Debbie snacks and cereals and other nutrition-free commodities. Four years old and already the perfect mindless American consumer.

But hunger, as the proverb has it, is the best sauce, even for finicky four-year-olds, and Kelly reluctantly yielded to the new regime. She had no choice, for her father, the few times Kelly had pleaded her case to him, had taken Diana's side when she'd shown him how much she was saving on the grocery bills. Then, too, Diana knew how to entice as well as punish. She would not buy Oreos, but she would bake up a batch of oatmeal-raisin cookies from scratch, with Kelly helping at every step. And then the cookies would be meted out as rewards for good behavior. Children are all, at Kelly's age, as easy to train as Skinner's pigeons. The carrot and the stick would do the trick.

Beyond that it was simply a matter of putting the house in order. Janet, who had always rebelled against the idea of cleanliness, order, or even beauty (there wasn't one potted plant in the house, not a picture on the walls that hadn't been inherited), had been the most perfunctory housekeeper, not to say a slob. There were cobwebs anywhere you wouldn't directly walk into them. The carpets were crusted with dirt. You could write your name with your fingertip on the windows.

January was not the ideal time to cope with such problems, but Diana went ahead and did a spring cleaning in the dead of winter. She shampooed the carpets, washed the windows *and* the curtains, and scoured what looked like a decade of grime from the bathtub and the sinks.

Carl was not unaware of the transformations she wrought, and he would regularly, in a polite way, take note of her improvements and proffer a figurative pat on the head. He never (she'd noticed) touched her; he had that much good sense. But he avoided spending time at home. He would show up for meals, and would spend some time with Kelly, and then he'd disappear. Probably to a local bar. Diana had no way of knowing where he'd gone. He didn't bother to tell her, and she wouldn't demean herself by asking.

She would hear him vroom up the driveway at eleven or twelve o'clock, and then he'd head straight to his bedroom. If Diana was still up watching the TV, he might ask, "Everything okay?" before he clomped up the stairs. Otherwise she would listen, tensely, in the dark, in her narrow bed, while he opened the door to Kelly's room, and then, too long later, go into the bathroom and draw a bath.

Everything was *not* okay. Something, in fact, was very wrong, but it was not something she could speak of to Carl. Or to anyone else, unless it were Brenda Zweig, but Brenda had gone off on a long vacation, to San Miguel de Allende, in Mexico, and wasn't responding to her answering machine, despite Diana's messages that Brenda could phone her collect. Is *that* what friends were for?

Everything was far from okay. Oh, the days were fine, with all the bustle. While the sun was shining and there were tasks to tend to and Kelly to look after, there were no problems. But after dinner, after Kelly had been put to bed, and Carl had driven off wherever he went to, and she was alone in the house, it was another matter. Then, as the darkness gathered, despite all that every lamp and lightbulb in the house could do, she would begin to feel . . . something wrong.

A hunger. But not her own hunger, strong as that could be sometimes. A hunger *outside* the house. As though, as in the fairy tale of the three little pigs, there were a wolf huffing and puffing at the back door. *Something* that wanted to come inside.

She would hear the noises that came at night, all the knockings and tappings and moanings that you wondered about, and she would ask herself: Is it the furnace? The icebox? Mice? What could it be?

A hunger that was (though she did not want to think so) sexual.

One night, when the fear, with all its irrational urgency, had become too much to bear, she thought she must confront it head-on by going outdoors to feel the humbling reality of the January cold. If this was just some fancy kind of anxiety, the cold would do away with it.

It was below zero. The winter had settled in to stay. She put on her down parka and zipped it up to her chin and slipped snow boots on over the moccasins she wore around the house. But she didn't pull the parka's hood over her head, because she wanted to *feel* the cold. She wanted the cold to tell her she was being foolish.

But the moment she stepped outside the house, her fear intensified. She knew, as it touched her skin, that the cold and the fear were one and that they were just the wind of what was behind them, the unseen force whose source she could sense above her, on the hill, where the moon shone on it.

The smokehouse.

No, she told herself, I will not go there. But already her rubber soles were squeaking on the afternoon's inch-thick increment of snow. No, I do not believe there is anything there. It is all in the past, and I reject what happened then. He has no power over me. He's dead.

But he was not dead.

He had, undead, felt her presence these many numberless hours within the house, bustling about, ordering things as she saw fit, and, when she slept, calling to him, incessantly, incestuously, insisting that he answer.

He had as little choice in this as she. He hated her, as only those who have been murdered hate those who have murdered them, but he had to answer her longing.

The longing, strangely, strengthened him. Quickened what had been, so long, mere latency. Before this moment he had drawn, or repelled, the meat that moved through the woods. Bats, wasps, owls—whatever could tremble within the range of his elsewise impotent fury. But *she* was now within that range; *she* could tremble. She could be, because he desired her, because of the lie she had told, his, at last and again.

She fell to her knees before the door of the smokehouse and pressed her face against the snow, first one cheek, then the other. She licked the snow. She spoke his name.

"Daddy," she said, remembering, at last, the moment that had united them so terribly, "I hate you. I hate you. I want you to die."

"You're mine," he whispered, without words, "and now I will destroy you."

11

Just as certain configurations of electric power lines produce powerful magnetic fields that, over the course of time, cause a variety of malignant tumors in tissues that have long been irradiated by those invisible and malign energies, so in the spiritual realm there can be conjunctions of moral events that act to spawn and to nurture those malignancies of the spirit that are lumped together under the heading of supernatural or psychic phenomena—hauntings, premonitions, the sudden flaring up of grotesque impulses, or the gradual wasting away of vital energies. Usually the confluence of forces that allow such things to be is so brief that we are able to write off the result—the stab of irrational grief, the sudden suicidal impulse, or the hand's reflexive grasp of the haft of an axe—as no more than the mental equivalent of a muscular spasm. No sooner do we see the apparition than it has vanished into the hallway's darkness.

But there are some apparitions that linger, and reappear, and become strong, and develop powers of speech. If we are so unwise as to enter into communication with these spirits, they can infuse us with strengths and powers that are like their own, but, because our physical selves are the conduits of these energies, the power we can exert—call it witchcraft—is exponentially greater than the power the unmediated spirits might command. In doing this we become, in a sense, the tools of these entities. We suppose we have been given powers, but in fact we have been given to them.

Most of the rites and rituals connected with witchcraft—the abracadabras, candles, and incense—are simply a form of theater, which the medium uses to put her soul into a state of entranced receptivity. In the age of alchemy, weeks might be spent elaborating such pomps. In our own time, a cigarette and the right music on the stereo can accomplish the same essential purpose with a fraction of the effort. Because the essential thing is not the physical ambiance—the runes and chanting and such—but a certain harmony between the moral environment and the soul of the would-be sorcerer; an equivalence of evils, so that the larger and pervading evil of the age finds in the soul of the witch a perfect embodiment, a mirroring of microcosm and macrocosm across whose quicksilver surface energies may flow.

In the soul of Diana Turney that balance had been refined to exquisite parity at the moment, not yet a month gone by, when she had confided to Brenda Zweig how she had been sexually abused by her father at the age of twelve. As they'd talked at Brenda's kitchen table, within the cone of incandescent brightness defined by the Tiffany lamp, as the sordid details emerged from the gloom of the past, Diana had felt a strange kind of empowerment. Strange, because shouldn't it have been just the other way around? Shouldn't such memories reawaken the shame and fear of that first occasion? Instead, Diana's pulse quickened, and her whole frame was atingle with that adrenaline charge you feel in the first moments after leaving a sauna or a hot tub. If she had been a man and accustomed to such things, she would have been ready to spar with a boxing partner for the pure physical pleasure of trading blows.

She told Brenda of forced caresses; of being compelled to fondle Wesley's sexual organ slimed with sexual discharges; of kissing him, and of his tongue's trespasses on her twelve-year-old body; of his penetration, abrupt and merciless, while he held his hand over her mouth to prevent her outcry; of being locked, afterward, in the filthy smokehouse where the acts were done, nauseated, weeping, bereft.

In telling Brenda these things, they became as real to Diana as if the same crimes were being committed on her flesh anew. She could feel each raw emotion as the child had felt it: her initial dismay, her mounting panic, the anguish of her actual violation, and the terrible despair that followed it. So real, so heart-wrenching, so painful, that by the time Diana fell silent, she had come to believe every word of it herself. She might have been lying (as, in a strict sense, she was), but these lies seemed, beneath the light of Brenda's Tiffany lamp, more full of truth than the dry dust of old facts.

Indeed, Diana had long since relegated those crumbly old artifacts to her mental attic, where, should she ever choose to sort through them, she might discover a few surprises among the brittle snapshots. Memories that were not so much "repressed," in the sense Diana claimed for her memories of incest, as tucked away in a dark, cobwebby corner: not forgotten, but unvisited. Which, in practical terms, amounted to the same thing. Out of sight is out of mind.

Did she feel anything like guilt in the matter of her father's death? No, nor had she even dreamt, in her adult life, of his body hanging within the smokehouse, inverted, like the body of the Hanged Man on the tarot card, the blood flowing down from the crotch of his blue jeans and across the front of his flannel shirt, and beginning to form thin rivulets down his neck and across his cheeks. Her ears were deaf, now as then, to his choked voice, as it pronounced the single syllable of her name: "Di!" She might have said the same to him as she'd closed the smokehouse door.

Those uglinesses were no part of the past Diana chose to remember. It is the survivors, after all, who write the history books. In effect, it had not happened and she had not seen it. But until that night at Brenda's, Diana had not thought to paint over those deleted memories with images of her own invention. Even then it was not as though she'd *thought* to do it. It had happened to her, in the way that poems are said to happen to poets: by an inspiration, a kind of wind filling the sails of speech and sweeping her away.

Cannot lies, like poems, represent a kind of higher truth? It was one of the ancient Fathers of the Church who said that he believed *because* the thing he believed was impossible. Otherwise faith would be nothing special. One doesn't need faith to believe in the grime in the sink. But to look up into the mirror, and smile, and see there the beauty invisible to everyone else and to believe in the ultimate triumph of that beauty, that's what faith is for.

12

Jim Cottonwood's cellmate, Patrick Bryce, had been a Roman Catholic priest. In the joint he came to be known as Father Rat—not because he was thought to be a snitch, but just because it rhymed with the Father Pat he'd been outside. He was also, having been a pedophile, Pat the Bunny. But only to the guards. On the yard he insisted on being addressed as Clay, and since he was quite capable of flying off the handle for the least abridgment of what he considered his due respect, that is what the other cons called him, to his face.

Pedophiles generally have a hard time of it in the joint, where there is an Old Testament sense of justice and the wicked have done unto them as they have done unto others, often on a daily basis. Clay had managed to make himself an exception to that rule by sending one of the first men who'd gang-raped him to the infirmary and another to the hospital in St. Cloud. Clay himself had incurred a broken tooth and lacerations about the face and neck, but he had established a reputation as someone who isn't fucked with, and he had not had to defend his honor and his asshole another time.

Clay had settled down to his twenty-five-to-life as one to the criminal underclass born, taking to the tank like a fish to water. He had the talk; he had the walk; he even had, across the knuckles of both hands, crude self-inflicted tattoos of LOVE and HATE.

There were a few details that didn't sort easily with his new persona. Clay came on like someone a good thirty years younger than the fifty-something Father Pat. Most of the cons who were up in their fifties had served so much time they'd lost their bounce. They had the wiped-out look of dead-end bureaucrats the world over. But Clay, despite that he was going gray and getting paunchy, had the attitudes and nervous energies of someone still tuned, internally, to MTV.

Even more anomalous, and what made Clay, for all his flakiness, an ideal cellmate, was the range of knowledge and general couth that he had inherited from Father Pat. Jim accounted himself a good *Jeopardy* player and figured that he still might qualify someday as a contestant. But he was no match for Clay. In most categories, including even pop-culture trivia, Clay could come up with the right answer before any of the contestants had buzzed in. The capital of Ghana. What is Accra? Okay, anyone on *Jeopardy* is going to bone up on capitals and presidents and that kind of shit, but what about the eighteenth-century Frenchman who was the father of modern chemistry? That drew a blank from all three contestants on the show, but Clay came up with it just like that: Antoine Lavoisier. Guys made book on whether or not Clay would be able to answer the Final Jeopardy question. He did better than three out of five.

He was also an ace Scrabble player, and that was rare in the joint. He knew all the funny two-letter words like "ut" and "re" and "nu" that were basic to high-powered Scrabble, but he also had a shitload of fancier words that were in Webster's, even if he didn't know exactly what they meant. "Quale," which is "a property, such as whiteness, considered independently of things having the property."

From the Latin, naturally. The guy had been a priest, even if he claimed that whole part of his life had been lived by someone else. The words were there but not, he claimed, the memories. Whenever such knowledge surfaced, Clay seemed just as surprised by it as Jim. The guy was a flake, no doubt about it, but not a fake.

It was in one of the Scrabble sessions that they'd hit the word "mandragora." It was right at the start of the game. Jim had had to go first, and his letters were impossible. One vowel, an A, and then Q, G, S, S, R, and V. He wasn't going to waste an S on GAS, so that left one possibility that he could see: RAG. Eight fucking points.

Clay stared at the board, which was just a sheet of paper that Jim had drawn up from memory, and stared, and stared, rubbing the stubble of his buzz cut, and then he smiled and said, "Eureka!"

He put down all seven of his letters, one by one, and then, before Jim could raise an objection, he said, "'Mandragora.' Sixty-eight points. It's in the Bible, and I think it's in Shakespeare, too, so it's got to be in Webster's. It's a plant. Look it up."

"I will."

Not that Jim doubted it would be there. And "mandragora" was there, though all Webster's said was "mandrake." But "mandrake" was the very next word, and just as Clay had said, it was a plant, which, to Jim's dismay, Webster's defined as "a poisonous plant of the nightshade family, found in Mediterranean regions." The definition continued: "It has a short stem, purple or white flower, and a thick root, often forked, used in medicine for its narcotic and emetic properties." After that was a second definition, "the root formerly thought to resemble the human shape," and a third, "the May apple, native to North America."

"Shit," said Jim.

"Sixty-eight points. Write it down."

"Yeah, right." He set down the sixty-eight points, then leaned back in his bunk and said, "Christ."

"Hey, the game's just started."

"Yeah, I know. The thing is, mandrake."

"It's there, in the dictionary."

"No, I got no argument with that. It's not the word. It's the plant, mandrake. I've been using it."

Clay chuckled. "No shit? For its emetic properties?"

"No, for the sweat lodge."

"Oh, come on. That's impossible. Like the dictionary says, it's Mediterranean. It's famous over there. You must have got hold of the other mandrake."

"Maybe, but I don't think so. 'Cause I've been using this root, and the first time I saw it I thought how it looked like the lower part of a guy's body. If the legs were twisted round."

"Where'd you get it from?" Clay asked.

"Through the chaplain. That's how I get all the stuff for the sweat lodge. Sage, mainly. Cedar. Sweet grass. And then this mandrake. The chaplain isn't all that happy to order it, but he has to. There was the Indian Religious Freedoms Act, in Seventy-six, just after I got sent here, which said that every prison had to provide a sweat lodge as part of our religion. So I got in touch with this medicine man at the Wabasha rez, where I knew some guys, and he sent me this list of things to use for the tea in the sweat lodge."

"Tea? You drink *tea* in the sweat lodge?"

"We drink some of it, but mostly it gets poured over the rocks. When it hits the rocks, the smell of it is something else. But then, after you've breathed it in a while, you don't notice it that much. The sage is the main element. Demons can't stand the smell of sage. A lot of the guys can't either. Probably 'cause they got demons in them. Anyhow, it's powerful, the sage. But it's not just the sage that's in the tea. There's cedar, and sweet grass, and, like I said, this mandrake."

"You know, I think your chaplain may have got things confused. Or someone did. There's May berry that grows in Minnesota, but that could be like hemlock. In America there's hemlocks that are like a kind of pine tree, but they're not the same as the hemlock that Socrates drank, that killed him. Or robins—what we call robins here isn't what robins are in England. The people who came here applied the old words they knew to the plants that were here. You must have got hold of the real thing. The Mediterranean variety."

Jim laughed. "And it's an emetic? It gives you the shits?"

Clay smiled in the sinister way he had sometimes. When he smiled that way, you could imagine how he could have actually done the shit he'd got put away for. "It can do more than that," Clay said.

"How do you mean?"

"It's an aphrodisiac. At least by reputation. In the Bible, they call it love apples. And that's before tomatoes had the name. Which are also in the nightshade family, the same as tobacco. Who knows what's an aphrodisiac? Some people think oysters do the trick. But mandrake must do something special. There's a story somewhere about a general who leaves a lot of wine around where he knows the army he's going to fight will find it. And he doses it with mandragora. So they drink it, and they nod out, and the general wins the day. It's a legend, probably. But hey, there's a better legend than that. The root of the thing when you dig it up is supposed to let out a scream. And if you hear it, you go crazy. So, in order to avoid that, what you have to do is, you tie the root to a dog, and you have the dog pull it up while you have got wax in your ears and blow some kind of horn, so you won't hear the scream. But the dog hears it, and the dog dies. How about that?"

"Sounds crazy."

"Ask the dog."

"But a lot of people did believe that?"

"A lot of people will believe anything, Jim. Me, do I believe it? You got some of the stuff, I'll test it out, and then I'll tell you. But not if it means I got to fast two days before I go into your sweat lodge. Anyhow, I don't need an emetic. Or an aphrodisiac. And I got sixty-eight points, bro. Write 'em down."

13

It had been years since the possibility of suicide had crossed Diana's mind. She'd come to think she'd put all that behind her. Now the blackness had returned like an unwelcome lover, someone you hated but at the same time could not resist. Come in, you tell him, come in, and there he is, a permanent guest, with his suitcase in your closet and his shoes under your bed.

It was there like the moon, noticed only at intervals, but always present, even when you couldn't see it, pulling at her. Telling her, you're mine, you've always been mine. Your very name is my name, too. Diana.

It was with her day after day, unrelenting, like this winter, the worst in decades. The snow piling up higher week by week, with never a thaw, one blizzard after another. The drifts on the north side of the house had built up to the level of the windows, and they were solid, impacted, unshovelable. On the coldest days, Carl's Chevy wouldn't start, despite every kind of pampering, and so he would borrow Diana's Camry, and she would be marooned in the house for the rest of the day.

She tried to read, but her mind wouldn't stay focused for more than fifteen minutes at a time. She would watch the TV, but then she would begin to hate herself for becoming just another damned housewife, glued to the soaps and snacking constantly. In the five weeks she'd been back at the farm, she'd put on ten pounds. At that rate, by April she'd be back to her all-time worst. What was really awful was she didn't care. Not about the weight. Not about the meat she was eating, along with Carl and Kelly, almost every day. Not about the way she was slacking off on every good intention that she'd formed before she'd finally agreed to come here. *Anna Karenina?* Seventeen pages. She *had* read Jane Smiley's *A Thousand Acres*, and it had shattered her, but that was the only book she'd read in five weeks. Some intellectual.

When she thought about it, the bottom line was, in the words of Martha Washington: Fuck that shit. Martha Washington was not the wife of our first president, but an African-American woman that Diana had got to know at Thursday-night meetings of Adult Children of Alcoholics (ACoA), back in Willowville. Martha had an ability, which Diana greatly envied, of saying exactly what she felt. Martha's verdict on all sorts of matters that other people at the meeting would get wrought up about was, quite simply, Fuck that shit. It was a formula that solved almost any otherwise intractable problem. But what if you considered it as a philosophy of life? What if nothing mattered, really? What if the best idea was just to walk out the exit? What if death was what it seemed to be when you were drunk and listening to the right music? Beautiful all by itself.

In this, the worst winter of the century—the worst, anyhow, that Diana could remember—the weather itself seemed to point the same moral. The snow, especially when the moon printed the shadows of the trees across it, was beautiful. The total blackness of the sky on cloudy, moonless nights—that was beautiful, too. And what was most beautiful was the silence when she stepped outside the house and tuned in to the absolute zero of winter. A silence that asked you to join in, as though you were at a Quaker meeting, where there were no hymns or sermons, only the immense, unspoken admission that there was nothing that needed saying, nothing that needed doing, nothing better than nothing at all.

Life disagreed, of course. Life bundled up against the winter and bided its time, certain that eventually things would start to stir. The snow would melt. The moon would sink in the west, and the sun would take charge, and the old cycle of eating and breeding would kick in again.

The Goddess, for all her sometime cruelty, was a goddess of life; of seeds and growth and new beginnings. And Diana knew what Martha Washington would have said about giving in to depression and trying to make something romantic and beautiful out of death. She *wanted* to be on the side of the Goddess and Martha Washington. But when she went out the back door and felt the sting of the cold, the idea would return, like a tune that wouldn't stop playing inside her head.

And, indeed, that was the case. Like a radio that could not be turned off, she was receiving signals. It was her father who spoke to her in the gleamings of the snow, in the shadows cast by the moon, in the deathly silence of the February nights. She had helped him to his death, and he meant to do the same for her.

It would not be an easy task. Diana was tenacious of life, and she resisted any direct awareness of his presence, even though he was now so near her. When he exerted his influence, she would look the other way. She would feel an encroaching darkness, but she did not give it his name.

But if not her death, the ghost insisted, then another must be exacted. There *must* be a death. Many deaths. This is the one thing ghosts insist on. The only thing they know.

14

Back when he had had a *Star-Tribune* paper route, Alan had ridden by Navaho House every morning, or trudged past the place if it was weather like this, too treacherous for two wheels. But all the time he'd had the route, he'd never gone up to the front door and asked if they wanted to have the paper delivered. There were six or seven old ladies living there on county assistance, and on summer evenings you could see them all lined up in a row on the front porch. Like the ragged odds and ends that got dumped in the box of things you could take for free at the garage sale at his grandpa's church. Nobody ever took away any of it, and after a while, seeing the same stuff every Saturday, week after week, you got to feeling sorry for all that junk. Electric can openers that didn't work. Old flannel shirts with most of the buttons missing. Tin ashtrays. Peculiar-shaped glasses.

He'd felt the same about the old ladies on the porch at Navaho House. Sorry, but at the same time a little queasy about any kind of contact, as though there were some kind of contagion in them. He'd no more have thought of asking them to take out a subscription than he'd have considered approaching the Good Shepherd Funeral Home two blocks farther down the street for the same purpose.

Which made it seem all the stranger to have become almost a regular visitor to the place. Unless you thought about it. Because wasn't that where he always wound up? In the same take-it-away box with the people no one else had any use for? The nerds who can't get a date to the prom, who can't make it as jocks *or* as brains? Who have skateboards they can't ride and computers they can't fathom? If he ever got a tattoo, it should be BORN TO LOSE. Or maybe just LOW AVERAGE.

Boy, was he in kick-me mode today. If self-pity were snow, he'd have been part of the landscape. One blizzard after another with no thaws in between, all piling up and turning into ice, so if you didn't get out there and shovel every time, it got to be like this pathway. There was no telling how thick the crust of ice was over the concrete. No telling if there even was a sidewalk down there at all. The old ladies were *trapped* inside Navaho House. Only they were so decrepit they probably didn't know it. Even in summer the porch was probably the farthest from the place they ever got.

He knocked on the back door, waited awhile, and knocked again. Unless there was someone in the kitchen, a knock wouldn't do any good, so he opened the door and called out, "Mrs. Cottonwood?" When there was no answer, he called out louder, "It's Alan Johnson." When there was still no answer, he scraped his boots on the welcome mat and went inside.

His glasses misted instantly, solid, like hoarfrost on a storm window. So when the old lady who owned the place came in the room, he had only the blurriest impression of her face. She looked like a raccoon, with black rings around the eyes.

Even blurred there was no mistaking her for anyone else. "Mrs. Turney," he said, "I was looking for Louise." He took off his cap.

Mrs. Turney removed the cigarette from her mouth. Alan couldn't recall ever seeing her when she wasn't smoking. "Yeah, I heard you shouting. So you're back to being Alan Johnson again? Last I heard you was Cottonwood, like Louise. The name didn't stick?"

Alan blushed. He didn't want to get involved in the whole explanation of how he meant to have his name changed back to what it had been, which he still hadn't done legally. There weren't that many people who knew him as Cottonwood anyhow, and he hadn't thought Mrs. Turney was one of them. Louise must have told her.

Mrs. Turney didn't wait for the explanation. "Well, Louise had to go out to the Shop 'n' Save, and she won't be back for a bit. We've run out of almost everything, and when there was a chance of a lift to the store, she took it. You don't look like you did when you was here last. When was that? No more than a week ago."

"I got my hair cut."

"I can see, I'm not blind. This one's an improvement. I'm not against long hair on principle, but some people it don't suit that well. Butch Larsen was your barber, wasn't he?"

Alan nodded.

"I could tell. Well, it'll grow out. It was the right basic decision, just the wrong barber. You must be looking for a job."

"Yeah, I have been. Louise told you that?"

"No, I'm psychic." She snorted out a derisive stream of smoke from her nostrils. "Any kid with long hair gets a haircut like you got, he must be looking for a job. But up here, this time of year, it'll take more than a haircut. I'm surprised you haven't moved down to the Twin Cities. That's what everyone else does, as soon as they finish high school. If not before."

She emitted a mirthless caw of a laugh and plopped down on a kitchen chair. "Well, don't just stand there. If you want to wait around for Louise, wipe your glasses off and sit down. I'd offer you some coffee, but the urn is dry. And the icebox is empty. We are living on Lipton's tea and mustard here."

"Thank you," said Alan.

He sat down, unzipped his parka, and de-iced his glasses with the flannel of his shirt, doing this at a discreet below-tabletop level. When he had his glasses back on, Mrs. Turney looked less like a raccoon. She even looked sexy in a weird way. Usually he wouldn't have associated sex with a woman of her age, but she did have big breasts, and the sweater she was wearing seemed to make a point of the fact. Plus, her face had a lot of makeup, which must have been the reason she'd made him think of a raccoon. All that mascara, but also some of the skin around the eyes was kind of purple in the same direction.

Mrs. Turney didn't say anything, just puffed on her eternal cigarette and waited for him to take the initiative. Which, for Alan, was never easy, even with people he knew well.

He went for the old standby. "This is some winter, huh?"

She lowered her eyelids and then raised them, as a comment on his powers of conversation. But then she agreed, "Uh-huh, some winter."

Alan tried to think of something else to talk about than the weather, but before he could, Mrs. Turney said, "It's going to ruin me."

"I hope not," Alan offered. When that got no response, he ventured, "The heating bills?"

She shook her head. "I wish that's all it was. The county picks up those. It's creeping ice."

He gave a blank look.

"You don't have creeping ice? Then you're lucky. I should have had the gutters cleaned in the fall, I guess. But it never happened before, or never as bad as this. See, what happens is the gutters fill with ice, and then, because of the heat in the house, the snow closest to the shingles melts, then turns to ice, and the ice backs up into the shingles. And a leak starts. The heat in the house keeps melting the snow on the roof, and the melt-off penetrates the roof, and starts coming down the walls—inside the house. And all that snow that's up there, instead of going down through the gutters, it comes into the house."

"Damn," said Alan.

Mrs. Turney focused her raccoon eyes on Alan in a calculating way. "Poor Louise. She's got the worst of it."

"How's that?"

"The wall of her bedroom is like a waterfall anytime the temperature rises even a little."

"You should do something," said Alan. "Take off the ice that's built up."

"I've tried, I've tried. But you know what they want? Seventy-five dollars an hour—where am I going to find that? Just to go up there and shovel off the snow that accumulated."

"Up on the roof?"

"It would probably just *slide* right off," said Mrs. Turney, "if you gave it a nudge."

"Maybe I could do it," said Alan.

"Hey," said Mrs. Turney, "I bet you could!"

He was suckered into it as easy as that. A few minutes later—with the help of a wonky aluminum ladder, which first got him up onto the roof of the porch and from there, by a real exercise of his utmost, onto the main roof of the house, snow shovel in hand—he was there, feeling capable and a little scared.

Never before in his life had Alan been up on the top roof of a house this size. A porch roof, yes. And a garage. But this was so high up that, with the rise of ground that Navaho House stood on, he could see, through the bare branches of the trees, as far as the water tower at the other end of town. The whole world looked different from this high up.

"I feel great," he thought, which for him, these days, was not a feeling he was used to. It wasn't just the elevation. It was knowing that he could do something for someone that might actually make a difference. He could solve the problem of creeping ice.

Standing spraddle-legged on the rooftree, he chunked the shovel down into the crusted snow and pried up a solid mass of it, which slid, with satisfying logic, down the steep slope of the roof, to impact on the drifted snow below. He proceeded, chunk by chunk, across the rooftree, releasing with each decisive tilt of the shovel another satisfying *whump!* as, unseen by him, the mass of the loosed snow hit the snowdrifts along the side of the house.

It felt good, as the exercise of power generally does. But then he hit a stretch where the snow, more impacted, did not as readily yield to his shovel's insistence.

He insisted more. He changed his footing. Only slightly, but enough. An avalanche resulted. An immense mass of snow cascaded down the roof.

Very impressive. He advanced and tried the same maneuver, but the shovel stuck. He waggled it. He changed his footing slightly and *pried*. It began to give.

He tried harder and it yielded, but as it did so, so did his footing. He tried to adjust, but he was slipping with the snow, and he grabbed for what was there, which was a long-defunct TV antenna.

The antenna snapped at its base, and he found himself sliding down the roof in the mass of loosened snow, riding it on his belly like a toboggan, still clutching the snapped antenna. He tried to jam the toes of his boot into the snow still left on the shingles, but that only had the effect of swiveling him round so that he was sliding down headfirst. He could hear the first hunks of hard snow hit the drifts two stories below, and then just before he figured he'd go over the edge of the roof himself, he could *see* the snow hitting the ground some thirty feet below.

And then, with his head and his left arm already beyond the lip of the frozen gutter, he stopped sliding. A few more hunks of snow spilled over the edge and dropped to the mound created by the avalanche from the roof, but he didn't go with them.

The antenna, still firmly gripped in his mittened hand, had saved him after all. He twisted his head sideways and squinted (he'd lost his glasses as he fell) and could just barely make out the taut length of wire connecting the antenna to the brick chimney at the center of the rooftree.

Okay, he told himself, I can do this. I've just got to swivel round to where I can pull myself back. The wire's secured to something up there, it'll hold.

If only he could get a grip on the gutter with his left hand and just push himself back a few inches from the edge of the roof. He shook off the mitten from his hand gently and then felt around for some kind of handhold. But the gutter was smoothly crusted with the ice that had built up all winter long, and the only result was that his left hand was soon stiff with the cold.

He was going to need help. He took a deep breath and bawled out, "Mrs. Turney! Hey, Mrs. Turney! Can you hear me? Hey, Mrs. Turney! Phone the fire department—please!"

His yelling didn't do a bit of good. The house was sealed up tight for the winter, and the old ladies, those who weren't completely deaf, were probably watching TV along with Mrs. Turney herself. There was nobody outside in this weather, and he was on the side of the house facing away from the street, so even someone driving by wouldn't have seen him. He might as well save his breath.

The thought finally couldn't be avoided: he could die. If he sledded over the edge of the roof headfirst, he could break his neck. If he didn't die, he might be paralyzed for the rest of his lousy life. Maybe the snow would cushion his fall, but that didn't seem a good bet. The snow that had come off the roof was as hard as ice. He could see it just below him, piled up in jagged hunks like the ice alongside a river after the first thaw. That snow was no featherbed.

He knew what people would say. "Did you hear how that Johnson kid killed himself? He shoveled himself off a roof." And they'd laugh. There was no one who'd feel the least bit sorry for what had happened. His mother might pretend for a while, but all he'd get from Grandpa Johnson was a final scowl.

It actually helped to think of Grandpa's reaction. Alan didn't want to give the old fart the satisfaction of presiding over his funeral, and from the reservoir of family hatred he drew new strength. He still had a grip on the antenna wire. If he rolled to the side and got his other hand on it, he could haul himself back to the top of the roof, hand over hand.

He thought each motion through a couple times, and then, as smoothly as he could, he shifted himself over onto his right hip and grabbed for the wire with his left hand. His body started sliding again, but both hands had a grip on the wire, and the wire took his weight.

It was the chimney that gave way. The mortar was old. A bad wind could have knocked it over. First it was just a few bricks, but then as the wire stapled to the side conveyed the force of Alan's desperate effort, the whole thing yielded at once.

Alan could see what was going to happen, and he let go of the wire. Before the chimney could hit him he was over the edge. And out cold.

15

By the time they got back to Navaho House with the groceries, Diana had had it with Louise Cottonwood. The expedition to Shop 'n' Save had been as exasperating as a field trip with a busful of second graders. Louise was stubborn as a mule. Diana would point out that rutabagas were going for only twenty-nine cents a pound, but Louise just shook her head and said the old ladies wouldn't eat rutabagas. Diana told her that she knew a wonderful way of fixing up rutabagas with evaporated milk and nutmeg so that you'd never know what they were, it would be like a pudding, but no, Louise wouldn't hear of it. Louise wouldn't hear of anything that wasn't already graven on her mental shopping list like one of the Ten Commandments. She insisted on buying a big cellophane-wrapped package of corn muffins at a ridiculous price even after Diana had pointed out how much it was possible to save by making corn muffins from scratch. Of course, at Shop 'n' Save you couldn't buy corn meal in bulk, and organic produce was not an option. And that was probably just as well, since from Navaho House's point of view the object was to cut corners and pinch pennies. But Louise actually favored canned vegetables over frozen, even though Diana could show her, from the unit pricing, that some of the frozen ones were cheaper. No, she would say, the old ladies prefer canned. And since Louise was the expert on what the old ladies would or would not eat, there was no arguing. Finally, Diana had just given up and gone out to her Camry and waited for Louise to get done.

They would have driven home in silence, but Louise (who, typically, refused to buckle up) turned on the radio, and there, on a station Carl must have tuned to the last time he'd appropriated the car, was Rush Limbaugh. So for the whole fifteen-mile stretch they were regaled by the wit and wisdom of America's number-one male chauvinist pig. Louise didn't even seem to be listening. She sat with her hands resting on her kneecaps, staring at the highway (which was treacherous the whole way), stony-faced.

This is the last time, Diana told herself, that I go out of my way to do a favor for her, Native American or not. Between Limbaugh and the recollection of all the good suggestions that Louise had categorically refused to heed, Diana was in a really foul mood by the time they got back to Navaho House.

"There's a visitor," Louise remarked as Diana pulled up in back of a rust-pitted Olds, which had occupied the only parking space on the road that accessed the shoveled path. (The driveway hadn't been plowed since early January.) "It's that Johnson boy. Good Lord."

"What Johnson boy is that?" Diana asked, forgetting to maintain the blockade.

"The one who thinks Jim is his daddy. He's a nice kid, but he's a *dumb* sonofabitch."

Diana had to repark, because Louise's door was blocked by the mound of snow the plows had built up along the street. Then Louise declined to take *two* bags of groceries up to the house, though it would have meant half as many trips, and Diana, miffed and careless, almost took a spill on the icy path.

Louise set down her bag on the kitchen table and returned at once to the car. Diana called out, "Mom?" and her mother appeared at once, with her usual cigarette. Talk about secondhand smoke: Navaho House was a plague pit.

"Is that kid here who parked his car outside? Maybe he could help bring in the groceries. We've got eight bags."

"The kid? Oh, right. I thought he must have gone off. Isn't he on the roof?"

"On the roof?"

"He went up there to shovel off the snow."

"When was that?"

"I don't know. While you were away. He came by, wanting to see Louise, and I told him about the creeping ice, and he volunteered to help out. Then he disappeared. I forgot all about him, to tell the truth."

Diana went back out into the cold and trudged into the deep snow to a point where she could see the whole roof. There was no one there, but something seemed wrong. She could see that some of the snow had been cleared from the very top of the roof, but that wasn't it.

The chimney wasn't there.

Christ, she thought. He's toppled the chimney over and now he's disappeared. But then why was his car still parked in front of the house?

She walked round to where she could see the roof of the porch, and there was the aluminum ladder, propped against the main rooftree. Which meant that whoever had used the ladder should, logically, still be up on the roof. Christ, she thought again, and this time she could feel her adrenaline kicking in.

Adrenaline or not, the snow made it impossible to run round to the other side of the house. The crust was hard enough in places to take her weight, but then, after three or four strides, she'd smash through it and be up to her knees. She trudged on grimly, with more snow getting into her galoshes each time she broke through the crust.

Rounding the corner of the house, she could see what she'd been dreading. There was the boy who'd been up on the roof, belly down in the snow, and the chimney, too, the pieces of it, right beside him. She paused where she was, undecided whether to go back into the house and call for an ambulance or to trudge the extra distance through high-drifted snow to see if an ambulance would be necessary. He might already be dead.

Louise solved the problem. Returning with a second bag of groceries, she'd seen Diana head round the side of the house and followed her. "Miss Turney, is something the matter?" she called out from close by the kitchen door.

"Tell my mother to call for an ambulance," she shouted back. "There's been an accident. Someone was up on the roof, and it looks like he fell off. He's just lying there."

"That Johnson boy?"

"I suppose so. I'll see if there's anything I can do."

But when she got to him at last and could see that he was alive—his breath was visible in the winter air—what could be done that she could do? She was not a nurse, and the only rule she knew in such a situation was that the injured should not be moved. In any case, she hadn't the strength to carry him across the snow and into the house.

In her very helplessness she felt a kind of calm and comfort. She could do nothing and was free simply to look on, and what she found herself looking at was the blood that speckled the snow. In making ceramics it was just that effect she'd tried to get, little spots sprinkled irregularly, like freckles on pale skin, like the petals of anemones.

But where had the blood come from? There was no visible wound on his head, which was bare and shorn close to the scalp, except across the pate. He had blond hair, lighter than her own, which was mousy. Whatever wound had decorated the snow so becomingly must have been on the side of his head that now lay upon the snow. She wondered if she should try to lift him just enough to turn his head, but no, that was the reason for the rule. His neck might be broken. Let the paramedics, or whoever came with the ambulance, make those decisions. If she touched him, she might become liable.

She began to be able to look at his face, and she found it, in its own way, as strangely affecting as the bloodstains on the snow. Not beautiful, as the blood on the snow was beautiful. His features were too coarse for ordinary beauty. Conscious and on his feet, she wouldn't have given him a second glance. A clod, a yahoo, an average resident of the area, like her own brother-in-law. But in these exceptional circumstances, poised (for all she knew) on the brink of death, he possessed a vulnerability she could not resist. Even an ugly man, when he is asleep, has a kind of beauty, a childlikeness that could speak to her. There had been men she'd wished she'd never met whom, nevertheless, when she'd seen them in the morning beside her in bed, she had, for that moment, loved with a love she'd never understood. For it vanished the moment their eyes opened and they became their familiar, boorish selves.

This one—what had Louise called him? the Johnson boy? how archetypal!—was like those others. But he was not simply asleep—he was unconscious, perhaps on the verge of the great abyss, and so, on that account, more beautiful. If helplessness—her own and his—is an element of beauty. It is in children. And men, when they are helpless, become children again. And this one was neither man nor boy, but poised somewhere between.

Then, as the poignancy of blood-speckled snow and the plumes of the boy's breath bore in on her, she remembered something Brenda had said, not at her last tarot reading, but the one just before—that she was to meet a man, neither dark nor fair, a younger man than she had ever known in a carnal way, whose name began with J, and he would profoundly alter her own destiny.

This boy, whose name was Johnson, who was neither dark nor fair, and who might be dying even now, must be the man foretold.

He opened his eyes. They were gray, only tinged with blue, like her own.

He smiled and said, " 'You will be showered by attention.' "

At once the spell was broken. "Beg pardon?" Diana said.

" 'You will be showered by attention.' That was my last Winner'qus fortune. And the one before that was 'A new friendship will cast a spell of enchantment.' Holy shit."

"You fell off the roof," Diana said by way of trying to restore a sense of order to what was happening.

"I guess I did. My name is Alan Cottonwood. Or maybe it's not. Probably not. I'm not dead? I thought maybe I was dead."

"You don't seem to be dead." Diana smiled. The boy was almost as charming alive as he had been when she thought he was dying. "Are you in pain?"

"You better believe it. But it's like—" He took a breath, and another breath, but she waited, knowing he'd continue. "It's like there are two of me. One feels the pain, the other's talking to you. I fell off the roof."

"I know. I had someone call for an ambulance."

"'The concern of others will make your trip a delight.' That's another one. I thought the chimney was going to fall on top of me, but I guess it didn't. I'm lucky."

"I'd say so."

"'New experiences and new friends will enrich your life.' It's weird—it's like I can remember all of them. I never thought they made a speck of difference. It's like believing in fucking fortune cookies."

"I'm sorry, I don't really know what you're talking about."

"How could you," he said, and then he blacked out again.

She envied him. She would have liked then and there to do just the same. Oblivion, and the same smile accompanying it. It was against all reason for this to be happening. He was probably still a teenager. She must be twice his age.

Nevertheless, she was in love.

Louise appeared around the corner of the house. "Is he all right?" she asked.

"I think so. We talked awhile, but he was delirious."

"Dr. Karbenkian is on his way here."

"Dr. Karbenkian?" He was the doctor who treated the old ladies in Navaho House. Diana had no more confidence in him than in a veterinarian. "I said to call an ambulance."

"I know. But Mrs. Turney wanted him. She said she didn't think it was that serious."

"She didn't think—! She's worried about her liability, that's what she's thinking!"

"Probably," said Louise dryly. "Anyhow, with luck, the boy'll be all right. You said he was talking to you?"

"Yes, you heard what I said!"

Louise just stood there, looking put upon. Then she said, "Anything you want me to do? A blanket or something?"

Diana looked down at the boy lying in the snow, then at the blood freckling the snow. "No," she said. "He'll be all right till the doctor gets here."

"Okay if I get the rest of the groceries out of the car?"

"Sure, go ahead. I'll stay here."

Louise didn't move. "Your mother said she'd like to talk to you."

"Then she can come out here."

Louise emitted a scornful huff. She knew, as Diana did, that nothing short of a fire would get Mrs. Turney out of the house in this weather. She was probably already back in front of the TV with the rest of the old ladies.

"Then I'll go get the groceries. Or they'll freeze right there in the car."

"You do that, Louise."

Louise went away.

Diana removed her glove and touched the boy's forehead. It was icy cold. His cheek the same.

"Are you awake?" she asked, tilting his chin toward her.

Nothing. He might have been dead.

She bent forward. Hesitated. And then, with a snowflake's gentleness, she kissed his unresponsive lips.

16

From his birth—no, even before, from his conception—the boy had been a thorn in his side. A wound that would not heal. And now the wound was festering. That was a problem for which Matthew—chapter 5, verse 30—offered the best solution: *If thy right hand offend thee, cut if off, and cast it from thee.* Jesus was no milktoast liberal. He did not believe in half measures, he didn't say on the one hand this but on the other that, no sir. Jesus hated the lukewarm. What Jesus said was, *I say unto you that except your righteousness shall exceed the righteousness of the scribes and Pharisees, ye shall in no case enter the kingdom of heaven.*

On that particular count the Reverend Martin Johnson and Jesus were in close agreement. In the matter of loving enemies and turning the other cheek, they were sometimes at variance. Jesus Himself often seemed to be of two minds in such matters. The Gospel didn't say what was to be done with a boy who would not accept correction, unless the parable of the prodigal son was to be understood in that light. But even there the sense of the parable seemed to be that the prodigal was to be allowed to go his own way until he'd learned his lesson. Wasting his substance with riotous living, in the words of Luke.

Reverend Johnson had hinted to Alan of such possibilities. Not riotous living, of course. Just the Marine Corps. Alan had been approaching high school graduation at the time. His grades had not suggested he was college material, and he had formed no other noticeable ambition. When he wasn't watching TV, he played games endlessly on his computer. You could hear him at it in his bedroom: a steady succession of muffled pings and blips. This was a way of wasting one's substance that Luke had never foreseen. So, Reverend Johnson had put it to his grandson at their Sunday dinner: had he ever considered a military career?

It had been a poorly chosen moment. He should have known better than to bring up the matter in front of Judy. His daughter, who ordinarily didn't have that much to say at the dinner table, became shrill and abusive. She had thrown out hints and made veiled threats, and finally Reverend Johnson had been obliged to order the boy to leave the table and finish eating his dinner in the kitchen. Which he had done, obediently, but not before shoveling another helping of potatoes and gravy onto his already overloaded plate. That had always been the boy's way. He didn't sass back. He did nothing that could be construed as open rebellion. He just glowered and went his own way, like a Negro in the old days. What was the word for it? Passive resistance.

And all the while, it now turned out, the boy had been scheming against him with diabolical cunning. Once again he'd got in contact with the authorities at New Ravensburg, and this time, because he was eighteen, he'd been allowed to meet with the prisoner James Cottonwood. That would have been bad enough in itself, but it seemed that Alan was in cahoots with the prisoner's attorney to prove that Cottonwood was not his biological father and, therefore, that his conviction for rape should be reversed and he should be set loose. Reverend Johnson had no way of confirming these things with the new warden, who knew nothing of the background of the case (and who was a Democrat), but Reverend Johnson's informant, Avo Kubelik, who was on the state board of corrections and a fellow board member of the Minnesota chapter of the Christian Coalition for Family Values, had counseled him that his grandson's bizarre initiative could conceivably bear fruit. "But only," Avo had added, "if the DNA tests support his case."

Reverend Johnson knew very little about DNA tests, but he distrusted them on principle, as he distrusted other alphabetical ploys of the radical left: AIDS, MTV, the ACLU, the NEA, UNESCO. There was no end of them. Anytime someone had a liberal agenda he wanted to disguise, he turned it into a set of initials. The whole point of DNA testing seemed to be to help convicted criminals get out of prison, so obviously it was just one more bowl of the liberals' alphabet soup. Avo had agreed but then added a caution. Once the machinery was set in motion, there was no arguing with the results. You had to nip a situation like this in the bud.

Reverend Johnson did not want James Cottonwood released from prison. The man posed a danger—to Judy, primarily, but also to Alan and, possibly, to himself. When he spoke to his daughter, Judy agreed that Alan must, on no account, be allowed to proceed with his effort to help James Cottonwood get out of New Ravensburg. Without any prompting on his part, Judy's immediate concern was for her own safety. "You know what he'd do, first thing," she'd said with conviction. "He'd come after me."

"Probably," Reverend Johnson agreed.

"Alan can't do this," she said. "I won't let him."

"Maybe you can control him, Judy. He doesn't listen to me."

"He'll listen to *me*, all right!" Judy declared with one of her clench-jawed smiles that always reminded Reverend Johnson of her mother, Emma, dead these many years. It was not a smile he liked to remember, but it was potent. He would let Judy take charge of the situation and handle it her own way.

The boy had driven off somewhere early in the morning without saying where. Judy made a couple of phone calls trying to track him down, and when that failed, she began to empty all the clothes in his closet into suitcases, which she lugged down the stairs and deposited on top of the snowbanks on either side of the front stoop of the rectory.

"Judy," he counseled, "do you think this is wise? Shouldn't we try to talk to him first?"

"He'll get the message. He can't do this. It's crazy."

"Yes, that may be so. But—"

"Fuck but!" Judy said. She stormed upstairs again and began filling cardboard boxes with the rest of Alan's private effects.

When she was in that sort of temper there was no contradicting her. At moments like this, when she became unusually energetic, Judy became beautiful again. In her teenage years she had been extraordinary, but even then, hers had not been the deceiving, thin-lipped beauty of conventional high school girls who starve themselves thin until they are married and then become sows. Judy was a true Johnson—large-limbed, broad-shouldered, a body framed for chill winters and hard work. Northern stock. You had to be of kindred stock to recognize the beauty in such women. They were not to be seen in Hollywood movies or on the covers of supermarket magazines. They more nearly resembled the statues that the pagan idolaters of Greece and Rome carved in marble and erected in their temples. A few such statues had found their way to the Minneapolis Institute of Art, where, twenty years earlier, as part of a tour group, Reverend Johnson had confronted them and been made to marvel.

"This is Venus," the tour leader had explained with a prim smirk, "the goddess of love. And behind her is another Venus, and there to the left, with some clothes on, is Hera or Juno, the goddess of home and marriage." The tour leader had hastened to the next gallery, but Reverend Johnson had lingered among the pagan statues quite as though they were, indeed, gods and goddesses and he had fallen into their punishing power. It seemed to him that the headless, one-armed torso of the larger Venus was his own Judy—not in its exact dimensions but in some deeper way. In the tilt of the hip and thrust of the bosom, in the shamelessness and boldness of the bare flesh (it was hard to think of it as stone), in the smooth curves that seemed to insist on the touch they forbade. Seeing this fragment of the pagan past, Reverend Johnson was overcome with a sense that St. Paul might have seen this same statue himself—that, indeed, he must have. These were the very idols Paul had denounced before the people of Athens and of Ephesus. Not golden calves or metal serpents, as Reverend Johnson had once imagined, but these beautiful abominations, these hymns to lust, which were still being adored in the temples of the Secular Humanists—their museums and institutes and universities.

He'd known it was sinful to linger among the idols, that simply to look upon them was a kind of worship, but he could not tear himself away. Better to marry than to burn, even Paul had advised. Meaning that some tribute must be made to the flesh. Not worship, as the pagans had worshiped. More a kind of tithe, a rendering unto Caesar, an admission that the flesh is weak. While Emma had been alive, these matters had not been a source of distress, for Emma had never denied him his conjugal rights. But when Emma had died . . . Knowing it was unwise to dwell upon such things, Reverend Johnson had exited the Minneapolis Institute and waited in the chartered bus for the tour group to reassemble.

For an hour, for two hours, Alan's belongings stood on the mounds of shoveled snow to either side of the front door—two canvas suitcases (his high school graduation present from Reverend Johnson, packed now for the first time) and two cardboard cartons brimming with junk emptied from drawers and bookshelves. Lunchtime went by without any sight of him, and then, just before two, a white Camry pulled up in front of the house, and Alan was in the passenger seat. He stayed in the seat while the driver, a woman in a knee-length sheepskin coat, went round to open his door and help him out of the car.

"Would you look at that," said Judy, who was standing beside Reverend Johnson at the parlor window. "He's got his arm in a sling. And his head's bandaged. Well, that isn't going to change a thing."

"Who is the woman with him?" Reverend Johnson wanted to know.

"Never seen her before," said Judy, but then, squinching one eye closed: "No, wait. That's Janet Kellog's sister, the one who went away and became a teacher."

"What's she doing with Alan?" Reverend Johnson insisted.

Judy gave him a look. "You'll have to ask *him* that one."

"I don't want to engage in a family quarrel in front of strangers," Reverend Johnson declared.

"His stuff's out there in the snow, and he's probably already seen it. It's too late now to avoid an argument."

Alan started up the narrow snow canyon to the front door with the woman following close behind. They stopped beside the cardboard boxes, where Alan got down on his knees and began picking through the contents with his good arm.

It couldn't be helped or put off. Reverend Johnson squared his shoulders and went to the front door. He took a scarf from the coatrack and wrapped it round his neck, but he didn't take the time to get into his overcoat, though he was usually careful not to take a chill. He went outside and stood upon the stoop, his arms folded across his chest. Judy was right behind him.

"Grandpa?" the boy said.

"I think you know why your things are where they are, young man. You can just take them away with you. You're not coming into this house."

"Reverend Johnson," the woman who'd come home with Alan began in a placating tone.

He scowled. "This has nothing to do with you, young woman. I would appreciate it if you would just return to your car—and drive off."

"I'm afraid you don't understand the situation, sir," she persisted. "Your grandson has just sustained a serious injury. He shouldn't even be on his feet. Whatever this quarrel may be about, this is surely the wrong—"

"There hasn't been any quarrel yet, and if there is to be one, it does not concern *you*! Now, please leave. I've asked politely."

"If this is your idea of polite, I'd sure hate to see rude."

Alan emitted a little bark of laughter. Reverend Johnson found himself at a loss for words. He glared at the woman, and she glared right back.

Finally it was Judy who dealt with the impasse. "I'm sorry if we don't seem hospitable, Miss . . . Turney, isn't it?"

The woman nodded, but she didn't take her eyes off Reverend Johnson.

"But this is a family situation here. We need to speak to my son privately."

"It looks to me," the woman said, "like you mean to turn him out on the street—and he's just thrown his arm out of joint, he's got a possible concussion, and his car is back at Navaho House on the other side of town. And you're suggesting that I drive off and leave him alone in this situation?"

"That's exactly what I'm suggesting," Judy said. "Because this is none of your damn business."

"I know what it is," Alan blurted out. "Someone from New Ravensburg called you, didn't they? They told you about the DNA tests, right? Right?"

"Alan," said Judy, "we're not discussing this out here in the cold."

"I don't know, it looks like we are. All my stuff is out here, and Grandpa says I *can't* come in the house."

"We've put your things outside to teach you an object lesson, Alan."

"What you mean is, I've got to stop helping Jim Cottonwood, right?"

"Alan," Judy said through gritted teeth. "Not—out—here."

"God, the two of you, it's like—" Alan shook his head. Then, with a grin of devilish triumph, "Anyhow, guys, it's too late."

"How's that?" said Judy.

"The results are in. And Cottonwood was right all along. There's no possible way he could be my father. There's not even like a one in six million chance. Which means that *you* had to be lying. You had that man sent away to prison all this time knowing he hadn't done what he was sentenced for."

"You little shit," Judy said.

"So where do the rest of my genes come from, Mom? Got any ideas?"

"Get out of here," Reverend Johnson commanded.

"You know what the final result might be, don't you? *You* might go to prison. For perjury. That's what the lawyer told me I should be aware of."

"Out of here! Or, by God, I'll—" Reverend Johnson raised his fist.

Alan turned to the Turney woman and asked her if she would help him get his belongings back to Navaho House. She said she thought that was a good idea and insisted on carrying the suitcases to the car herself.

Alan turned back to face Reverend Johnson. "You got my computer in there, too. I want that."

"Your computer!"

"I bought it with my own damned money."

"The parish mailing list is in that computer. It stays right where it is."

"There's thirty names on your damned mailing list. I'll send you a printout any time you like. The computer is mine, I paid for it."

Reverend Johnson stood in the doorway and glowered. Judy put her hand on his shoulder and whispered into his ear, "Do you want me to go get his computer?"

He shook off her hand. "I'll get it. You stay here. Don't let him in the house."

Anger is an intoxicant. It can make us do things we would never do in a sober and reflective frame of mind. We strike out without regard to the consequences. Reverend Johnson was seething with anger, and when he saw the screen of the boy's Wang computer, sitting there on its white Formica ledge, it was as though its blank screen were the boy's face—smug and silent, with all its nasty little secrets packed inside. He ripped the electric cord from the wall, but he found the thing was still tethered to another piece of equipment from which it was not as easily disconnected. That was the last straw. He tightened his right hand into a fist and gave it a whack.

The screen disintegrated like a shattered light bulb, littering the Formica shelf and the rug beneath with splinters of thin gray glass. Reverend Johnson didn't even notice the blood on the back of his hand, or feel the pain, as he grasped the screen and yanked it free of its moorings.

At the head of the stairs he stopped to catch his breath. He realized that he was beside himself. He went down the stairs with a special caution, placing his feet precisely on the center of each step. But once he reached the front door and saw Alan, the same fierce anger took control of him again, and he lifted the shattered computer to chest level and hurled it into the snow.

Alan went over to the computer and knelt beside it. Was he going to shed tears over it? Reverend Johnson wondered.

With his free hand Alan reached down and picked, from within the broken screen, a shard of glass. "You seem to have cut yourself, Grandpa. Look"—he held the shard up—"there's blood."

Reverend Johnson looked down at his hand and realized that Alan was right. Droplets of blood were trickling down from the cut on the back of his hand and curling round the knuckles to drip onto the fabric of his pants.

"That was a dumb thing to do. Really dumb." Alan was removing other shards of glass inside the broken screen and placing them in a handkerchief.

The Turney woman had carried all his other things to the car, where she was waiting for him. She honked, and called to Alan: "Come on, Alan. It's broken, just leave it where it is."

"Right, right!" Alan called back, getting up from his knees. He placed the handkerchief wrapped about the shards of glass in the pocket of his coat.

"And where do you think you're going with *her*?" Reverend Johnson demanded.

Alan laughed. "It pisses you off, doesn't it, that I've got anywhere to go at all? You thought you really had me over a barrel. Instead"— he patted the pocket of his jacket—"it's just the other way around. Maybe—huh?"

"I don't know what you're talking about."

"Well, that's par for the course."

The boy turned on his heel and walked toward the car, and Reverend Johnson went back in the house with a frustrated sense that the boy had somehow got the better of him even as he was being evicted.

Judy helped with the cut on his hand, which wasn't as bad as he'd feared at first. She washed it and sprayed on antiseptic, and then bandaged it with the last two Band-Aids left in the medicine cabinet.

17

When Diana got back to Navaho House and the Johnson boy was still with her, Louise Cottonwood didn't raise an eyebrow. When the boy had shown up at the back door two years ago, looking like a second grader inflated to grown-up size, she'd had a feeling that, whatever kind of fool he turned out to be, he was going to complicate himself into her life and Jim's and the Turneys' till he was lodged there solid. He had that kind of needy look in his eyes that's worse than love, because with love it's not so hard to turn the other way. People get over love fast enough, and if they don't, it's because they enjoy their broken hearts. But this boy wasn't after love, not in particular. He just wanted any scrap of attention he could get—a scratch behind the ears, five minutes with a cup of coffee, or just someone remembering his name. How do you say no to that kind of pure mongrel hunger?

So here he was back again, a bad penny, and it hadn't even taken that much persuading on Diana's part for Mrs. Turney to agree to let the boy move in—"temporarily," of course—to one of the empty upstairs rooms on the corridor alongside her own. So while Diana and Mrs. Turney clucked over the boy at the kitchen table and tried to find out what had got his grandpa so fired up, Louise was getting the room ready. The mattress had a musty smell, that couldn't be helped. But before she made up the bed, she tucked a plastic sheet round the mattress to keep the damp out of the bedclothes. The old ladies always complained that the plastic sheets were crinkly and uncomfortable, but the ones who complained the most were also the ones who were the worst bed-wetters.

When the bed was made, she cleared out two drawers of the dresser that were used for storing the old ladies' surplus flannel nighties. Then she unlocked the closet door and pondered whether there was time to clear out all the stuff drying there before the boy moved in. There looked to be about two boxfuls, maybe two and a half, and she knew where there were some good-sized boxes in a room down the hall, from when she'd unpacked the presents that Mrs. Boise's nieces in Fargo had sent all the old ladies at Christmas. Every one wrapped in its own box with a tag for the name to go on. What a commotion that caused. Just when you think the world's rotten down to the core, somebody comes along and does something as nice as that.

When she came back with the empty boxes to the room she was getting ready, there was Diana standing in the doorway of the unlocked closet. What a nose the woman had for things that didn't concern her. "Louise," Diana said, "I thought I'd come up and help."

"Thanks just the same, but I got the bed made. I'll just get this closet cleared out and he can move in."

"I didn't know you were an herbalist, Louise."

She used the same wheedling tone of voice she'd used on the drive to the Shop 'n' Save. It was probably the way she talked to the kids in her classes. Louise wondered if it got on their nerves the same way.

"It's just some stuff that's drying out," Louise said. "The chimney's right behind there, so things dry out nice in the closet. You wouldn't think so, as damp as this bedroom gets. That's one reason, the damp, that I thought having the closet open might be a good idea. Dry the place out. The stuff that's been in the closet is good and dry now, so I can load it all in these boxes, and we'll be squared away."

"I'll help," Diana insisted. "I'll take them down from the hook, and you can pack them in the boxes. Or did you want to wrap them in tissue first?"

Louise shook her head. "No, they don't need tissues."

"It has such a unique scent, Louise. It's some kind of root, isn't it?"

Louise nodded. "Yeah, it's a root."

"Oh, you are a tease, Louise. What is it *called*?"

"Honestly, Miss Turney, I don't remember. Some foreign name. I don't grow it for myself."

"Well, what is it *used* for?"

"You'd have to ask the doctor at the rez about that, Miss Turney."

"Aha! It's some kind of tribal secret, is it? Have I poked my nose where it doesn't belong?"

Louise let Diana figure out the answer to that from her silence. After the lesson had time to sink in, she said, "Well, let's get it into these boxes, shall we?"

When the first box was packed, Louise carted it off to her own room, so that Diana would have a chance to snitch as much of the stuff as she had a mind to. It was obvious she was going to anyhow, one way or another, so why not make it easy for her? It probably wouldn't do her any real harm, unless she brewed up a whole quart of tea and drank it down all at once.

She didn't know what exact purpose Jim used it for in his sweat lodge, and he probably didn't either. It was just a recipe he'd got hold of, and she'd had to do the shopping for him. And in this case the growing as well, though it pretty much took care of itself till it was big enough to dig up. The soil suited it, and no bug would touch it.

One thing Jim had said was that a little of the stuff boiled up and drunk hot would work for constipation problems. When Louise had tried to test that out on the old ladies, only one of them would take more than the tiniest sip. It brewed up into a real lip-puckerer. But the cup Mrs. Corby drank down had worked like Drāno. So if Diana took what wasn't hers and decided to test it out, she might get an unexpected lesson in tribal medicine.

And it would serve her right.

18

February is nature's prison. People slow down, and stay put, and brood. Seeds and roots are sheathed in ice. Life has no choice but to hoard its resources and serve its time, counting the days to parole. Not that there's any hope that March will be better. It will probably be worse, with sleet and the year's worst blizzards. But the numbness begins to depart sometime in March. The blood quickens and hungers stir. The ravenous deer forage through the woods. Sudden thaws flood basements and slick the roads with ice. Tempers unravel. Business picks up at the bars, and the fights in the parking lots are more serious. March is waking up with a hangover and wishing you were back in the blackout and oblivion of February.

All through February Diana had marked time, doing the absolute bare minimum required to keep things on an even keel. She got meals cooked on time. Everyone had clean socks and underwear. Beyond that it was as though she were on strike. She let Kelly watch the trashiest cartoon shows on TV, or anything else that would keep her quiet. She started to *rely* on the microwave. She would notice cobwebs in odd corners and do nothing about them. She didn't bother making her own bed in the morning. Instead, she just closed the bedroom door. She put off changing the water filter until you could taste rust in the tap water and the bathtub started to turn orange.

Love got put on hold. If that's what it was between her and the Johnson boy and not simply the worst embarrassment of her adult life. A teenager. It was hard to believe. In fact, for a while she'd almost convinced herself that it hadn't happened, or that she'd mislabeled her feelings and confused a natural concern for his well-being with love. A maternal solicitude. Except that each time she'd driven the icy roads to see him again—he was still squatting at Navaho House—she'd felt like there was a cyclone of hormones whirling through her bloodstream. A hollow feeling in her chest, sweats and palpitations. Sudden tears over any dumb song on the radio. And her tongue, her whole mouth, so hungry for the taste of him that it was worse than dieting. Then, when she'd got there, and neither her mother nor Louise had any idea where he might have gone off to ("Alan? I don't know. Isn't he in his room?"), the devastating disappointment. The long wait, the simmering anger, and finally, on the long drive back home, with Kelly whining every mile of the way, the sheer humiliation of it.

She was certain he must be trying to avoid her. Except she'd never given advance notice of her visits. Certain that her very hunger had driven him from her. He was just a teenager, after all. A virgin, most likely. He had that kind of shyness. A full month went by without her once seeing him, but she had only to close her eyes and she could summon his face, the gray eyes, the tentative smile, the pallor of the skin—and the blood speckling the snow, like a Kirlian photograph, his aura made visible.

Early in March, during a window of opportunity when the plows and the salt and a brief thaw made most of the main roads reasonably drivable, Carl announced that he'd arranged to spend the weekend with Janet in the facility her prison provided for spousal visits. He would take Kelly with him, and Diana could have the weekend to herself. She had forgotten what a blessing a weekend could be, its promise of freedom from the daily grind, with every Friday or Saturday night a New Year's Eve in miniature. Just the prospect of a trip into the Twin Cities was such a tonic that she made her first entry in the appointment book that had come in the mail as a Christmas present from Brenda Zweig. TO DO she wrote in large block letters on the page facing the frowning marble face of Athena, the goddess of wisdom.

Then, momentarily, she was stymied. Not that she didn't have plans already laid out for what she meant to do, but *those* plans did not need to be set down in so many words: get drunk, get laid, pig out, in no particular order of preference. Then she remembered the plastic bag of dried roots she'd taken from Navaho House. She'd hoped that Brenda might be able to say what they were, and what they did, at a glance, but Brenda was still basking in San Miguel. Maybe a visit to the university library might solve the problem, or she could see if there was some botanical whiz at the Natural History Museum who might know—though probably not on a weekend.

"Roots?" she wrote at the top of the list, and then, as though loosened by a spritz of WD-40, the worthy purposes stacked up into a column of respectable length:

> Roots?
> ACoA (8pm meeting)
> Bookstore:
>   Freddie the Detective
>   Bingo Palace (for Alan)
>   Secret Survivors (for Janet)

Jojoba
Toenail clippers
Bloodstains on coat?
Check oil in car!
Extra-virgin olive oil, balsamic vinegar

At D & R Auto Service in New Ravensburg, she had the pleasant surprise of finding out, from Ruben, that Carl had checked the oil the last time he'd borrowed her car, put in two quarts, and never even mentioned it to her. Typical of a man to be more attuned to the needs of machinery than of other people. But she must, in any case, remember to thank him.

She turned the trip odometer back to zero and checked her watch. The button that controlled the display had got stuck on the 0-to-24 system just after she'd moved back home, and she still had to do the arithmetic: 15:45 seemed meaningless as a time of day; 15 minus 12—it was 3:45, so for all her rushing around, she wouldn't get into the Cities before dark. There'd be an hour of night driving on the throughway at rush hour. On the other hand, she'd have time to check into a motel before the ACoA meeting.

It had been a bright morning and early afternoon, but by the time she was on her way the sky was a solid gray, the air misty, the snowy fields on each side of the road the same dreary gray as the sky, flat and shadowless. All the northbound traffic had their headlights on, and Diana took the hint. Her car, being an off-white, achieved near-invisibility in such weather if the lights weren't on. She deliberately eased back on the gas pedal. In weather like this you can't be too careful.

Even so she almost had an accident as she turned up the sharply curving entry ramp to Route 371. Because of the snow banked on either side of the road she didn't see the carcass of the deer until she'd nearly driven into it. The crows that had gathered, as surprised as Diana, took to the air with caws of indignation. She backed the Camry away from the body without thinking to look in the rearview mirror. Fortunately there was no one close behind her. What to do? The deer was sprawled across the road in such a way that she would have to drive over its front or hind legs to reach 371, or else get out of the car and pull the thing out of her way. The first option was too cruel, the second too dangerous, not to mention messy. The deer's legs were crushed and bloodied, either from the collision or by other drivers less squeamish than Diana, and the crows had already set to work on its guts.

They had perched on the phone wires strung along the county road behind her, an orderly row of them, like children lined up waiting for the school cafeteria to open. "She's all yours," Diana called to the crows as she shifted into reverse and slowly backed down the ramp. "Just give me half a minute."

She'd backed almost the whole way back to the county road before a pickup turned into the ramp and came to a stop behind her, blocking the way out. She rolled down her window and called to the driver, "There's a dead deer blocking the road." In reply, the driver honked his horn.

She had to get out of the car and walk back to the pickup, a slate blue Dodge Ram. The driver took his time stubbing out his cigarette before he rolled down the window, releasing a gust of stale smoke into the pure winter air. "What's the problem?" he asked, a gigantic, pockmarked farmer in a grimy red-and-black plaid jacket with a matching grimy cap. "You break down?"

"No. There's a deer blocking the ramp. It's right in the middle of the road."

"A deer? Can't you pull it off to one side?"

"It's a large doe. And all bloody."

"Can't be that large."

"If you'll let me back out of here, you can deal with the matter any way you want. I'm not dressed to cope with a bleeding carcass."

"Whatever you say." He rolled up his window and let the pickup roll back to the road, backing into the eastbound lane. Diana, therefore, had to back up into the other lane, which set her facing the wrong direction. Or did it? She'd best check the roadmap in the glove compartment.

While she did that, the pickup headed up to the ramp, stopping where she'd been stopped and scattering the crows a second time. The driver got out and squatted down beside the deer so that only his visored cap was visible above the snowbank, one glint of red among the misty grays.

According to the map, she could drive west for two miles or so and turn onto Crow Wing Road, which paralleled 371 to the next entrance twenty miles south. Of course, it might be easier just to wait until Paul Bunyan cleared the deer's carcass off the road, but that idea grated against Diana's sense of independence. She did not like men tipping their hats to her, or opening doors she could open for herself, and this seemed to be in the same category.

In any case, Paul Bunyan was not just clearing the road. He had lifted the deer by its hindquarters and was dragging it to the back of his pickup. The crows, it seemed, would have to look elsewhere for their dinner. Diana was sure she was witnessing some kind of illegal, even obscene, act and did not stay to see more.

The road beyond the ramp was one she'd never driven and not at all the beeline indicated by the map, even though the land was flat on either side—a marsh to the right with rotted stumps and cattails penetrating the snow; to the left a shallow scrim of scrubby pines masking, in all likelihood, another dismal swamp. She punched the trip odometer again and, after a mile and a half, slowed down to thirty-five so as not to miss the turnoff onto Crow Wing Road.

The Camry fishtailed on the icy gravel road, not dangerously but enough to make her uneasy. The treads on the back tires were low, and if Crow Wing Road was anything like this one . . . Then, as she approached another bend of the road, she thought she saw something behind her, only a shadow at the edge of the rearview mirror, and only for a moment. As the road curved, the shadow vanished from the mirror, but there was nothing worse, on a road like this, than to be tailgated by someone wanting to go faster. She increased her speed, but even so, when the car came into view again it was much closer, and worse than that she could see it was the blue Ram pickup. Was he *following* her? No, surely not. He had the carcass in the bed of the truck, so he wouldn't want to be seen on the highway. He was returning home, that was the logical explanation. But logical or not, she'd been spooked, and she increased her speed to fifty.

And then she saw the unmarked turnoff ahead and braked, but not in time, for as she made the turn, too fast, the Camry did a full one-eighty spin, and the car plowed backward through the snow mounded on the left side of the road and over the shoulder.

There was a jolt and then, to her horror, the airbag inflated and she was pinioned to the seat. She tried to push it to the side, but it pushed right back, all but immobilizing her. And she did not know how to deflate it. This had never happened to her before.

She heard the pickup come to a stop in front of her and felt relief, humiliation, and dread, all in a single rush of emotion. The driver knocked at the side window and asked, "Can you open your door? It's locked."

She twisted her left arm around until she could lift the latch. Then, at his bidding, she released the seat belt, and he was able to push the bag to the side till she could wriggle out of the seat.

"You okay?" he asked.

She was shattered. But she said, "I'm fine. I mean, I don't think I've been hurt."

"That's good to hear. But it looks like you've got a flat. The left rear tire. You hit that pothole. Probably a lucky thing. It kept you from going over the shoulder with both wheels. And maybe rolling over."

"I've got a flat? God damn."

"Yeah, wherever you was headed, you won't be getting there tonight."

"Well, I guess I should be thankful it's nothing worse. Thank you. That airbag . . . I panicked."

"Hey, anyone would. You must be Carl Kellog's sister-in-law."

Diana's alarm bells went off. "How did you know that?"

"I work with Carl at the Ravensburg lockup. Fact, we carpool together, so I been in the backseat of your car three or four times. And I'll tell you, there ain't much legroom for someone like me. I'm Tommy W., by the way." He pulled his sheepskin glove off his right hand and held it out.

She looked uncertainly at his huge hand, raw with cold, the knuckles swollen. Then she realized he intended a handshake. She took off her own glove, accepted his hand, as cold as her own, and numbly shook it.

"It is *cold*," he said. "Tell you what. I live just half a mile down Crow Wing. I can tow you there myself, and if you don't mind, I can change your flat myself, too."

"There's no need to do that. I can phone Ruben at the Mobil station. Triple-A will pay for it."

"Well, yeah. But I'd rather not have Ruben see what's in the pickup. He's a deputy constable, and no buddy of mine. I can have you back on the road sooner than him. If that's okay with you. Where were you heading anyhow?"

"Down to the Cities."

"Well, I wouldn't advise that tonight. It'll be dark before you hit 371, and you must be kind of shaken. That's up to you, of course. Anyhow, the first order of business is haul you out of here before there's another accident. Right?"

She nodded reluctantly.

"Don't worry," he assured her. "I done this plenty times before. I got chains and rope, and you facing in the wrong direction actually makes it easier. Go have a seat in the pickup and let me take care of this. Okay?"

"I can't tell you how much I appreciate this, Mr. . . . W?"

He laughed. "Call me Tommy."

19

"Here," said Tommy, sweeping a tangle of clean laundry from the plush recliner facing the TV and depositing it on the threadbare loveseat beside it, already piled with newspapers and magazines. "Have a seat. The phone's over there if you need to make a local call. But if you want to call someone in the Cities, I'd appreciate you calling collect."

Diana had been known to ask the same thing of visiting strangers, so she could not very well take umbrage. The man was acting like a genuine Good Samaritan, and if his cabin was a chamber of horrors, that was none of her business.

"I got to go out and bleed that carcass before it freezes. Shouldn't take long. If you want some coffee, there's a pot on the stove that might have some left in it."

She nodded acknowledgment and sank into the recliner without removing her coat. The cabin was not that warm. "Thank you. I'll just rest a moment."

Outside the huge black German shepherd was still barking. It hadn't let up for a moment since the pickup, with her Camry behind it, had pulled into the blacktop driveway. Though it was less a driveway than a small parking lot. Typical.

"Beast!" the man yelled from the back doorway. "Shut the fuck up!" The dog went on barking, and the man yelling. It was demented pedagogy. You can't yell at children to make them quiet, and the same surely held true for dogs. Finally, a loud *thwack* silenced the dog. Momentarily.

She closed her eyes so as not to have to be aware of her surroundings, but when the dog began again, she knew there was no way she could compose herself in such a situation.

If you ignored the guns (four of them) in the rack beside the front door and all the hunting trophies mounted on the pine-paneled walls (fish, ducks, a moosehead, and a variety of antlers) and concentrated on such things as cleanliness and order, Tommy's cabin was probably an above-average bachelor environment. The pile of clothing on the loveseat was, after all, *clean* clothing. The floor was swept. The sink she'd passed by in the kitchen area was not full of dishes. There was no noticeable odor, except the lingering aroma of woodsmoke from the stove at the far end of the single open space. The carpentry was all very do-it-yourself, with a staircase up to the sleeping loft constructed of two-by-fours and raw planks, and only a portion of the insulation between the ceiling rafters had not been covered by sheetrock, which meant that the cabin was still in progress and probably of his own construction. This was how all men would live, she supposed, if there were no women. The macho version of *Good Housekeeping*.

The dialogue outdoors between dog and man shifted in tenor, and a short while later, Tommy came in the back door to ask, "Are you okay with dogs? I mean, do they scare you? The thing is, the deer out there is driving Beast crazy. If I bring her in the house, she'll behave fine. Like they say, her bark's worse than her bite. She'll stay where I tell her, no problem."

"No. I mean, I'm not afraid of dogs as such. If *she* doesn't mind my being here."

He nodded. "'Preciate it." He gave a jerk to the chain he was holding, and Beast allowed herself to be led from the kitchen area and across the room to the woodstove.

"Sit!" Tommy commanded, after taking off the chain. Grudgingly, Beast sat.

"Stay!"

Beast laid her large head down on her extended paws without seeming in any way to relax. Her eyes were fixed on Diana, while Diana did her best to keep from constantly glancing in the dog's direction and advertising her own unease. She tried not to think of the work Tommy would be returning to, while Beast (she imagined) could probably think of nothing else. Diana believed that the intelligence of animals, like that of children, was much greater than they are usually given credit for.

"Hey, you're still in your coat. Is it that cold in here? I'm in and out so much that I usually keep my coat on most of the time and don't notice if it gets down under fifty. You want me to get the stove going?"

"No, you take care of what you've got to do. I can get a fire going. Unless . . ." She glanced toward the dog and thought better. "Really, it's not that cold."

"I won't be long," he promised.

So she sat there quietly, thankful that she'd worn her sheepskin coat, despite the bloodstains on the hem and sleeve, thankful that the accident had been no worse, and thankful for Tommy W.'s hospitality, despite the certainty of how, inevitably, all this would get back to Carl. Gradually, she could feel her adrenaline diminish, her pulse quiet, the tension ease. And she realized she needed to go to the bathroom. She leaned forward in the recliner, which had already been tilted halfway back when she'd sat down.

Beast lifted her head.

"No," she said, as to a second grader, pointing her finger authoritatively. "Sit. Stay. I'm just going to the bathroom." And she got up and walked directly toward the door, near where Beast rested, that had to lead to the bathroom.

And so it did. She slipped off her coat and hung it over the bathroom door and, after spreading toilet paper across the seat (which seemed reasonably clean), she relieved her bladder.

And then she must have simply blanked out, for the next thing she knew the man was knocking on the door. "Are you okay in there? Can you hear me? Are you okay?"

"Yes, thank you." Though, in fact, she felt invaded, as if he'd opened the door. And indeed, because the coat was hanging on the door, leaving it ajar by a good four inches, he *might* have looked in.

"Is there anything you need?"

"No. No, I was just . . . freshening myself." She flushed the toilet to end any discussion and, when she'd zipped her fly and cinched her belt, emerged with what dignity she could muster.

Beast's eyes met hers at once, but there was no sign of Tommy W. He called down from the sleeping loft, "I'm up here, just getting something."

Closing the door after retrieving her coat, she crossed the room and draped it over the recliner. Beast's eyes never left her.

Tommy thumped down the plank staircase with a bottle of Jack Daniel's in his hand. "I don't know about you, Miss . . . Sorry, I don't know your name."

"Turney. But call me Diana. I think we must be on a first-name basis by now."

"Okay. Diana. Anyhow, you'll be glad to know that everything's squared away. I changed your tire. But you should get some air in that spare. It's a little low, but it should get you home okay. Before you head off, I thought you might like some of this." He held up the half-full quart bottle. "To unwind."

Diana looked at the uncurtained window above the kitchen sink—it was pitch-black outside—and then at her watch. "My God, it's seven o'clock."

"Yeah, well. I knocked earlier, but you just mumbled. So that's when I went back outside and changed the tire. I figured it was just shock or like that. You're feeling okay now though?"

She laughed. "Actually, I feel like it was seven *a.m.* It's weird."

"I guess this whole day has been pretty weird." He smiled and tilted his head. "I was hoping you might want to stay and have dinner."

Dinner and what else? she wondered, knowing the answer.

And knowing the answer, she said, "That's very nice of you. I'd love to. As long as it's not venison."

Tommy laughed.

Beast growled.

"Beast!" Tommy reprimanded. And then, to Diana, "She's jealous. She's used to being the only female in the house. As for dinner, it'll have to be spaghetti. The cupboard's pretty bare. That's one reason I was heading down to Stockholm."

"What was the other?"

"I usually hang out at the casino there on Friday nights. And lose money. *This* is a much better idea." He held up the bottle. "Let me get glasses."

He got glasses, and poured their drinks, and even thought to ask if she wanted hers neat or with ice. "Not ice, not today," she said with a rueful smile. Tommy squatted down beside the recliner (the loveseat being filled with the laundered clothes), quite like another Beast. He had that kind of large-framed, lumberjack body that reminds you that humans are, basically, just another species of large mammal.

They clinked glasses, and it tasted good.

This is providential, she thought. The very reason, really, she'd been driving to the Cities. She'd been hoping, she'd been certain, that Jack would be there at the ACoA meeting, and there was no reason to suppose that this fellow would be any worse than Jack. She liked large men. Often enough they were actually gentler, as though their size made them shy. Tommy seemed that type. The only reason to refuse what Fate was offering was that he worked with Carl, and no man could be counted on to be discreet about their so-called conquests. But, as they say, what the fuck. It wasn't even the whiskey saying it. She'd had only a sip. It was a decision she must have come to hours ago at some point between the accident on Crow Wing Road and their arrival here. Her intuitions were always ahead of her conscious choices, sometimes uncannily.

"You like saunas?" Tommy asked.

She offered a noncommittal "Mm" and took another, grateful sip. "Why?"

"'Cause I got one. And it's heated up. I started it up just for myself, while you were in there." He nodded to the bathroom. "Then it occurred to me, you might like one too. I mean, we could take turns."

"You have your own sauna?" she asked, evading a direct answer to his proposition. "That's amazing."

"Well," he said, untying the laces on his boots and prying them off, "I had a choice. I had the money where I could build a garage or put up a sauna, which would cost a lot less, 'cause it's more of a sweat lodge really. At the lockup I had to help build one. It was state-mandated, would you believe it? Part of the 'Native American' religion. I'll tell you, they got an easy life there. But can *we* use the thing, the C.O.'s, when it's sitting there idle thirty days out of thirty-one? No way. It's holy fucking ground now. Excuse the language. So I've got my own. You want some more Jack?"

She handed him her glass. "A little, thank you."

While he played host, Diana untied her own laces and loosened them, but she didn't take off the boots. Just the loosening was enough to inspire a sigh of relief.

"You have gorgeous eyes, Diana." He handed her the replenished glass.

She sipped, and smiled coyly. "So does Beauty."

"Who?"

"Beauty." Only after she'd repeated it did she realize the nature of her mistake. They laughed in unison, the friendly laughter of a shared perception.

He turned to the dog. "Hey, Beast, you hear that? You got yourself a new name now. You're Beauty." He turned back to Diana, smiling. "Truly, she is a beauty, and I might call her that from now on. Beauty. Only thing is"—he refilled his own glass—"she's fierce. You expect that in a German shepherd. They're bred for it. But whoever trained her first . . ." He shook his head. "She's a great hunter, I'll give her that, but I swear she must be part wolf. You can bet she's still got her mind on that deer out there. From the moment we got here, even before she could see it in the truck, she was in a state."

"She was," Diana agreed.

He sipped his bourbon with his eyes on Diana's face again but his mind still on Beast, or Beauty, whichever she was to be. "I got her from Ravensburg, they couldn't handle her. She ran down a couple of escapees, and deserves a medal for that, but she got to the second one before her handler did and tore him up pretty bad. There was a lawsuit, abusive whatever. So they were going to put her away, but I said let me have her. I figured she'd be a good hunter, and she is. And usually well behaved. It was the smell of the blood that got her all riled up." He paused, then shifted gears. "You want to try the sauna now?"

"In a bit," Diana said. "Tell me, why are you Tommy W.?"

He lowered his head with a modest smile, pleased to be asked about himself.

"The W is for my middle name, Wagner, after my grandpa on the mother's side, Tommy Wagner. See, my other grandpa was also a Tommy, last name of Gilbertsen, and my older brother was named for him. So, growing up, he was Tommy G. and I was Tommy W. And it stuck. I guess I wouldn't recognize myself by another name."

That's so sweet, she thought, though she knew better than to make any kind of comment. It was as if he'd told her his closest-held secret. Like Rumpelstiltskin.

"I need to get something from my purse," she said. She looked around the room. "Where is it?"

"By the back door," he said. "I'll go get it."

"No, no, stay where you are. I'll get it."

It was her diaphragm she was after. She knew it would be best to have that taken care of before they went into the sauna. If that was, in fact, in the cards. And yes, there was her purse. Another visit to the bathroom, and . . . But as she headed that way, Beast lifted her head and *growled,* and the shock of it (she'd forgotten Beast was there) was such that she started back, stepping on her loosened bootlaces—and fell over backward.

Everything in her purse spilled across the pine boards of the floor.

Tommy crawled forward from where he was sitting to help her gather up the contents of the purse. She got to the diaphragm first, and then her keys, her coin purse, the Maxipads. But it was Tommy who lighted on the plastic bag with the still unidentified roots.

He held it aloft, as earlier he'd brandished the bottle of Jack. "God damn, I know what this is. How in hell did you get hold of this?"

"You know what it is? What is it? I've been trying to find out."

"It's called mandrake. They use it in the sweat lodge at the lockup. It's got some other Italian name, too. Every so often the medicine man from the reservation delivers a supply of different herbal stuff that gets boiled up together, and then when the rocks inside are super hot they slosh that brew on them. It's got a nice smell, when you get a whiff of it outside. Mostly it's sage. I got some of that brewing out there already. It's a funny thing to be carrying around. What do *you* use it for?"

Diana explained how she'd found it drying in the spare room at her mother's nursing home, and the little that Louise had told her about it, and how she'd brought the sample with her to see if there was someone in the Twin Cities who could tell her what it was and what it was supposed to do.

"Well, I guess I saved you that trip. It's mandrake, all right. Like Mandrake the Magician in the old comic book. I'm no botanist or anything, but the chaplain keeps the sage and this stuff in a locker in his office, and every time they get the sweat lodge fired up, I go to the locker and measure out a few ounces. I could be wrong, but it sure looks the same—the color, and the way the roots twist round each other like little snakes. And from what you said about that Louise, she sounds like an Indian."

"She is."

"Yeah, well then. What do you say we add this in with the sage that I put in the kettle out there?"

Her first impulse was to demur, but hadn't Fate almost ordained it? Perhaps the Goddess (whose realm includes a cupboard well stocked with herbs and simples) had elicited the growl that made her stumble just so this would happen. "Why not," she agreed.

"And if you want something that will be comfortable in the sauna, try this on." He rummaged through the pile of laundry and produced a white terry-cloth bathrobe. "It's one-size-fits-all and fresh from the dryer. And before that from the Radisson Hotel. We had our convention there last year."

"Does that mean I'll be abetting a crime?"

He grinned. "I hope so."

Beauty gave another growl, right on cue, and they both laughed.

Then he went outside, and Diana slipped off her boots and went into the bathroom to change into the purloined robe.

She never ceased to be amazed at how these things happened, the people you might end up with. Her first impression of Tommy, when he'd honked at her and she'd yelled back at him, surely wasn't the stuff romance is made of. When he'd rolled down his window and she'd had her first close-up view of his pockmarked face, along with the whiff of stale smoke, she'd thought him anything but good-looking. And certainly hostile. Just moments ago, when he'd knocked at the bathroom door, rousing her from her faint or black-out or whatever it had been, her first thought had been that he'd been spying on her. And now she was actually putting in the diaphragm. Was it pheromones—pheromones and nothing more?

If so, was that a bad thing necessarily? Smell is the most basic sense, the one closest to ESP, the one that connects to the roots of our animal nature. That was the logic behind aromatherapy—and shamanism. You couldn't explain such things in the language of science, though people tried. But the Goddess understood, and guided, and when you sensed her guiding hand, then you must simply take her hand and follow.

When she had finished changing and had cinched the belt of the Radisson Hotel's bathrobe about her waist (the hem came to just above her knees, like a chiton), Tommy had already taken off his clothes and wrapped himself in a sheet from the pile of laundry. "Ready?"

She nodded.

They polished off the bourbon left in their glasses and headed out into the shock of the winter air. It wasn't below zero tonight (except on the Centigrade scale), but it was colder than just bracing. Walking on the compacted snow of the driveway and through the trampled drifts on the path to the sauna was a mild form of masochism—but that was part of the ritual of the sauna. A rite, literally, of passage.

The dead deer had been strung by its hind legs on a wooden frame beside the path. Its head rested in the snow next to the tub that held its entrails. It was not an unfamiliar sight. She'd seen many gutted deer before, in her childhood, and on visits to Carl and Janet in later years. But it had never struck her before in such a solemn way, as though she were witnessing a kind of pagan sacrifice and not a violation of nature. She did not linger over it, but neither did she glance away.

The deer had not fazed her, but her first sight of the sauna as they rounded the bare branches of a large, low willow gave her a start, for it seemed almost the twin of the smokehouse on the Kellog farm—the same gray and weathered walls, the same crudely shingled roof. At second glance it was not the same at all. It was larger, the size of a small camper, and the log fire roaring in the pit at the near end did not vent *into* the structure. The smoke and sparks rose directly through a freestanding stovepipe into the night air, and the light of the blaze turned the snow cover for yards around into something altogether spectral. Diana got close enough to the fire to enjoy its warmth and the smell of the steam rising from the blue metal five-gallon pot on the grate.

Sage. With a tinge of something indescribably else.

"You go inside and take a seat back from the rocks," Tommy told her. "Then I'll bring in this tub."

"Is that safe? It's scalding hot."

"I'll be careful. I've done this before when I've had a lot more to drink than tonight. Don't worry."

She didn't. She was in that pleasant condition of feeling completely trustful—in him, and in her own Higher Power, which could arrange for accidents to be the source of good fortune. The Goddess was in charge tonight.

She entered the sauna, which was lighted by a battery-powered lantern set on a low table in front of two wooden stools. She didn't sit down until Tommy appeared with the tub of steaming water. He was using the sheet draped over his shoulders as potholders, which allowed a glimpse of his private parts. He already had an erection, but not one, to Diana's relief, of Paul Bunyan proportions.

Tommy set the tub down beside the rocks at the farther end of the sauna, closest to the fire outside.

Diana, unbidden, closed the door and fastened a hook into its eyehole to keep it closed, then took a seat on the nearer stool. Tommy dipped up the fragrant water with a long-handled ladle and, at arm's length, poured it over the superheated stones. At once, with a loud hiss, the water was transformed into steam that filled the sauna.

Diana could feel it penetrate every pore of exposed skin. And then, with her first inhalation, her lungs and, by degrees, her whole body. You could actually feel the change, the metamorphosis, cell by living cell. Awakening impulses, stilling anxieties, making mind and flesh mesh.

Tommy had slumped forward, elbows propped on his knees, oblivious of anything but the impact of the heat and the steam. The sheet covering him had molded to the contours of his body, and his hair had become a garland of ringlets. He looked like a statue in a museum, Greek and geometrical. An archetype.

Neither of them spoke. What they were sharing was better than speech. A preparation for something that would also (she hoped) be better than speech. From time to time he would add more of the tea of sage and mandrake to the rocks, and the lantern-lit steam would become denser, more obscuring, lovelier.

Slowly their bodies adjusted to this new atmosphere. He raised his head and swiveled it to the left and right. She admired the elegance and naturalness of the motion. He seemed at home in his body in a way that Diana never had been, even at moments like this.

"You did the right thing," she said.

He raised his eyes to meet hers, with an open regard that dispensed with the courtesy of a smile. "How's that?"

"To build the sauna and not a garage."

"Yeah. I know. Sometimes when I'm in here I'll think of those guys in the sweat lodge there in Ravensburg. And it's like, I don't know, we're all in the same situation together. We're all in these *bodies*. You know?"

"I think so, yes."

"It's all they got, in a way. The one good thing."

"That's sad. For them."

"Mm-hm," he agreed, slumping forward again.

Then, with a deep breath, he pushed himself to his feet. "What do you say we head back to the cabin? It's not good to stay in here too long. It can knock you out."

"You're right," she agreed. "Let's go inside."

She led the way. The shock of the cold seemed less extreme this time, for her body retained, for a while yet, the sauna's heat. This was the moment true believers would take a roll in the snow. But Diana had no such intention. She sprinted to the door of the cabin and, once inside, hesitated over whether to leave the door open for Tommy, who had paused beside the gutted carcass of the deer. She left it open and crossed to where she'd left her clothes neatly folded on the recliner. As she was considering whether to get dressed again, she heard Tommy come in the back door with a crash.

He had stumbled over the doorjamb and was on his hands and knees. He must have been more drunk than she'd thought. "Oh, dear," she said, "let me help you."

But as she stepped forward to offer her hand, he reared up—and he was no longer Tommy, nor entirely human. Antlers had sprung from his head, and the hands by which he tried to raise himself had become hooves. Even as she watched, transfixed, his eyes grew larger and darker. He bellowed in alarm, and shook his no longer human head, striking the neon light fixture with his antlers and shattering it.

His dark lips writhed, but they could no longer produce human speech. He had risen to his full height, and the sheet had fallen from his torso to reveal the body of a mature stag.

Beauty attacked without warning, sinking her teeth in the stag's front shoulder and trying to pull him down with her own weight. But the stag rose up on its hind legs, and the dog lost her grip. The stag's hooves came down on Beauty's back, and she backed away with a yelp, then whirled round to take a defensive posture, baring her teeth in a snarl.

The stag tried to escape through the back door, but his wide antlers struck the doorframe. The stag that had been Tommy spun round to face the dog, lowering his head, snorting a hopeless defiance.

Beauty began to stalk the man who'd once controlled her and led her about on a chain, edging alongside the sink and stove, her head lowered, growling. The stag, reluctantly, moved back from the doorway and any hope of escape, backing toward Diana, who stood clutching her bundled clothes, paralyzed. Not with horror or fear, but simply wonderstruck at her own power. She knew that the Goddess was working through her to bring about this violation, and fulfillment, of nature, and there was a glory in that knowledge.

The stag had backed away from the dog step by step, until he stood in the far corner of the cabin, between the stove and the bathroom door. Beauty made a feint, and the stag tried to rise again, to strike with his hooves, but his antlers struck the ceiling of the sleeping loft.

Beauty made a rush and locked her teeth in her victim's throat. The stag fell sideways, knocking down the stove and sending a cloud of soot from the disconnected pipe. Beauty lost her grip, and the stag managed to scramble to his feet.

Their eyes connected for a moment, Tommy's and Diana's, and his seemed to ask, without accusation but with a wonder equal to hers, why she had done this, why this betrayal, why there could be no love between them.

She looked away from him.

"He's yours," she told the dog, with a savagery now fully conscious and triumphant. "Finish him."

Beauty obeyed.

20

When the first knock came on the door, Alan rolled over in his bed and tried to hold on to the dream. A nice dream, but strange. He was inside a cloud, all misty and moist and very warm. There was a lady in the dream, all in white, with a white, pointy hat on her head, and he had laid his head in her lap and she was stroking the horn on his head, because he was a unicorn. And wasn't, at the same time. Because earlier in the dream he was just himself, and the lady was Diana, and she'd said to him, "You're a dear boy. Very dear." And he'd tried to tell her how much he loved and respected her, but he couldn't. Because he was a unicorn, and unicorns can't talk.

But you can't be inside a dream and figure what it means at the same time, and when the knock knocked again, he knew he'd left the dream and didn't try to get back there. "Yeah? What?"

He was still dreamy enough that when it was the voice of Louise Cottonwood that answered and not his mother's, he was surprised.

"It's your lawyer," Louise said. "He says he's got news for you. He wants you to call him."

All at once he was full of adrenaline. He pushed himself up from the lumpy mattress, and the dream, every trace of it, was gone.

"What *time* is it?" he asked, confused, because outside it was still, dimly, day. But Louise had already gone downstairs, and the electric alarm clock by the bed said 5:30, which did not seem possible. Then he realized it was 5:30 in the afternoon. He couldn't remember lying down to take a nap. He almost never took naps. And if he did, he didn't dream. And he had been dreaming, though he couldn't now remember anything of it, except that it had been about sex in some way. And Diana had been in it.

He was fully clothed, and (he checked) his fly was zipped.

He went down to the kitchen, where Louise was in the middle of fixing dinner for the old ladies. "My lawyer called? What'd he say?"

"To call him." Louise was opening a huge can of string beans.

"I was asleep." He thought he needed to explain that.

Louise just gave him a sideways look. "His number's by the phone."

Alan headed for the hallway, where the pay phone hung beside the front door.

"Not that phone," Louise called to him. "In here."

Alan looked at the phone on the little table at the far end of the kitchen, which only Mrs. Turney and Louise were allowed to use. Everyone else was supposed to use the pay phone.

"Call him collect," Louise said, answering the unasked question. "Hell, just call him. *She* won't know."

Alan realized that since it was a call from his lawyer, Louise was probably as much concerned as he was, since it must have to do with her son. So he dialed the number and got the lawyer's secretary, and this time there was no runaround, she put him right through.

"Alan. Good to hear your voice."

"Thank you. There's news?"

"There is indeed. As I've told you before, the lab's been equivocating about the results of the first tests."

"Pardon, sir?"

"Equivocating. Seesawing. One day it's yes, the next we can't be sure. But the *new* tests are positive. No equivocating with those. They say that it is your father's blood, beyond any doubt."

"The *new* tests? The blood that was on the little shard of glass?"

"Yes indeed. Now, you've never said whose blood that is. Am I to assume that it was from your friend Mr. Cottonwood? In which case, I'm afraid, our efforts have been in vain. And you, young man, know with a certainty few others possess just who your father is."

"Oh, Jesus," said Alan. He hung up the phone and looked up at Louise, who was already staring at him.

"Was it bad news?" she asked.

He nodded his head.

Louise sighed. "Well, you did your best, Alan. That's all any of us can do. I'm sorry. Sorrier than you, I guess."

He looked up, realizing how she'd mistaken his meaning. But how could he explain?

She set down the big tin of green beans and came over to him. "So it looks like you're a Cottonwood after all." She bent down and placed a kiss on the side of his head. "And I got myself a grandson. Well, God bless you, boy."

He could feel the tears coming to his eyes. He couldn't *tell* her. He couldn't say she was wrong, that he was not her grandson, that Jim Cottonwood was not his father. That his real father was a man he hated more than anyone else in the world, his own grandfather, the Reverend Martin Johnson.

"Now, where you going?" Louise asked. "At this time of night?"

It was a good question, and he had no answer. "Out," he said. "Just out."

"Well, put a jacket on anyhow. It's cold out there."

Alan did as he'd been told, feeling resentful but grateful at the same time. Was there anyone in the world who actually cared a damn for him besides Louise Cottonwood?

He realized there was, and that she was the only person in the world that he could talk to at this point.

Diana Turney.

She didn't know that he loved her, or how much. But she was kind, and he could talk to her, and where else was there to go? Who else would understand?

Who else was there to love?

21

It amazed her how much she was still in control. After all that had happened. And still might.

If only the Camry's spare didn't give out. Tommy had said it was low. How far had she to go to get home again? She looked down at the trip odometer. It registered only 6.7 miles. How could that be? Oh yes, she'd reset it after she'd backed out of the entry ramp to 371, where this whole nightmare had begun. Another 7 miles or so. She must drive slowly and watch for potholes.

Was there something she'd forgotten? Some telltale item of her own that had been left in that hellish cabin? No, no, she'd been quite careful. She'd taken her clothes, her purse. She'd washed the glass she'd drunk from, but there was no knowing how many other things she might have touched. But no one would think to look for her. No one had seen the two of them together. And *she* had not murdered Tommy. It was not even Tommy who'd been murdered.

A dog had killed a deer inside his house. A freakish accident. That's what would be discovered.

And yet she knew otherwise. She could remember every moment. How she had led him from the sauna toward his death, and called him "dear." She'd not meant "deer," not consciously. How could she have? But it had been a part of her witchcraft.

She was a witch. She'd always wished it, and now here it was, the capability, the power. The very deed.

She regretted the man's death, and she could not truthfully say she had not willed it. Beauty had killed him, his own dog. But had she not given the command? That much blood was on her hands. And on her clothes, a great deal more, quite visible, an accusation, for as the dog had torn Tommy apart—or the deer he had become— the blood of that contest had drenched her clothes where they had lain on the recliner.

She must burn those clothes as soon as she got home and forget what had happened, blot it out and never think of it again. One *could* do that. By an act of will. Just as now, by an act of will, she was driving her Camry home. Bad things might happen, but they might also unhappen. She would burn the bloodstained clothes. She would erase the horror from memory.

Here was the turnoff. She hung right and tilted her head back with a silent rejoicing. She checked the clock on the dashboard: 8:42. Could so much happen so quickly? It could. And there was her house, her home, safety.

She'd already thought out what to do. She would take the soiled clothes, everything she had taken from the chair in Tommy's cabin, and burn them on the grate of the smokehouse. There seemed an almost mathematical equivalence in that act, a biblical exactness of justice.

The moment when she stepped out of the car and the cold air hit her face and her bare legs was pure bliss. She had been burning up alive inside the car, even with the heater off and her wearing nothing but her shearling coat. Which she unbuttoned now and opened to let the chilled air minister to her naked body. It was like standing under a cold shower on a sweaty summer day, first the shock, then the shiver of pleasure—a shiver not of the skin but arising deep within, mounting her spine, like water surging from a fountain, until it hit the base of her neck and then exploded inside her brain like fireworks. It had been years since she'd felt this orgasmic rush of liquid pleasure course up her spine—always at moments of supreme drunkenness, and never singly but in waves.

When it had passed, the chill of the air no longer felt like a balm, and Diana wiped the tears from the corners of her eyes and cinched the coat closed with its belt. Brenda had a name for such moments, when your emotions seemed to move in the opposite direction to the real events in your life, depression after some big success or, like this, elation in the face of a major disaster: I.A.—inappropriate affect.

The clothes, she reminded herself. She unlocked the Camry's trunk and gathered them up from where they lay atop the flatted tire. There would be a lighter and starter fluid in the crevice of the barbecue, where the Kellogs burned their trash. And where Diana might more easily burn these clothes. Except that that rite had to be performed on the smokehouse grate. She did not know why that seemed so necessary, only that it was an essential part of her witchcraft to stand by the fire and bask in its heat. Tonight she would be Ishtar ascending to heaven, one piece of clothing at a time. The Snake Woman shedding her skin.

It was Wesley, of course, whose will impelled her, whose power was now so much greater that he could summon her without exertion. Day by day, as Diana had busied herself about the farmhouse, she had been tangling herself in the cilia of that swollen, invisible anemone that Wes Turney had become, that sac of blind hunger that at last was being offered nourishment. As Diana approached the smokehouse across the hard-packed snow, bearing her offering—her own clothes moist with the blood of her first victim—those cilia were all atremble.

She placed the clothing on the iron grate, doused it with the fluid, and applied the butane lighter at arm's length. It flamed with the first ratcheting of the wheel. A foot of the pantyhose caught fire, and the flame lengthened and brightened, spreading quickly to the heavier fabric of the jeans and shirt. Another wave of pleasure coursed through Diana as the fire flared up, and she let the shearling coat fall to her feet.

It seemed as though her flesh and the flames were a single entity, and that within the circumambient air was yet another entity, etheric but real, like the fires of Pentecost, a living Wisdom that entered her shocked flesh at each pore.

"Go to the door," Wes urged her. "To the door that you closed so long ago. Open it. Let me see what you've become."

When the flames within her flesh had diminished, she obeyed that prompting, thinking to herself as she did so that there might be something in there that would be stained by the soot. For our conscious thoughts, even when our actions are least our own, still have some little film of plausibility, like the reflective surface of a pool of water.

And yet, when she did open the door and saw her father hanging there, upside down, bleeding, in pain, she was neither surprised nor dismayed. For he appeared just as she had left him. It was not a winter night but an autumn afternoon . . .

. . . and she had *wished* his accident. She had seen him on the roof of the smokehouse, and all the resentment she had felt at lunchtime and for every waking moment for the past two weeks focused on his crouched body, hating him, wishing him dead. It was just then, as he brought his hammer down to nail another shake in place, that the main crossbeam collapsed and he toppled forward into the smokehouse. There was one sharp yelp of pain, and then a long silence.

It was what he deserved. She wasn't the least bit sorry for him. He had always been against her, always favored Janet, and today was just the crowning example. Janet was heading off with her Brownie troop for a weekend holiday in the Twin Cities, a $22 extravaganza including a Disney ice show, while Diana had to go with her mother to visit her grandmother in the hospital in St. Cloud and miss her best friend's birthday party because her father didn't have the time to come pick her up when the party was over. She would have to sleep on the couch in her uncle Maurice's trailer while her mother and uncle and his stupid friends got drunk. It was all hugely and horribly *unfair,* and there wasn't a thing she could do about it.

It was then that her mother, from the back of the house, had shouted out her name. "Di! Di, we're leaving!"

She hated being called Di. She hated everything about her life, but she especially hated her father, who now, from inside the smokehouse, also called her name. She could not resist the temptation. She went to the door of the smokehouse and opened it and took one look, and sealed her heart against him.

And closed the door.

When they were in the car, her mother and Janet and herself, her mother asked, "So, is your father finished up there?" and Diana had answered, "No, he's still pounding away."

And the next day, when they came back from St. Cloud and there was no sign of her father, and his pickup was still inside the garage, Diana didn't say a word. She left it to her mother to find him in the smokehouse hours later, hanging the way Diana had left him, with the meat hook lodged in the back of his knee and the blood that Diana had seen dripping down from his face all dried, and the flies swarming about. And even then, sneaking her second look while her mother blubbered into the phone, she had not felt the least bit sorry.

It was what he deserved.

"So," Wesley said, reading her thoughts, "I deserved to die? Because you couldn't go to a birthday party? Or because I raped you? Which is it?" The flies were swarming about his staring, upside-down eyes.

"You're dead," she told him.

"And you?" He answered the question himself: "You're a witch. Full of hatred. Always have been." He tried to spit at her, but his blood, even as a ghost, was clotted, and the red drool didn't reach escape velocity. It ran down his cheek and then along his eyebrow.

She offered no denial. She felt the old hatred firm in her heart again.

"You're *dead*," she insisted again.

"But I would be alive today—alive and lame—if you'd acted like"—one of the many flies flew into his mouth, and he spit it out— "like a daughter!"

"You break my heart."

"Your heart cannot be broken. It isn't there. You've become a witch. No love left in you. There was never much. Now there's none. You will kill everyone you once loved, as you killed me. And I'll help. I'll help."

"Go to hell," she told him.

"Where else?" he answered.

And was gone.

. . .

"Diana!" a familiar voice called out.

Familiar, but even so she could not recognize it. She stood there naked, freezing, aware, for a moment, of some awful emptiness and then of nothing at all.

22

He'd never seen a live woman entirely naked before—and there Diana was, the woman he loved, unconscious, spread out before him, the way he'd imagined her once: in a dentist's office, anesthetized, her mouth slightly open. In his fantasy he hadn't imagined the drool seeping out from the corner of her mouth. He'd imagined only their kiss, and then backed away from the daydream guiltily. But here was that daydream actually happening, and it was sinister much more than romantic.

"Diana?"

When that produced no results, he tried again, a little louder. Still she didn't stir. He wanted to know what had happened, why she was lying in the snow, naked except for her winter boots. But the first order of business was to get her in out of the cold. He got down on his knees beside her and tilted her forward and got her right arm over his left shoulder, then tried to lift her into a standing position. But she was too heavy, or he was too weak. He stooped lower and got his right arm under her knees and then, still kneeling, lifted her legs up separately and got a better grip on her upper body. This time he got her off the ground, except for her back end, but he was on his knees and could rise no higher with her in his arms.

At last, by tilting her forward into a sitting position, he was able to lift her up by her armpits and drag her along backwards with her bootheels tracing two lines through the fresh snow. He almost took a tumble when his feet tangled in her sheepskin coat, which was lying on the snow in front of the brick barbecue attached to the rear end of the little shack where he'd found her. Was it an outhouse? Was that why she had no clothes on? Why would an outhouse have its own barbecue?

She began to groan when they were halfway to the back door of the house. Alan was frozen from sheer embarrassment. For a moment he considered just dumping her there in the snow before she awoke and recognized him. And then he remembered how she had found him in almost the same way, unconscious in the snow. Just before the phone call from his lawyer had awakened him, he'd had a Winner'qus fortune message playing Taipei. It said, "Strange new experiences will add to your joy of living." Maybe his Taipei obsession was like believing in fortune cookies—or maybe, as Diana so often insisted, there are no coincidences and the world is full of signs and omens. Maybe, as another Taipei message he often encountered explained, unseen forces were working in his favor, prompting him, bringing him here at the moment Diana needed him most.

At the door Alan found himself with a new problem: it was locked. The key might be in a pocket of the coat he'd tripped over, or in her car on the ring with the ignition key. But he couldn't go on dragging her about through the snow while he looked, or set her down on the freezing concrete steps. He managed to shrug off his coat and position it underneath her like a cushion.

The keys were in the pocket of her coat, and soon he had her inside the house, slumped across the kitchen table, her sheepskin coat spread over her like a blanket. Strangely, her flesh seemed hot and was beaded with sweat, as though she'd just stepped out of a steambath.

Having accomplished this much, he could not think what else to do. Repeating her name did not rouse her, nor did gently shaking her shoulders. He looked about for a blanket or articles of clothing he could help her into, and returned with a pair of fuzzy blue slippers.

She woke as he was on his knees under the table, trying to position her left foot (from which he'd removed the boot) to accept the slipper. She shouted out, reared back in the kitchen chair, and kicked Alan in the face. He felt a thrill of gratitude to know that she'd returned to consciousness. "Diana!" he cried, backing out from under the table, "it's all right! I'm here."

"Alan?" She looked down at her bare breasts and pulled her shearling coat tight about her torso in a gesture of belated modesty. "What are you doing here? Where are . . . ?"

"Your clothes? I don't know," he said helplessly. "I found you like that outside that little shack behind the house. Lying in the snow. I couldn't wake you up. So I carried you in here the best I could. I hope I didn't hurt you."

"Hurt me? I don't understand."

"I mean I had to drag you through the snow. Why were you . . . ?"

Her eyes narrowed with suspicion. "I still don't understand why you're here. How you got in the house. Where my clothes are. Why you're taking my boot off."

"Something happened that I had to talk with you about. So I drove here. And when I got here, there were tracks up the driveway and your car was standing with the door open. I called out your name a couple times."

"We'll have to discuss all this later," she said, rising from the table, glaring at him. "I have to get some clothes on."

He remained as she'd left him, crouched on the kitchen linoleum, her fuzzy slipper in his hand. Did she think that *he* was responsible for her nakedness? Had there been some act of violence that had left her in a state of shock?

Had she been raped? The possibility so alarmed him, it seemed at once so likely, that he sprang up and ran from the kitchen to the foot of the stairs. "Diana! Are you all right?"

Halfway up to the landing she paused to remove her unlaced boot. It was then the lights went off all over the house.

"Alan! God damn you!"

"It wasn't me, Diana, I swear. A power line must have gone down somewhere. The snow's been piling up."

"Well, then," she said in her familiar tone of voice, "I'll change that to just God damn the snow."

"Diana? I'll tell you what. I'll just sit here on the stairs. You get some clothes on. It's kind of cold in the house. Maybe the furnace is on the blink. Is there a flashlight up there? Or candles? I better not go stumbling around or I'll knock something over for sure."

"You do that," she agreed.

He listened to her irregular footsteps. One boot on and one boot off. He fingered his jaw where she'd kicked him, and smiled. People behaved weirdly in a crisis. Why had he fussed with her slippers, he wondered now. Here was the boot she'd taken off and left on the stairs. He sniffed at the fleecy inside, and grimaced. A ripe smell. But hers, and so he sniffed again, and the second time it seemed almost pleasant. Maybe feet were one of those things like cheese or olives that you had to learn to like.

Upstairs there was a banging of drawers. She was angry, but she was coping with the problem, which was probably a good thing. In a couple more minutes she returned to the head of the stairs again. "It's so dark," she told him, "I can't see a thing. Sit on the other side of the stairs from the handrail. And just stay there till I get to the kitchen and find a candle. I don't want you crashing into the furniture."

"Whatever you say."

Each tread of the stairs had its own distinctive creak as she came down. He could feel her brush by him in the darkness, cloth catching at his shoulder, giving a momentary tug, then slipping away. He traced her progress toward the kitchen in his imagination—through the hallway, across the living room carpet, circling the big table in the dining room, and then a long silence broken by small purposeful noises. At last a candle flame appeared below Alan where he sat on the stairs, Diana's cupped hand glowing before it brightly like the shade of a lamp. No candle had ever seemed so beautiful before. He understood why Catholics used them for their services and the stricter Protestants didn't. They were sexy.

He followed the red candle like a moth. The smell was sexy, too. He was getting an erection. His erections were always like that, sudden and connected to something unconnected to sex—the smell of burning grease outside Burger King, the pop of a stubborn pimple, the tingle of snuff. This time, of course, there *was* a connection to sex, only Alan's mind veered away from thinking of it. He eased himself down into the chair Diana had pulled back from the table and took a deep breath.

She had lit the stove, perhaps to light the candle, but now there was a kettle over the blue flames. "I'm making a tisane," she told him.

He nodded acquiescently but then had to ask, "What's that?"

"An herbal tea. This one will guard against a cold. And warm us up. It *is* cold in the house. I turned the thermostat all the way down when I left earlier. I thought I'd be away for the night, and Carl has taken Kelly off to visit her mother for the weekend. And now we can't turn the furnace on till the electricity returns. We may have to snuggle on the couch just to survive."

She said that in what he thought of as her teasing tone of voice. She had different voices. When she was pissed off was one, and when she wasn't thinking about him at all was another. The teasing voice was friendlier than those, but there was still an edge to it that could make him feel uncomfortable. It reminded him of his mother when she was coaxing him to do something.

The kettle on the stove began to whistle, and Diana busied herself making the tea. When she was done, she brought the red teapot to the table. Steam rose from the spout, and the light from the red candle made a kind of halo around the pot. The different reds made Alan wish he were a photographer. He also wished he could see Diana naked again, instead of in the pink bathrobe she'd put on. He realized that this was the feeling older men had in mind when they joked about being horny.

And then, again, that teasing voice as she placed two big mugs beside the teapot. "So—do you want to tell me what brought you here at such an opportune moment?" She smiled and sat down in the same chair in which, so little time ago, he'd laid her unconscious body. And now she was asking him about *his* problems, as though none of that had even happened. It was a little unnerving.

"Oh, that doesn't matter. Right now I'm worried about you."

"Nothing bad happened out there. I've told you before, I'm a Wiccan. I was performing a kind of ritual. It's nothing to be alarmed about, but it's not something I can talk about either. Okay?"

"Okay."

Actually, it seemed insulting, in a way, to have the matter dismissed so lightly. But also mysterious, like some old black-and-white movie. You probably couldn't have it both ways. If she were completely open with him about everything, she wouldn't have seemed mysterious.

"Here," she said in a mothering way. "Have some of this."

She poured tea into the mugs and lifted one to her smiling lips. The steam veiled her face. The curling vapors gave off a minty smell and, mixed with that, something he could not put a name to. He picked up his own mug and tried to sip, but the water scalded his upper lip, and he flinched. "It's hot!"

She drew a deep breath and made a grimace of impatience. "Let's go in the living room."

Again he followed the candle flame obediently and sat on the couch. The cushion yielded under his weight, and he spilled some of the hot tea over his gut, catching his breath so he wouldn't yelp. She put the burning candle down on the end table, and her mug of tea beside it. Since there was no table on his side of the couch, he rested his own mug on the arm so that when she sat he wouldn't spill any more on himself. Where it had doused his shirt it still hurt.

"Let the tea cool," she said. "Tell me what happened."

"The lawyer called."

"And?"

"My father isn't who I thought."

"You've told me that before, Alan."

"But now I know who is. I sent in another blood sample. Not from Jim Cottonwood. And the DNA test says this other guy *is* my . . ." He could not say the word. "There's a match."

"And?" she insisted.

"Remember when you drove me home the day we met? And my grandfather threw my stuff out of the house? And broke the screen on my monitor doing it? Well, he cut his hand. That's how I got the sample of blood to send them."

"You don't think . . . ?"

"Yeah, it's him. I couldn't believe it either at first. I mean, she's his daughter. It's incest. And I always *hated* the bastard. Hated him. So maybe I always knew. Unconsciously."

Neither of them spoke for a long while. Then she took a sip from her mug of tea.

"But that man has been in prison all this time."

"Yeah, I know. The more I think about it, the more . . . I mean, it's awful."

"Yes, certainly."

The candle flame wavered, almost guttered out, then offered a sudden brightness and steadied. Alan remembered his mug of tea and picked it up and took a long sip, hot but tolerable. He closed his eyes—and found that he was crying.

"Have you *talked* to them?" she asked.

"No! I couldn't. To my mother? Or him? No! Not even the lawyer. *He* thinks the blood is from Cottonwood, and I let him go on thinking that. I'm the only one who knows anything. And now you."

"The beast," she said in a tone of cool and certain judgment.

"Yeah, it's terrible. But I remember your telling me that your father . . ."

"Oh, yes. He *touched* me. In ways he shouldn't have. But . . . there was no actual sex. I think he wanted to. I think many men do."

"I think maybe they do. I know that my fucking grandfather did."

As he admitted the likelihood of his worst doubt, Alan felt a terrible cramp in his stomach, just below where the tea had scalded him, and then the cramp became a kind of slithering underneath his T-shirt.

"You poor boy," she said. "Oh, you poor boy." And she leaned toward him and took him in her arms, and her embrace and the slithering sensation united, and he felt a terror (and yet only its first glimmering) such as he'd never known before. The flame of the candle shuddered, and her embrace tightened. He couldn't breathe or speak. Her arms had become the coils of a snake, pressing the breath from his lungs.

And then the lights in the house came on and she screamed, and he could breathe again.

The coils had released him. The terror just as suddenly was gone, but her arms were still around him, and her lips were pressed to his.

He loved her, with a shame and a desire and a pure devotion that were desolating and unbearable.

23

"I love you," he told her. "I love you now more than I ever have."

"Well, that's nice of you to say, but I don't believe it."

"It's true. I've had a long time to think about it. And at first I was pissed off, I'll admit. But the fact that you were actually willing to *kill* me . . . That's something you expect more from a guy."

She laughed. "You wouldn't think that way if you spent some time here. I actually have a higher credit rating among the other ladies and some of the guards for having gone after you and Dana."

"There's the same pecking order in the men's joint. Homicide's at the top, but attempted homicide still rates high, as long as it looks like a sincere attempt. And I think yours was pretty sincere."

"How *is* Dana these days?"

"You'll have to ask her. She and I are not speaking. She blames me as much as you. I didn't testify at the trial, and in her eyes that amounts to aiding and abetting."

"And how's your arm?"

"I still get twinges. Listen, we been through all the how-are-you's already. We better get down to business, honey. If they catch me here, we'll both be in a lot deeper shit. This place is off limits, for me especially. I could be canned."

"Well, then, get going. You're always ready at six a.m."

"'Cause I wake with a hard-on."

"Weren't you the one who just said how much you love me?"

"It's not the same thing. If you gave me a little encouragement . . ."

"You mean if I sucked your cock."

"Yeah, that's one possibility. Do you need a sex manual, for Christ's sake? I'm here for your sake, you know. You're the one who wants to get pregnant and have an exit visa."

"I know, I know. It's just difficult. I'm on edge, too. We've both got to try and get relaxed."

"Relaxed is not in the cards, honey. Try stimulated."

"Do you want to try doing it on the floor? You like that at home sometimes."

"In summer, or on a thick carpet. But have you tried walking around in this place in your stocking feet? You'd freeze your butt off."

She laughed. "Or you would, depending." She leaned sideways and gave him an impulsive kiss on the bristly side of his head. "You can be such a pig."

He grinned. "That's the sixty-four-dollar question right now, ain't it? *Can* I?"

There was a knock at the door.

"Oh, Jesus," said Janet with a stricken look.

Carl put his finger to her lips, then whispered in her ear, "Don't panic. I thought this out. My shoes and pants are both under the bunk, and I'll scoot down there, too. There's plenty of room. Just rumple the spread so it hangs down over the side, then deal with whoever it is and get 'em out of here. Okay?"

She nodded.

And called out, after a second knock, "I'll be right there. Just let me get decent."

"It's Officer Lincoln."

Carl was under the bunk. He gave her ankle a reassuring squeeze. Janet said, "Come in. The door isn't locked."

Officer Lincoln entered. She was wearing a black nylon uniform jacket, light gray slacks, with boots trimmed at the top with artificial fleece. No weapon (none of the guards at Mankato carried weapons), and no cap, so that her crown of black braids was dusted with snow. "Hi," she said. "Is this an okay time?"

"Okay as any," Janet allowed.

"I saw you hadn't come to the movie but your roommates were there."

"I've seen *Doctor Zhivago* a few times already. It's always on TV. Come in, close the door."

"Thank you." Officer Lincoln entered and crossed the room to sit beside Janet on her bunk. There were other places she might have sat, but none at a comfortable conversational distance. From Janet's viewpoint, if not from Carl's (for Officer Lincoln was a large woman), it was probably the best choice. As long as she was sitting on top of him, she couldn't look under the bunk.

"It's a wonderful movie," Officer Lincoln said, "but I've probably seen it enough times myself. But for a lot of the younger women it can be a revelation."

Janet nodded, hoping this was not the beginning of a conversation about *Doctor Zhivago*, which she'd never seen except for the first few minutes, and that only at Carl's insistence. He'd stayed up, she remembered, to see the whole thing. But he couldn't come to her rescue in the present situation. "How is that?" she asked.

"Well, very few of them have any idea how the whole thing in Russia got started. Even those who've got high school diplomas don't have much sense of history. That's a luxury these days." Officer Lincoln heaved a sigh and leaned back against the wall, unzipping her jacket as she did so. "You at least are a reader. There aren't many here. In Shakopee, yes. There are readers there. When I was there, that's three years ago now, we actually had a reading group that read *War and Peace* pretty much all the way through."

"No kidding. That's better than me. I think my husband read that one. I know it's there in the bookcase. It's a big one, right?"

"One of the biggest. So, how did it go with Carl today?"

"Just fine. He couldn't have been nicer. Considering. And Kelly, that's our girl, she was fine, too." There was a long pause until Janet finally thought to say, "I realized how much I miss her." And when this produced no response from Officer Lincoln, Janet added, "I was just thinking of writing a letter to my sister, Diana, to thank her for all she's been doing."

"You haven't written many letters while you've been here," Officer Lincoln observed.

Janet bristled at the woman's careless knowingness, as though everything she did was something Officer Lincoln would automatically be aware of. But she couldn't show her resentment. Ever. That was the first rule. And the second, and the third.

"I should start to make it a habit," Janet agreed.

"That's excellent advice for anyone. But especially for those here. We have to keep those bridges in place."

"You're right! I should sit down right now and start that letter."

Officer Lincoln recognized this as an invitation to leave. She stood up and then, in a casual way, asked if she might go to the bathroom.

"Sure," said Janet. "You know where it is."

Officer Lincoln went into the bathroom. After very little time, there was the sound of the toilet being flushed, and she returned.

Her mood had altered. She seemed miffed. "Well, it's been nice talking to you, Janet. You've been making excellent progress here. There are no demerits on your record."

"Thank you."

"So keep up the good work."

"Thank you."

Officer Lincoln went to the door, opened it, and turned around, scanning the room like a surveillance camera. Then she nodded her head and left.

"Don't say a thing," Carl cautioned from under the bunk. "Don't do a thing. Write the fucking letter."

Janet nodded her head. She sat at the table in front of the big picture window and went through the motions of writing a letter. She had no idea if she was on videocam, but she felt she might be. Sometimes that feeling could be overwhelming, which was why she had to get out of this place.

Dear Diana, she wrote on the prison stationery, *Fuck you! I am having the shittiest time of my life. I wish you were here instead of me. I wish I were dead. Have you been to bed with Carl yet? If not I expect it won't be long.* Then she took the sheet of paper and tore it into smaller and smaller bits.

"Okay," said Carl from under the bunk, "now turn off the lights. You know why that bitch asked to use your toilet, don't you?"

Janet turned off the lights. "She thought you'd be in there."

"Yeah. Well, I got a hard-on now anyhow. So that's no problem. You head into the bathroom, and don't lock the door."

"I can't."

"It's a pisser, ain't it?" But then he added, quite sincerely, "You know, I really do love you."

"I know. I love you, too," she said, no less sincerely.

24

Witches, so often credited with possessing the power of the evil eye, are also remarkable for their green thumbs. Their gardens are lush, their houseplants thrive, their lawns spontaneously yield pounds of mushrooms and asparagus. The two gifts rise from a single source, a keen and focused attentiveness to patterns and appearances. A natural witch, unaware of her powers and uninstructed in their use, is nevertheless able to pluck, as though they were harp strings, the nerves of any stranger her attention has lighted on. Let her sustain that gaze, and the object of her attention will be petrified into inaction or melt with servile compliance. Wherever sheer intimidation is at a premium, witches flourish. They have always been the best sales personnel and trial lawyers and the most effective nursery school teachers. This is doubly true of those who have become conscious of their gifts and know themselves to be witches—as Diana now did.

Of course, she could not simply walk about through the woods and meadows of Leech Lake township and gather a chaplet of herbs and simples specific to some witchy purpose. But her intuitions were quick and accurate in matters that directly concerned her, such as male lust. Ruben at D & R Auto Service always hastened to the pump when she pulled up for gas, and though the least talkative of men, he lingered by her window to offer his opinions on basketball and the last flurries of winter weather. It was the same with the teenage baggers at the Shop 'n' Save, who buzzed around Diana like drones around their queen. If she fixed her attention on any of these males, she could discern not only the auras of their lust but the tribe or totem inherent to their nature, the beast she could make them become if she exerted her powers.

Pigs were commonest. Two of the baggers at Shop 'n' Save were of that tribe, as were her brother-in-law and Alan Johnson. Even, probably, President Clinton, though with faces she knew only from photographs or TV she could not be sure if her taxonomies were based on a real witchy intuition or just ordinary hunches. Dogs, horses, and other domestic animals were also common among the denizens of Leech Lake, then the larger rodents and scavenging birds. Predators were rarely discernible in the general population. Perhaps the human personae of those who belonged to the tribes of tiger or fox clung to their human identities more tenaciously. Perhaps her vision was limited to prey and blind to other predators. She did not know her own nature as a beast. In the crude machineries of a mirror auras are not visible. She supposed her essential nature was feline, but she'd never seen herself so.

Many of the talents that have been ascribed to witches were not within Diana's range of powers. She had no special prevision of the future. Her evil eye might spook those, human or animal, with a special sensitivity, but except for the single, radical power of metamorphosis, she could not induce illness or injury by the sheer force of a baleful look. She'd focused all of her ill will on the squirrels that came to thieve from the birdfeeder, and she knew with the first trial that D-Con was not about to lose a customer because Diana had found herself to be a witch.

She could not read minds or leave her body to enjoy nocturnal flights, nor could she summon other spirits—though she might visit her father in the smokehouse if she was patient and he was in the mood. But this was not a power she was eager to exercise. Like the preserves in the food cellar, he was there for emergencies one hoped would never come.

Altogether, there seemed to be little practical advantage to being a witch. But it was undeniably an *empowering* awareness. Whomever she found herself with, Diana felt in charge. The whole world had become an elementary school, and she was its principal. In a sense, this had always been her relation to the rest of the world—if not effectively, at least wishfully. When she'd first majored in psychology as an undergraduate, before being persuaded to switch to education, that had been the attraction. One of the required texts in her junior year had been by a Frenchman with a thing for prisons. In his ideal prison, there was a central observation tower from which one could see all the prisoners in all their cells at the same time. Diana felt like the warden of such a prison. Indeed, this was no new observation, for

Diana's mother had often claimed she thought of the old ladies under her charge at Navaho House as being her prisoners, confined there by feebleness and poverty. "The Turneys," she would say, "are prison people. It's in the blood."

Diana's powers as a witch were limited in one other crucial regard. She could entrance a man's attention, but she could not compel his performance. She had tried, on the night of Alan's visit, when he'd found her unconscious by the smokehouse; she'd given hours to the task, and she had failed. When his lips barely brushed hers, she could feel his incipient hard-on straining at his blue jeans, but any determined effort to encourage a fuller erection produced the opposite result. Even to talk about sex had proven next to impossible, for Alan became morbidly shy at any mention of his own body, or hers. Did they make anatomically correct dolls for this purpose, as they did for children who had to be coaxed into discussing the trauma of abuse?

At last he had revealed that he was a virgin—not just in the sense that he'd never had sexual relations with another person. He'd never had an orgasm. Guilt and sheer embarrassment had kept him from trying to achieve satisfaction by masturbation, and his few dates, before meeting Diana, had never advanced beyond hugs and hand-holding. His nearest approach to an orgasm had been in wet dreams, but even then without the relief of spontaneous ejaculation. Diana had never known such a man, eighteen years old and still a virgin. Perhaps that was his secret attraction. Perhaps virginity affects the pheromones, intensifies a man's sexual aura and makes him more desirable.

For she did desire him, she could not deny that. Witches can feel every degree of need, of want, of hunger, of sexual appetite. But did they (Diana had to ask herself) experience love in the usual sense of the word? Diana had always supposed that what she'd experienced with the men to whom she was attracted was love. That was how people spoke of such things, that was what songs were about. It was the stuff of books and movies.

Tenderness, yes. She would often feel a tenderness toward her sexual partners, especially in the aftermath of their union, during the postcoital *tristesse*, when the man would lie there inert, or panting like a tired dog, mere meat. Their helplessness at such times could be so saddening, and when she'd first seen Alan, after his fall from the roof, she'd felt the extremity of such sadness.

But was that actually the same as love? She wasn't sure, but she was determined to find out. One way or another she was going to have his cherry. She realized that her new feelings toward Alan—the ambition simply to take possession—were the way she supposed men must feel toward women. The way rapists must feel—downhill with the brakes off. It was disgusting and piggish—and irresistible.

25

A spring drizzle hung in the air, light enough to allow the exercise oval to be used but thick enough to be a soothing balm on Clay's face as he did laps. The drizzle had turned the landscape surrounding the prison tower into a black-and-white photograph, with the mists above Leech Lake a single luminous, opalescent glow. The scrub pines of the Wabasha reservation were brush strokes of Chinese calligraphy on a painted scroll. Very spacey. Outside of dreams, the illusion of freedom here was as close as you could get in the joint, and Clay was not happy when, with ten minutes of yard time left, Carl Kellog cued him with a wiggle of his finger to leave the track.

Clay slowed to a trot and stopped in front of the C.O. "Sir," he said, his chest still heaving pleasantly. The first beads of sweat started to form across his forehead and scalp and trickle down to the collar of his sweatshirt.

"Hi there, Clay," Carl said in that officially neutered voice the guards used when they were performing some official function.

"Sir," Clay repeated, in his own zombied-down, I'm-just-a-number-here voice.

"I was wondering if there was anything you could tell me about this fracas outside the Lutheran Church."

"No, sir. I was not there. My knowledge about events outside the prison is limited to what we're allowed to see on television."

"Mm-hm. So, you would know nothing about the protesters?"

"No, sir."

"Or what they expected to accomplish?"

"I've never talked with any of them, sir. But if you're asking me if Jim knows anything about it, I would guess not. He was taken to the hole on Sunday afternoon, and he's been there ever since. I don't know for what infraction. I do know that there's been *concern* among the men here. I would say the concern has reached only a low simmer at this point. There's speculation. I guess that's unavoidable."

"To what effect?"

"Some guys think if a guy goes to the hole, there must be a reason. None has been given. Did he commit some infraction? Is he in protective custody? From whom? The guys are puzzled."

"If you need to know the reason, there have been harassing phone calls to local citizens."

"And you think that Jim made those calls from here in the facility? I thought security was tighter than that."

"The calls were made on his behalf. The protesters at the church are protesting on his behalf. The warden believes Jim knows who's behind it all."

"But if he doesn't know? It's not as though he *needs* a protest. Because Jim is a remarkably patient guy. He's bided his time for over eighteen years. Does the warden think he can get him to withdraw his appeal at this point? The word is out, Officer Kellog. Jim doesn't need to stir up that bunch from the rez. They were out there last Sunday just for the hell of it—that's my guess. No doubt some of the older people outside the church remember the trial. Even back then, Jim tells me, a lot of his people thought he was set up, and now it looks like they were right all along. So when the shit hits the fan, they want to be sure that Judy Johnson is covered with her fair share of it. I mean, if it turns out she was lying, and it sure looks that way from what I hear, then she's responsible for Jim Cottonwood's false imprisonment for eighteen years. I assume it was her or Reverend Johnson getting the harassing phone calls?"

"It's for me to ask the questions, Clay."

"Oh, absolutely, sir. I don't want you thinking *I'm* some kind of agitator. I'm just telling you what the 'tude is here, as I understand it. And it's a combination of suspicion that Jim is about to get shafted and a feeling that he can take care of himself."

Carl nodded a dour concurrence.

Clay cracked his knuckles, avoiding eye contact by focusing on his tattoos. "Anything else, sir?"

"Uh, yes. But it's not official. In fact, the warden would be pissed off if he thought I was meddling in this. But when you see Jim again, which'll probably be tomorrow at the latest, you can pass it along— but don't say where you heard it—"

Clay nodded. "When I see him again . . . .?"

"Tell him the Johnson kid is still busting his balls for him. There's been pressure from some of Reverend Johnson's friends at the state capitol, but you won't see the warden caving in to Avo Kubelik. Jim'll get released, but what the kid tells me Jim's lawyer is saying is that there'll have to be an appeal for clemency. The rape conviction may be overturned, but Jim racked up another fifteen years during the ruckus back in Eighty-eight."

"He saved a guy's life. That was another setup, and everyone here knows that. Anyhow, Jim's already served eighteen years for something he didn't do. And when he gets out of here, he's going to be able to sue this place for millions."

"Personally, I hope he gets it, though it's a long shot. No one's saying it wasn't a fair trial, so the State of Minnesota would be off the hook, liability-wise. But where Jim might stand to gain some money is from the Johnsons. Judy perjured herself. The statute of limitations has passed on that, but—"

Clay lost his cool momentarily: "You mean, because it was eighteen years ago that Judy told her lies, the meter's expired? He's been rotting here, and she could have let him out anytime she found her conscience."

"Hey, Clay, I didn't write the law. That's what Jim's lawyer told the Johnson kid. He says Jim has a good chance of suing Judy *and* Reverend Johnson in civil court. So Jim might end up owning the church and rectory. I understand that when the higher-ups in his church wanted to close the place down ten years ago, he finagled a deal to buy the buildings off them real cheap. Anyhow, none of that is official information, though it's common knowledge. But if you'd pass it along to Jim, I think he might feel a little easier in his mind."

"Basically, you don't want him stirring up trouble. Is that it?"

"Out there or in here. Right."

"Sure, I'll pass it along. Oh—and while there's still some yard time, has there been any word about Officer Wagner?"

"That's a subject we're not supposed to discuss, Clay."

"It's a weird situation. All that mayhem, and him just disappearing at the same time."

"I can't talk about it, Clay."

Clay acknowledged this with a nod and, returning to the track, went through the motions of jogging until the bell sounded half a lap later.

26

In the middle of April, just as daylight saving time was kicking in and short sleeves were an option, word was passed down to Carl from on high that he had to lose forty pounds or else. He deeply resented being told what he had to weigh, but the union had agreed to the state prisons' Personal Appearance Code when they'd negotiated their health-care package back in 1986, and who would have thought back then that Carl, with his thirty-four-inch waist, would ever blimp up to his present XXL dimensions? But he had. The flab had spread down his torso like a fucking glacier. So now, when he passed along the cafeteria line at 3 a.m. (he'd just been moved to the grave-yard shift), his lunch was waiting for him wrapped in its film of Saran Wrap: cold cuts and sliced tomato on Mondays, fruit salad on Tuesday, and on Wednesday, which was today, a tiny can of tuna fish with half a grapefruit.

Diana, when she looked over his list of suggested dinners, told him that the prison nutritionist must have copied out the Scarsdale diet, invented by Dr. Herman Tarnower back in the '70s. The elderly Tarnower had been the victim in a celebrity murder case of that era, when his uncredited coauthor and jilted lover, Jean Harris, avenged herself for this double sleight with a pistol. Eating the prescribed daily menus (Diana adhered faithfully to the prison nutritionist's list), Carl felt as though Jean Harris were still enjoying her revenge through him. This morning's dinner had been a miniature lamb chop and a mouth-puckering salad that was basically just lemon juice on lettuce. Carl was already wired on black coffee from working the night shift, and booze was prohibited, though he did allow himself one vodka tonic as a sedative before he went to bed at 11 a.m. He'd never had a problem adjusting his sleeping patterns to fit the prison's schedule before, but this time he was lucky to get three or four hours of sleep before it was time to get up, fix breakfast (half a grapefruit, one slice of unbuttered toast, and the first cup of his daily river of black coffee), and watch the ABC news on channel 7. Diana shared the news and *Jeopardy*, and then he'd catch the last of the daylight outside with Kelly, futzing around in their so-called garden. Carl believed in growing all his own produce, but the garden rarely yielded more than those crops that grew themselves. At some point during the summer, his life would get too busy, and the garden would self-destruct.

By the time he had to head for work, Carl was grateful for even the meager distractions of the graveyard shift. It was only six weeks out of the year that he had to work on the skeleton crew that kept the joint running during the hours the rest of the world was asleep. The system of video monitors was state-of-the-art, so there was no need to patrol the corridors of the cellblocks. From the desk of the monitor station each cell was open to surveillance twenty-four hours a day. Some patrolling was still required, more for the sake of keeping the guards alert than from any other practical necessity, but for a good part of the shift he was allowed to read.

The problem was that Carl had less of an appetite for reading these days. He used to be able to settle down with a book for hours at a time. The C.O.'s had dibs on all the prison library's recent acquisitions, so Carl got to read all the best-sellers while they were still fresh—Grisham, Clancy, King, Crichton. Lately, however, since Janet had been put away, and especially since going on the diet, he couldn't focus on anything but the newspaper for fifteen minutes before his attention would get derailed.

He knew what it was. It was sex. Or, rather, the lack of sex, combined with the lack of calories, and the new rule against smoking anywhere in a public building in the state of Minnesota. He was just one big twitching Hunger, with no likelihood of satisfaction anytime soon.

His one shot at getting Janet knocked up when he'd visited Mankato in March had misfired. Three weeks later she let Carl know that she'd had her period right on time, and by then it was too late to try again. There was no way they could claim that a new pregnancy predated Janet's arrival in Mankato. They would know that Carl had flouted the rules, and that would mean the sack. So he would just have to go on being horny until Janet had served out her full sentence, which would be early next year. (She'd already forfeited any time off for good behavior when she was caught sneaking smokes from a secret stash and then caught again, in a sting, buying a carton. Mankato ran a tight ship.)

In hindsight Carl could see that having another kid would not have been a great idea. Neither he nor Janet was exactly an ideal parent. Diana, that was another matter. If they could keep her on as their own private Mary Poppins, another kid would have been a snap. Carl had come round to thinking of Diana as a major convenience. She'd completely cured Kelly of her temper tantrums, something neither Carl nor Janet had been able to do. She kept the house shipshape, and she was a super cook: his waistline was proof of that. Carl still had his little spats and boundary wars with her, but they no longer escalated into major quarrels. The fact was, Diana was easier to live with than Janet—smarter, better able to cope, more interesting company.

And even (Carl reluctantly admitted to himself) sexier. She'd filled out since she'd moved in, but in all the nicest ways. Her flesh was no glacier of flab; it was fruit, ripe for plucking. Even overripe sometimes. She was definitely one of those women for whom deodorants were not optional. Last night when Carl had come in from his stint of quality time with Kelly, Diana was curled up on the couch with a book and giving off a smell of pure Roquefort funk. Half toe jam, half crotch sweat, the smell seemed to wrap itself around him. During the entire drive to the prison the smell never left his nostrils and she never left his thoughts.

That morning at six, as he was clocking out, he had his first slip from grace. There was a dispenser in the corner of the C.O.'s lounge that offered, for seventy-five cents, a choice of regular or barbecue potato chips, Fritos, Cheez-Its, or pretzels. His first choice was Fritos, but the dispenser had been cleaned out of them. It was as though the god of diets was giving him one last chance to turn back, but instead he went for the Cheez-Its. In the time it took to get to the parking lot he'd wolfed down the whole bag.

"I'm off the diet," he informed Diana when he got home two doughnuts and a half-pint carton of chocolate milk later.

"No, you're not."

"I am. Really. Maybe if I weren't on the night shift. But sitting around twiddling my thumbs, I can't think of anything else but the hunger. It's driving me crazy."

"I've been on a diet, I know all about it. But I've got something for you. And it works. Brenda Zweig, my astrologer, just lost thirty pounds when she was in Mexico. It's this herbal tea, and she swears nothing else kills your appetite like this stuff. Brenda's short, so thirty pounds off her would be like fifty off you."

"An herbal tea?"

"Oh, don't worry, it won't turn you into a Democrat. Just try it. I knew you'd crash, so I brewed up a half-gallon in advance. It's in the bottle at the back of the fridge. Pour yourself a glass and just chug it down. It tastes awful, but it does the job. What have you got to lose? Except your job."

What was the point in arguing? She was right. He thought to ask what it was brewed from, but Kelly came into the kitchen in her pajamas just then, and he was caught in the routine of getting her ready for school while Diana started his dinner: Thursday, broiled chicken, with the skin removed.

But first a glass of herbal tea.

27

When Diana Turney hit her with a broom and told her to lie down by the refrigerator, Judy Johnson snarled, but she did what she was told. Her father had used his belt to the same effect. As a child, Judy could never be reasoned with, but she could be bullied into submission. She lay there, belly on the linoleum, still tense, still quite alert, but pretending to be interested in the birds darting back and forth about the feeder hanging outside the kitchen window. She hated Diana Turney (as she had hated her father), but the woman was in charge. How she had come to be in charge, Judy was not sure, any more than she could have said at age seven how her father came to have the belt and the right to whip her. He was bigger, and that was that. Eat your dinner! No back talk! Go to bed!

Diana went to the back door and, as she exited, turned round and pointed at Judy. "Stay there!" she commanded.

Judy stayed there. Not because she had to—she was free to move about just as she liked—but because she had no other compelling purpose. She would explore the Kellogs' house in due course. She'd enjoyed poking about in other people's houses back in her baby-sitting days. Their bathrooms and closets could be especially interesting. Once, in the old Knudsen farmhouse, which a city family had bought and fixed up as their summer cottage, she'd tried on the most gorgeous red silk dress. Or maybe it was rayon, the label didn't say. But it felt so slinky! It was a little tight on Judy, but she didn't force the zipper. Even so, that family never asked her back to sit for them again.

One smell in the kitchen had primacy over all the others, a dead-mouse smell that issued from under the icebox. The mouse was not there now, but it had died there (you could still see a telltale cache of greenish D-Con pellets between the oven and the icebox), and its remains had mummified before they were found. Now its smell was wedded to the tiles of the floor like the weeds in an asphalt driveway. Not an appetizing smell, especially, but interesting in its own way.

Diana returned with a little girl. "Kelly," she told the girl, "here's your surprise."

"But I wanted a kitten!" the girl protested. "Not an old *cat*!"

"Well, they didn't have any kittens at the pound, and Ginger isn't an old cat. She might have kittens herself someday."

"She's a lady cat?"

"No, not this one. She's a female but not a lady."

Diana chuckled, and Judy bristled with resentment, as she did whenever someone treated her as trailer trash. Her father was a fucking minister of the gospel, and that should count for something.

"Why don't you pet her?" Diana suggested to Kelly.

"Okay." The child approached Judy and squatted down beside her. She reached out to stroke her head.

Judy reared back and snarled.

"Ginger!" Diana pointed her finger. "None of that, or you'll get taken back to the pound. And you know what happens there."

"What happens there?" Kelly asked with a grin.

"Bad cats meet sad ends."

"They kill them?" Kelly asked solemnly.

Diana nodded.

Kelly reached out again, and this time Judy allowed her fur to be stroked.

"I think she understood you," Kelly said.

"Of course she did. Cats are very smart in their own way. Now, you take her outdoors and show her around the property while I get started on dinner."

"Is she going to be *my* cat?" Kelly wanted to know.

"Yes, if you take care of her. See that there's always water in her bowl, and kitty litter in the box I put in the bathroom."

"Can she sleep in my room?"

"No, I think it would be better if she slept under the porch. During the warm weather anyhow. There's an old basket up in the attic that we can fix up as her bed. She'll be comfy."

So out they went, with Judy leading the way and Kelly tagging behind. Judy knew, the minute they were out the back door, that there was something *wrong* out here, and she knew just where it was to be found—just as she'd known where the mouse had died under the icebox. Kelly seemed dimly aware of it as well, for they both headed in the opposite direction until they came to a cluster of fruit trees, where Kelly got into an old tire strung from a tree limb and tried to tempt Judy into her lap. Judy sprang up into the tree instead, and from a high branch she watched Kelly arc back and forth.

It seemed perfectly natural to be looking down at the world from that vantage point and, at the same time, entirely weird. Judy was a cat now, and in some sense she'd always been a cat, or had possessed a catlike nature. But her transformation had come over her so suddenly and so unexpectedly that she still thought of herself as human. It's not an uncommon attitude among cats, especially those who've only lived with people and not known the company of other cats. Like them her frame of reference was human and indoors. The prospect from here in the tree was feline, outdoors, and *confusing*, a pandemonium of smells and noises intensely interesting but profoundly mysterious. It was as though Judy had found herself all at once in the middle of a foreign country—France or China or one of those—where everything had a French or a Chinese name and all the old American names had vanished.

"Come along, Ginger," said Kelly, wriggling out of the O of the swing. "I think Daddy must be up now."

Judy climbed down out of the tree and followed the child back into the house, where a fat, potently odorous man was sitting in front of the TV eating a bowl of milk and breakfast food. The milk looked delicious.

"Daddy," said Kelly, "look at this. I've got a cat."

"I see." The man gave Judy a very unfriendly look, like the guard at the entrance to the Mall of America in the Twin Cities.

"Her name is Ginger."

Judy rubbed up against the cuffs of the man's trousers, by way of marking her claim. She began to purr. When the man did not object to this, she leapt into his lap and curled herself up in the warm, spongy softness.

"Off!" he said, trying to scoop her up with one hand. But she got purchase on his pant leg first. With his other hand he grabbed the scruff of her neck and lifted until the only contact between them was her clawhold on his pants, which, reluctantly, she released.

"I see you've met Ginger," said Diana, bringing a mug of coffee into the room and setting it down beside the man.

"Yeah, she's already started molesting me."

"Molesting!" Diana protested.

"That, or sexual harassment. Did we need a cat?"

"Cats make the best mousetraps. And Kelly needs a pet."

"Well, as long as I don't have to open the cat food cans, okay."

And so it was settled. Judy became a member of the household and a presence in the house, gliding from room to room, listening from the shadows, sniffing the air. Her chief concern, as ever, was for her own comfort and convenience, and she had few complaints on that score. There was an abundance of choice scraps from the table, and if she kept a low profile in the evenings she could avoid being evicted to the basket under the porch. Doors were a nuisance, but she seldom had to sit long by the back door before someone would let her in or out. Kelly could be a brat, grabbing Judy by her flea collar and pulling her about, or dressing her up in doll clothing. But a good snarl and a flash of her claws usually put an end to those indignities.

It would have been an entirely tolerable life if it were not for two things. One was the malign presence concentrated in the little building behind the house, a presence that had a way of becoming pervasive at odd hours of the night, like the odors arising from a landfill. Judy had a toxic reaction that resembled nothing so much as a migraine headache, accompanied by blurred vision. The reaction would come on quite suddenly and then gradually abate, and there was nothing she could do but just hunker down and wait for it to stop.

The other major unpleasantness she had to put up with was that her son was a regular visitor. Coming only when Carl and Kelly were out, he would either visit with Diana inside or hammer and saw away at a big wooden fence in the area of tumbledown sheds behind the hill in back of the house, the area where Judy's migraines came from. Judy had never been one to ponder the reasons for her likings or loathings. She experienced them like the weather, and how she experienced Alan, when he would turn up, was with aversion and a barely controlled rage. Her hatred was as specific and pointed as the nails his hammer would drive into the wood of the fenceposts. Were he a mouse or a bird, she would have liked to sink her claws deep into his gut flesh and lick away the blood like ice cream as it seeped down the side of a cone. It annoyed her that he could not recognize the depth of her rage, much less its source. Indeed, she only imperfectly understood why she hated him so. That he had ruined her life she knew. She had been human once and now she was not, and he was to blame. Perhaps Diana was more directly to blame, but Judy could not—as one in thrall to Diana, and her familiar—focus her hatred there where it most was due. Even against her son she could not express her spite when he was inside the house, within the protective circle of Diana's influence. There Judy might glare and glower, but to spit or snarl was denied her. She would listen to the two of them as they necked and petted, Diana urgent and encouraging, he shy and fumbling, and writhe inwardly at the spectacle of a courtship that amounted to nothing but endless hours of grooming. What a spineless creature to have for a son!

There was some comfort in knowing that his intimacies with Diana could only bring harm to him. Diana had become a force like the black whirlpool labeled "Drugs" in the videocassette that the Christian Coalition for Family Values had sent for her father to show the parishioners. Anything that came within a certain distance of the black whirlpool was sucked in and disappeared.

Diana was the same. She was evil in the same contagious way as drugs. It didn't make any difference if you were good or bad. If you were bad, the whirlpool would get you in one big slurp, the way it had got Judy. But if you were good, it would get you, too. You might circle around for a while, like a leaf in an eddy, but each circle was a little tighter than the last until it was too late and you were pulled down to wherever whirlpools took you.

So all Judy had to do, really, was to sit on the sidelines and watch Diana do her job. Of course, she would have preferred to have a share in the boy's undoing, but she would take what she could get. Diana understood that, and sometimes when she and Alan were involved in one of their tepid sessions of grooming and licking and kissing, Diana's eyes would stray to where Judy sat in the shadows, watching them, and they would share a glance of complicity.

"You like to watch, don't you?" Diana said once when Judy had hopped up into the bed and settled into the dent Alan had left in the pillow.

Judy purred.

"All in good time," Diana assured her. "He'll get his. Just be patient."

Judy rubbed her head against Diana's bare hip and gave herself over to luxurious thoughts of her son's soft, pale torso streaming with blood and streaked by the long lacerations of her claws.

"Who's my darling kitten?" Diana asked her, tickling her ear. "Who do I love?"

28

Reverend Martin Johnson was beside himself with rage, with righteous indignation, with sheer mortal dread, and there was no one he could take it out on, no one he could punish or shout at. For his daughter had left him and gone off with his secret (and pitifully small) emergency cash fund of $123,500—all that he had to show for a lifetime of service to the church—and he couldn't report the theft to the police, because it was money he officially was not supposed to have so long as he received a monthly stipend from the Lutheran Pastors' Assistance Fund. Those people were as bad as Medicare in making sure you were a complete pauper before they'd lend a helping hand, and Judy knew that. She'd witnessed his affidavit. If he reported her, she'd report him.

Judy had taken off in April, just after the first protest outside the church, and there hadn't been a word from her since. Her clothes were still in her closet, her mail (bills and invitations to open new charge accounts) stacked on her mirror-topped vanity table.

Reverend Johnson's Cutlass, which had disappeared with Judy, had finally turned up in a trailer park outside Sturgis, South Dakota, but the teenage girls who had been living in it claimed to have "found" it parked outside the Greyhound station in Brainerd, suggesting that Judy had driven it only that far and then abandoned it with the keys in the ignition, an invitation to be stolen. Such, at least, was the theory of the state policemen who'd returned the car to Reverend Johnson. The two young thieves had been returned to their families, and the police had refused to press charges. Unless he pressed charges against the original thief, his daughter. No one at the Greyhound station remembered anyone resembling Judy. She might be anywhere now.

Before she'd gone off, Judy had said many unkind things, all true and, for that reason, unforgivable. She'd said that Reverend Johnson was "in denial" about his grandson, for Alan was in fact his son. Alan knew that now, and soon all the world would know it, too. Reverend Johnson had ordered her, in the sternest tones, to be quiet, but she'd continued to jeer at him, and when he'd struck her, she'd hit him back, with her fists, and knocked him to the floor. Then, as she'd stood over him, she'd told him that he was not a Christian, for there had never been love in his heart but only lust and greed and spite, and that if there was a hell, as she hoped, it would be his certain destination, for his sins had congealed in his soul like the plaque in his arteries, making it impossible for him to repent or ask forgiveness. She had railed at him like a preacher possessed by Pentecostal fire, and each accusation had the ring of God's truth and His wrath. She'd told him that he was unloved and had been all his life, that his wife, Emma, had hated him for his cruelty and despised him for his weakness and failure. That only those parishioners as mean-spirited and stupid as himself remained with him, and that even they would rejoice to see him unmasked as a hypocrite and the abuser of his own daughter. She'd said that the press and TV would make him as famous as O. J. Simpson. That even little children would recognize him on the street or shopping in a store, for he was too ugly to escape unnoticed in a crowd. Finally, he had simply crawled out of the room and taken refuge in the church. When he'd returned, at nightfall, she had taken the keys to the Cutlass and the money from what he had thought was the secret compartment in his desk, leaving behind her poisonous truths.

He'd had no dinner that night and slept in his clothes on the living room sofa, for the upstairs rooms seemed haunted by the ghosts of those who'd fled from him—Emma, the boy, and now Judy, whom he'd always counted on to be irrevocably his, united with him by a sin that could never be confessed. He would have gone without breakfast, too, but hunger had overcome his pride. He'd made oatmeal, scorching the pan and producing a kind of gluey paste that he'd managed to get down with the last of the milk and several spoonfuls of sugar.

Reverend Johnson had never learned to cook. Indeed, he felt a doctrinal contempt for men who usurped the role of women in the domain of the kitchen. Emma or Judy had cooked his meals, and when illness or absence had made them unable to perform that task, he had simply done without or driven to the diner in Leech Lake. The diner was no longer an option. Reverend Johnson could not even bring himself to go into the Shop 'n' Save, and so for the next two weeks he'd lived off the diminishing resources of the cupboard and icebox. For Sunday dinner he had had a can of chicken noodle soup. Since then there had been nothing left but canned or frozen vegetables and a box of spaghetti. But even if he made the spaghetti, there was no sauce for it.

But the Shop 'n' Save was an even more intolerable prospect now than when this whole thing started. Perhaps he should follow Judy's example and just vanish into the sunset. He still had the car, and two uncashed checks from the Lutheran Pastors' Assistance Fund. But he had no confidence that he could survive on his own in the larger world beyond Leech Lake County. Somehow he was sure the police or the liberal media would track him down, and the disgrace that Judy had predicted would be visited on him.

And so he decided to kill himself.

Once that decision was made, he felt an immense relief. A great weight had fallen from his shoulders. He felt like himself again, capable and decisive. His anger returned, and his wonted sense of righteousness.

He knew how to set about it, thanks to the book he'd taken from one of his parishioners, Clara Munz, a self-help manual on suicide. The book explained just which pills to ask your doctor for and how many to wash down with a bottle of brandy. Clara, who was suffering from stomach cancer, had confessed her desperate intention to her minister, and he had demanded that she give him the book and the pills and even the bottle of brandy, for Reverend Johnson insisted on a strict teetotalism from his flock. Clara's cancer had killed her not long after her aborted suicide, and Reverend Johnson had felt a special glow of virtue when he'd officiated at her funeral, knowing that he'd saved her from the certain damnation awaiting suicides. Now those pills would do the job they'd been intended for.

First, however, he must draft his will, something that had never seemed necessary until now. Who would his heirs have been but Judy and her boy? And they would inherit what little there was in any case. But they were now, as the special agents of his ruin, precisely the people he did not want to benefit from his death.

He wrote it out on lined notepaper:

The Last Will and Testament of
Reverend Martin Andrew Johnson.

I leave all my worldly possessions, including my house at 34 East Second Street and the neighboring Church of the Holy Redeemer, to James Cottonwood, now in the New Ravensburg State Correctional Facility, as a result of my daughter's false accusation of rape. I realize this cannot begin to compensate him for the years he has been falsely imprisoned.

Reading it over, the last sentence sounded too much like an apology, so he crossed it out. The important thing was to prevent Judy or Alan from being able to contest the will.

He signed and dated the paper, then folded it, put it into an envelope, and addressed the envelope to Bruce McGrath, the lawyer representing James Cottonwood, from whom he'd received a series of letters insisting that Reverend Johnson contact him in connection with making a deposition required by the appeals court. Reverend Johnson was pretty certain he knew the kind of questions McGrath would be asking him. Well, now he had his answer.

He walked the letter to the mailbox at the corner of Second and Main, the farthest he'd been from the house since Judy left home. It was a gray, overcast day, and people's lawns were starting to come back. There were even some potted daffodils in bloom on the Oxenburgs' porch. But nothing in that familiar view cried out to him to stop, to think again, to thank the Lord for the gift of life. He knew that was the line to take with someone talking of suicide, and he'd seen how little effect it usually had. When your life is just one long punishment, what is there to say thank you for? It astonished him that he'd never thought of killing himself before. Now it seemed the logical answer to an otherwise insoluble problem.

Running off must have seemed like that to Judy. For Reverend Johnson, who rarely considered how other people might see things differently than he did, this was a real leap of the imagination, but it did not lead to any further insights. It did help steel his nerves. If Judy could resolve to act, then so could he.

He fetched the pills and brandy from their hiding place, in a locked cupboard drawer in the church sacristy. From another part of the drawer he took out a ceramic cup that a visiting politico had donated under the mistaken idea that the church shared communion wine at its Eucharist services like the Episcopalians. It did not, but the price tag had been left on the underside of the cup—$60—so although it had never been used, it hadn't been thrown away either. Reverend Johnson had saved it for a suitably solemn occasion, and that occasion had finally come.

The cup had a handmade, cumbersome look, the sort of thing you'd expect a child to bring home from school with a boast of "Look what I made!" The outer surface was a coppery brown mottled with silver flecks. The inside of the cup was a pale-yellowish gray, also flecked. Reverend Johnson couldn't understand why it was so expensive, because it seemed ill-made.

He filled the sixty-dollar cup to the brim from the bottle of apricot brandy. "This is my blood," he thought, not with any sense of irony but conscious that the quotation was more than usually appropriate.

Reverend Johnson was not an experienced drinker, but because of its fruit flavor the brandy was not as difficult to swallow as he'd feared from a previous experiment with whiskey. He put one of the little blue pills on his tongue, took the smallest sip of brandy, just enough to ease the pill on its way to the back of his throat, then forced himself to swallow. Another pill, another sip, another swallow. Six times in quick succession. Then, as the book advised, he took a break.

On the silver-plated communion tray he carried the pills, the cup, and the brandy into the church. For all the time he'd spent here, the place did not evoke any special sensation in his soul. It was a drab, dark space, with pews and pulpit of dark wood and an oak choir stall that was supposed to match the veneer of the electric organ but didn't. The white paint on the walls had darkened in irregular patterns. The only element of the interior that could have been thought decorative was the windows, with their alternating lavender and amber diamonds, except for the one window that had been broken by a falling tree limb five years ago and been replaced by panes of opaque white glass. He had never liked the stained-glass windows and would have had them all replaced if there'd been money in the budget for such an extravagance.

Reverend Johnson sat down on the topmost of the three steps leading up to the pulpit and washed down another half-dozen pills. This time he was more liberal with the brandy, and when he was through, he drank some just for its sweetness.

It occurred to him to wonder whether, if he had been a drunkard like his older brother Henry, he might not have had a happier life. Henry had wasted his in beer joints and Indian casinos and died at the age of forty-two of lung cancer. But between the two of them, wasn't Reverend Johnson actually the worse sinner? Henry's sins seemed piddling by comparison. There was nothing to be envied there.

Six more pills, six sips of brandy. He was halfway through the pills but had not progressed so well with the brandy. He made himself swallow an entire cupful at one go. His eyes teared from the effort, and the tears, once started, continued to trickle down his cheeks. But they did so without any discernible emotional connection, neither sorrow nor self-pity, nothing but an agreeable numbness, a tiredness in his neck and back that prompted him to slump back until he was resting against the wood panels of the pulpit.

He filled the cup again and lifted it to his lips. He wondered what his life, his afterlife, would be like in heaven, then remembered with a start that he was not bound for heaven. That thought, grim as it was, was bracing, like the first taste of the weather as you stepped outdoors in the depths of winter. Somewhere he'd read that hell might be a place of cold and darkness rather than fire and brimstone. That would be his sort of hell.

He realized that he'd spilled brandy down the front of his jacket. Perhaps he was becoming drunk. Or perhaps the pills were beginning to have their effect. He poured out a handful from the bottle, lapped them up with his tongue, and sloshed them down with the brandy.

Would there be people in hell whom he'd recognize, as one recognized old friends and family members in heaven? Would Judy be there eventually, cursing him again, kicking him when he'd fallen to the icy pavement? Somehow he was sure she would be. He remembered how she'd looked down at him the last time he'd seen her. Snarling.

He'd lost the pills, but there was still some brandy left. He drained the bottle and felt such peace as he could not remember feeling in his entire life.

The next Sunday morning he was still there, curled up inside the wooden shell of the pulpit. From the entrance of the church not even his shoes were visible, and in any case no one had come inside. The church was empty of parishioners, though the protesters still paraded back and forth on the sidewalk, enjoying their triumph—for the headlines of yesterday's Brainerd newspaper had finally broken the scandal. The county prosecutor's office had announced that DNA tests had shown that James Cottonwood could not have been the father of Judy Johnson's child. Further scandal was promised. The paper said that the identity of the child's true father was known to Cottonwood's attorney and to the prosecution, and would be revealed at a suitable point in the appeals process.

The nave of the church was large, and the spring weather unusually cool. Reverend Johnson's corpse decayed sedately, shriveling rather than bloating. There was no great stench. Anyone who might have thought to poke his head in at the front door would have noted only that the usual mustiness had intensified. But no one did. There were no Sunday services anymore, the protesters stopped showing up, and it seemed only natural to the neighbors to suppose the Johnsons had left town.

29

The crows began to be a nuisance after the first delivery of corn to the newly constructed corncrib. Alan had built it himself almost from scratch (the concrete foundation was already in place), based on a design in an old textbook, *20th Century Agriculture*, that Diana had found at a garage sale, and he was dismayed when he realized that the crows had virtually free access to the corn. However, a visit to Leech Lake Lumber provided a quick fix. The corncrib was swathed in sturdy plastic netting that kept the crows from the corn, though they continued to perch on the roof and complain.

Diana felt like one of the original covered-wagon pioneers when Alan had finished the job and the sty and its compound were habitable. She'd done little of the work herself, only pitching in when Alan needed another pair of hands, but the idea had been hers, and she'd paid for the labor and materials out of her own pocket (with a little help from the windfall of cash she found in Judy Johnson's valise). There is nothing so gratifying as seeing a pile of raw lumber and spools of wire and rolls of tar paper slowly shaped into real buildings and fences, declaring a human purpose in the midst of nature's muddle.

And Alan had been shaped up by the same process. The pudgy teen who never was far from his computer screen lost his pallor and gained an early tan, lost flab and gained muscle, and lost *some* of his wallflower modesty and gained a modicum of confidence. Diana dealt with him like his physical trainer, scolding his posture, praising exertion. And he was at that wonderful age when his body responded to exercise like a tomato plant to Miracle-Gro. You could almost see the muscles plumping up in slow motion.

Carl was another matter. He was plumping up, too, but it was not his muscles that were growing. The Scarsdale diet hadn't worked (Carl must have cheated every time he was out of the house). He'd lost a sum total of three pounds in his first two weeks of dieting, and gained twelve as soon as he started drinking after work again. Diana did not nag, and though she served high-protein meals with lots of fiber, as per the instruction sheet from the prison dietician, she also stocked the icebox with lots of Carl's favorite snacks, cheeses and bean dips and thick yellow cylinders of liver sausage. Plus, now that he was back on the day shift, they shared drinks before dinner as they watched the news, and more drinks after Kelly had been put to bed, or what was left of the magnum of wine from the dinner table.

Diana saw what she was doing as a traditional maternal and/or wifely task: fattening up adult males for their first coronaries and thus preparing for a comfortable widowhood. She was doing it a little faster than some of the young matrons she saw pushing their wire carts about the Shop 'n' Save, but it was essentially the same job.

Of course, she had an edge over most other women in that, as a witch, she could *see* what she was accomplishing. She only had to adjust some internal psychic wire (it was like popping your ears to hear more clearly) and Carl, who always got his minimum daily requirement of mandrake root, would go fuzzy in front of her and then come into focus as though his destined transformation had already been accomplished. There he was across from her at the dinner table, a virtual Porky Pig, equipped with only those human attributes required to handle silverware and slouch forward in his chair, but his face already metamorphosed to pig, tusks jutting up over his upper lip, snout quivering with pleasure, ears pricking up or relaxing as they carried on their small talk.

"What happened to Kelly?" he asked one night, snuffling down a big forkful of Goya Rice and Black Beans (a standby whenever they had ham steaks). "She's got this big [snuffle] bandage on her shoulder."

"Oh, it's nothing to worry about. She went a little too far with Ginger. Ginger doesn't like being teased. I put some iodine on the scratch. She'll be fine."

"More wine?" he asked, holding the magnum poised over her glass in his cloven hoof.

She nodded. "Thanks."

He filled her glass, then his, and slurped with satisfaction.

"Anything on TV tonight?" he asked, shoveling in more rice and beans.

"Not a thing, really. But we still have that tape we made the other night."

"The Belushi program? Hey, great."

John Belushi was Carl's favorite comedian. Diana herself liked him well enough, for that matter. Back at school she had been thought a stickler for what was politically correct, but she was not without a sense of humor. Perhaps Belushi was a little too gross sometimes, but since she had discovered her powers as a witch, Diana was less finicking in such matters. Good taste, bad taste, what difference did it make which was which? Or good and bad, for that matter?

So they watched the tape, zapping past the commercials with the remote. Carl got steadily more sloshed and uproarious. Diana giggled more than she guffawed, most of her mirth inspired by Carl himself in his piggish persona, not by the program, but Carl wasn't clued in to that.

It was delicious having all these secrets. All her life Diana had loved the feeling of knowing what others could only guess at. Knowing how her father had died. Knowing what had become of Tommy W. Knowing where Judy Johnson had gone off to. Knowing Carl to be a pig.

She would, she decided, complete the process tonight. The moon was out, and Carl was drunk, and she felt her powers strong within her. They were like the breath that comes when one has been skating hard in February weather, the lungs seared to their depths by the cold, the fibers mapped by each inhalation.

At the end of one of Belushi's samurai routines, Diana paused the VCR and said, "Come outside a moment. There's something I want to show you."

"Outside? Now?"

"Mm," she said, and led the way to the back door, where Judy Johnson was waiting to be let out.

The moon was just past full and halfway to its zenith. A few wisps of cirrus, high up, formed fleeting counterpoints to the fixed stars, constellations with no stories.

"Don't you want to put shoes on?" Carl asked.

"The grass is damp. It's perfect weather for bare feet. Come along."

The trees were finally in full leaf and cast bold, black shadows slantwise across the hill before them. Off in the distance a small chorus of frogs rehearsed for the summer's diapason.

A breeze of voluptuous vernal mildness caressed Diana's skin as she undid the knot of her bathrobe and let it spread open to each side. Reaching the top of the hill, she turned to face Carl, still some paces behind her, and let the bathrobe fall about her feet.

Carl's piggish face was a comic mask of surprise, and then, as her invitation sank in, of lickerish hunger. Unbidden, he slipped out of his own shirt and pants and advanced toward her, half pig, half man, all hers. He put his arms about her and pulled her down to the ground. There were almost no preliminaries. His thick tongue pushed its way into her mouth. His thicker cock squirmed against her crotch, seeking entry.

"Carl," she told him, pulling her mouth free, "you are such a pig."

"Yeah, you got it," he agreed as he achieved penetration. "I am a pig."

"And what sound do pigs make?"

"Oink," he answered. "Oink-oink." With each oink the shaft of his cock sank in a little deeper.

"Oh, you can do better than that. Give me a Belushi oink. Put your gut into it."

The pig in Diana's arms bellowed with lust and then, as the metamorphosis gelled, a second time in terror and outrage.

Diana broke away and got to her feet.

"You really are a pig now, Carl. Isn't that amazing? Or perhaps it isn't, really. In so many ways it's what you've always been. I think you'll enjoy it. Most pigs seem to. What's the expression? Happy as a pig in mud. And *there's* your surprise." She pointed to the newly renovated sty and its fenced compound. "Your new home. Come, I'll open the gate for you."

She led the way down the hill.

Judy and Carl followed, with that complacent acceptance of the present moment and its changing weather that only animals seem to enjoy. Unless the noises that Carl made as he trotted along could be understood as a kind of grumbling. But really, what had he to grumble about? His stomach was full, he'd just shot his load, and the weather could not have been nicer.

Diana opened the gate, and Carl entered the sty that had been built for him.

"You mustn't go behind this fence. Do you understand?"

Carl nodded.

Diana returned to the house, unpaused the tape, and watched it to the end while she finished off the pitcher of daiquiris that had been waiting in the freezer.

30

Shortly before noon the next day there was a phone call from someone asking to speak to Carl. Diana told the caller that Carl was at work.

"But he's not," the caller replied. "That's why I phoned—to ask why he hasn't shown up. This is Barney Williams, from the personnel office at New Ravensburg. Are you sure he's not there?"

"Let me go check." She went into the kitchen and returned with what was left in the Mr. Coffee. "Well, he's not sleeping late, I can tell you that," she told the man, "but his car *is* still in the driveway. But that's not unusual. He's in a carpool, so his car is here more often than not."

"Can you think where he *might* be?"

"Honestly, no. If he was anywhere near a phone, he'd certainly have phoned you. And if he got a ride from someone else and there was an accident, someone would have phoned here."

"Well, if you do hear anything . . ."

"I have the number," she assured him.

Carl was now officially missing, but it seemed too early to report his disappearance to the police. She would call Barney Williams again in the afternoon, after the school bus brought Kelly home, and ask his advice on how to proceed.

And what would happen then? She had no idea and had made no plans. Oh, yes, she'd had Alan prepare the sty for Carl's arrival; in that sense her enchantment had been no mere improvisation. But she'd made no calculation of the likely long-term consequences—for Kelly, for Janet, for the running of the house without Carl's salary. Or for Carl, for that matter. At this point, she was simply playing with her power, the way a child might play with a chemistry set. Here's a little bottle with yellow powder, and here are little crystals: if you mix them in water, what will happen? Of course, it was not as innocent as that. It was more like a child's first experiments on kittens and bunnies: here, Fluffy, drink this!

For the rest of the morning Diana busied herself with the laundry, including the sheets from Carl's bed and seven pairs of his shit-stained underpants. A blessing to be done with *that* task! Though in another sense cleaning up after Carl would be a nastier chore than ever. Pig shit is notoriously noxious and plentiful. She hoped that Carl would still have some control over his sphincter even as a pig, and be able to dump his loads in a single latrine area. Some pigs are kept as indoor pets, and that suggested that they *could* be toilet-trained. She'd find out soon enough.

While the first load of clothes was in the dryer, she spent fifteen minutes on the exercise bicycle, which had been bought ostensibly for Carl's weight-loss program, though he'd scarcely sat his fat ass on it once. She used only a modest resistance, but by the time she was done she'd worked up a healthy sweat. A second load of heavier clothes and towels finished the spin cycle in the washer, and she took them out and pinned them on the clothesline. Gnat season had begun, and the insects formed a cloud about her as she worked.

For lunch she had half a canned peach with a dollop of cottage cheese. Now that she no longer had Carl as an excuse, Diana was determined to cut down on the calories. She'd done it before and could do it again. She might never fit into a size six again, but there was no reason to settle for Bette Midler when Bette Davis remained a possibility.

After lunch she phoned Navaho House and chatted with her mother (mentioning, by the bye, the phone call from the prison inquiring after Carl), then asked to talk with Alan. But he'd gone to the State Employment Office in Brainerd by way of indicating his immediate availability for work, a ritual he had to perform at monthly intervals.

Then, for two solid hours, she enjoyed the luxury of a book: Marion Zimmer Bradley's *The Mists of Avalon*, an utterly absorbing retelling of the story of King Arthur from a feminist point of view, with the good witch Morgan le Fay as its heroine and all the patriarchs of Christendom as villains. The book had been waiting on the shelf for years, but suddenly the time seemed ripe for her to read it. As the cover promised, the pages turned almost of their own accord, and Diana was spellbound.

Shortly after three o'clock Kelly got home and Diana announced, "Don't take off your jacket. We're going outside. I've got a surprise I want to show you."

"A surprise? What is it?"

"If I tell you what it is, it won't be a surprise, will it?"

Judy was waiting by the door. Cats *must* be psychic, Diana thought, because Judy was always on hand when she wanted her. Diana opened the door, and the cat and the child stepped outside. Then, as Diana stooped down to rebutton Kelly's jacket, Alan came round the corner wearing the suit and tie he'd put on to go to Brainerd.

"Alan! What a nice surprise."

"Hi. Your mother said you'd called. So I came over to tell you my news."

"Which is?"

"I've got a job. At least I think I do. I'll find out on Friday."

"Oh, that's wonderful. At least, I hope it's wonderful."

"It is. I'll be working with computers. What I do is go around for this operation called CyberWeb and help people get set up on the Internet. If I can sell them some of the extra services, I get a commission, but that goes on top of the basic salary, which is a hundred-fifty a week. Plus an allowance for the car. Neat, huh?"

"Yes, since it's what you like to do anyhow. That's the best kind of job."

"Where's the surprise?" Kelly insisted impatiently.

"Oh, the surprise!" She smiled at Alan. "I'd almost forgot. *We* have a surprise, too. Come on this way, both of you."

"I want a ride," Kelly demanded of Alan.

"Kelly, he has his *suit* on," Diana scolded.

"That's okay." Alan got down on one knee and boosted Kelly up so that her legs straddled his neck piggyback-style. "Okay," he said, rising. "Where to?"

They proceeded up the hill in single file, the cat leading the way, then Diana, then Alan with the child on his shoulders. Diana was wearing a full maxi dress of thin cotton in a floral print, which the wind swirled and unfurled like a banner in an old-fashioned painting. When she reached the top of the hill, she looked like Morgan le Fay herself, a woman glamorous in the original, occult sense of that word. Alan couldn't look away from her. He was enthralled—and in her thrall.

"I don't see any surprise," Kelly complained.

"I think he must be hiding from us," said Diana. "But I know he's there."

The cat looked up at Diana inquiringly and then, obedient to her unspoken command, trotted toward the willow tree by the sty. They followed, but even as they stood beside the refurbished fence, there was no sign of Carl.

"Soo-ee! Soo-ee!" Diana cried, and Carl appeared from inside the little outbuilding that opened to the compound, responding to the traditional summons to the trough.

"It's a pig!" Kelly cried.

"It's a *big* pig," Alan agreed.

"Are you surprised?" Diana wanted to know.

"Is he going to *live* here?"

"Yes. Why do you think Alan has been going to such trouble all this while?"

"He *is* big," Kelly observed. She seemed more dismayed than pleased.

"That's what one looks for in a pig," said Diana. "The bigger they are, the more money they bring in."

"You actually intend to run a commercial operation here?" Alan asked. "Not just . . . the one pig?"

"When I was a girl, we had fifteen or twenty pigs. We've got the room, and the water, and Kelly will be in charge of feeding them. She'll be a proper farmer's daughter now. She'll enjoy that. Won't you, darling?"

Kelly regarded the broad mass of her father dubiously. "Are there going to be a *lot* of pigs?"

"In due course, I suppose, yes. For now there's just this one. Do you want to give him a name?"

Kelly shook her head.

"Alan? A name?"

"Well, he's evidently a boy pig. How about"—he grinned—"Hamlet?"

"Hamlet he is!"

Judy, who had been brushing up against Alan's trouser cuffs, suddenly sprang up and alighted on the top railing of the fence.

Diana regarded the two little families before her with the quiet pride of a 4-H exhibitor at the county fair. Father and daughter, mother and son.

If only she had a camera.

31

Kelly was crying. She was all alone in her bedroom, having been put to bed early as a punishment for misbehaving, but she was not crying for effect. She knew there was no one on the other side of the door listening. Someone who might say, "Kelly, you can come down and have dinner. Everything's okay." Because it wasn't. Her mother was in prison, and her father had gone away somewhere, and there was no one left at home but Aunty Di, and she *hated* Aunty Di, and Aunty Di hated her right back. But Aunty Di was in charge now.

Kelly had seen it coming for a while already. The first time was when Aunty Di took her into the Shop 'n' Save and said no, she wasn't going to buy the box of Froot Loops, and when Kelly put it in the shopping cart anyhow, Aunty Di put it back on the shelf, and when Kelly made a scene and threw herself on the floor and screamed, Aunty Di just pushed the cart somewhere else and left her there on the floor kicking and screaming until she finally stopped and had to find where Aunty Di had gone to. She was standing at the checkout counter bagging the groceries as the woman at the register rang them up. "Oh, *there* you are," Aunty Di had said, "I was wondering." And ever since it had always been oatmeal for breakfast, or Cream of Wheat. Maybe with raisins or bananas, but usually without. And only one spoonful of sugar, because Aunty Di said sugar was a bad habit.

And now she had to feed the pig. Twice a day, once before the school bus and again as soon as she got home, she had to take a bucket of this stinky yellow powder that made her sneeze and mix it with a lot of water so it turned into goop that got poured in the trough. The stuff would spill out of the bucket and get on her clothes, and the pig made awful noises. Kelly had always thought pigs were cute, but those were the pigs in books. This pig was enormous. Its head came as high as Kelly's shoulders, and when it reared up, with its front feet on the trough, it was taller than she was. Of course, she didn't go inside the trough. She climbed a little set of stairs alongside the fence and poured the glop down to where the pig was waiting for it. But the pig was always so hungry, and made such noises, that it was scary. And it didn't make any difference what the weather was like, she had to bring the pig his food, including a trip to the sty after dinner if there were lots of leftovers. She was only five. She didn't know any other five-year-olds who had to feed pigs. It just wasn't fair. So this afternoon when she got home, she *didn't* feed the pig. She forgot. And when Aunty Di asked if the pig had been fed, she nodded her head, and somehow Aunty Di knew she was lying, and when it was time for dinner—a chicken pot pie, not frozen but made from scratch—Aunty Di said, "Do you remember the story of the Little Red Hen?" Kelly knew what was coming next. There was no chicken pot pie for her because she hadn't fed the pig and then lied about it. "There won't be any liars in this house," Aunty Di had declared.

Sometimes, if Kelly had done something really bad, such as the time she'd broken the recliner by rocking it too hard, she had been sent to bed without dinner, but her mother had always brought up a tray eventually. With Aunty Di it wasn't like that. No dinner meant no dinner. Stay in your room meant stay in your room. It meant no TV. She could play with her Trolls, but she didn't *want* to, and besides, her favorite Troll, Orangey, was missing, and Kelly was certain she knew what had happened: Ginger had gone off with her. Once she'd caught Ginger biting Orangey. Maybe the cat thought Trolls were like mice. Her family had disappeared, and now the Trolls were disappearing, too.

Later, when it was dark outside, the phone rang. The phone calls were always for Aunty Di, so Kelly did not pay much attention, but then Aunty Di called upstairs: "Kelly, it's your mother. Come say hello."

When she got to the phone, Aunty Di put her hand over the part you talk into and said, "I didn't tell your mother that you'd been sent to your room for lying, so there's no need for you to say anything either. Okay?"

Kelly nodded.

Aunty Di handed her the phone.

"Hello? Mom?"

"Hello, darling. How are you tonight?"

"I'm okay." She couldn't think of anything to say to her mother except what Aunty Di had just told her not to. Finally she thought to ask, "Mom, when are you coming home? Daddy isn't here."

"I know that, sweetheart. And I wish I were there with you right now. But it isn't up to me. You know that."

"You're being punished."

"You got it, sweetheart. What's happening there?"

"We have a pig."

"A pig? A live pig?"

"Yes, and he's really big, too. And I have to *feed* him."

"For heaven's sake. Why?"

"Because he's hungry all the time."

"Yes, of course. I mean, why do you have a pig?"

"Well, first Alan fixed up the old pigpen, and then the pig came to live in it."

"Who is Alan?"

"The guy who lives with Grandma Turney. He named the pig. We have a cat, too."

"You've told me about the cat. Her name is Ginger, right?"

"And the pig's name is Hamlet." Without any warning, simply because everything was so awful, Kelly started crying. And in her prison, off in Mankato, her mother started crying, too.

Aunty Di signaled for Kelly to give her the phone. "Janet?"

Kelly strained to hear her mother's reply, but without having the phone against her own ear the separate words didn't register.

"Janet, things'll be okay. Kelly misses you, that's only natural. But you'll be back, maybe sooner than you think. Your lawyer says there's a good chance you'll be let off early if Carl doesn't show his face pretty soon."

There were more words at her mother's end, to which Aunty Di responded with an "Mm-hm," and then again, "Mm-hm," and then, to Kelly, "Upstairs, young lady."

When Kelly got to the top of the stairs, there was Ginger, outside the door to her room. As though the cat knew where she was supposed to be, as though the cat were like Mrs. Waller, the old black woman at school who was in charge of things when the teacher wasn't there.

32

Judy had found that in her dreams many of her old, human capabilities were restored. She could sit down at a table and eat with a knife and fork; she could drive a car; she could put on makeup; and best of all she could talk. She remained a cat all the while, but the other figures in her dream treated her like a person, not an animal or a child. The worst part of being an animal (or a child) is being ignored or taken for granted.

It must be much the same to be put in prison. Until her enchantment, Judy hadn't given much thought to prison or the man she'd put there. Now she *was* in prison. She chafed at every restraint, at every enforcement, as though they were chains. When Kelly dragged her round by her collar, or Diana scooped her up in her arms and dumped her outside, she would fume—but, except for a hiss of protest, she could not complain. If someone said something stupid, she could not say, "I don't agree with you there." Speechlessness was a kind of muzzle. She would open her mouth to say something, but the words weren't there. She couldn't even *think* the words—except in her dreams.

Summer had begun. The dreary days were longer, the nights shorter but richer in life. She could roam free, responsive to the lattices of vagrant scents that might lead to prey or to nothing at all. Her world widened, her territory expanded. Some days she did not return at all to her customary station beneath the farmhouse porch, but drowsed away the hot afternoons in hollows cushioned by moldy leaves beside a sun-drenched rock deep within the woods. It was here, far from the farmhouse and the shadow of her servitude, that she would become, in her dreams, almost human again.

And it was here that her father appeared to her in his new, so much diminished form as a spider. She had studied this particular spider often back at the farmhouse, in the little space it had staked out for itself between the windowpanes above the air conditioner in the master bedroom. There, among the husks of flies stuck to the cobwebs in that narrow space, it had spun new tapestries and bided its time. Judy, as a cat, had not recognized the spider as her sometime father, but she had felt the same morbid fascination in his quiet toil that she had felt as a teenager, curled up on a sofa in his study, watching him write his sermon for the next day, awaiting the signal for sex. He rarely spoke on those occasions, but the silence they shared was the closest they ever came to a feeling of intimacy, for their sexual relations were abrupt and hurried. A smile was the most that could be hoped for, and even then it would be a careless, absentminded sort of smile.

Such a smile as the spider directed at her now. "Judy," said the spider. "You've changed."

"I could say the same, you know."

"But you would be wrong."

"You're dead now, Daddy. That's one big difference."

"*You* thought I'd go to hell."

"Being a spider is better?"

For a long while Reverend Johnson said nothing. He was a very small spider, and his mental powers were even more limited than they had been when he was human. There were certain people he still wanted to hurt: his daughter, their son, the woman who—all unaware—had whisked his spirit from the place where he had died. Only in these corners of his diminished psyche, which could still hate in the old, accustomed way, did the spider have spirit or spite enough to muster words that would express its thoughts.

"I know whose slave you are now," he told his daughter with satisfaction. "I've seen her command you."

To that Judy could make no reply. A cat is powerless against the truth. She could only stare at the small creature with its nervous legs and swollen abdomen.

"And I know what she will do to you. In the fullness of time. Do you? Have you guessed?"

Judy remained mute. She had her suspicions but wasn't about to share them with the spider.

"She'll kill you, too," the spider went on cheerfully. "She will never allow you to be human again, you may be sure of that. You say that I am dead, but is your life now any better than my death? She'll keep you about for a while longer, to play with, as you might play with a mouse. But she will grow bored with teasing you. She will kill others, too. Her hunger grows by feeding. Yours does, too. And mine. We are all killers. Thirsty for blood. There is so little blood in a gnat. And even in you, how much? A quart, at best. But in your son, just think! There must be gallons."

"I have no son," Judy lied. (For cats *can* lie.)

"No?" the spider replied. (For spiders, liars themselves of the subtlest skill, can detect less capable impostors.) "Why, then, I'm wrong. And yet I'm sure that one way or another his blood will flow. But if he's not your son, or my son either, then that is no lookout of ours, is it? He'll die, you'll die, we all die when our time has come. But it's not true, you know, that cats have nine lives. They have just one, and it is usually quite short."

"Even if I wanted to, I couldn't leave. I'm bound to her."

"But the bond is weaker where you are now, so far from the house. Go farther off, it will be weaker still."

"She feeds me."

"I fed you, but you were able to leave me."

"Why do you tell me this?"

"Oh, not to help you save your life. To do *her* a mischief. If you could do her any worse harm, I would urge you to do that. If you leave her, she will begin to doubt her power."

"If I leave, it will be to get away from you."

"Perhaps *that* isn't possible. We are like magnets, the two of us. If there is a hell, I'm sure we'll be there side by side. But perhaps hell was all a false alarm."

"Don't count on it, Daddy."

The spider smiled and wriggled its hairy palpi. "Even now," it confided, "you excite me. I would like to spread my sperm across your eggs and watch all the little creatures that would hatch."

Judy hissed at her father with deep-felt loathing, and he took that opportunity to leap forward and sink his clawed mandibles into the pink tip of her nose. She shrieked, and the spider laughed and skittered off to a safe distance.

She awoke then. It was twilight, and a waning moon hung above the western horizon. She understood what she must do. She must follow the moon where it beckoned, as she'd first intended when she'd taken her father's money. She'd been a fool to drive to the Kellog farm to have a final talk with Alan. That last flickering of maternal feeling had been her undoing.

She had always been a stray, whether as a human or a cat. She should have gone west long ago. To California. Or Nevada. And she would have, except for her father. But that bond was broken now, and there was nothing left of it but an annoying itch on the tip of her nose.

33

Merle Two Moons was not a believer in anything that had to be believed in for it to work. He was sure as hell not a Christian. He'd seen from a variety of directions how that didn't work any better than bingo for most things that mattered, even when the belief was bone-deep. The best it could do for you was to make you think your miseries had some higher purpose. Thanks, but no thanks. On the other hand, though he had some of the powers of a shaman, he was no believer in tribal bullshit, most of which was just superstition and fairy tales. You couldn't control those powers any more than you could depend on the currents of a wide river. You could ride them while you were lucky, but then watch out. Life is a crapshoot, simple as that, and while there are times the dice will obey you like a dog, there are other times when they will turn on you like a wolf. Finally, as the Bible says in its more candid moments, there is nothing certain but the sun rising and setting. And there was a kind of evenhanded justice in that: you could have luck, you could have brains and good looks (and Merle had his share of both), but in the long run fate will find its way to fuck you over and even make you feel responsible for your own bad luck.

And yet, weirdness happens. For instance, here, buckled round his wrist, was this leather collar that had come off a cat's neck. He could remember trying to reason with the cat while he was taking off the collar. "You want to be a free cat, do ya, Ginger? Want to live in the wind? Here, hey, hold still. There you go."

That much had to have been an accurate enough memory, because here was the collar on his wrist. But after that he must have slid into a dream while he was lying atop the rock with the cat curled up across the crotch of his jeans. He'd been well lubricated, and the moon unusually eloquent, so it had seemed in no way strange when they struck up a conversation, Merle and the cat. Like a pickup at a bar, the kind when you know you're just exercising your tongue. At that point his companion was no longer a cat, or not entirely. Her name was Judy Johnson, and she was the daughter of the minister he'd read about in the papers, and she was running away from home.

It's often the way with cats in the country that they will run off and we never find out what becomes of them. The same holds true for lots of teenage girls from the same background. But can we call them feral simply because *we've* lost touch? In their own ongoing lives they are wives or hookers or welfare workers, the same as the rest of the women around them. Except that their family life has been radically simplified. They have no past, the way Eve has no navel. Anyhow, that was the attitude Merle tried to encourage while they'd talked, as best he could remember.

He'd drift back into the dream or into the floaty space around it, and when he'd wake again, the cat would still be there, warming his crotch, and the moon would be sailing along through wispy clouds, and he would take a sip from his pint of Old Crow, and as the liquor radiated through him he'd be back in the bar with the whining Judy Johnson. She was complaining about her old man and saying the rumors going round were true, he'd knocked her up way back when, and then got her to blame it on a boy from the rez, Jim Cottonwood. All that was black-and-white fact, and some of the young bloods were pretty heated up about it, since Cottonwood was still serving time on account of what this Johnson girl had testified to in court back when. Merle was too young to have known the guy who'd been put away, but his older sister had gone to grade school with him, and she'd sworn even back then that he was being railroaded.

Merle had no reason to suppose she was wrong on that score, but he was not someone to get swept up in righteous causes. Jim Cottonwood was not the first red man to have been swallowed up by New Ravensburg, and he would not be the last. You could figure that every two years on average the prison would claim one life off the rez just the way Leech Lake did. You had to believe there was some justice before you could complain about the lack of it, and that was another belief Merle lacked.

So why this dream that was all blinking red lights and alarm sirens? Why did this cat's collar buckled on his wrist fill him with such a panicky dread? If this was a shaman dream (and he had to sup-

pose it was, since the rock here had its own dark force in that direction), what was it trying to tell him?

Finally he asked her, "Judy, why are you telling me all this?"

"Well," she said, holding her cigarette up to take a light from the
tip of his, "I'm worried about my boy. Alan. He's involved with this
woman who is . . . evil. You're probably thinking the pot is calling
the kettle black, and I'll admit I've got a lot to answer for."

"The Cottonwood guy."

She nodded her head and released two little spumes of smoke
from her tiny nostrils. "But I didn't do that to be mean. I did it to
save my skin. Whereas the woman Alan is involved with *is* mean. She
thinks she's in love with him, but that won't make a difference in the
long run."

"I know the type," Merle assured her. "I just don't see what you
want me to do about the situation."

"Well, what I was hoping was that you might kill her."

Merle huffed a one-syllable laugh of incredulity.

"Seriously. And not for Alan's sake. Because it isn't just Alan. She's
going to be your problem, too. And it's not as though you've never
done it before, is it?"

"I don't know what you're talking about."

"Oh, I'm not trying to trick you into a confession, Merle. But I do
have a nose. And so do the crows who are always circling that rock.
It's pretty obvious that someone is planted there. Was she a friend, or
just a pickup like me? Did you even know her name?"

"Tit for tat, honey. You tell me all about you and your old man,
and I'll tell you about my career as a serial killer. Deal?"

Judy crinkled her nose. "Oh, you are such a crude asshole. Well,
don't say I didn't warn you. That woman is dangerous, even for
someone like you. Maybe especially for someone like you." She
jumped down from the vinyl seat of the chair and padded off across
the linoleum floor of the bar, a cat again entirely.

And when he woke, the dawn had gone beyond a glimmer, and
four crows were circling in the little funnel of leafless space high
above the rock. There couldn't have been that much of an odor left
at this point. He'd planted Bonnie here after the first good thaw,
back in April. The rock must have turned her to instant hamburger

when he lowered it back down on her body, after which nature would have taken its course. By now she'd be a bony, sodden hulk.

The bottle was empty, but he still had one cigarette left. With the first drag, the dream had disintegrated into a single image of the ginger-colored cat darting off under the tables at the bar.

He remembered that there'd been a warning—some woman he should be worried about. But whether that woman was alive and still ahead of him or dead and buried under this rock, he wasn't sure. The only thing he knew with complete certainty was that he had a hard-on like a fucking piston.

That cat was lucky it had taken his advice and run off, because at a moment like this Merle wasn't answerable.

34

When the stylist had finished, Diana felt transfigured. Her hair had never been ash blond, or so short, or, simply, so chic. "Feathery" was the word. To be the woman with this hair, she would need an entire new wardrobe. Even in this outfit, which she'd found in Janet's closet, where it had lived for years with the sales tag still attached, she looked like someone from another lifestyle. The rayon blouse was the female equivalent of a Hawaiian shirt, and the skirt a slithery, iridescent second skin. By her own standards of a year ago she was positively garish, a tramp, a floozy. Oh, if her friends could see her now!

But that wasn't likely to happen at an out-of-the-way mini mall in Bloomington. It had been many months since Diana had been in touch with her colleagues at the Perpich school, none of whom were likely to turn up where she was headed to later tonight, the Frequent Flyers Club, a singles bar near the airport. And even if she did run into someone she knew, it wasn't as though she were committing a crime. None that they'd ever know about, anyhow. A man might disappear, but that wasn't news. Men disappear all the time without making headlines, if they're young and single. It was a male prerogative.

Feeling extravagant, and flush with the cash she'd found in Judy Johnson's valise, she agreed to the stylist's suggestion that she have her nails done. It was fun being pampered. The final reckoning, after she'd tipped the stylist ten and the manicurist five, came to seventy dollars, the most she'd ever spent at a beauty parlor. Then, in her new pagan glory, crested and taloned, she paraded down the arcade to the bookshop at the far end of the mall, where she browsed for a while, first among cookbooks (she skimmed, but didn't buy, a neat little do-it-yourself guide to making home-cured hams) and then in the true-crime section, where from a ceiling-high bookcase of black-spined paperbacks she selected Christie Cahn's *The 39 Ladies*, a collection of bios of all thirty-nine American women currently awaiting execution on death row. Ever since Janet had been sent off to Mankato, Diana had taken a morbid interest in anything to do with prisons, so this seemed a promising accompaniment to dinner at Lemongrass, her favorite Thai restaurant, which was only a few miles away.

Some ten minutes later, she was there. When the hostess who led the way to a table seemed not to recognize her, Diana smirked inwardly. Despite the fuss she made to have her usual seat alongside the aquarium, where the light was best for reading, not a glimmer. Diana had been a regular customer at one time. She really was a different person now.

She ordered a shot of Stolichnaya on the rocks, and once the waiter had gone round to the other side of the aquarium, she added, from the flask in her purse, a tincture of home-brewed mandrake spiked with oil of peppermint. She winced at the first sip. What to call such a cocktail? Eye of newt? Toe of frog? Or simply hellbroth? This was the downside of witchcraft, but a necessary evil. It was like using a tuning fork to tune a violin. To use the mandrake on anyone else, she had discovered that she had to have it in her own system.

While the concoction simmered in her innards, Diana concentrated on *The 39 Ladies* (ignoring, as best she could, the blood-red talons clasping the paperback's pages). The ladies' stories were arranged in the chronological order of their homicides, starting with Pamela Lynn Perillo, who, stoned on angel dust, strangled a man who picked her up when she was hitchhiking with two girlfriends. She was bad, but the schizophrenic Priscilla Ford was a lot worse. Priscilla had crashed her Lincoln Continental into a sidewalk full of people watching a Thanksgiving Day parade in Reno, a deed in which she took great satisfaction. Several of the ladies had done in their spouses and boyfriends (it was hard to see why that was reckoned a capital offense rather than a simple crime of passion), and as many more had been in Diana's mother's situation, caregivers at hospitals and nursing homes, where they acted as angels of death. It was dispiriting reading. So few of the women had committed crimes of any imagination or daring. And once they got to death row, they all went into denial, except for feisty old Priscilla Ford. Even the lady who'd injected drain cleaner into the veins of the teenager she and her husband had abducted got all weepy in her interview with the author: "I'm innocent, God damn it! Yeah, all right, the drain cleaner. But it was Sweetheart who shot her before that, and raped her, and did all the rest. And *he's* only serving life. Is that justice? It was me who led the cops to the body in the canyon. I should get *some* credit! I love Jesus. He is my Redeemer. I have been born again right here in the joint. Praise Jesus! And fuck Alabama. (Don't print that last part.)"

When the appetizer came, a plate of six barbecued ribs, Diana set aside the book and enjoyed the bliss of yielding. Eating under the influence of the mandrake was like bulimia without the vomiting. There was the same conscious cannibal carnality. Only a really committed vegetarian can appreciate spareribs in their essential nature. Already the mandrake was kicking in, and she could see the diners at the adjacent tables in *their* essential nature as well. The jowly lady of a certain age whose breasts were veritable udders. The man across from her with sad, brown, basset eyes. The three pigs in suits and ties toasting one another with bottles of Heineken. It was Old MacDonald's farm, with a moo-moo here and an oink-oink there.

The thought of that song, which she had sung along with so many toddlers, mooing and oinking and clucking, put Diana in mind of Kelly, who would be spending this evening with her mother in

Mankato, thanks to the ever-pliant Alan Johnson, who'd volunteered to act as chauffeur. Kelly had not adapted well to her father's disappearance (his *seeming* disappearance), and Diana hoped that the visit to her mother's prison would put the apples back in her cheeks. In the long run Kelly would be better off without her pig of a father, but right now, even with Alan around, it was hard for her. And Diana, truth to tell, had not been an ideal foster parent. It was not a role that gibed well with the practice of witchcraft. She could not resist teasing the child, and from time to time she would yield to impulses of petty cruelty—usually in the guise of "discipline," but Diana knew what she was doing and so did Kelly, probably. It was good to be away from the brat for a little while.

The main course arrived in a covered bowl. Diana lifted the stainless-steel cover and savored the aroma of the butterfly shrimp. Each shrimp was wrapped in a strip of bacon before broiling. Scrumptious. She had the waiter bring a glass of white wine and dug in. That she could indulge her appetite this lavishly without any fear of piling on the pounds appeared to be one of the special perks of being a witch. Her metabolism seemed to have been running at a higher rpm ever since her night with Tommy W. She always felt slightly feverish nowadays and couldn't bear any bedclothes but a single sheet, and no matter what she ate she didn't put on weight, for which blessing, whatever its source, she had to be truly thankful. The freedom to eat should be on the Bill of Rights.

Again and again she would sip at her doctored vodka, revise the flavor with a swallow of wine, then bite into one of the celery-crisp shrimps, while the fish in the aquarium beside her performed their underwater ballet. One of them—a black, eely thing with a dorsal fin like a feather boa—was especially sinuous and snaky and seemed to move in sync with the easy-listening harp recital on the PA system.

It was at just this moment of lushest pleasure, halfway through the bowl of butterfly shrimp, that John Klepfennig smiled at her through the aquarium walls. The little hairline mustache below his snout became a precise horizontal underscore as he lifted his glass in a toast that also asked the question, "May I join you?"

"John," she said amiably. "Of all people."

"Diana Turney. I didn't recognize you at first. I saw you and thought to myself, *Who* is that glamorous woman? What is she doing here? Why isn't she in Hollywood? And then I realized I *knew* that glamorous woman. You are looking mah-velous!"

His delivery was a good approximation of Billy Crystal's. People who didn't know him always supposed John Klepfennig was gay, but from what Diana had heard, his effeminacies were a kind of protective coloration, a Stealth persona that allowed him to slip through most women's radar. Plump and cuddly and endearing as a teddy bear, John could slip into anyone's bed almost without their noticing. He would probably never return, being a classic Casanova in that respect, but then one probably wouldn't want him to. Unmarried, childless, feckless, and jobless for as long as Diana herself (he substituted for sophomore and junior English classes), John seemed an ideal candidate for Diana's sty.

"Flattery will get you everywhere," Diana assured him. "Here— you're an expert in these things." She raised the tinkling tumbler of hellbroth so that it almost touched his lips. "See if you can tell what's in this."

"An expert, am I?" He bowed his lips and sipped. "Bleh!"

"Seriously, John. What is it?"

"Peppermint schnapps and . . . motor oil? It's vile."

"It has a strange aftertaste. Try it again."

He rolled his eyes, but took a second, polite sip. He shook his head, a perfectly porcine head now. "This is a popular drink in Thailand? God help the Third World!"

"No. This is my own home brew. And it's an aphrodisiac. Can't you tell?"

The pig across the table gawked. "You are *not* the same Diana Turney."

"No, I'm not. But I hope you're the same John Klepfennig. You have a reputation, you know."

"Amazing."

"Here." She pushed what was left of the butterfly shrimp across the table. "Polish it off. Then let's split."

He finished his martini at a gulp, then pulled the paper wrapper off his chopsticks and began to wolf down the shrimp. Diana signaled to the waiter and handed him her Visa card. By the time John was done, Diana had her receipt.

"Finish that off, too," she told him, nodding at the hellbroth. Which he did, quite as though he were already entirely under her dominion.

"My place or yours?" he asked as she led the way to where she'd parked her Camry, out of sight behind a Dumpster at the far, dark corner of the lot. When they got there, she clicked open the trunk with the remote on her key chain.

"How about a kiss?" she suggested, standing in front of the door on the passenger side.

"You don't waste time, do you?"

He bellied up to her and, as their tongues said hello, she opened his fly and got hold of his cock. He squealed with surprise, and then, when she whispered into his ear, "You know what you are, don't you?" and answered her own question, he squealed more loudly as his forelegs, cocooned in his gray silk summer sport coat, slid down the smooth sides of the Camry.

Diana couldn't help laughing at the spectacle he made, splitting out of his clothes. He shook his head frantically as though that might restore him to his human shape.

"Into the trunk," she told him, lifting the lid so he could get in.

It took him more than a single lunge, tangled as he was in his clothes, and Diana had to help get his hind legs inside along with the flapping trousers.

She hadn't considered the problem of closing the trunk. A Camry's trunk is not designed to accommodate the girth of the hog John Klepfennig had become. It took all the strength she had to press down the lid so the lock would engage. Poor John must have felt like a can of Spam.

Halfway along the drive home Diana became aware of an odor familiar to her from her dealings with Carl. John had emptied his bowels in the trunk, and the smell had penetrated the interior of the car. She turned off the air conditioner and rolled down all the windows, but even then the stench of the pig shit was inescapable. She decided that it would be wiser to conduct any future swine-hunting forays closer to home, and preferably in Carl's Chevy.

35

Since he'd started with Hamlet, Alan continued in the same vein when he christened later pigs who came to live in the sty. The next one, who was already in residence when he returned with Kelly from Mankato, became Gravedigger, because that was the role Billy Crystal had played in the Branagh movie of *Hamlet*, and for some reason the cute new pig, with his humorous snout and Porky Pig–pink coloring, put Alan in mind of Billy Crystal. It was also the case, Alan had learned at a Web site called www.pigfancier.com, that the ancient prohibitions on eating pig flesh sprang from the fact that wild boars *were* gravediggers. They would dig up fresh graves and eat their contents. So in eating a pig, you might have been eating an ancestor at just one remove.

Hamlet and Gravedigger were good buddies so long as they were by themselves, but when the third and fourth pigs came to live with them—Laertes and Fortinbras—things got hairy. It seemed to be with pigs the way it is with people: two's company, three's a crowd, and four's warfare. Pigs in groups have to establish a pecking order, and they do that by fighting. They chew off each other's tails and shred each other's ears and butt into each other like the bumper cars at an amusement park. They would probably be as bad as Serbs and Bosnians if they were better equipped for killing, but they can do harm enough the way they are, especially if their tusks have never been clipped, which was the case with Fortinbras. Fortinbras quickly established himself as king of Denmark, and poor Hamlet wound up at the bottom of the pecking order, eating whatever scraps were left him when the other three pigs had had their fill. In short order Hamlet had developed a mopey, woebegone demeanor, cringing when Fortinbras would make a sideways swipe at him for no good reason except to be mean.

Alan was fascinated by the pigs' behavior. It was just the way he remembered high school, where he'd always been low man on the totem pole. You had to feel sorry for the Hamlets of the world, the ones onstage *and* the ones in the sty, but in both cases it was hard to look the other way while the spectacle was going on, with its fore-gone conclusion death, and on the way there, assorted slings and arrows, such as when Diana read in her book on pig raising that the traditional solution to the problem of excess aggression among older penned males was castration. She called up a vet in the Bunyan area, and he got all four pigs tusked, ringed, and castrated in a single morning. The pigsty was a lot quieter for the next few days while the four stags (which is what you call a boar who's lost his balls) recuper-ated from the trauma of surgery.

Diana had helped the vet with the tusking, securing a noose over each pig's snout while he cut back the tusks with his hoof nippers, and she'd stayed around as a witness while Alan and the vet did the castrating, which was not as gruesome a procedure as Alan had feared. First, you wound a kind of tourniquet with fishline all round the scrotum, then you made a slice down the middle with an old-fashioned single-edge razor blade. The testicles popped right out. Then, when they'd been pulled out, the wound was plastered over with baking soda to prevent its getting infected. The vet scolded Diana, in a playful way, about not having had the job done sooner. The best time to castrate was before a piglet was weaned. "It's no more trouble then," the vet declared, "than squeezing a big pimple."

On the night of the four castrations, Diana came into the bath-room while Alan, who'd never felt so filthy in his life, was in the tub. She had one of the thick blue rubber bands that had held together stalks of broccoli from the Shop 'n' Save and wanted to put it around Alan's scrotum, as though he were going to be next in line for the vet's services. Alan was still shy enough about her touching him down there as it was (she'd never managed to help him get a full erection, to his considerable embarrassment and chagrin), and when she wouldn't lay off, they both got drenched in the scuffle. She was laughing like it was all some kind of prank, but Alan became rather upset, and instead of spending the night there, as he'd planned, he drove back to Navaho House and spent a long time playing hearts with the old ladies. He felt like he was right where he belonged, in a human scrap heap of the stupid, the ugly, the incapable and impotent.

Love, when you are impotent, is more of a torment than a pleasure. To have the opportunity and lack the means is so shameful. Diana had gotten to be so beautiful lately, and she swore it was all for him, to rouse his passion, for which, of course, he had to be grateful. She looked so sexy, with her hair like some movie star, and the way she had of twisting round at her hips to look sideways when she might have just turned her head. He'd memorized her body, all her little gestures, the way she walked, the flick of her tongue across her lips before she began to eat. The softness of her flesh, so different from his, as though she were made of butter. He *adored* her body the way the ancient Greeks and Romans adored the naked statues in their temples (a subject which his grandfather had dwelt on in many of his sermons), but he was just as unfit to make love to her as if she'd been carved from stone herself.

No wonder she had fantasies of cutting off his balls. In some deep Freudian way that was probably what she'd like to do with him at this point. Her frustration must be equal to his. Sometimes he had suspicions that on nights when she brought Kelly to stay over at Navaho House she went out to a bar or the big casino on Mille Lacs Lake. She would only volunteer some vague excuse, like she was "seeing a friend." He couldn't have blamed her if she was having sex with some stranger in a motel, because she wasn't getting anything from him, but even so the thought tormented him. He would keep coming back to it, the way you have to keep scratching poison ivy until your arms are bloody.

At ten o'clock that night, desolate, he phoned to say he was sorry and to beg to be allowed to come back and spend the night. But the line was busy. He decided he would wait ten minutes before he called again—but before the ten minutes had elapsed, the phone rang, and he picked it up in a flutter of thankfulness, thinking it must be her.

But it wasn't Diana, it was Lucille McGrath, the wife of Jim Cottonwood's lawyer, calling to explain why Alan hadn't heard from her husband for the past week. He'd gone on vacation and had a skiing accident and was laid up in a hospital in Utah. Mrs. McGrath assured him that he had nothing to worry about on Jim's account and that he would be released in due course, and that the system was deliberately dragging things out because, at Bruce's advice, Jim was refusing to sign a waiver of his rights to sue the state for false imprisonment. She added that with regard to his own legal problems concerning his grandfather's estate he should contact a local lawyer. The whole tone of her conversation was *Stop bothering us!*

Alan had mixed feelings about that estate. Ever since Reverend Johnson's desiccated corpse had been discovered curled up inside his pulpit like a mummy in a mummy case and the county coroner had declared him a suicide, Alan had been unable to cope except by pretending nothing had happened. If it hadn't been for his feelings toward Diana and a lingering sense of responsibility toward Jim Cottonwood, he would have probably pulled a disappearing act just like his mother. Reverend Johnson's insurance and savings hadn't amounted to that much, and while the church and the house might have been worth a tidy amount, they would probably go to his mother, in the absence of a will. And if his mother didn't show up, they would just sit there till the county decided to auction them off to pay delinquent taxes. Alan didn't really give a hoot about all that. He would have been happy to see both buildings burn to the ground. He had no wish to inherit anything that man had owned. It was bad enough having his genes.

But Diana felt otherwise. She thought he should sue to take possession of Reverend Johnson's estate as next of kin, and she knew a lawyer who would take up his case on a contingency basis, only taking a fee when and if Alan was able to sell the house or at least get a second mortgage. If nothing else, such a windfall might pay his way through college (except that he had no plans to go to college).

But if Alan took the old fart's leavings, he would feel even more like he'd murdered him than he already did. No matter how righteously Alan presented himself before the court of his conscience, the fact remained that it was his actions that had driven the man to kill himself. And the man had been his father! In the Greek legend, it's Oedipus who kills his father. In Alan's case, it's Oedipus's son who kills Oedipus. But either way it's a sorry situation, and Alan wasn't coping all that well with the aftershocks. He was not, in one of Diana's favorite phrases, dealing with life on life's terms.

The job with CyberWeb, for instance, had so far *cost* him money, because to earn the basic hundred-fifty-a-week salary, he had to connect up a weekly quota of new customers, and there weren't that many people in the area who wanted to be on the Internet who weren't there already. Which meant that his franchise fee had to come out of his own pocket. Thanks to the work he'd been doing for Diana, he'd put enough aside that he could afford to pay for the privilege of having a job, but the job itself had begun to look like just one more humiliation.

Sometimes it seemed like his grandfather had had the right idea but it had just taken him too long to implement it. Alan had snuck into the house once after Reverend Johnson's body had been discovered and the house was locked up. He resented not being allowed to use his own key, and he'd always known how to get in through the window over the back porch, so he went there one night in early summer in violation of whatever law had put the place off-limits and just looked around inside. Nothing much had changed except for there being almost nothing to eat in the pantry. But the one interesting thing he found was an instruction book on how to commit suicide without hurting yourself. It must have been the book his grandfather used to do the job.

Alan took it away with him and read it cover to cover, and late at night, when he would lie in bed awake, he would imagine different ways he might kill himself. Sometimes he would see himself getting dressed up for it like it was a holiday occasion. There'd be a bottle of champagne to wash the pills down with, and candlelight, and E. Power Biggs playing something sad and solemn on the organ.

But then that approach began to seem like bullshit, and the scenario changed to a shotgun in the mouth, like Ernest Hemingway. Blam! He would do it somewhere fairly public, where they'd be sure to find the body soon afterward, because he didn't like the idea of lying out in the open a long time all wormy so that when he was discovered people would just be disgusted. What he really wanted was for people to feel sorry. A funeral with people crying quietly and asking each other why he'd done it and whether there wasn't something they could have done. And Diana would be standing at the back of the chapel, dressed all in black, with a veil over her face so that no one but Alan could see her tears.

He knew it was a ridiculous fantasy and nothing but the worst kind of self-pity, but he kept returning to it, alone in his bedroom, in the dark, crying to himself as though he were watching the saddest movie ever made.

36

It was a distance of seven miles as the crow flies, or twelve miles along the connecting roads, from the rock under which Merle had buried his half-breed cousin Bonnie Poupillier to the Kellog farm. Merle had made that journey only *as* a crow, and so he had no idea how to get there in his own skin. Nor did he feel the magnetism that the place exerted except as a crow, among other crows.

Wes had no such difficulty abridging that distance. The geometry of the afterlife is non-Euclidean. From the smokehouse where his spirit was centered to the rock beneath which Bonnie rotted was a hop, skip, and jump from Wes's vantage point, and had been even before Bonnie's interment, and before his own recent invigoration, when he had been a mere blind vapor sniffing out some taint of evil like a dog trained to detect drugs. For Bonnie's rock had served the young men of the rez as an altar on which a hundred virgins had been sacrificed. It was well suited to that purpose, thanks to the solitude provided by the crescent of swampland that made a natural moat about it, and by its spooky beauty, which gave it a B-movie glamour. Mists rose from the swamp even in otherwise clear weather, and loons emitted their little foghorn hoots and coos from dusk to dawn. If you were going to lose your innocence anywhere, this was the place to do it.

Now, at midsummer, a sweet rot of decaying pines scented the moist air—and disguised whatever scent of Bonnie Poupillier that still lingered. Lying atop the rock, with crows overhead, Merle had the beginning of his buzz for the day and was trying lazily to draw them close enough to grab a free ride. The crows were wary, but curious, because the idea he was using for bait was an image of Bonnie the way he'd seen her last, her face bloated beyond recognition and frozen solid. Crows are drawn to carrion in all its grossest manifestations, just as some children are. They wanted to know what Merle knew.

Merle had killed three women in his life, but Bonnie was the first he'd killed just for the sake of killing. The first couple of times he'd simply done what the situation required; they were crimes of caution or retribution, not passion. But with Bonnie there had been no practical necessity for what he'd done. She wasn't a witness who had to be silenced or a motel whore with sticky fingers, just another junkie out for fun. For her share of Merle's booze she would spread her legs and even go through the motions of pretending to love it. "Oh yes, oh baby, oh Merle, you make me feel so good!" Merle had always been curious about what it would be like to kill someone at the same time you were screwing them, since the movies made such a big deal about it, and what he'd found out was that all those movies were pure speculation. Murder wasn't more exciting than an ordinary fuck. That had to be good news, since who wanted to be a serial killer, always wanting something that could get you put away for life? That was one degree worse than being a junkie, and Merle had always had the good sense to resist that temptation. But good news or not, it had left him with the problem of what to do with Bonnie's corpse. For a while he'd stashed it in the deep freeze in his garage, along with some fifty pounds of venison that had been there a couple years. Then, late in March, a small tornado had solved the problem by toppling a pine that had stood close by the rock. The pine came to rest on the rock's natural overhang, and when the ground was softened by the spring rains, the weight of the fallen tree gradually tipped up the other end of the rock as though it were a teeter-totter, making a natural niche underneath just the right size for Bonnie. Merle had hauled the frozen, bundled body along the path in a wheelbarrow on one drizzly April night, wedged it in place beneath the rock, and then lowered the rock back to its original position by sawing through the pine. When he was done, he felt like some pharaoh who'd put the finishing touches on a monument that would last a thousand years or longer. That rock would just sit on top of Bonnie until a new ice age arrived and a glacier pushed it somewhere else.

The bait finally worked. A crow glided down and lighted on the top of a sumac to study Merle. *He* was not the carrion but the source of carrion signals. Where was the carrion? the crow wondered, and then it wondered nothing at all, for Merle had pushed its keen, meager mind to one side and established his own temporary residence in the crow's body. He flexed his wings, flicked his tail, and then lifted off, with an awkward flap, flap, flap, like a camper from the city who's rented a rowboat and has to learn how to work the oars all over again.

Ah, but what glory once he was well above the trees and circling with the others in the dance hall of the sky! Was there any higher pleasure, any finer freedom? It didn't come without a price, of course. He had to be empty of other purpose, a blank slate, weightless and without ambition. But wouldn't he have been all of that in any case? Merle could never hold a job. He liked money, but he would rather steal it, so long as his thievery did not become another kind of job. He liked sex and had sowed his share of wild oats, but he would never have considered settling down and becoming the paternal compost in which his own little family took root. No, he'd lived loose, and this was his reward. Shamans didn't have to be good: loose was enough.

The first time he'd taken flight as a shaman had also been the first time he'd tripped on acid, and he'd supposed, afterward, that the experience had been no more than a particularly vivid hallucination. But how, then, could he account for the fact that the tidbits of information he picked up during flight time always proved accurate afterward? The cabin by the lake that always stood empty and unlocked in the early afternoons, the car keys hung in the darkest corner of a garage? No, the magic was real enough. The catch was, you couldn't force it. Not every crow would give him a ride. Not every night-visiting voice would tell the truth. Not every dream came true.

The dreams, indeed, were trickiest. The deceit seemed to be built in, the way it is in some women, the ones who fall in love only with people they'll wind up hating. They never told an outright lie. They told you the lies they told themselves, sometimes with passionate conviction. And there was always *some* part of the dream, or the woman's lie, that turned out to be true.

The crows' circle broke up soon after Merle joined, and the

whole convocation of them started heading north in a ragtag bomber formation. Over the swamps, over meadowlands no longer mowed, over an abandoned cabin that local teens used as a motel, across the shallow waters of Fishhook Lake, sweeping close to its shore in the hope of dead fish, then along County Road B with an eye peeled for roadkill. His wings worked now with the same easy rhythm as his fellows', as thoughtless as a typist's fingers.

As the tower of the New Ravensburg prison came in sight they hit the first thermals and rode them, corkscrewing upward on extended wings until the air no longer buoyed them, then the long glide to the next thermal.

And that is how Merle found himself clutching the strand of razor wire mounted along the periphery of the prison rooftop and exercise yard, not five feet from the staring eyes of Jim Cottonwood. Merle stared back, knowing that Jim wanted what he had, the crow's body and time aloft.

Merle was not about to give him that opportunity, even if he were able. He'd never encountered anyone else with shaman powers when he was in that mode himself. But he acted *as if*, which was the only way to go when the juice is flowing. As if Jim would understand him, he said, "Sorry, buddy. This car's already rented."

The staring eyes blinked once, and you could see they were a crow's eyes in just the way that Merle's were. Then, without moving his lips, the guy said, "Do I know you?"

"No, but I think we got a friend in common. You're Jim Cottonwood, the guy that's been in the papers—right?"

Jim nodded his head.

"I'm surprised you're still in the joint. I thought they were supposed to let you out a while ago."

"You'll have to ask my lawyer about that. But I don't think I caught your name."

"Crow will do. Old Crow. I wasn't planning to come here. But sometimes it's like you dial the phone and when they pick up at the other end it's someone other than who you thought you dialed. But you know them anyhow. It's like that."

"So, how is it you know me?"

"We have a ladyfriend in common. Judy Johnson. Remember her?"

"I heard Judy disappeared."

"Well, she's changed a lot. But I saw her not that long ago. And she was worried about her boy. Alan. You know him."

Jim nodded.

"That's it. That's all I know. But I don't suppose it's any accident I flew this way. I figure that was something I was supposed to tell you. A warning."

"While I'm in here, there's not much I can do for that boy. They don't even let him visit anymore. Are you in contact with him?"

"I've seen him once or twice. But only, you know, on the fly." Merle unloosed a self-appreciative caw.

"Find out more if you can," Jim Cottonwood said. "And let me know."

"How? You got visiting hours?"

"You'll know when. We seem to be tuned to the same wavelength."

"I'm not your friend, you know."

"I didn't think you were. But I've got a feeling you'll be back."

Merle felt perplexed, and then, the way you can be deadlocked in an arm-wrestling contest for the longest while and suddenly your opponent has this surge of power and the back of your hand is on the table, Jim took possession of the crow, and Merle found himself back on the rock with a monster headache, staring straight into the sun.

37

The conversation at dinner was strained. Just before they were ready to say grace there had been a phone call from Janet, who'd spent most of her time talking to Kelly, and then just a couple minutes with Diana. But that had been long enough to put Diana into a temper. Her end of the conversation had been too tight-lipped and monosyllabic for Alan to be able to figure out the nature of the disagreement, but he figured it probably had to do with Kelly and the pigs. On their visit to Mankato Kelly had complained bitterly to her mother about having to slop Hamlet every day, and Janet had seemed sympathetic. So was Alan, for that matter, especially now there were four pigs, though he'd never said anything to Diana, from a sense that he had no business interfering in how Diana laid down the law for Kelly.

Not much was said while they ate. It was canned lentil soup, corn muffins from a mix, and carrot salad. Kelly became a little whiny, not for the first time, on the subject of Ginger, who had been missing now for three weeks. Had she got lost in the woods? What would she live on there—birds and mice and chipmunks? What if she'd been hit by a car? Kelly never saw a roadkill these days without insisting that the car slow down until she was sure the victim had not been Ginger. Diana was unusually brusque in dealing with her questions, but Kelly persisted—not so much from a concern for the cat (it seemed to Alan) but because she knew her questions rubbed Diana the wrong way.

After a perfunctory dessert of Mott's applesauce sprinkled with cinnamon, Diana told Kelly to go up to her room and play with her Trolls. There'd be no television tonight. Kelly pointed out that she hadn't taken the scraps out to the pigsty.

"You won't have to do that anymore," Diana told her. "Your mother thinks you're too young for that much responsibility."

"But won't the pigs be hungry?"

"Perhaps they will. But their hunger won't be your concern any longer."

"I'll take out the scraps," Alan offered. "It's no big deal."

"There, you see," said Diana, "the pigs will be fine. Now, up to your room. I'll come up before bedtime and read you a story."

Kelly left the table with an air of conscious victory. Her whining had won the day for once.

"Come into the living room," Diana said to Alan as he started collecting dishes from the table. "I've got something important I have to ask you."

When he was about to sit where he usually did on the couch, Diana shook her head and patted the recliner's headrest. "No, you take Papa Bear's chair tonight." When he was seated, she scrunched down on her knees beside him.

"I've got a proposition," she told him.

"Yeah? What?"

"Let's get married."

He looked at her dumbfounded, and then laughed.

"You think I'm too old," she said.

"No, of course not. It's the last Winner'qus fortune I had playing Taipei. It said, 'Accept the next proposition you hear.'"

"Well, there—you see! You've got God's own green light."

"Oh, it's just a computer game, you know that. But as soon as you said, 'Let's get married,' I couldn't help thinking of it. I can't believe you're serious. I mean, after all the problems I've been having."

"Maybe you wouldn't have those problems if we were properly married. But that's not the reason I asked."

"Why did you, then? I mean, I love you, you know that. But . . . I'm only eighteen, and I've got no job, no education. I don't really think of myself as a grown-up. You must know all kinds of guys back in the Twin Cities who'd make a better husband than me. And God knows you're not marrying me for my money."

"And what about love, Alan? Shouldn't that have something to do with it?"

"Of course. But. I'm just so amazed. Like, I never dared even imagine you'd want to *marry* me. *Why?*"

"I thought I just answered that question."

Alan went on for some time protesting his incredulity while Diana just repeated the one argument against which he had no answer, love.

"Tell me this, then," she said at last. "Do you *want* to marry me? Forget about should and shouldn't or what people will think or where we'll live when Janet gets back."

"Damn, I hadn't even *thought* of that! Where *will* we live?"

"How about the church?"

"The church!"

"Unless you want to get ordained somewhere and open it up for business again. Does the furnace work?"

"Uh-huh."

"And it's got plumbing?"

"There's a whole big kitchen in the basement. It hasn't been used for a while, but it works. And two toilets."

"So, it wouldn't be a whole lot of work to convert it into our own home sweet home. We can make a sleeping loft where the altar is. It's a perfect place for kids, and—"

"Kids?"

"You *want* kids, don't you?"

Alan marveled at the notion and the careless way she put it forward: marriage, children, a home.

"I guess it's what I'd like most of all. That is, besides you." He looked down at her hand, which was resting on his knee. He lifted it and kissed it with exaggerated reverence like a priest kissing the relic of a famous saint. "I'll have to get a ring."

"Well, there's a jewelry store in Brainerd. We can stop there tomorrow before we see the justice of the peace."

"Tomorrow!" He was amazed all over again.

"Why wait longer? It's not as though we have to hire a hall and a caterer. But I guess we should get some film for the camera. I'll wear that white dress with the yellow flowers, and you've got your blue suit. We'll look respectable. Would you like Kelly to come along? That way we'll have a bridesmaid at least. But I *don't* want my mother there. We'll bring back a nice big bakery cake and share it with Mom and the old ladies at Navaho House. But Mom will just be a nag if we tell her beforehand."

"She'd be against the idea, I guess."

"She's against *any* idea that isn't hers originally. I expect your mother would have been against it, too, if she were still around to run your life. I am almost exactly twice your age. In fact, I must be a year or two older than her."

Alan shook his head with a woeful look. "It's not much of a family you're marrying into, is it?"

"Well, I don't foresee any *problems* with them. Do you? Somehow I don't expect your mother to turn up again anytime soon. Which is something of a nuisance from a legal point of view. You can't sell any of the property without her approval, but you can rent it—the lawyer was clear about that. We'll live in the church and rent the house."

"You've thought the whole thing out. It's amazing."

Diana smiled, and patted Alan's knee, and got to her feet. She *had* thought it all out, and he didn't know the half of it.

38

What Alan chiefly did not know, and what even Diana could not easily have put into words, was that they were not the same people they'd been when they'd first met. In his case there was simply a loss of innocence, something one is always bound to lose once one ventures forth into the open seas of love, but for him there had been no attendant gain. Sex was simply a new way to fail. Gone was the charm of his guilelessness, gone the sunny, skittish temperament that makes even the crustiest grown-ups smile at the antics of puppies and kittens. The careless youth who'd had no thought for the future had become a worrywart, still without a map or plan but aware now of that lack. When he looked in a mirror, he was dismayed by the face he saw there, and looked away. His only comfort was that somehow Diana seemed to see a different person than he did, and he was grateful for her least smile, the touch of her hand, any kind of attention.

Diana had changed, too, but in the opposite direction. Her crimes had given her an unexpected, tardy bloom. In the midsummer of her life she'd spread her petals and released an aroma as potent as the most drop-dead perfume. And the petals did not wilt as the summer wore on, but continued to bloom, like the white, waxy flowers of some desert shrub. Evil, in those who have consciously made that choice, imparts a real strength and a charisma that those, like Alan, who lack such self-awareness and definition find mesmerizing. They swarm to it, like ants to sugar. How else explain Hitler, the matinee idol of evil?

Charismatic evil is much less common in women than in men, for women are rarely *dedicated* to an evil purpose. They tend, more often, to slip into their wicked ways without knowing it, all the while protesting their essential virtue as mothers, or as victims of a patriarchal society, or simply as being unlucky in love. Rarely do they revel in their crimes like some mad emperor or marauding warlord. Diana even now maintained a womanly habit of self-extenuation. In her relations with Alan she thought herself a paragon of romantic passion and self-sacrifice, heroically rising above mere animal desire, a source of love and nurturing despite his impotence. As to those men who'd tasted her enchantments in a less benign way, well, they *were pigs*, weren't they? Their transformation was the confirmation of their essential nature as male chauvinists; they'd got what they deserved, and were still getting it, and would get more. In that resolve Diana was remorseless—the staunch champion of all women, a darker shade of Joan of Arc. In this sense of herself as a vengeful Fury, she did begin to approach evil in some larger and more heroic way. She was Woman: goddess, witch, nymph, all female archetypes, indeed, but mother—and that was a role she had no wish to be cast in. Whatever maternal fulfillment she might need had been sufficiently provided by her career as a teacher. From that job she had learned one essential lesson: all grown-ups are fossil children, with the same flaws and failings, the same ingrained stupidities, the same piggish anthem of Me, Me, Me, all the way home.

Grown-ups are children, and children are animals. Indeed, dogs and cats and pigs and all their mammalian tribe are brighter than toddlers. Just how much brighter was on record in thousands of psychometric studies. People take a longer time learning to be people than animals take learning to be animals. In their nests and dens, baby animals are a simple Pavlovian stew of appetites and impulses that grasp and crawl, gurgle and crow—alive in the Eternal Now, nearer to God but further from the complex machineries of capable knowledge.

That's why, when we imagine gods, they so often take the form of infants or of animals, the two Others nearest us in nature. And that was the root of Diana's power, of her witchcraft. She could lay hold of that primal connection between what is human and what is animal. To turn men into animals she only had to make infants of them again.

She had outside help, of course. No witch can work without some mediating power. Diana had Wes assisting her. As his power had grown, hers had grown in proportion, which in turn swelled his—a resonance phenomenon that had gradually favored Diana, so that now, in a practical sense, her strength was greater. Yet his power still underlay hers with a dumb brute force, the way the sea buoys up a swimmer. He amplified her strength but did not direct her acts. *He* had no animus against Alan Johnson, was aware of him only as a sometimes irksome presence among the swine within the sty, of whom Wes had a much keener awareness. He could sense *their* doom, for in some ways it resembled his own. And he hungered for it. He wanted their blood to soak the ground, as his had. Ghosts notoriously thirst for such libations.

Wes was not the only unquiet spirit in the Kellog household. Another had come to dwell there, his presence unknown to Diana, though she had brought him there. It was not Tommy W., though his death had stained her hands. Tommy's spirit, never strong, had ceased to exist soon after he'd been killed, his soul evaporating like a shallow pool of rainwater in the summer heat. It was the Reverend Martin Johnson who had come to live with Diana now, in his devolved, posthumous form as a spider of the genus *Erigone*.

The *Erigones* are spiders who build small webs in the grass and among dead leaves, where they live unnoticed and almost unnoticeable (so small are they) except in the months of October and November, the season of "gossamer summer," at which time they become airborne, lifted by long threads extruded from their abdomens. They rise to great heights in this manner until at last the threads tangle together and they plunge to earth like a billion Icaruses.

Reverend Johnson was an exception among the generality of arachnid reincarnates in that he maintained some tiny remnant of human consciousness and purpose: that his only son should die, as he had, in despair and bitterness of spirit. This dream was like one of those filaments the *Erigones* release to the wind in gossamer summer—infinitesimally thin but as strong as iron chains and sufficient to bear his entire weight. His hatred sustained him even in the meager circumstances he had come to inhabit, as nuns of especial holiness have been rumored to live on no other nutriment but communion wafers.

Now Reverend Johnson's purpose was becoming Diana's as well, as her soul began to resonate with his. It was she, all unawares, who had brought him home with her, as she might have brought home the virus of a cold. For the evil, when they die, remain for a time contagious, and she had had the misfortune to be exposed to the contagion when she had found the letter Reverend Johnson had tried to send to Bruce McGrath. A postal clerk had judged there to be insufficient postage on the envelope, and it had been returned to Reverend Johnson's home. There Diana had found it in the little mound of unrecovered mail under the letter slot of the front door.

She had gone there in May, shortly after she'd found the cache of money in Judy Johnson's luggage. Perhaps (she had speculated) there would be other booty in the Johnson home. In any case, she had been curious as to what had become of the old man. She'd not discovered his corpse, for she hadn't gone into the church, but booty there had been, if not in any form she could have expected.

By taking the will, she had removed Jim Cottonwood's claim to Reverend Johnson's estate. Alan would be the old man's sole heir. At that time Diana had not foreseen that she might soon be Alan's wife, and possibly his widow. Taking the document and squirreling it away had seemed only a kind of prudence, and a kindness to Alan. The boy's murder had been far from her thoughts.

39

"It's your Jews and your Catholics who are the big rollers," Merle was explaining to the lady beside him at the bar of the Taco-Nite Casino. "They both believe in luck, but in different ways. Jews believe in smart luck. They figure the odds at the crap table, try and count the cards at blackjack, and fold their hands half the time when they play poker, 'cause the numbers don't compute according to some complicated table of statistics they keep in their heads.

Catholics, on the other hand, believe in dumb luck. Jews lose their money slowly and carefully, but Catholics go for broke. Catholics think God's gonna help them get rich, just to make up for all the times before when he didn't. They love the roulette tables. They'll bluff on a pair of jacks. One or two drinks in them and they'll pump the ATMs dry from a firm conviction that *this* time they'll hit the jackpot.

"So that's why these casinos up here won't ever get off the ground. Outside the Twin Cities, where's the Catholics and Jews in Minnesota? We got Lutherans and Indians, and all of them dirt poor. Lutherans mainly don't gamble at all. Might as well open state brothels for all the money any Lutheran will shell out for sin. It's not that they don't sin, but they can't stand to pay money for the privilege." Merle blew a puff of cigarette smoke in the other direction from the lady beside him, who was not a smoker and obviously resented his smoking, though not enough to move farther off.

"Now, most Indians believe in dumb luck just like the Catholics, but we're so damn poor that there's not a lot of money to be made off us. The money Indians drop at Taco-Nite *came* from Taco-Nite. What a name, huh? Sounds like a special offer from Taco Bell."

This was not the right lady for his too often recycled joke. She offered a polite smile and turned her attention to the casino floor. Did she feel she needed rescuing and was looking for her date? She wasn't one of the Taco-Nite regulars, the hookers and the blackjack and bingo addicts. Merle figured she must be up from the Cities, staying at one of the resorts. And how many of her type were going to venture this far north on their own to catch walleyes? There must be a husband or a boyfriend around, but the crowd was pretty sparse this early on a Wednesday night, and he didn't see any likely candidates. She just didn't compute.

"There are never clocks in casinos, are there?" she said. "Do you have the time?"

"No, not in the way I guess you're asking. This here"—he turned his wrist to show her—"is just a collar off a dead cat."

She laughed at that plain fact as she had not at his joke. "Really?" she marveled. "A dead cat? Yours?"

"Well, no. It must have been a stray. I found it pretty deep in the woods."

"Just the collar, no cat attached?"

He nodded, annoyed by her curiosity, and then it came back, the dream he'd had, where he was in some other bar, talking to another woman. No, to the very cat they were talking about. Who'd run off, in his dream, and when he woke, the real cat had run off, too, leaving her collar behind. Which he'd buckled round his wrist, 'cause he liked the look of it.

And he was *sure* there was some connection between that dream and this lady here, staring so intently at the red leather collar he'd taken off that cat. He removed the collar and handed it to her.

Immediately she looked at the inner lining of paler leather, on which someone had written GINGER in childishly awkward ballpoint letters. He could see a glint of recognition and then, as she handed the collar back, the feigned indifference.

"Ginger," she said lightly. "That's how you can tell it was on a cat. There must be a thousand cats called Ginger."

"There must be," he agreed. "Hate to think of what must have happened to this Ginger, though—with just her collar there in the woods." He took a meditative drag and didn't bother directing the smoke another way. "I guess you must be a cat lover yourself."

"Me? Oh no. I'm almost the opposite."

"An ailurophobe?"

That got a rise out of her. She didn't come right out and ask where he'd got a ten-dollar word like that, but he could see it registered. He'd finally caught her interest.

"My name's Merle," he said, slouching her way and offering his hand.

"Diana," she said, accepting his handshake reluctantly.

"And what's your game? If I may ask."

He'd ruffled her feathers, but she replied, with a backward tilt of her head, "I'm a schoolteacher. Though I'm on a leave of absence right now. And yourself?"

He grinned. "The same—I'm on a leave of absence. Though that wasn't what I was asking. I meant—what's your game here, at the Taco-Nite? Blackjack? Roulette? I don't see you as the bingo type, but I could be wrong. I only do the slots myself. Bingo's too slow, and the other games get too expensive. I never got better than a C in arithmetic, but that was enough to take in the fact that the odds favor the house. Yourself?"

"A's usually," she said, loosening up all at once, seeming almost friendly, "though again that's not what you were asking. My game? I'm here to play . . ." She offered a smiling, what-can-I-tell-you? shrug, ". . . the field?"

Was she putting the make on him? Merle wondered. It would not have been the first time he'd been beaten to the punch. There was a whole class of ladies who came to the casinos looking for some affirmative action with boys from the rez.

"You know, if there was a band, and we were dancing, this is the moment when I would slip the bandleader five bucks and ask him to play 'Let's Spend the Night Together,' one of my all-time sentimental favorites."

"Mine, too," she agreed. "Though I'm not sure five bucks would do the job these days."

"Then we got a problem. 'Cause in the classic choice of my place or yours, you would not be very happy with my place. I know I'm not. But I'm near broke, so that rules out a motel. So, where are you staying? And are you here by yourself?"

"My place is possible, but it's a ways away. Almost fifty miles. And I wouldn't want to drive you back here after the date."

"I'm the same," he assured her. "Shy about making commitments. But how's this for logistics? I follow you home on my bike. We spend the night together. I grab some sleep. You provide breakfast. Does that sound like love at first sight?"

"It sounds possible."

They got off the bar stools in unison, and Merle could swear that at just that moment he could see Ginger, with her red collar on, scoot across the linoleum floor in the direction of the bingo hall.

They exited the casino through wheezing pneumatic doors and entered a summer evening that featured June bugs sizzling in the bug lights and a full-scale aurora beyond.

"Jesus," said Merle. "We don't get many as good as that."

Her head swiveled sideways, like a television monitor, and a tongue slid out from her lips that was not a human tongue. Thin, and split at the tip, the tongue of a snake.

"It is beautiful, isn't it?" she agreed, making her voice sound deep and sexy.

But it was too late. He knew her for a witch. And she didn't know he knew that. Had no suspicion.

And he knew something else: this was the woman Judy Johnson wanted him to kill.

"Merle, would you excuse me a moment? It's a long drive. I'd better hit the ladies' room first."

"Sure. Just point the way to your car, and I'll get my bike ready."

"It's the white Camry at the far end of the lot."

"I see it."

She hesitated a moment and then, on tiptoe, her tongue human again, gave him a kiss, quick but not so quick as to seem perfunctory.

Would he kill her? He couldn't decide. The shaman in him seemed to favor that impulse. His hands itched to be at her throat. But first another itch had to be taken care of.

He'd never felt so incredibly horny in his life. He felt like a slot machine poised on the brink of a jackpot. One touch and he'd be all lights and sirens and an endless blissful flow of silver dollars. The aurora was no accident tonight.

40

In a toilet stall that still had its doorknob and lock intact, Diana bolted down the mandragora cocktail she'd brought along in a miniature plastic vodka bottle. The sight of a whole mob of strangers seen in their animal aspect could be unnerving, so she no longer prepared for her hunting expeditions by taking the hellbroth before she absolutely had to. But now that she and Merle were on their own, she was curious to know his secret identity and the totem of his tribe. He was no pig, surely, so she would not be adding to her sty's resident population. No Rosencrantz or Guildenstern tonight. Nowadays, even without the magic spectacles a sip of her home brew provided, she could often catch a glimmer of a stranger's inner unperson, but not this guy's. Merle was opaque.

And he remained so when she spotted him behind her Camry, helmeted and already mounted on his bike. Perhaps she hadn't given the cocktail enough time to do its stuff. As she'd exited the casino, she had seen one or two beastly gamblers on the floor, but not the mob of them there might have been if she'd been viewing the casino at full optical power.

She slowed her pace, considering her options. She did not want to arrive home and discover she'd made a date with a horse or a weasel or something nastier. Should she back out now or take her chances? Perhaps the mandragora was losing its efficacy. It didn't come packaged with an expiration date, and she was not yet an expert in dosages. But she didn't *need* to add to the sty. So if, on arrival, Merle remained merely human, they might just have a conventional one-night stand. For he was, in his human form, a sexy guy. The type she'd rarely been able to entice in her prewitchcraft days. Not smooth John Travolta sexy, but craggy Nicholas Cage sexy. But that was good enough.

"Ready to go?" he asked as she came within speaking distance.

She smiled and wet her lips with her tongue, an invitation to be kissed. "As ready as I'll ever be."

He nodded but didn't accept the invitation. "Then let's hit the road." He pulled the plastic visor down over his face.

There had been a glint in his eye at that last moment, and she thought, I shouldn't be doing this. But her sense of simple good manners prevented her acting on the impulse. She got into her car and they set off, she in the lead, he close behind, the beam of his headlight shifting position in her rearview mirror with each least bend in the highway. Mostly it never wavered, for the land was flat and the road seldom curved.

She felt she was being a fool, that there was some basic caution she'd neglected. A foolish virgin who hadn't taken her pill but lacked the power to resist puppy-dog eyes and a wagging tail. Yet that was part of the excitement, too. Witch though she was, she could still find a thrill in danger.

And, it occurred to her as the highway's dash, dash, dash of white lines flashed by, the thrill of adultery as well. She was a married woman now, a member of that tribe she'd always so despised. It had been only a few hours since she'd sent Alan packing after another dutiful wifely attempt to rouse his limp dick. Oh, she'd been an exemplary wife all through this first week of their official marriage, full of encouragement and the wisdom of *The Joy of Sex*. And he had tried so hard and failed so miserably. With never a reproach from her. But tonight she'd informed him, after his most effortful failure yet, that she had a terrible migraine and had to be alone and undisturbed, so he absolutely must not phone her, and he had promised not to.

To think that only last winter she'd thought she was in love with the little dork. And not (to be honest with herself) just thought it: she had been. What changes she'd been through!

Yes, and what changes were still in store? What new powers might she still discover in herself? As a witch she was just a fledgling. There were still bits of eggshell in her feathers.

But there, already, was the sign signaling the turn to County Road B, and she had to brake rather too quickly, and the headlight in her rearview mirror approached more quickly still. They both barely made the turn, but they did, and now it was only two more miles, without the white flashes of a median line. Home again, home again, jiggety-jig.

She pulled into the gravel driveway, eased to a stop, and was out of the car before Merle's headlight held her in its monocular beam.

Then his headlight went out, and she was momentarily blind in the darkness. The night had misted over, and the aurora's light was at an end. No way to know what he would look like when he took off his helmet. A bear? A bulldog? A bull?

But no, he took off his helmet and was still the Merle she'd met at the casino. No magic tonight.

"God damn," said Merle, "it's a good thing they don't post cops on that road. You must have been doing ninety all the way here."

"I was?"

"You were."

"I better slow down, then."

"Oh, it's too late for that, lady. Keep your foot on the pedal. We haven't got started."

And then there was a scream.

"What in hell was that?" said Merle, taking a step back.

It was one of the pigs. Carl, she was almost certain, for Carl was the one the others most often attacked, even now that they'd been castrated and should be milder-tempered.

"It's one of the pigs, I think," she said.

"You got *pigs* here?"

"Only a few. Over the hill, behind the house. Usually you never hear them at this hour."

"Pigs," said Merle.

"You're in the country," said Diana. "People raise pigs."

Merle made no response but headed, on his own, toward the back door of the house, and then veered right, up the hill, toward the sty.

"Merle!" she called out. "Merle, where are you going?"

Halfway up the hill he turned round and called back, "I know this place. I been here." He continued quickly up to the crest of the hill and stopped.

"You've been here?" she said when she caught up to him.

"Yeah," he said. "I know your whole spread. The sty, the corncrib. Over there, the smokehouse. But I've only seen it from *above*. That's why I didn't realize till just now where I was. God damn."

"From above? Oh, you're . . . a pilot?"

"You could say that. Yeah, I got my own private craft. Come here."

She still might not have. Her instincts were against it. But she did. Whereupon he put his hands about her neck and gripped her firmly.

"Lady," he said, "I know what you are. You're a snake."

She would have laughed in his face, but his grip was too strong. She could not breathe, nor speak any word of protest.

"A fucking snake," he insisted.

She writhed in his grip, but she could not bite him.

"A god-damned snake. Yeah, right, look at you. Well, it looks like you met your match, lady. You got no power over *me*. I'm the boss now. Right?"

She could only flail in his grip.

"Right?" he insisted, tightening the hand that held her throat.

"Yes!" she hissed.

"Yes, what?"

"Yes, Sir!"

"I could kill you right now, lady. But you know what? I never met anyone like you. A witch, I guess you could say. I always wanted to meet my female equivalent. I met a man once who had the same power. Almost. But never a witch."

His squeeze became more powerful. She was being strangled.

"I could kill you, you know."

She writhed in assent.

"So you got to agree you won't ever even threaten me. You got to *submit*."

She nodded. But that was not enough.

"Suck it," he told her, and forced his cock into her mouth.

When he'd come, he let go, and she could breathe again.

"That felt good," he told her.

She lay in the grass, exhausted, and wished she could kill him, but she knew she never would be able to do that. She could hate him but not hurt him. Because now she was his.

41

The whole house was full of mosquitoes because right in the middle of dinner one of the old ladies, Mrs. Witz, had keeled over into her plate of macaroni and cheese and died, prompting a mass exodus from the dining room to the front porch, and then, with the house all lit up, a constant coming and going and banging of the screen door as Dr. Karbenkian and then the police and the county coroner came by to make the death official. Once Mrs. Witz had been taken off to the funeral home, every mosquito in the neighborhood had found its way indoors, and the old ladies were helpless against them. They just didn't have the reflexes to swat fast enough. Mrs. Turney had heard once that pine-scented room deodorants were as effective against mosquitoes as any of the bug bombs that cost so much more, but now she knew for certain that that wasn't true, because the house reeked of the deodorant but the mosquitoes were still in charge. Alan and Louise did the best they could with the flyswatters, but it was obvious they were outnumbered and the mosquitoes would win.

That was when the phone call came from the sheriff's office in New Ravensburg. They wanted to talk to Alan, and Mrs. Turney, certain that they must be calling for some reason connected with Mrs. Witz, assured them that Alan had no connection with the old lady, that all the paperwork was taken care of and the body had been taken to the Good Shepherd Funeral Home.

They still wanted to talk to Alan.

"Hello?" Alan said when Mrs. Turney finally surrendered the phone to him.

"Alan Johnson?"

"This is he."

"You reported your mother Judith Johnson as a missing person some while back. Yes?"

"Well, it was just a formality. I figure she just took off without leaving a forwarding address. I don't really know if that counts as missing. Why?"

"Because we've found a body we think may be her, but we need someone to come in and make an identification."

"She's dead?"

"Assuming it's her. If you're free now, we'll send a car over there to pick you up."

"Oh, I can drive to New Ravensburg myself. Where was she? How did she die?"

"I'm not allowed to discuss this any further until there's been an identification. The car's on its way there now."

"They found your mother?" Mrs. Turney asked, with ill-disguised avidity, when Alan hung up the phone.

"They think so. They wouldn't tell me any more than that, but I don't suppose it's liable to be someone else."

He wanted to call Diana, but she was having one of her migraines and had asked him not to phone. Anyhow, what could she do to help? He wasn't even sure it was his mother yet. And if it was, he wasn't sure how he felt. He'd already been through so many feelings about her disappearing the way she had—anger, hurt, resentment, even some grief. Now he'd have to reshuffle the whole deck and deal it out again like a new game of solitaire.

In fact, his feelings about almost everything else were in the same state of chaos. He still hadn't adjusted to the idea that he was married. Which he wasn't, except in a legal sense, since the ceremony in Brainerd hadn't worked any magic on his sexual dysfunction. The real wedding ceremony took place in private, with just the bride and groom attending, and that ceremony was permanently pending.

For a while he sat and stewed, but Louise was still going around whacking the mosquitoes, so he took up his swatter and joined her, and in no time at all he was completely absorbed by the job at hand and leaving a trail of bloody splotches all over the wallpaper in the downstairs rooms. *Blat! Blat!* It was like a virtual reality arcade game.

His score had mounted to 27 by the time the police car arrived. There were two officers, and they were no more communicative than the man on the phone had been. It seemed to Alan that he was being treated like a murder suspect. They hadn't read him his rights or put him in handcuffs, but what he felt, sitting by himself in the backseat of the police car, was pure panicky fear.

Then, when he thought things could not get worse, something *really* awful happened. The police car's radio crackled to life and said to watch for a speeding car heading their way on the highway, a white Camry, license plate SVS 329, with a Yamaha motorcycle behind, both pushing ninety. The officer radioed back to say he was already on assignment and would not be able to respond, but he did slow down enough, as the headlights of the speeding car approached from the opposite direction, that Alan was left with no doubt in the matter. The car was Diana's Camry, and it was speeding like crazy in the direction of the Kellog farm, with a guy on a motorcycle close behind, almost tailgating.

He hadn't actually seen her behind the wheel, but he wasn't jerk enough to try to think of some way another person might be driving her car. The situation was pretty clear-cut—she was having sex with someone else, and probably had been right along, and their marriage was even more of a fraud than he'd supposed.

He sagged back against the stiff vinyl cushion of the backseat with the sense of weirdly blissful release that can come in the wake of total disaster—a tornado that's leveled your house, or the news that you have an inoperable brain tumor. The police seemed to suspect him of killing his mother, and the newlywed wife he'd never had sex with was having an affair with a biker. And it didn't matter! It was all okay! Because *he* knew he was innocent. Dumb, maybe, but he'd done nothing to be ashamed of. He was a genuine example of what his god-damned father was always sounding off about— a righteous man. And the promise to the righteous was there in the first Psalm: "For the Lord knoweth the way of the righteous, but the way of the ungodly shall perish." There it was, plain as could be, just after the Book of Job, which finally made sense to him, now that he was in the same situation: all you need is a clear conscience, and whatever shit may happen, it'll all work out in the end. That's what Job believed, and it was probably what had kept Jim Cottonwood sane all those years in prison, and now Alan believed it, too.

When he got to the coroner's office, it was ten-fifteen, and ten-thirty before the coroner got there. Alan waited in the basement corridor of the county courthouse with one of the policemen while the other went off to fetch the coroner. There were no benches. One of the two fluorescent lights flickered and made a sound like bacon grease. The policeman never once tried to start up some small talk, which Alan found amazing, unless he was under orders.

At last the coroner arrived and opened up his front office and then the little half-room behind it where there was a special refrigerator for corpses, like a deep freeze, only instead of white enamel it was the color and texture of a galvanized-steel bucket.

The body inside was covered with a white sheet, which the coroner lifted and pulled back. The body seemed to be completely naked, although the breasts had not been exposed. Everywhere the skin was shredded or chewed up, as though animals had been at it.

"Well?" said the coroner. "Is that your mother?"

Alan couldn't think what to say. Finally he managed, "I . . . I don't know. I mean, the face is all . . . messed up. What happened to her?"

The coroner exchanged a significant look with the policeman, and the policeman answered, "That's how she was found."

"Is it your *mother*?" the coroner insisted.

"Honestly, how could I tell? There's just . . . meat. I guess the hair could be hers. Was she wearing any kind of jewelry? Mom's ears were pierced."

"You refuse to make an identification?" It was the policeman this time.

"I don't *refuse* to. I *can't*. Would you know if it was *your* mother?"

"Don't get smart, kid."

"Smart? I'm sorry, I'd like to leave. You won't tell me anything, and I can't help you identify her. I'm not used to looking at . . . anything like this. Plus, the smell is getting to me."

The policeman heaved a sigh and signaled to the coroner to close the lid on the cooler. Then he announced to Alan that he was being arrested on suspicion of murder, and that he had the right to remain silent. In the police station across the street from the courthouse he was told he could make one phone call. He couldn't trust himself to phone Diana, but he did try to reach Bruce McGrath at his home number, which he knew by heart. But he only got an answering machine. So it looked like he would be spending the night in jail.

The cot in the cell he was locked in was no more uncomfortable than the one he'd been sleeping on at Navaho House. Even so, he had a little trouble getting to sleep, but after he recited the 23rd Psalm a few times he popped right off.

42

Magic is like knitting a sweater, a patient, persistent intertwining of a single purpose shaped in the form that the moving needles have insisted on. But let that single thread be snapped at any of its linkages, and the whole fabric is at peril: the sweater may unravel to become a mere skein of yarn again.

So it was with Diana's witchcraft. The first break in the yarn had been Judy Johnson's disappearance, which Diana had given little thought to at first. Cats will run off, or get run over. Some stay on longer than others, but even the luckiest are not much sturdier than houseplants. It is part of their charm that they *don't* have nine lives but only one, and that one likely to be brief if they are free to range the countryside and highways.

It had been a milk delivery truck that killed Judy as it backed out of the Minnawichee Dairy garage early in the morning. She had spent the night beneath the truck, lured there by the sweet stench of spoiling milk and the lingering heat of the engine. Her feline body was found later that day and deposited in a trash bag, which was taken to the local transfer station with the rest of the dairy's garbage two days later. As luck would have it, the trash bag was not at once buried beneath each day's tons of new garbage but came to rest at the top of a mound slated to be bulldozed into a waiting pit. It waited too long. First the crows and then the rats tore the trash bag open to feast on the cat's carcass. And then, before the remaining scraps could be plowed under, the weakened thread snapped altogether and Judy, in death, reverted to her human shape, although her corpse still bore the ravages inflicted by the truck and the vermin at the landfill. Alan was not being cagey when he insisted that he could not identify her remains. Only a forensic scientist could have done that with any certainty.

All Diana's magic had not been undone at once. Only the weakest link had snapped. The four pigs remained in their sty, and remained pigs—at least to the eye of a casual observer. But they had undergone, it seemed to Diana, an inward change. Their behavior seemed less piggish when she approached the sty to slop them. They did not fight for precedence at the trough, but hung back, looking at her. It can be unnerving to be stared at by four large pigs. She did not know to what degree each of them might be aware of his changed condition. She had been assuming they were pigs through and through, mere dumb brutes, but now those mere dumb brutes seemed more like the inmates of some prison camp, caged in the sty—and caged, as well, in their own porcine flesh.

Finally it was Merle who proposed the simple obvious solution to the problem. The pigs had to be slaughtered. They weren't pets, after all, or lodgers, like the old ladies at Navaho House. They were food for the table. Merle had friends who had the necessary equipment—the block and tackle, a scalding vat, barrels for chilling the carcasses in brine, and the various items of heavy-duty cutlery— hooks, saws, cleavers—needed for the butchering. Diana already had a working smokehouse and a functioning freezer in the garage that had stood empty for years waiting for just this occasion.

She had not told Merle how she had come to be raising the pigs, but he seemed to understand their special character without her having to spell it out. Sometimes when he visited, he would study the pigs from a distance as they were being fed, and perhaps he caught glimpses, as Diana sometimes did, of the men they had been before their transformation. What explanation did he need, after all, when he possessed the same powers she did—and had already exercised them against her? His interest in the pigs seemed professional, like that of a physician looking on during a colleague's surgery, making no comment but alert to assist.

Of course, Diana had always intended that the pigs be slaughtered, but she'd been daunted by the prospect of undertaking the work herself on her own or (which amounted to almost the same thing) with only Alan's assistance. She was no longer as squeamish as she'd once been about the shedding of blood or dealing with the larger cuts of meat one might bring home from a supermarket, but she was not confident that she could kill and butcher an entire animal larger than, say, a rabbit or chicken. But when she heard the news that Judy Johnson's body had been found at the local landfill (and *she* had no doubt it was Judy's body), it led her to wonder if the same reverse transformation might take place with one or other of the pigs after they'd been slaughtered, so that where a butcher had hung a fresh-cured ham one day he might return to discover a human thigh and buttock. It seemed prudent, in light of such a possibility, to store the meat from the butchered swine where she could keep an eye on it until such time as it was to be cooked. Four pigs represent a lot of meat, so the ladies at Navaho House were in for some nice barbecues.

The more alarming possibility, which neither she nor Merle spoke of, was that the reverse transformation she dreaded might take place *before* the pigs had been slaughtered. She did not like to imagine how her prisoners might behave if they were suddenly to be set free from the Bastille of their altered flesh. She would not want to be on hand for the rejoicing.

There was one further reason for conducting a slaughter ASAP. Prompted by Carl's continued unexplained absence, the state parole board had arranged for Janet's early release from prison. Could Diana turn over the charge of the house and of Kelly to her sister and continue to live on the premises? Even if Janet extended such an invitation, Diana shrank from the prospect of such a painful transfer of power. She had got used to being the boss. It was bad enough being subservient to Merle, but to Janet?

When she'd begun to raise the pigs, she had let herself assume that the status quo might be sustained indefinitely, that as her power as a witch grew, her luck would grow with it. Even now, she had not really abandoned that assumption. She might yet become the sole owner of the farmhouse she'd grown up in—in addition to those properties that Alan would now inherit without dispute. She had never imagined herself a woman of property, but the prospect was tempting. She only needed to exert herself. The power was there if she would summon it. It was there in the smokehouse, smoldering. It was there trembling in the dirty cobwebs above the air conditioner in Janet's bedroom. It was there in the gravel of her heart.

43

A lot of the time lately he wasn't in the sty. He was back in the lockup, but not at New Ravensburg. In a vast dirt compound surrounded by barbed wire. And he wasn't a guard now, just one of the cons. There was a mob, thousands, and they were being starved to death. The warden was a woman with light blond hair in a feathery crewcut and she would preside at the cafeteria counter in the food tent at the far corner of the compound, dispensing dollops of shit-brown mush to each of the prisoners as he passed by. When he left the food tent on the way to mess tables, he'd be attacked by a gang of other cons who were after his little bowl of slop, so he'd be left with nothing. This had happened many times.

After lunch there was a lecture by the warden, who, using a pointer and flip chart, explained the theory of the corrections system in the state of Minnesota, the object of which was to terrorize and brutalize the inmates until they had become animals. Daily rape by the stronger inmates and regular beatings by the corrections officers accomplished this purpose best, as was shown by various bar graphs and tables of figures. To illustrate the same basic point, the warden offered humorous anecdotes from her own career in both public and for-profit institutions. Then, becoming more serious, she wanted to know which of the men were born-again Christians. They all raised their hands. From those who'd raised their hands she chose four for castration.

These were dreams. He could understand that afterward when he found himself back in the sty, baking in the mud, grateful to be a pig again. Once he'd thought it was these hours wallowing in a mire of mud and shit that were the nightmare, that he belonged on the other side of the fence with the guards who brought his feed. But there were too many proofs to the contrary: his ragged ears, the infected stump of his docked tail, the burning itch all about his scabbed and empty scrotal sac. And the other, human world was worse—its tortures crueler, its cruelties more extreme. In that world there were no mercies, no remission of the horror.

Here, although he had to fight for his place at the trough, there was almost enough food, and sunlight to drowse in (if he could keep from falling into the horrors of sleep), and the presence, from time to time, of a friendly guard. His favorite had been the girl who'd brought his feed when he'd first been put into the sty. Such a pretty thing. She'd seemed afraid of him at first. He could understand that, for she was such a dainty little thing, with such a pleasant smell, though sometimes, without thinking, he would snap at her. But gradually, as he came to associate her with mealtime, a liking had developed, even a fondness. Hogs are not usually noted for their affectionate nature, even toward their own young. Indeed, boars regularly devour their young, like the elder gods of Greek mythology, but Carl had retained a benevolent temperament even as a pig. It was in his nature.

What he liked most in the girl who fed him was not the daily ration of mash mixed up with titbits of household garbage, but the fact that she would sit down on her side of the fence and talk to him. He could not understand the words, for his brain simply did not process human language. But he could catch her tone, which was one of melancholy and muted suffering, feelings with which he could easily empathize. Besides the mash she brought, those conversations had been Carl's only solace during his months of captivity.

But then she stopped bringing him his food, and he was slopped by one or the other of the two full-size humans—either the female, who appeared in his nightmares as the warden of the prison colony (and whom he dreaded as though she were divine), or the male, toward whom he had come to have a certain fellow feeling, not as strong as what he felt for the girl but similar. The woman fed him (he knew) because she wanted him fat, and he knew why she wanted that. The man fed him from a sense of duty, and even, a little, of sorrow, as a prison guard will often pity the creatures under his charge.

That Carl's frame of reference so often drew upon his experience at New Ravensburg, even though he could not remember his human life in its particular details, did not strike him as puzzling. He was a thoughtful sort of pig, but thoughtfulness in pigs has definite limits. He knew what he knew, what he liked and what he loathed, just those essentials. And what he loathed now more than anything else in his shrunken, sty-bound life was the new guard, Merle. That was the name *she* used to address him, and by the way she intoned the name Carl knew she had submitted to Merle's authority, as Carl submitted to hers.

Carl *had* to obey her. He had no more choice in that than he did in where or when he shat. But Merle was another matter. Merle had not forged his fetters. Merle controlled him more by brute force than by psychic compulsion. For that reason Carl could offer some resistance to Merle, ineffective as it might be against Merle's boots, his prod, his cigarettes, and his deep reservoirs of spite. Carl had known C.O.'s like that, especially at the old lockup, before New Ravensburg was built and staffed from scratch. But he'd never appreciated how terrible it was to fall into the power of such a man, to live at his sufferance.

And then, to die at his command. For that day had finally arrived. Carl knew, as the equipment was moved into place, that his and his companions' fate was sealed. He did not understand how the work was to be done, how each engine was to be employed, but he knew that the path to his death had been mapped and strewn with gravel.

And when no mash appeared in the trough at the end of the day, he knew that was no accidental omission. They would be starved for a little while before they were slaughtered.

Carl tested the gate, but with no more success than when he'd butted against it a hundred times earlier. With the flick of a finger any human might have lifted the noose that secured the gate to the post of the fence, but that simple act was beyond his power. He might as well have wished for a machine gun.

And then, as the moon lifted above the crest of the hill, the girl appeared, luminous as the angel who visited Paul in his prison cell.

"Oh, Hamlet," she said, "I thought you'd still be awake. And I am, too. *I* have to go away tomorrow, so I won't be here when they . . . do that stuff. I'm not even supposed to know about it."

Carl was wonderstruck, for he understood every word the child said. And he knew who she was: his daughter, his only child, Kelly.

The knowledge was an anguish almost beyond bearing, but his terror was greater still. He squealed in a way that was a plea for mercy, for salvation, for the child to recognize him in turn.

"I'm so glad Mommy's coming back. I just *hate* Aunty Di! I hate her. And Merle, too, he scares me. But they'll go away, and it will be just Mommy and me. And maybe Daddy will come back, too. Alan says he thinks he will. Anyway, I just came to say good-bye. Okay, Hamlet?"

Carl squealed, but he had no larynx that would transform his pain into speech.

Kelly sighed. "I know you want to get out. It's just awful. But if I did let you out, would you go away? You'd have to hide in the woods, I guess. And not come back here when you get hungry. Aunty Di says a pig that escapes from its sty will always come back when it's hungry enough."

Had she understood him, as he'd understood her? Would she answer his prayer? She was tall enough to reach the noose and lift it from the post.

She had understood him! For she nodded her head and said, "Okay, Hamlet. I'll do it for you, but not the others. You were always kind of special. But you got to be quick. Here." She flicked off the noose and pulled open the gate just wide enough to allow him through.

He trotted away, unthinking, at his fastest pace, until he realized that he was heading straight toward the smokehouse. He veered at once in the opposite direction, almost knocking Kelly off her feet, before he vanished over the crest of the hill, in the direction of the rising moon.

44

"I'm sure she'll turn up any moment," Officer Lincoln insisted brightly. "She can't have gone far. I didn't turn my back two minutes."

"Please," Alan said placatingly, "don't be upset. If it's anyone's fault it's mine. I just wish I could go out there and help look for her."

"I can understand," said Officer Lincoln, touching her crown of tight braids as though it might somehow have become disarranged. "But unfortunately, since we've put the grounds on alert, we can't allow that. Everybody's been ordered to their rooms so we can do a check cabin by cabin. If Kelly—that's her name, Kelly?"

Janet nodded grimly. She'd said almost nothing since learning that her daughter had disappeared from the prison's playground while she was being processed for departure. She just glowered. Alan didn't think she was really that worried or pissed off and was actually enjoying the situation in a way, since she was unarguably in the right and the System at fault.

"If Kelly has gone *into* one of the residences," Officer Lincoln went on, "—and honestly, I can't think where else she *could* have gone, since the surveillance cameras can spot anyone who's on the grounds—then she'll be found by one of the residents."

"Unless she's hiding," said Janet.

"She does love to play hide and seek," Alan volunteered. "And she doesn't always hide in obvious places. And she loves to climb. So I don't know, I'm not sure you're going to find her that easy, until she wants to be found."

"She may not even be on the grounds anymore," Janet pointed out. "Have you thought of that?"

"Yes, and there are cars—unmarked cars, of course, in the immediate neighborhood who are helping to look."

"Maybe you should issue some kind of announcement?" Alan suggested. "You must have some kind of system for that as part of your security system."

Officer Lincoln winced. "I think it would be premature to send out a sound truck. We don't like to alarm our neighbors needlessly. It's not as though Kelly poses a danger."

"Not to anyone but herself," Janet commented. "And maybe the staff here—if she's not found."

"Mrs. Kellog, she *will* be found. But I do understand your being anxious. So right now I think it might be better, less stressful, if I left you here in the visitors' lounge with Mr. Johnson. Feel free to help yourself to the coffee and any of the pastries over there. I'm getting signals on my beeper that the warden wants to see me. Probably for a chewing out." She stood poised by the door. "Okay?"

"If the warden chews you out?" Janet asked. "It's okay with me."

Officer Lincoln rolled her eyes expressively but didn't insist on having the last word.

When they were left alone in the lounge, neither Alan nor Janet could think of anything to say. Alan had fixed his attention on the big handpainted mural on the wall behind the dining area, which showed a family of deer and assorted forest creatures beside a brook of turquoise blue. There was another mural almost exactly the same in the visiting area of the New Ravensburg prison. Alan imagined the painter going from prison to prison all over Minnesota painting the same greeting-card animals, the same smudgy leaves and pastel sky.

"Would you like a coffee?" he asked at last, poised to push himself up from the low, orange vinyl, many-sectioned sofa.

"No," said Janet. "I'd like a beer. That was the first thing I was going to ask for as soon as we got out of here. A can of Budweiser. No, make that a six-pack. I figure that would last most of the drive home. How long does it take?"

"We were on the road about four hours coming this direction."

"Right now we'd be passing by St. Peter, even if we'd stopped to pick up the beer. If Kelly hadn't decided to disappear."

"I can imagine it must be frustrating. You've been released but you're still *stuck* here."

"But there's no rule says we have to wait here in Bambi Hall till they find Kelly. I'm sure they *will* find her. In an odd way this is probably one of the safest places a kid could get lost in."

"Yeah, but we still have got to sign out with the guard at the main gate. And I don't figure they're going to want to check us out to go get a beer, and then check us back in when we come back for Kelly."

"We don't have to say *why* we're going out. You've got a cellular phone. So the minute they find Kelly they can call you. I just want to be on the other side of the gate. In the free world. Please?"

How could he say no? So they went and got his car in the lot and the guard at the gate didn't give them any hassle. She took down the number of Alan's phone, and they set off in the direction of the shopping strip north of town. It seemed funny to Alan to be leaving Kelly in prison, but was it that different, really, from dropping her off at day care?

"So—how are things back at the ranch?" Janet asked once they were beyond range of the grounds of the prison and she'd swiveled round to watch the road ahead of them. "Kelly didn't seem that happy when I saw her earlier."

"To tell you the truth, Janet, I'm just as glad to be away from there today myself. Today's the day they're slaughtering those pigs.

And Diana was kind of upset this morning because one of the pigs is missing. In fact, she blamed Kelly for letting it out of the sty deliberately. She really got on her case. For a while I thought she wasn't going to let her come along on the ride."

"*Did* she let it out?"

"Probably. I told Diana it was me, but I don't think she believed me. But she had to pretend to and let up on Kelly. But, boy, was she angry! I never really saw that side of her before. I don't know what it is with those pigs and her."

"How long will they be at the slaughtering? It's not exactly my idea of the ideal homecoming."

"They'd already got started before we left, but they'll still be at the butchering when we get back there. Unless they take a really long time finding Kelly."

"Then let's hope they do. There!" She pointed to the 7-Eleven they were approaching. "Pull in there. They'll have beer. There's even a picnic area. We can sit outside with the beers and I can have a cigarette."

"I thought you gave up smoking?"

"In the joint I was a god-damned born-again Christian, and so is everyone else. We're all *nuns* in the joint. But that is over now. Praise Jesus!"

The way she said "Praise Jesus!" made it sound like a curse, but rather than argue with her on the subject of smoking, Alan just pulled into the parking lot at the 7-Eleven and took a space near the two metal picnic tables. Janet unbuckled the seat belt and took up her purse.

"To be able to spend my own *money* again! Do you know what it *feels* like to never have anything but small change for candy bars and toothpaste? You just can't imagine." She opened the car door. "Anything I can get for you in there?"

"A Coke would be nice."

She nodded and, halfway to the door of the 7-Eleven, called out, "Grab one of those tables."

For all their obvious differences, they were so much alike, Diana and her sister. The way they both ordered him around like he was a waiter in a restaurant. Never so much as a please or a thank-you. The way both of them just surrendered to their appetites. "*Grab* one of those tables," Janet had told him. They were grabbers, and Kelly was growing up to be another. It was an enviable quality, unless of course what they were grabbing belonged to you. It must be hard to live in a family of grabbers.

Janet emerged from the store with a plastic bag bulging with purchases, which she proceeded to spread across the mottled, sticky tabletop: a can of Budweiser for her, a Coke for him, a big bag of barbecue-flavored Doritos, two packs of Kents, and a Reuben sandwich heated in the store's microwave and oozing cheese into its clear plastic wrapping. "We'll stop for a proper meal later," Janet assured him, "but when I saw this in the dairy case, I just couldn't resist. Here—" She undid the wrapping and pulled the sandwich apart, careless of the melted cheese, globs of which dribbled out, along with sauerkraut, and added to the deposits on the table. "Half's for you."

Alan held the sandwich in his hand and watched as Janet washed down huge, half-chewed mouthfuls with her beer. Only when she'd finished did she notice that he hadn't started. "Is something wrong with it?"

"You know, I think this morning turned me into a vegetarian. Don't ever watch pigs get slaughtered if you like bacon."

"It's corned beef in the sandwich, not pork. But if you don't want it . . ."

He handed her the sandwich and went on: "I shouldn't have gone to watch them, but I was curious. God, I am so glad I didn't have to be involved. At first Diana was planning that we'd do it ourselves, just the two of us. But when she'd read up on it, she realized it was just too big a job. So she brought in this friend of hers from the rez. Merle. And two buddies of his."

"I don't remember her having any friends on the rez."

"He's a new friend."

"But not a friend of yours?" When he didn't reply at once, she said, "I'm sorry. It's no business of mine."

When he still said nothing and started to cry, she said, "Something is wrong, isn't it? Not just watching those pigs get killed."

He blew his nose into one of the napkins that came with the sandwich, then wiped at his tears with another. But the tears wouldn't stop.

"Alan, what *is* it?"

"It's something I can't discuss. I promised Diana."

"Is it the thing with the police and your mother? Diana told me that was all cleared up."

"It is. They never booked me, after the one night I spent in jail. And I was never all that worried, really. All they had was their suspicions. And I was the only one they *could* suspect."

"But it must have been upsetting. Jesus, I remember what it was like when they came and arrested me."

"Yeah, but—" He didn't know how to say it politely.

"But I was guilty as charged. Yeah, that would make a difference."

"It was upsetting to see her so smashed up. Nobody knows how it happened, or even *what* happened. It looks like she was hit by a car and then crows and rats got at her, so it might have been just an accident on the highway at night. Except she didn't have any clothes on, and they can't figure how she ended up at the landfill. *Someone* must have brought her there."

"Then what is this deep dark secret? What does Diana have to do with it? You're in love with her, aren't you? That was pretty obvious last time you came here with Kelly. So, did you have a falling-out?"

"No. Just the opposite. We got married." The moment he said it, the tears stopped and he felt one hundred percent better.

"I don't believe it," Janet said. "You and Diana?"

"Yeah. Beauty and the Beast, huh?"

"Well, I might agree with that, except I think you mean Diana to be the Beauty."

"Oh, you haven't seen her lately. She is gorgeous."

"And she made you promise not to tell me? Why?"

"We haven't told anyone. We went to Brainerd, to the justice of the peace. That was back in June. And everything was fine till then. We had problems, but we were in love. Now . . . there's just the problems."

"Problems with sex?" Janet wanted to know.

Alan nodded.

"She's frigid, isn't she?"

Alan smiled ruefully. "No, the problem was never hers. It's me. I can't do it. I'm . . . impotent."

"No, you're not," said Janet confidently. She opened up one of the packs of Kents, took out a cigarette, lit it, and filled her lungs with smoke. "No," she said, exhaling, "the problem is her. She has that effect on men. She did in high school, and she did with Carl when she came to live at the farm. I don't know for certain if they had sex after she moved in, but I know that when he came here last winter to visit he couldn't get his engine going, and that was the only time he ever had that problem. There *are* women like that. They may seem real sexy—'gorgeous,' I think you said—but the bottom line is, they will break your balls. Why do you think she's never been married, or even had a steady boyfriend?"

"Boy, you really don't have much use for your sister, do you?"

"No more than I would for a pet snake." She finished her can of Budweiser, pitched the empty in the direction of the trash can, missing it, and popped open a second.

"Hey, maybe you should slow down. You don't want to be drunk when we go back to get Kelly."

"Do I seem drunk to you?"

"Kind of, yeah. You're out of practice. And there's a lot of bad feelings stored up. So it's understandable."

"Okay, you're right." Janet aimed the full can at the trash can, and this time she scored. "I'll hold off till we're out of Mankato. I *might* explode. But if I do that, let me ask a favor in return."

"Sure, whatever."

"I'm not up to facing my sister tonight. And I don't want to arrive while those people are there doing the butchering. So let's spend the night in a motel somewhere outside the Cities. Have a nice dinner at a restaurant. Bring a bottle back to the room. And get to know each other. Okay?"

"Hey, I'd like that."

"Diana will be pissed off, but Kelly's disappearing act is a perfect excuse."

It was then, as though by magic, that Kelly woke up in the backseat of the car, where she'd gone to sleep on the floor, unnoticed under Alan's nylon windbreaker.

After the explanations and a good laugh all round, Janet suggested *not* calling the prison right off the bat with the good news but making Officer Lincoln and everyone else go on looking for Kelly the rest of the afternoon. Alan persuaded her that that would be unkind, and she agreed to let him phone right then.

She even agreed to throw away the two packs of Kents. It didn't make sense to take up smoking again after she'd kicked the habit for more than six months.

"I can't tell you," she said, once they hit Route 169, "how beautiful this is."

"This? The highway?"

"No. The freedom." She leaned sideways and kissed him on the cheek.

He blushed, and smiled, and stepped on the gas until they were doing seventy.

45

This was the third day of Jim's fast, and it was hard to think of anything but food. Food remembered, food imagined. The meat people eat, the carrion of crows. How leather is chewed to soften it. Clay had told him once that in times of famine books were boiled for the glue in their bindings and wallpaper was stripped from walls for the same purpose. His mother had told him of winter famines in her childhood, snowbound in the cabin and half starved.

He had never lived in such times or places. The hunger of fasting was the closest he'd approached starvation, and there was an essential difference in knowing that he might stop fasting when he chose. There was even an element of bravado in holding steadfast to the resolve—the clenched-jaw glory of the marathoner or the anorexic.

All such thoughts—of food, of his own willpower—were at odds with the purpose of the fast, and he did his best to let them scud along their way through the blue skies of consciousness, observed but not obsessed over. For the purpose of the fast, beyond its being a preparation for the sweat lodge, was clarity. It was as though, far off and faintly, he could hear a tapping, like the tapping of the raven in Poe's poem, but what it meant, where it came from, he could not tell without the acuity that would come from the fasting.

Meanwhile, one of the new screws had summoned him from his cell to take him down to the visiting room, and the passage along the Y-block corridor was a slow-motion moonwalk, another side effect of the fast. Each swing of his leg, each hinging of elbow or knee, took unaccustomed effort and was stretched beyond its real duration as his mind swept up the kind of details you usually only have time to pick up on in movies: speckles of paint, the flicker of a fluorescent bulb, the way the C.O. who checked the pink passes outside the visiting room had nicked his chin shaving. Each detail glimmered with some out-of-reach significance like the clues in a Sherlock Holmes mystery. Jim realized that the fasting had induced a kind of auto-intoxication. But getting high was not what he was after. He was after clarity; this was a drunk's illusion of clarity.

And there, already stationed on the central orange vinyl sofa, was his mother, squat and dowdy, with a face that seemed made of welded iron, each wrinkle a testament to some decision formed deep in her genes a century or two before the great collision between the Wabasha and the white man. She did not acknowledge his presence until he had sat down before her, and then she said, in their own language, "I see you are well."

Like the code-speakers of World War II, they spoke in their own tongue, haltingly, and fused with lots of basic English that had no quick equivalent, but the final mix would surely have baffled anyone monitoring the mikes.

"Very well," he answered.

"It amazes me that you still have to be here."

"It amazes me, too. But they want me to sign papers that I won't sign." (This was a statement, it occurred to Jim, that must often have been made in the language of the Wabasha.)

"To promise you won't sue them?"

"I don't intend to. But they won't believe that."

"They are afraid of you now."

"It's only a matter of weeks until the court will be forced to release me. I can be patient. I've learned that living here."

"There is another problem that brings me to you. The Johnson boy is in trouble."

"Yes, I've heard. They found his mother. It seems she was murdered."

"They suspected him, but they had no evidence. Now there's evidence. One of our ladies died a short while ago, and I had to go up to the attic to fetch her suitcase down. When I did, I noticed a suitcase I didn't remember. A tan canvas bag with a name tag on it that said J. JOHNSON. J for Judith, I thought. Of course, it might have been used by Alan when he moved in, but I remember he came with just one suitcase, and it's under his bed. I looked inside the new suitcase, and it had a lot of women's clothes. Also, an envelope addressed to Jim's lawyer, Mr. McGrath. Inside was Reverend Johnson's will, just a scribble, but it was clear enough, and I'll bet it's legal. He left his house and the church to you."

"To me? He hated me."

Louise shrugged. "He must have hated his daughter and Alan even more."

"So how did Alan . . ."

"That was my first thought, too—that Alan put the suitcase there, and that he must know how his mother had disappeared. I thought the two of them must have found the will and kept it secret, and then he'd killed Judy so that he wouldn't have to share the inheritance. I thought of calling the police."

"Alan wouldn't do something like that," Jim said confidently. "He is not so mean—or so bold a spirit."

"I know, and that's why I didn't call the police. But they came anyhow. They had a search warrant. They looked in Alan's room, and then they asked to look in the attic. Where they went through all the guests' suitcases."

"But they didn't find Judy's?" Jim asked.

"I'd taken off the name tag and put her clothes in the duffel with other things that will go to the Methodists' garage sale. I put Mrs. Schermer's collection of old *TV Guide*s from the '60s in Judy's suitcase. The will is in a safe place. The police took away the boy's computer, nothing else. But their coming to Navaho House, and the way they knew just where to look in the attic, made me think that the suitcase had been put there not to be hidden but to be found. I think someone told them where to look and what to look for."

"Who would want to do that?"

"Who *could* do that? It had to be Mrs. Turney's daughter Diana. She comes and goes as she likes, so she could have planted the suitcase where I found it. How *she* came to have it, and that will, I can't even guess."

"Why would she try to get the boy arrested? Last time you told me they were in love."

"They were. And he's still always sniffing after her. A puppy. But she's changed since she went to the farmhouse. You know how a person can change if they win a lot of money up at the casino? How the money can charge them up?"

"I can't say I do, Mom. The guys here don't get to the casino much."

Louise smiled ruefully. "Well, she's like that. But it's not money with her. I don't think it's sex either, or not exactly. I don't understand the situation. But it has a bad smell. I think she's up to no good, and I'm worried for the boy."

A chill breeze sprang up just then, ruffling Louise's hair and making the leaves shimmer in the mural behind her. Jim heard the caw of a crow, and then, in the pastel sky of the mural, the bird appeared— first as a simple V-shaped brushstroke, then, as it drew nearer, assuming the features of the crow he'd spoken to not long before in the exercise yard on the roof of the prison.

"Jimbo," the crow greeted him, "I said I might come during visiting hours. I'm keeping my word."

"You said you'd find out more about my friend Alan."

"No. That's what *you* said, buddy."

"Tell me about this woman he's in love with. Diana Turney."

"She's his wife now. Would you believe it? But somehow I don't see that marriage lasting a long time. Or him either." The crow lifted its wings in preening menace.

"Tell me about the woman," Jim insisted.

"She is a witch." The crow spread its wings again, not preening now but wanting to fly off. But Jim's gaze tethered it to the branch of the tree on which it had alighted.

"Tell me more, Old Crow. What kind of witchy things has she done?"

The crow cawed, but it could not refuse to answer. "Remember that screw called Carl? Carl was her brother-in-law. And the other guard, Tommy, who disappeared last winter? He was her first. Then there was that old flame of yours, Judy Johnson: *she* disappeared. I think your friend Alan would have already disappeared himself by now except for one thing. He's still a virgin, so her magic don't work on him. A gun would work, but the lady is gun-shy. But *you* just gave me an idea, buddy. Hunger. You been fasting, haven't you? I can feel it, the hunger, like bees in the air. And it would be right for that kid, don't you think? I mean, he's *all* hunger."

"Jim," said Louise anxiously. "Jim, are you all right?"

Jim's attention shifted to his mother's face for only a moment, but that was time enough for the crow to slip loose and hide itself in the dense viridian tangle of foliage shadowing the stream.

"I'm fine, Mom."

"Are you sure? I thought for a moment you were having a stroke or something."

"I'm fine. But I need to ask a favor. Can you get in touch with Gordon Pillager at the rez?"

"Not very easily. Gordon doesn't have a phone."

"But you know where his cabin is."

She nodded.

"Tell him I need my medicine."

"What medicine?"

"He'll know. Tell him I need it tomorrow."

"You want me to go to that cabin of his *tonight*?"

Jim nodded. His eyes had returned to the painting. Where the fawn had stood behind its mother, there was now only a boulder mottled with moss and a few speckles of vermilion, representing blood.

"Time's up," the C.O. announced.

Louise got to her feet, then bent down so that Jim could kiss her cheek.

It was to be their last farewell.

46

For Janet's homecoming dinner the leaf had been added to the dining room table. There was a white tablecloth and six place settings, five of them with the Orient Fantasy china that Janet and Carl had got from Mr. and Mrs. Turney, who'd received it themselves as a wedding present from Grandma Turney's parents, the Iversons, way back in 1957. There would have been a full complement, but Kelly had broken the sixth dinner plate just today when she was setting the table for dinner, and so *she* would be eating off her own everyday dinner plate with the portraits of Princess Di and Prince Charles, which Diana had bought for her at the Methodists' Saturday garage sale.

Kelly had not got much of a scolding for breaking the plate, because they'd just got home after the long drive from Mankato and everyone was walking on eggs. Last night, when Janet had phoned Diana from the *second* motel they were staying at, Arrowsmith Motor Court, the two sisters had got into an argument. Diana had thought they should just keep heading for home, since they were only two hours away in Sauk Centre, to which they'd made a detour in order to see the grave of Sinclair Lewis. But the cemetery was closed when they got there, so they'd had to stay over. Diana didn't think Sinclair Lewis was important enough to justify postponing the homecoming dinner, which was already in the oven, but Janet refused to be bullied. "I'll get home when I get home!" she yelled into the phone, and then hung up without listening to any further objections. Kelly was delighted to see her mother standing up to Diana. It was something she couldn't do herself.

Kelly spent the night in her very own room at the Arrowsmith Motor Court, and the next morning they all had the deluxe breakfast at McDonald's, with pancakes and sausages and everything else, using coupons Kelly had clipped from the Sunday paper. For only 89 cents extra Kelly got a souvenir Pocahontas tumbler. Then they went to the cemetery, where Kelly took a picture of her mother and

Alan standing in front of the granite monument for the whole Lewis family. For the rest of the drive home they listened to the tape recording Alan bought at the museum of the book Sinclair Lewis wrote about Sauk Centre, *Main Street,* and every few miles Alan would start laughing for no reason at all, and then her mother would, too. Kelly didn't understand why Sinclair Lewis was supposed to be so funny, but she figured *Main Street* had to be full of dirty jokes that were over her head. It made it a long drive.

When it was time for everyone to sit down to dinner, Diana pointed to the chair at the head of the table, where Kelly's father used to sit. "Merle, you sit there," Diana said. "And Kelly, you're next to Merle, and, Mother, you'll be here beside me." She placed her hands in a proprietary way on the back of the chair at the other end of the table from Merle.

"No," said Janet, "I think Mother should sit at the head of the table, and I'll sit at the other end. That's always been where I sit, and this is my homecoming, right? Alan, you sit between me and Kelly. Now, Kelly, do you want to say grace?"

Kelly dutifully bowed her head and clasped her hands in front of her Princess Di plate, but she couldn't remember the exact words of the prayer, since lately they had not been saying grace as a regular thing. "O Lord . . ." was as far as she could get unassisted.

"O Lord," Alan prompted, "for what we are about to receive . . ."

"Make us truly thankful!" Kelly chimed in.

They all said "Amen," and Janet and Diana went into the kitchen to get the food.

The four remaining at the table couldn't think of much to talk about until Grandma Turney said, "Well, Kelly, it sounds like you had quite an adventure in Mankato. Everyone was looking for you like you were an escaped convict."

"Uh-huh," said Kelly guardedly. Her mother had said it would be best not to talk about how she'd been in the back of the car all the time. The motels they'd stayed at were another topic to avoid, since they didn't want Diana to get all heated up again. But that didn't leave much she *could* talk about concerning the trip.

"I got *this* at McDonald's," she said, holding up her Pocahontas tumbler.

"Oh, yeah?" said Merle. "Tell us about it, kid."

So Kelly told them about the deluxe breakfast, and how Janet had to argue with the manager about the coupons because it was almost eleven o'clock, and then about the Pocahontas headband that she got for free, and how Alan's head had been too big for his headband to fit, and Grandma Turney made a comment about when she first knew Alan and he thought he was an Indian. Alan said, "Hey, let's not go into that."

Merle laughed out loud and then said, "Sorry," with a big smirk. "I was just imagining you dressed up like Pocahontas."

Alan gave him a nasty look.

Kelly felt she'd said the wrong thing and could not be coaxed into any more news about the trip to Mankato. Grandma Turney was reduced to praising the weather before she, too, joined the silence.

The silence was broken by a scream from the kitchen, followed by the crash of something heavy and metallic. The scream was Janet's, and the crash, Alan saw as he reached the kitchen, the first to get there, was the pan in which the pork roast had been cooking. The pan and the roast itself were on the floor, as was Janet.

"Are you okay?" Alan asked, bending down to help her to her feet. "Did you burn yourself?"

"No—but *I* did!" Diana announced in an aggrieved tone. She was wiping her leg with the sponge from the kitchen sink. The skin had already blistered.

"I'm sorry," Janet said, almost in a whisper.

"Sorry doesn't help. What in the *world* possessed you?"

"It was the roast."

"The roast!" Diana repeated. "Oh, my God, Merle, get the roast back into the pan. But don't burn yourself."

When Janet, limping, had been helped to a chair beside the kitchen table, Merle used the carving set to return the pork roast to the pan and got the pan on top of the stove. Grandma Turney busied herself with paper towels, sopping up the pool of hot grease from the floor in front of the oven.

"Everyone back to the table!" Diana commanded, taking the roll of towels from her mother and using it as a baton to steer Kelly out of the kitchen. "The crisis is over. Merle, stay here and carve the roast. The rest of you, out!"

Janet made no protest as Alan led her back to her place at the dining room table.

"What *happened* in there?" he wanted to know. "You fell down getting the roast out of the oven? Or what?"

"Or what," Janet replied. "Would you get me my drink, Alan? I left it on the TV."

"I don't know if that's such a good idea, Janet," Diana said from the doorway to the kitchen. "*Maybe* you've had enough already."

"Thanks, *Officer.* Maybe I'm old enough to decide that for myself."

"Hey, it wasn't me who fell on my butt just now. I don't know *how* you did it."

"Get off my back!"

"Girls, girls," Grandma Turney scolded.

Janet leaned over toward Alan and whispered something in his ear.

"Would you excuse us a moment, Mrs. Turney?" Alan said. "Janet and I have something we need to discuss."

When Janet and Alan went out to the front porch, just Mrs. Turney and Kelly were left at the table. "Good Lord," said Mrs. Turney. And then, "I think I need a cigarette. Would you get my purse, dear? It's on the coffee table in the living room."

But it wasn't, so Kelly had to think where else it could be, and the likeliest place was in Alan's car. But that meant going out the front door, and that was where Alan and her mother had gone to discuss what they couldn't talk about at the table. Her mother was crying.

Alan said, "Hey, hey, it must have been upsetting, but you *know* that's not what you *saw.* I was in the kitchen, I saw Merle get the roast back into the pan. It was just a pork roast. Maybe a little burned."

"I know that," Janet said.

"You're upset," said Alan. "That's understandable."

"Why is that Merle here? Who *is* he?"

"Hey, maybe the best thing is for you to go upstairs and rest. You can say you hurt yourself."

"I *did* hurt myself!"

"So it wouldn't even be a lie. The rest of us will have the dinner—except I'm not having any of that damned pork roast—and then if Merle doesn't get the message, I'll ask him to drive Mrs. Turney home."

"Would you?" said Janet.

And then Kelly saw them kissing, and at the same time Janet saw Kelly.

"What are you looking at!" Janet shouted at her, pulling away from Alan.

There is nothing quite so unfair as being blamed for knowing something about someone that they don't want you to know. Kelly was more upset by the way her mother shouted at her than by having seen her and Alan kiss. Hadn't they slept in the same bed at the Arrowsmith Motor Court? She knew that when grown-ups slept in the same bed they were kissing each other all the time. She hadn't *seen* them do it, but she wasn't stupid.

"I'm sorry," said Kelly, hoping that would do the job. Then, "Grandma sent me to get her cigarettes."

"Dinner's ready!" Diana called out from the dining room.

Janet plunked down on the big chair that was losing its stuffing and had been moved out to the porch. She folded her arms over her chest. "Make up any kind of excuse you want," she told Alan. "I'm not going back in there. The whole place stinks of that roast. It makes me sick."

"Okay," said Alan, taking Kelly by the hand, and tugged. "Back to the table, Kelly."

"But Grandma said—"

"She can do without her cigarettes for five minutes."

So they went back to the dining room and took their places at the table. Every plate had a big slice of the pork with a glob of mashed potatoes beside it and thick brown gravy over the whole thing and a slice of black, burned-up onion for decoration.

"So where's the Homecoming Queen?" Diana asked.

"She's not feeling very well," said Alan. "She asked to be excused."

"She said the smell of the pork roast makes her sick," Kelly volunteered, knowing she shouldn't but unable to resist passing along the snub. "It makes me sick, too."

"So, suddenly we're all vegetarians here, are we?" Diana said, with a significant glance at Alan's plate.

"Now, Diana," said Mrs. Turney, "it wasn't all that long ago you wouldn't touch so much as a bite of potato salad if there was any bacon in it."

"Hey, if people aren't hungry, they don't have to eat. Right?" Merle sliced into his slab of pork, sloshed it around in gravy, and held it up for the table's admiration. "Me, I'm famished."

Everyone watched as though he were performing a trick as he started chewing on the pork. It seemed to take an unusual amount of chewing. "Mm," he commented, nodding his head. "Mm."

Then, with no warning, he vomited into his heirloom dinner plate.

Kelly was the first to burst into laughter, then Alan and Mrs. Turney, and finally even Merle joined in, partly to be a good sport and partly because the thing had tipped over the edge from awful to ridiculous. Only Diana, scowling at the gray gruel of vomitus spread like a second gravy over Merle's pork, did not join in the general, dismayed merriment.

47

The sweet odor of the burnt sacrifices had penetrated even to the space between the windowpanes inhabited by the little *Erigones* spider that had been Reverend Martin Johnson, who believed with his diminished but still tenacious faith that these sacrifices were made on his behalf. His hunger was aroused to the degree that he left the stillness of his retreat, skittering up the rope within the window sash to stand in a beam of sunlight. The heat excited his silk gland, and his spinnerets began to extrude a long thread that floated in the faint updraft by the air conditioner. "Oh," he thought, "he's near! He's near! He's mine again! Come closer, my boy." It was as though he were a spider of the female sex, scenting a male presence, eager to kill. In fact, it was his son's proximity that Reverend Johnson sensed just behind the bedroom door. Alan entered the room, to plunk down heavily on the bed beside the woman who was (the spider noticed now) already in the room.

Alan and the woman talked in earnest, hushed tones, but Reverend Johnson took no interest in their conversation. Trembling with desire, he let himself be lifted by the thread of gossamer and sail through the room, unseen by the couple on the bed, a mote among a swarm of other motes and molecules of smoke, the incinerated remains of the savory sacrifice. He alit on Alan's shoulder, broke loose from the thread that had borne him there as an aviator sheds his parachute, and made his way quickly across the fabric of Alan's jacket and the collar of his shirt to lodge in the shadowy hollow of his ear, where Alan experienced his presence as a brief annoying tickle. But too late now and too deep inside his ear to be got at by the thrust of his little finger.

"What shall we do?" Janet's voice boomed as though in an echo chamber. "I can't *stay* here!"

"Why not?" Alan's voice resounded like the membrane of a drum, and the words, amplified in this way, made a kind of emotional sense to Reverend Johnson, a fear that agreeably mingled with the smoke of the burnt offering. "It's your house, isn't it? You could just tell her to leave."

"I'd rather leave myself. With you and Kelly. I don't know what it is, but I don't feel safe here."

"You're being irrational."

There was a knock on the bedroom door.

"Diana, would you *please* just leave me the hell alone?" Janet shouted at the door.

"It isn't Diana, darling. It's your mother, and I have to talk to Alan. I know he's in there."

"Can't it wait a moment, Mrs. Turney? Things are a little hairy right now."

"I don't think it can wait, Alan. It's the police again. Louise just called to say the police had phoned, asking for you. She told them she didn't know where you were. They wouldn't say what they wanted. But maybe it wouldn't be a good idea to go back to Navaho House right now. That's what Diana says."

"What does Diana have to do with it?" Janet fumed.

"Well, she was right there beside me when I talked with Louise. And she actually had an idea of what might be the best thing for you to do, Alan. Merle says you can stay at his place. He says the police might come round here looking for you, but they wouldn't think to connect you with him. Does that make sense?"

"Merle and I are not exactly good buddies, Mrs. Turney."

"Well, we find out who our friends are when we're in trouble. And I don't know what else to suggest. Unless you *want* to go to the police."

"What do you think, Janet?" Alan asked.

"The last thing I would do is go to the police," said Janet.

"Merle, then?" He was asking himself more than Janet.

"A friend in need is a friend indeed," said Mrs. Turney, still on the other side of the closed bedroom door.

Alan sighed his submission, and the eavesdropper inside his ear stridulated with instinctive eagerness, like the spider's bride as she feels the bridegroom's first tentative plucking at her web.

48

"Did you torture your pets when you were a kid?" Merle asked Diana as he watched her scrunched over in a half lotus trimming her toenails.

"I wouldn't say I tortured them," she answered. "Teased them perhaps."

"Did you tease them to where they'd bite and claw?"

She looked up with a grin. "Why? Is that what you think I'm doing? Taking my claws out?"

"That hadn't occurred to me. No, I was just wondering how some people are like the name of that movie, natural-born killers. I always figured, even when I was a kid, that someday, somehow, I'd kill people when I was older. The way some kids know they'll be dads and moms. And when one of these kids takes a machine gun to school and lets loose on his classmates, I always think: hey, there but for the grace of God."

Diana laughed. "You're one to talk about the grace of God!"

"I know," he said with a lazy smile, leaning back against the headboard and reaching for the lit cigarette in the ashtray on the nightstand. "But I've always been a big believer. In our situation, when you've actually got some connection to the power that's out there, you can't really help being a believer. The difference is, *we* have to figure out what to believe for ourselves. 'Cause the regular theories people get taught at Sunday schools and catechism classes, if you grow up Catholic like I did, don't hold water. The Indian stuff fits the facts better."

"You mean Native American," she corrected schoolmarmishly. "Not Hindu."

He afforded her pedantry a derisive snort, then reconsidered. "They got a handle on something, too, those Hindus. That tantric yoga, I read a couple books on that shit."

Diana finished with her toenails and folded up the clippers. She flipped her head back, as though to get her hair out of her eyes. She still had all the little habits that went with longer hair. "I guess there is a connection between sex and the power we've got, whatever you call it."

"How about witchcraft?"

"Witchcraft," she agreed. "If the connection weren't there, I suspect Alan would be hanging from a hook in the smokehouse with the rest of them. It was always such a temptation to zap him. I'm sure at some point I would have given in. I *tried* a couple times. 'Alan,' I told him, in this very bed, 'you are such a little *pig*.' And I'd tickle him, and stroke him, and say it again—in an affectionate way, really. Pigs can be darlings. I loved that movie *Babe*. And I had flashes when I could *see* him with his little snout. But the magic never was there. I realized finally it was because he was a virgin. It was the one crucial wire that wasn't connected."

"It'd work now," said Merle with a knowing smile.

Diana's eyes widened. "You mean that he and . . . ?"

"Your sister, yeah. I thought you knew. It seemed pretty obvious to me. I thought that's why you were so pissed off with her when they got here. You could smell it on him. And he had that little smile guys get when they've just lost their cherry."

She nodded. "Yes, I did notice that. But I'm just so used to the old Alan, it didn't occur to me. With Janet!" She shook her head ruefully.

"It's a pisser, ain't it? You do all the work, and she reaps the reward."

Diana forced a laugh, grateful for the balm of his sarcasm. She had every reason to be jealous. Alan was her husband, and Janet her younger sister. A classic betrayal in both directions. "Where is he now?" she asked.

"Oh, he's safe as money in the bank," Merle answered. "He's down in my root cellar. On this big workbench with bolts in it, and him chained to the bolts. He can thrash around with his legs, but it won't do him any good. Or bang his head."

"Was there a struggle? You never said anything but 'Well, that's taken care of.'"

"Uh-huh. I was wondering when you'd ask. There was a *brief* struggle. But it was more like I sucker-punched him. He wasn't expecting to get attacked, not right after we went in the back door. I was behind him and had the bottle ready, and once he'd swallowed just a bit of it, he didn't have much fight left."

"You've done that to other visitors?" she asked.

He nodded. "A couple times. Your boy was the easiest. The other times they were more cautious, I had to be sneakier. But it's always fun. More fun than duck hunting, that's for sure. You can freeze your ass off waiting for something to happen in a duck blind."

"I've never been duck hunting, but I've done more ice fishing than I care to remember."

"Yeah, you're more the big-game type, I guess." He leaned forward in the bed until he was able to cup his hand round the back of her neck and pull her closer. She got up on her knees accommodatingly and gave him a questioning look. But he wasn't after sex just yet. He only wanted to talk about killing. That was his foreplay.

"You know that lady in Canada, in the book you was reading about all the different women on Death Row?"

"Mm," she said. "I think I know the one you mean. Karla Homolka—who drugged her sister, and then she and her husband together raped her and tortured her to death. But that was another book, not the one about Death Row. They don't have capital punishment in Canada. They're too civilized."

"Well, we might consider doing the same stuff with *your* sister."

Diana shook her head. "No way, Merle. And you wouldn't get off on it either, any more than you did with that girl you buried under that rock of yours."

"Yeah, yeah," Merle agreed. "Just daydreaming." He considered the smoke curling up from his cigarette for a while. Then: "Hey, speaking of capital punishment: you know that song? 'Whatcha gonna do when they come for you?' When they come for *us*, we should head for the border."

"Except that we don't have the death penalty here in Minnesota either."

"But did you ever think about that? What you'll do when your number's up and the cops are closing in?"

"Oh, yes. I'll say I was sexually abused. It's quite true, you know. My father abused me all the time."

"You say that so *sincerely*. But you can't bullshit me, sweetheart. You're forgetting: I'm your evil twin."

"Well, that's what Karla Homolka said, and she was able to plea-bargain a minimal sentence. She'll be released in just a few more years."

"You going to tell them *I* corrupted you?"

"Who else can I blame? It worked for her. I'll say you compelled me. I was the helpless victim of your insatiable lust. But this is all so hypothetical. We haven't even *done* anything yet."

"Well, we've abducted your husband, and your sister's conked out in the next room."

"She asked for a sedative, I gave her one."

"So, what I want to know is: what *are* we going to do with them? Will it be quick? Or slow? You want to repeat what you did with your brother-in-law and those other pigs?"

"I don't think I could, not with Alan anyhow. You know how if you strike a match two, three times, after that it just won't ever light?

Alan may not be a virgin anymore, but it's like he's been vaccinated. Do *you* have any bright ideas?"

He nodded. "Uh-huh. You know that guy they're looking for in Serbia or whatever the fuck they call that area now? The guy with the unpronounceable name?"

"The guy who ran the concentration camps there?"

"Yeah, that one. I'd like to do what he did."

"A pig farm I can handle, Merle. A concentration camp would be beyond our limited resources."

"I just mean I'd like to starve him to death. I think that could be really interesting. No physical torture. Just keep him chained in the basement like they did in the Middle Ages. For as long as it takes."

"That could be months. And I think eventually you'd start feeling sorry for him. Or I would."

"Well, if that happened, we could just finish him off quick, like at a vet's. Anyhow, that's my idea."

"Well, he's yours to do with as you like. Only at the end we have to make it look like a suicide. I want them to find the body."

"So you can be the grieving widow—and inherit. Right. What about your sister and her kid?"

"Oh, I wouldn't want to harm Kelly. Would you?"

"Not especially. Maybe if she were like two years old and really whiny. I've wanted to swat kids that age. But it's not like I've got this urge to put as many notches in my gun as I can. No one's keeping score. Killing people should be a pastime, not a job."

Their eyes met, and there was a further brief discussion conducted only by glances. It didn't take any deep intuition to know what he wanted as he lay there with a hard-on. A nod from him, and she got started. With Merle sex was always as quick and straightforward as a Big Mac. No need for preliminaries, no pretense at tenderness. But she did wonder, when he came, what he was thinking about. Was it Alan, or Janet, or even Kelly? It wouldn't have been herself, she was pretty sure of that. Usually you can tell if someone is thinking of you when you have sex with them.

49

Carl was not that old, in human years, but even so, when he'd last seen his human face reflected in a mirror, he'd been aware that he'd grown thicker and coarser. He was prematurely middle-aged, just like Janet. Not that either of them had been any great prize to begin with. By thirty-four, the boy who'd played right wing on his high school hockey team, the Gordie Howe of north-central Minnesota, had just about disappeared, like the kids on milk cartons. Yet there were moments, even during his recent battle of the bulge, when the two faces had merged, the old face of back when and the older face of here and now.

And so it was again: he would lower his snout to drink from the water of the bog and see, in the dark water, a flicker of his human face. There was no joy to be had in such moments, no glimmer of some redemption up ahead, for he had no hope of becoming human again. He was like those poor sods who get sent to the joint for life without parole and know they'll rot there. It would be easier to be just an animal, as he had been in the sty. Or like the deer he would encounter in the woods and swamplands, with no other thoughts than the endless, anxious quest for the next bite to eat.

That, of course, was Carl's quest, too. What could he eat, where would he find it? The deer, at least, had some clue to these questions. Carl had none. Most of the grasses and weeds he rooted up and chewed and swallowed served only as emetics. He stumbled through the woods and boglands, leaving a spoor of vomit and watery, ocherous shit. The only thing that seemed to offer real nourishment was the roots of the water lilies that grew at the edge of the swampland, but to get at them he had to risk being swallowed alive in the mire, and now the one area where they grew in any abundance had been exhausted and he had had to forage farther afield. Perhaps if he'd known more about edible weeds and mushrooms and such stuff, he might have fared better, or perhaps not. The North Woods were not a natural habitat for wild boars. He would probably meet the same fate as the prisoners who'd made it out of New Ravensburg back before it was escape-proof. They'd been able to hide in the woods, but not to survive there, and they were eventually recaptured once they resurfaced in civilization, breaking into someone's pantry or a convenience store.

Carl had come close to making the same classic mistake when he'd returned to the farmhouse where he'd lived as a man and been penned as a pig. The door to the sty had been left open, and a plastic pail had been set beside it filled with prime leavings from the dinner table. He had been strongly tempted, until he got close enough to see what was on the menu and realized it was the charred remains of his recent companions at the trough. Not that he had any compunction on that score, for he was very hungry, but it reminded him of the larger situation. He was sure that this offering was a kind of bait and that there must be a hook inside. The food might be drugged or poisoned, and sure enough, when he refused the bait, Merle appeared out of nowhere and took aim at Carl with a shotgun. Carl's own shotgun, he figured at a later, calmer moment. He took three pellets in the butt and counted himself lucky.

The neighboring farms were careful with their garbage from a concern for raccoons and other scavengers, so Carl had no other recourse or resource than what nature and the highway provided. He found himself in competition with the crows for roadkill and kept his eye on the skies above County Road B, especially where it curved around the tip of Turtle Lake. The crows dining on wheel-burgers would scatter as a car approached and could be seen circling above their interrupted dinner. Once Carl lucked into a freshly killed yearling and was able to drag it into a ditch beside the road and eat till his gut was full. The crows were furious. Briefly he enjoyed the once familiar pleasure of a decisive social superiority, which he'd known as a C.O. "Eat shit!" he would have jeered at them—if pigs could talk.

No one is ever lost in the woods, for they follow, like water, the course of least resistance, traversing the paths made smooth for them by the deer and other denizens of the wilderness. Those paths may not lead where they would like to go, of course. They will lead to some deeper, safer solitude, where fear may hide itself and they can risk sleep where peril is least. So it was that Carl often found himself by the rock that served as Bonnie Poupillier's unmarked grave, having followed the tight northwestward meander of the trail first blazed by the unquiet spirit of Wes Kellog. Wes sniffed for evil; the deer followed where he led, and Carl did now as well, until he had reached that rock within its crescent of solid ground, moated round with bog. It was close by that he'd discovered the stand of water lilies whose roots had sustained him in the worst days of his long hunger. They were gone, but the rock itself, with its shadowing ledge, offered its own cool comfort. He would wriggle in under the ledge, where the soil was cool and moist, and rest with a sense of sanctuary, and there quietly long for oblivion. Not death, for he feared death as every animal must. He craved, like every other derelict, the peace that mimics death. A satiety that blots out the need to be ever on the move. An evening coolness and dimming of the light. A brief reprieve from the prison of daily life.

Imagine, then, his dismay when he came to that sanctuary and saw Merle on top of that rock he'd thought his own, secure refuge, the man who'd twice tried to kill him. Carl froze, knowing he could be seen, fearing he would be heard if he tried to run away. Merle had only to turn his head.

But Merle had other matters on his mind, and a pint bottle of whiskey in his hand. Perhaps he was drunk. Carl shared the local opinion concerning the Indians on the rez, all of them drunkards who couldn't handle their booze like a white man. Whiskey was their fatal weakness, the reason so many wound up in New Ravensburg or at the bottom of Leech Lake.

Slowly Carl moved back into the obscuring undergrowth of the woods. Merle had not heard him. He lifted the bottle once, and then a second time, draining it, and then lowered himself so that he lay supine on the rock, gazing up at the midafternoon sky, streaked with motionless wisps of cirrus.

High up, no more than a fleck in the blue, a crow appeared. It neared, spiraling down toward the rock and Merle, to alight on the highest limb of a nearby spruce. For a while it gazed at Merle, then, of a sudden, cawed and flapped its wings spasmodically.

The crow flew away, but Merle still lay atop the rock, motionless, and somehow Carl knew that Merle was not there, that he had left his body to become the crow. The human Carl would never have supposed such a thing, but being under an enchantment himself, he could sense magic when it was in the air.

He approached the rock. Merle did not stir.

He made a snuffling sound, to which there was no response, and when he raised himself, bracing his forelegs against the rock, and snorted as loudly as he could, Merle still lay there, inert, entranced— and wholly vulnerable.

But out of reach.

Carl circled the rock, looking for some natural terrace of steps by which he could mount it. But there was none. On its south side, opposite the declivity in which he took his naps, he could scramble up to within inches of Merle's right hand, five little sausages pulsing with blood.

Mere inches.

Merle was safe from even the hungriest pig, but Carl was more than a pig. A human spark remained—enough to allow him to pause and consider what must be done.

He began to build a platform. From the deadwood that lay all about he dragged the likeliest branches and piled them, one on another, beside that part of the rock nearest the hand he sought to make his own. The branches would snap beneath his weight, but he would bring more branches and add them to the heap, and finally, by the simple, patient piling up of one layer on the next, he was able at last to catch Merle's pinky in his teeth and then to tug the limp hand to where he could chomp down securely and pull Merle's unresisting body off the rock.

He dealt with his hand first, because it was already in his mouth, and because its small bones yielded to his jaws with such satisfying *resistance.* He chewed the hand to shreds before he paused—not for thought, but from pure satiety and satisfaction. In his famished state the blood was an elixir, altogether apart from the satisfaction of knowing it was Merle's blood.

How, now, to dispatch him? He was inclined, at first, to do for Merle what had been done for him. But Merle's private parts were sheathed in Levi's, and Carl had, in any case, a squeamish feeling about attacking Merle's cock and balls with the only weapon he possessed.

He went for the neck. It took three lunges and much shaking about before he finally was able to rip open the main vein. The dark blood spurted in a steadily diminishing rhythm into Carl's face.

He blinked, and licked his snout, and would have laughed, if pigs could laugh, and then he simply gorged.

50

Merle, meanwhile, aloft in the borrowed body of a crow, had no notion that he was, in effect, dead. Like an investor ruined in the bankruptcy of an S & L of which he is as yet unaware, he flew his private jet with his usual sense of sheer, soaring glory. Up, up, and through the blue ether, fueled by that glory but also, today, by a sense of sheer unmotivated evil, a devilishness that beat even the best drunken rage hollow. Because he was more or less sober the whole time and able to savor his cruelties as he piled them on.

The idea had finally sunk in to Alan's brain that Merle was his executioner and really did mean to kill him by slow degrees, that there was no exit from the basement where he lived, starving to death, amid a steady babble of television idiocies. Merle varied the programming from the dumbest cartoons in the morning to the shopping channel all through the afternoon and porn tapes after dinner, when Merle would often watch the performance with his victim. When Alan ventured to cuss him out or to beg for mercy or, in his fuzzy-headed, desperate way, to *reason* with him, Merle would let him go on for a while and then zap him with the cattle prod he kept handy for the purpose. But Merle didn't punish him when he just blubbered quietly. He figured that was probably beyond the kid's control at this point. Anyway, after almost a week with just a ration of water and other cocktails of Merle's devising, his energy was on the wane for any kind of vocal display. Sometimes just to spice things up Merle would give him a little pick-me-up of crystal meth. Then he'd get him talking, asking all about him and Diana and her sister. The kid thought Merle was jealous and tried to reassure him that it was all over between him and Diana, that they'd never had sex, that she was Merle's now, Alan had no claim, et cetera and so on till the meth wore off and he realized that Merle was just making him jump through hoops and it would dawn on the kid that the essential situation hadn't changed: he was roadkill.

Merle had never seen or heard a skylark, but he knew about them, how they rose up in the air, singing their guts out. And that was how he felt now, a skylark, except that instead of singing he cawed, and when he did, other crows took heed and headed in his direction. He was the leader of the pack.

He speeded up, as though he were on his bike. They followed. He cawed, and they answered in a raucous chorus. And soon, ahead, there was the tower of the prison, and there were other crows already assembled there, swirling about like black Ping-Pong balls in some ultimate lottery drawing.

He did not consider why there would be a great convocation assembled before he'd led his own smaller throng there, for he was not, now, in a considering frame of mind. He was far from his dying body now; his human blood was draining into the dirt about the rock. But he was alert enough to notice that an ambulance had drawn up on the lawn near to the sweat lodge that had been erected on the prison grounds. The crows were whirling in a great gyre centered on the sweat lodge, outside of which Merle could see, with a crow's keen vision, the familiar figure of the man he'd visited here twice before. Jim Cottonwood was stretched out on the sere grass beside the lodge, surrounded by several prison guards.

Dead? he wondered. Was that why he'd felt such a powerful impulse to take to the air just now, so that he could be here for the fucker's death?

But almost as though in answer to that thought, he heard a caw among the other cawings of crows about him, and he knew Jim Cottonwood was not dead. The body that was even now being carried into the ambulance was like his own (as he supposed) on the rock, unoccupied, and Jim Cottonwood was part of the commotion around him. He had escaped the prison. How, Merle didn't know, but he had heard his voice.

He tried to rise, but he could not find an updraft. His wings seemed leaden, as though he'd tried to press too heavy a weight too many times. The ambulance was leaving the prison grounds, and the crows were dispersing, not as a single flock but randomly.

Merle alighted on a telephone wire and tried to take stock. He was not thinking clearly. He wanted to be with Diana. He needed her strength. But to do that he must return to his own body.

Wearily he lifted off and winged his way homeward. It seemed a long journey. He was not the leader of the pack now. No one followed where he led. Several times he had to interrupt his flight from sheer weariness.

But when he arrived, there was already a flock assembled. When he saw them, when he saw himself, his crow nature asserted its primacy, and his last act, as the Merle who'd been but had ceased to be, was to join the crows assembled at their feast and to dine on his own corpse.

51

Vegetarians who blame the bad behavior of the meat-eating majority on their diet are being simplistic. Hitler, after all, was a vegetarian. Squeamishness in prospect of a rare T-bone is no more a virtue than a tendency to constipation. However, in some ways the old saw is true that diet is destiny and we are what we eat, especially in the spiritual realm. There, indeed, every molecule is encoded with its own arcane significance, so that the process of digestion is a kind of alchemy, transmuting the roots of turnips into the tissues of our lungs, the insect residues in our breakfast food into big biceps and rippling abs—and the blood of quick-witted, wicked Merle Two Moons into duller, porcine neurons and dendrites in the brain of Carl Kellog. Without an ongoing supply of Merle-ness in his bloodstream Carl would have been his usual metamorphic self, but while he could still taste Merle's blood Carl was a much brighter pig.

When, in his widening search for something to eat, Carl had first come upon Merle's cabin, set well back from the main road, he hadn't thought whose place it might be. He'd noted only that the lid was off the garbage can, which contained only some beer cans and glass bottles. Now, with his mind quickened, he remembered the motorcycle on the dirt drive beside the cabin. He remembered, as well, the roar of the revving engine that he'd heard occasionally in his last days in the sty when Merle had appeared on the scene. This cabin was near the rock where he'd found Merle and murdered him. It seemed to compute that the place might have been Merle's. If so, it belonged to no one now, and any food that might be found inside was up for grabs.

He found his way back to the cabin with no difficulty. Merle had virtually blazed a trail through the woods. And there was the motorcycle, its kickstand braced against a steel plate planted in the dirt. Carl knocked the bike over on its side for spite, as a vengeful cat might piss on a piece of furniture, but he wasted no more effort vandalizing the machine. Its owner would never get the message.

The door to the cabin was closed, but Carl doubted it would be locked. He didn't bother trying to manipulate the doorknob with his snout. He simply rammed into it, linebacker-style, and the latch popped at his first assault.

He found himself in a typical backwoods bachelor pad: a single open space with separate areas for sleeping, watching TV, cooking, and eating. Spartan but a cut above plain trash. He'd known C.O.'s who lived worse. The bed, for instance, had been made; the linoleum on the floor was reasonably clean; the tabletop wasn't littered with a week's food scraps and empty beer cans. Merle seemed to look after himself pretty well, so Carl was hopeful as to what the refrigerator might contain.

He was able to get the door open easily enough by propping himself against the side of the refrigerator and clamping his teeth about the handle. One backward jerk and the door swung open.

Even from the perspective of a human thief the pickings would have been slim. Two six-packs of Bud on the lowest shelf, some bottled condiments, a tub of margarine. But nothing in the way of fresh fruits or veggies, no leftover takeout, no bakery or deli treats. No cheese. No cartons of milk or cream. Merle was clearly more redneck than yuppie. His home was not his own private 7-Eleven.

Of course there was still the freezer compartment, but that was at the top of the refrigerator, its handle tantalizingly out of reach. Carl looked about the room for something that would serve as a stepladder to extend the reach of his snout by the few extra inches he needed. The two chairs by the kitchen table seemed too rickety, the recliner facing the TV too bulky and hard to maneuver. But over beyond the potbellied stove was just what he needed, a big old army surplus footlocker. And just to make it easier to handle, it was sitting on top of a rag rug. Carl sank his teeth into the fringed end of the rug and started tugging it and the footlocker toward the refrigerator. His progress was inchmeal, but hunger is a great motivator, and his brain was revving now at an almost human rpm. Maybe he could find work as the first pig furniture mover.

And then he froze. For he could hear a voice, faint but not that far away. "Hello," at first, and then another, "Hello, is someone up there?"

Carl peered at the door and then, stupidly, at the raftered ceiling, festooned with dusty cobwebs. Why "up there"? Because (it dawned on him) this shack had a basement. In fact, the footlocker on its rug had been covering the trapdoor that was its entrance.

"Please! I'm down here. I need help. Please . . ."

It was a man's voice, and somehow familiar. But very weak. Carl decided it posed no danger, and returned to the task of opening the freezer compartment. He had to reposition the footlocker back from the refrigerator so that he could prop his forefeet on the upper inside shelf, and then, with a quick tug, he had the freezer open—and here was a whole trailer-trash Thanksgiving dinner. Pizzas. A half-gallon of Hershey's maple walnut ice cream. Two Hungry Man meatloaf dinners. What looked like a whole lot of sunfish in a big plastic Baggie. Something wrapped up in aluminum foil, and something else in a plastic tub. He took hold of the shelf with his teeth and pulled it loose. The pizzas and ice cream and four ice cube trays avalanched to the floor. Carl cleared out the rest of the freezer's contents with two swipes of his snout and then, not very gracefully, dismounted from the footlocker. Mission accomplished.

Then the voice started in again. "Please, I know you're up there. I can hear you. I need help. I'm . . ." The voice fell silent, and when he tried to start again, it was like turning the ignition key on a battery that's gone dead. "I'm . . . please . . ."

Carl recognized the voice. It was the kid who'd worked as Diana's gofer, who'd slopped the pigs in the sty—and sat down outside the fence and talked to Carl. He couldn't remember what he'd talked about, but he'd been friendly in his way, as friendly as anyone is ever going to be to a pig.

Somehow that kid was trapped down in Merle's cellar and begging for help.

Even as a pig Carl had a conscience, not to mention curiosity. The spoils of the freezer were scattered all about the floor of the cabin. But they wouldn't go away. In fact, all that stuff would be tastier if it thawed a while.

He would do the right thing.

The trapdoor to the cellar posed a much bigger problem than the refrigerator had. It had to be lifted *up*, and it was not easy to get a purchase on the brass handle with his teeth. Again and again it slipped loose after he'd succeeded in raising it an inch or two, but at last he was able to slip his foot into the crack before the thing slammed down again. It hurt like a motherfucker, but with the proverbial foot in the door he got the thing tilted back against the wall.

Except for the light that spilled down the stairs, the cellar was dark, but Carl, without even having to puzzle it out, looked where a light switch should be, on the wall of the stairwell, and sure enough there it was. He nuzzled the switch, and the cellar was filled with light. And his mind felt the same way, electrified. The refrain came back to him from the storybook he'd read so often to Kelly: I think I can, I think I can.

He took the stairs too eagerly and too fast, and halfway down, one of the rotted steps broke beneath his weight and he tumbled the rest of the way down with a squeal of pain.

The boy who'd been his jailer—and it was him, Carl had not mistaken the voice—lay atop a crude platform of pine planks on the cellar's dirt floor, directly beneath the bare bulb hanging from the ceiling. His wrists and ankles were fastened to the planks with chains, and his face, turned sideways toward Carl, was a sorry sight, sores and scabs and a two-week scruff of beard.

"Who is it?" he asked in a hoarse whisper.

He'd heard Carl tumble down the steps. He'd heard him squeal. And he was looking right at him. So why did he ask, in a tone of bleak surrender, "It's you, isn't it, Merle?" Was he blind? Carl's eyesight as a pig was not what it had been, and he had to come quite close before he saw the gauze mat of spiderwebs that covered the boy's face. Not just his eyes, though they were thickest there, but in his nostrils and all about his ears and through the stubble of his hair and beard. Carl was not squeamish by nature, and his life as a pig had rid him of any qualms he may have had as a human. Even so, he was dismayed. He couldn't think what Merle had been up to, but his first unconsidered impulse was to clean away the gruesome mummy wrappings that Reverend Johnson had so patiently been weaving across Alan's face.

Alan quailed at the first swipe of the pig's rough, wet tongue, and then he had the good sense to close his eyes tight as Carl continued his crude cleansing. With each lick he would wipe off as much of each clotted mass of cobwebs as he could, using the boy's shirt or his own hoof, afterwards, as a napkin. Really, it was no worse than chewing tobacco, though as with tobacco you had to be careful not to swallow. But pigs don't have a human facility for spitting, and once or twice he did swallow, and the last such swallow, after he'd licked away the tangle over Alan's ear, represented the final extinction of Reverend Martin Johnson, who entered Carl's stomach to mingle his own meager juices with the blood of Merle Two Moons and the various enzymes of Carl's digestive tract. The spider knew a brief flash of terror as it died—such as the reverend had often described to his parishioners in depicting the fate of sinners who fall into the hands of a vengeful God—and then, as its tissues dissolved, it entered its own spidery eternity, where its first terror blossomed endlessly into larger and brighter terrors, beyond the imagining of any spider, or any Lutheran minister, for that matter.

At the moment Reverend Johnson entered his own private Hades, Alan opened his eyes and saw what his situation was at that moment. He felt no terror, only a profound astonishment.

"Hamlet," he marveled feebly.

Carl tried to smile, but he lacked the muscles that would have made such reassurance possible. He did manage to nod his head up and down, as though to say, "Yes, it's me, and I'm here to set you free."

"Hamlet," Alan said again. "God damn. This is so . . . Merle said you were . . . That Diana had . . ."

Carl lowered his head, admitting what Merle had said and Diana had done.

"But I thought he was crazy. And he is. Crazy . . . and dangerous. And he's going to be back here any moment."

Carl shook his head, slowly and decisively: No, Merle would not be back.

"He won't?" Alan asked, believing and not believing. "You can understand what I'm saying?"

Carl nodded, and Alan, with a little more thought, began to laugh. Very weakly, and for only a short while.

He accepted the situation. His life had been an education in doing just that, and being chained down and starved had been the finishing school.

"I'm hungry," he told the pig. "That Merle wanted to kill me."

Carl nodded. He understood that very well.

He mounted the stairs slowly, trying to place his weight away from the center of each step. The step he'd broken on the way down presented a challenge, but he was careful. Up in the cabin he took a survey of the scattered contents of the freezer, and item by item, by nudges and kicks, he got it all across the room to the edge of the steps. The ice cream, as being the likeliest first course, he carried down with his teeth clamped about the cardboard box.

He'd always loved maple walnut.

Feeding the boy was not that easy. Carl had no hands, and the boy's arms were chained to the wooden platform. Carl managed to spread open the ice cream carton by tooth and hoof, and he positioned it so that Alan could lick up the softening ice cream as though it were a big cone. But pressure had to be exerted so it stayed in place where Alan could get at it. Alan was ravenous, and Carl feared he would strangle from the sheer joy of feeding. But though he did, once or twice, start to choke, ice cream, in its nature, is easy to get down. The carton was emptied in a few minutes, and Carl allowed himself the luxury of licking up the residues left on the carton.

"Thank you," said Alan afterward. "That was wonderful."

Carl acknowledged this with a curt nod. He was already thinking ahead to the next course. The sunfish? That would have been his own choice, after they'd thawed a bit. The mystery leftovers? No, probably a pizza. It would thaw the quickest and be easiest to chew.

But before he could devise a pizza-delivery system, the phone rang. Carl had become so human in his thinking that his first impulse was relief. The burden of care would be off his shoulders: help was on the way. Then he realized that he couldn't answer a telephone, and even if he could, he wasn't sure it would be a wise thing to do. Anyone calling Merle Two Moons might be a similar demented scumbag. In fact, it might be Diana.

He looked to Alan for advice. Alan was also paralyzed, but his eyes were fixed on the phone, which was in what must be Merle's corner of the basement, beside the one comfy chair, the VCR, and an old Magnavox TV.

Carl was an inveterate believer in his own good luck. He went to the phone and nudged the receiver from its cradle.

"Hello?" said the one voice he had longed most to hear again. Carl stared in mute reverence at the receiver where it lay on the dirt floor.

"Hello? Is somebody there?"

Carl remained silent. Any sound he might have made would only have frightened Kelly, who sounded frightened enough already. He looked up, promptingly, at Alan.

"Hello," Alan said as loudly as he could.

"Hello! Alan, is that you? I almost can't hear you."

Carl pulled the receiver by its spiraling cord closer to where Alan lay chained.

"Who is it?" Alan asked. "I can't hear. It's not Diana, is it? She calls here all the time. She knows what Merle is doing."

"Hello? Please, Alan, Mommy's in trouble. There's something wrong with her. She never comes out of her room. It's locked. Alan? You got to help us. Please."

"Help!" Alan called out, as loudly as he could.

There was a scream at the other end of the line, and then a banging sound, and then it was Diana on the line: "Merle, is that you? I've been trying to get in touch for days. Get up to your room, young lady! Merle, I know you're there. Don't start playing games with me. We've got trouble. Merle?"

"Help!" Alan called out again before Carl could pull the phone cord from the wall socket.

Alan, his face still smeared with the ice cream, began to cry—and Carl would have too, if pigs could cry. They were fucked now. Diana was probably already on her way here. And what could he do? As much as he hated her, Carl wasn't sure she didn't still have her weird power over him. He remembered how docilely he'd entered the sty when she'd told him to.

He gave a few well-meaning tugs at the chain securing Alan's ankles, but he knew from prior experience in the sty that his teeth would give before the chain did. It was bolted in solid.

He wished there was more he could do for Alan, but he was more concerned now for his daughter. And for Janet. Alan would have to look out for himself.

Before he headed back up the stairs, Carl managed to position one of the thawing pizzas where Alan could get his teeth into it. Even while he went on crying, Alan started to chew. Carl wished he could say good-bye. He wanted to be able to *explain* his betrayal—that he had no choice, that he was no match for Diana.

52

Insofar as he had had a plan, his plan had worked. He was out of New Ravensburg. The human body of Jim Cottonwood was lying comatose in the back of an ambulance, heading for the hospital in which it would await his spirit's return, a puzzle for the doctors. His crow body was winging its way above the reedy southern shore of Leech Lake, well beyond the perimeter that had limited his earlier flights above the prison to the aerial equivalent of the rooftop jogging track. Below him was the real world in all its lovely grunginess: Ki-Wa-Wa-Yun-Wa Christian Youth Camp, Don's Bait Shop and Gaseteria, Bailey's Tourist Cabins (with color TV in every room), Lakeshore Canoe Rentals, and a huge billboard pointing to the turnoff for the Wabasha Wonderland Casino—every bit of it brand-new to Jim and a source of wonder. It was as though all Leech Lake had been transformed into Florida during the time he'd been locked away, every ditch and bog offering its own little enticement for the tourists driving by.

How he would have liked to be a citizen of that country, where all human pleasures seemed so possible. But equally he enjoyed flying over that country as a crow, unenticed, inhuman, free.

He could be a crow forever if he chose. Or for whatever part of forever a crow could look to. It was a temptation, but the human part of him knew that even a life locked up in the joint was a better deal than being any kind of animal. If you weren't bred to be slaughtered, then you were going to be hunted by something larger and faster. And the drum that beat out the rhythm of the whole endless dance marathon was hunger. He could feel it now at the core of this crow, like the purr of a car's engine, the sustaining hum of its hunger. Oh, it was great to be able to fly, but did crows know that? Jim could feel no elation like his own resonating from the crow's meager mind, nothing but the dumb one-two, one-two drumming of its heartbeat as it set the pace for its wings' unceasing effort.

He reached the point where the main road diverged from the lakeshore, and there, standing propped against the tailgate of his pickup and sending up smoke signals from his Swisher Sweet stogie, was Gordon Pillager. Jim banked and rode the air in a slow downward spiral until he landed atop a burlap feedbag in the bed of the pickup.

Gordon saluted him with a tight little smile that didn't disguise the fact that he was missing most of his teeth. "Yo, crow," said Gordon. "Like the man says on TV, I got good news and bad news." He paused for effect, and Jim tilted his head sideways to signal that he was listening.

"Good news is, you're a free man. That's why there was the long delay after they got the body in the ambulance. You are no longer a ward of the state, or whatever the fuck they call it. You been released. I got the feeling the paperwork was all done a while ago, maybe a couple weeks, but they just hadn't got round to telling you yet. No surprise there.

"Bad news is, the ambulance ain't heading for St. Cloud like we figured it would. You're not a prisoner now, so they can't send you to the locked ward there. So you're headed for somewhere in Duluth or close by, but even the ambulance driver didn't know where. First, a doc has got to figure out what's wrong, then they decide where you go. So, like you, it's all up in the air.

"I don't see you got any reason to panic. You can hop a ride with me inside the pickup and we could head to Duluth now. Or we can wait till we know where in Duluth to head to. They got to tell Louise soon as they know. She's going to have go along with the two of us anyhow, 'cause she's the one got visitation rights.

"So that's the situation. What I suggest, my friend, is just enjoy yourself. Ride the wind. But remember who you are. Don't get too caught up in being a crow. Each time you go to sleep inside that new skin it's a little harder the next day to remember you got another body to go back to. And don't mess with other crows. I mean, sex. I did that once. In my wolf years. Oh, that was fun, but I stayed too long at the party. And I almost didn't get home. Hang round outside Louise's place. I'll keep in touch with her. You do the same. Okay?"

Unthinkingly Jim responded with what he meant to be "Okay." A caw was as close as he got.

Jim took the news, both good and bad, calmly. It didn't really change anything, but it was good to touch base with Gordon. He'd been Jim's first guide in the Other World, as he called it, and the only genuine shaman Jim had ever known besides himself. Shamanism wasn't something you could sit down and learn. It was like music: you were born with it or you weren't, though if you were, there was a good chance that sooner or later you'd be spotted by someone else with the same gift, as Gordon had spotted Jim when he was sixteen and Gordon was already missing most of his teeth and a lot of his hair. All through the time Jim was in the lockup, Gordon had stayed in touch, and they'd worked out the escape plan years back, when Jim had begun to think New Ravensburg was going to be a lifetime residence. So this had been intended as his own private loophole, an exit visa to be used only in case of an emergency. A way to avoid the one thing Jim dreaded more than anything else, which was dying inside.

Better to leave the prison as a crow, and live a crow life as long as he could, than to die a prisoner. Gordon sympathized, and had agreed to do what he could in such a contingency. He had come to the prison parking lot on the day appointed for the sweat lodge, bringing his own convocation of five crows. The crows had circled the smoke that issued from the vent of the sweat lodge, and Jim, inside, had heard their calls. He went outside, signaling to the guards not to approach. Often those in the lodge had to take a breather. The guards stayed back, but one crow alit on the lintel of the lodge.

Jim had entered the crow, but even then he remained on the lintel, like Poe's raven on the pallid bust of Pallas (it was his favorite poem, he knew it by heart), for the whole time it took for the medics to be summoned and Jim's human body to be loaded into the ambulance and driven away. Even then he had not been sure that the old strictures that had limited his range of flight to the prison's own airspace would not still be in force.

But they were not. His human body was out of New Ravensburg, and his crow body enjoyed the same freedom.

He found the turnoff onto County Road B, not far from where Gordon had parked, and followed it, but at an altitude that let him whittle away some of the extra mileage between the prison and the Kellog farm, where he was headed. His mother had given him directions, but they were based on the signposts she used herself when she drove to visit him: an old barn with a sagging roof, a big fenced-off acreage destined to be landfill, a stretch of Highway Department spruces as regular as wallpaper, and then, at last, the turn left onto a gravel road. According to his mother's directions he was just about there.

The sky, though cloudless, seemed to grow darker. Without meaning to, he lost altitude and felt his wings wearying. He'd never flown this far, for such a length of time, and so the fatigue might have been just a fact of crow physiology.

But then the farm itself came into view, just the shingles of the roof, and he knew that the darkness, which was thicker now, had its source not in some trick of the atmosphere but in the presence, ahead of him, of some firmly rooted evil. It was as clear and unmistakable as a bad fart.

The smell of his enemy.

53

Diana had never been good at fixing things when they broke. Replace the little black rubber thingy inside a leaky faucet? As well ask her to install an automobile transmission.

Now it was the same with her magic, only there are no repairmen to call when magic goes awry. She'd talked about the matter some with Merle, but he had no inside information, no grimoire or secret formulas. His magic was all impulse and intuition. Like a laboratory rat who'd learned to run a maze, he did what had worked for him before. Put him in another maze, and he was lost. In any case, Merle wasn't picking up his phone. Diana was on her own.

The problem was Janet.

Even before Janet's parole, Diana had intended to do for her sister what she'd already done for Carl. There was no way the two of them could have lived together. Janet was a control freak. She wanted everything done her way. It had become impossible to discipline Kelly. Janet wanted the keys to Carl's Chevy, even though, while she was on parole, her license was invalid. She complained about Diana's cooking. She'd told Diana to stop using the smokehouse, though Diana had held her ground on that, insisting that all the meat was not yet properly cured and would spoil if she let the fire go out. Basically, Janet wanted her sister off the premises, and if she hadn't been on parole, she would probably just have pulled rank and told Diana to pack her bags.

So there had not been much choice. Diana had acted in the manner already proven effective. She had doctored Janet's liquor supply with her own essence of mandragora, and on an opportune occasion, when Janet was soused and in a foul temper, she had let rip. "You're a pig, Janet, do you know that?"

She'd seen Janet wince, and go red in the face, and swell within her dowdy housedress.

"Fuck *you*!" Janet responded.

Diana just ignored her. "A pig!" she repeated emphatically, "A sow!"

There were hooves now in Janet's slippers, but her face remained Janet's—familiar, hateful, jowly, dense.

"*You're* the pig," Janet had said in a level voice, even as she tottered forward, still unaware of her transformation, still with her human head planted ridiculously on her pig body. "Worse than a pig. A snake in the grass. I've always known it. I should never have agreed to let you come here. Get out now! Do you hear that?"

Diana had known then a moment of fear, or trepidation, or indecision, for she had bolted from the room, slamming the door behind her. Only then had she thought to secure her curse by a third, conclusive repetition: "A pig!"

The words had been followed by a howl from the other side of the door. Janet must have finally realized, then, the change that had come over her, for there were sobs and a single wordless squeal of rage and other noises. But among those noises, there were noises no pig could have made, and Diana knew, even before she opened the door again, that the magic had not taken. Not quite.

Janet had been chastened. She had wedged her thick body between the window and the bed, hiding her still human head, from shame, beneath the bedframe, like a guilty child. Diana could not see her face, but she had heard her say, "Go away." From that she assumed that the magic had not had its full effect. She'd turned her sister into one of those impossible monstrosities you read about in

Greek myths or see in the freak show at a county fair. Janet, the Pig Woman.

After taking thought, Diana returned with the key that she'd told Janet had been lost. Not that she feared Janet might try to leave the room, but she did not want Kelly going in.

But this, she knew, was a temporary solution, if only because it required Janet's quiet compliance. Shame, sheer horror, and a modest ration of white wine in a plastic bucket just inside the bedroom door could be counted on to keep Janet from open rebellion for a while.

But what *was* Diana to do if Janet became fractious, as she surely would? She could not simply go into her sister's room and kill her. Such dirty business was what men were for. The mechanics, the plumbers and electricians. The butchers, if it came to that. Merle had dealt expeditiously with *that* problem when it had come time to slaughter the growing population of pigs in the sty. But Merle had not been answering his phone. He had assured her, such times as *he* chose to call, that Alan was a goner, that he was almost gone, that the end was nigh. And she had enjoyed going back to her anxious, booze-sodden sister and assuring her that Alan was just fine but didn't want to talk with her just yet. It had seemed no more than a refined form of torture.

Had Merle been lying? Did he have some agenda of his own? Undoubtedly he did, but Diana had thought of him as dependably malign. What could be in it for Merle to keep Alan alive? Once he'd squeezed some juice from him, the risk of having him about would outweigh the little juice still to be had.

But what if Merle had gone off on his damned motorcycle and just left Alan to die on his own? What if, what if—there was nothing but what-if's so long as Merle kept avoiding her.

And meanwhile there was a different kind of problem, with Kelly.

Kelly was Diana's anchor to whatever was human in her own nature. Kelly was still, though difficult at times, a child, and Diana had appointed herself the child's mother. What else is a teacher, a *substitute* teacher at that, but, in the legal phrase, a loco parentis? Diana had a responsibility toward the girl: she must be spared the trauma of seeing that her mother had become some gruesome approximation of a pig.

The thought of a summer camp had occurred to Diana, that old standby for dealing with children who should not be witness to the behavior of the adults about them. But her first inquiries in that direction had been discouraging: she lacked the legal authority to have the girl shipped off. The bureaucracy of summer camp enrollment had become almost as complicated as that of the regular school system. In any case, it was better to be able to keep her eye on the girl.

Happily, Janet, after her first dismay, was not raising a ruckus. Kelly, however, was resistant to the idea that her mother didn't want to see her, but when Janet (at Diana's strong urging) assured her daughter, through the locked door, that she must be patient, Kelly remained docile.

Or so Diana had believed. Now it appeared that Janet and Kelly had been hatching their own little plot. She had known that the two would sometimes confer in whispers through the locked bedroom door, but this had seemed a harmless steam valve so long as Kelly did not misbehave.

Then, today, in the late afternoon, when Diana had gone upstairs to prepare Janet's evening bucket of cheap white wine, she'd heard Kelly's voice downstairs. *Who* could Kelly be talking to? If the phone had rung, Diana would have heard it. But if Kelly had dialed someone herself . . . ? Whom? Diana went quietly to the head of the stairs and strained to hear what Kelly was saying, and caught, "Hello! Alan, is that you? . . ."

It couldn't have been Alan, of course. Kelly must have called Navaho House; she knew that phone number well enough. But then, as Diana started down the stairs to put an end to the nuisance, she heard the girl say, "Please, Alan, Mommy's in trouble," and more to that effect.

Diana was incensed and did what she would not have thought herself capable of. She bolted down the stairs, ripped the receiver from Kelly's hands, and swatted her across the face. Kelly screamed and went tumbling backward in her chair.

"Merle, is that you?" Diana insisted. "I've been trying to get in touch for days."

Kelly, on her back in the overturned chair, began to bawl. Diana grabbed her by the arm and jerked her up to her feet. "Get up to your room, young lady!" Then, into the phone: "Merle, I know you're there. Don't start playing games with me. We've got trouble. Merle?"

The voice that responded wasn't Merle's. "Help!" was all he said, but that was enough. She knew Alan's voice.

"Alan?" she said, but the line had gone dead.

As she'd been doing for days with mounting exasperation, she pressed the redial button. As ever, the phone rang and went on ring-ing until Diana returned the receiver to its cradle. But her question had been answered. Kelly—probably at Janet's suggestion—had done what she'd just done herself, pressed redial.

And Alan, not Merle, had answered. And had called for help. Diana had not mistaken that nasal whine. And now no one was pick-ing up. But the fact that Alan had been able to speak to Kelly when she'd called was more than ominous.

Up till now she had avoided going to Merle's cabin to confront him about why he was avoiding her. Such prudence had become a luxury. She had to go there. But first she had to make sure that Kelly didn't make any more mischief.

Kelly had not gone to her room, as she'd been told. She wasn't anywhere upstairs, or in the house. Diana went out the back door and called aloud, "Kelly! Kelly, I have to talk to you." But if Kelly had taken fright (as she must have, after the wallop Diana had given her), then she must have hidden somewhere, and she had all out-doors to hide in. The girl was almost six and much more devious in the game of hide-and-seek than she'd been when Diana had first come to the farm last winter. There wasn't time to spare looking for her.

What Diana did instead was disconnect the phone, so Kelly could not use it again. She dumped it in the front passenger seat of Carl's Chevy, which she'd been driving lately for economy's sake.

Then she returned to the house to make sure Janet's door was locked. When Janet heard her twist the handle, she said, "Is that you, Diana? Is something wrong?"

"No, dear, everything is *fine*," she assured Janet in her most teacherly voice.

"I thought I heard . . ."

"Kelly and I had a little argument. But it's all over. I have to leave the house for a bit. But I'll be right back. If you talk to Kelly, tell her I've gone to get a pizza for our dinner. Okay?"

Janet said nothing.

"Okay!" Diana answered herself.

And thought: "I'm going to have to kill her after all." The thought distressed her, but what was more distressing was the thought she did not put into words—that she would have to kill Kelly, too.

Before she got the keys for the Chevy, it occurred to her that it would be wise to bring along the shotgun and a box of shells. She'd protested when Merle had insisted on teaching her how to load and fire. The recoil had almost dislocated her shoulder. Merle had smirked, but then he'd shown her a better way to hold the thing, and how to aim.

What a sorry state the world has come to when women have to learn how to use firearms!

54

"I'd like to see some ID," the state trooper told Diana once she'd rolled down the window on the Chevy.

"Of course," said Diana. After she'd made a pretense of looking at the seat beside her, where the shotgun and the box of shells and the telephone with its cord wrapped round it were all in plain sight, she said, "Oh. I must have left my purse at home."

"Uh-huh. How about the registration?"

"That's in here," she said brightly. When she opened the glove compartment, the pint bottle of Jack Daniel's spilled out, but the registration for the Chevy *was* in its little plastic envelope where it was supposed to be, thank heaven. She handed the registration to the trooper, who pretended to study it as he backed away from the door and took his gun from his holster.

"You're Carl Kellog?" he asked with a practiced neutrality.

"That is my brother-in-law. I use his car sometimes, and he uses mine."

"Step out of the vehicle, please."

What choice had she? She raised the lock, which she'd pressed down when the trooper had pulled her over.

"So," he asked, adjusting his classic mirror-shade sunglasses, "where's the fire?"

She took a deep breath. She could not afford to offend the man.

"Was I over the speed limit? I confess, I wasn't looking at the speedometer."

"Uh-huh." He nodded toward the passenger seat. "So tell me, what's that?"

"It's . . . my brother-in-law's gun."

"Yeah, I can see that. I mean, the bottle."

"Oh! Oh, it's not what you think. I *haven't* been drinking. That's a tisane."

"A what?"

"An herbal tea. I was bringing it to my mother. It's a stomach remedy."

"Yeah? I'll tell you, lady, *that's* one I haven't heard before."

Diana smiled an entirely beguiling smile. "I know what you must think. But open it. Smell it. Taste it, if you like. It's not alcohol."

"Right."

"Smell my breath if you like."

"No, thanks," he said, but he did reach into the car and retrieve the bottle. He screwed off the cap and sniffed and yes, yes, he sampled it! And puckered his lips with dismay.

"Was I lying?" she asked him, and now there *was* a taunt in her voice. Her back solidly against the wall, she could afford bravado.

"Put your hands on the side of the car, please."

She did not comply, but looked him in the eye, and said, "Do you know what you are? You are a pig."

She had made no threatening gesture, and he showed no alarm, only a mild amazement.

"A pig," she repeated, as a gambler at Vegas might have asked for a single card, hoping to fill an inside straight.

And then, though there was no alteration in his features and he remained only the state trooper who meant to arrest her, she said it again, a third time, with cool conviction. "A pig."

The shudder of metamorphosis passed through his body. He fell forward, his pistol dropping to the asphalt, his hooves scraping furrows in the Chevy's paint.

They're all pigs! she thought triumphantly. All of them!

And the magic still worked.

She had to help him out of the tangle of his uniform, then sicced him off into the woods along the road. "Run!" she shouted after him. "As fast as you can! And keep running!"

When he'd vanished into the undergrowth, she picked up the fallen pistol and tossed it into his patrol car. Then she took the keys from the ignition and flung them in the direction in which he'd disappeared.

It felt good to know that she still had the power of her magic. She was Woman. She was Invincible.

Even so, she kept her eye on the speedometer the rest of the way to Merle's cabin.

55

For a little while Carl had thought he was human again, that he'd done something animals can't do. In a choice between love and duty, he'd followed the path of duty. Instead of hightailing it home to help Kelly, he'd stayed in the vicinity of the cabin to see what he could do for Alan. Alan's case had seemed the more desperate, and Carl, by profession, helped those in the most desperate situation of all, prison. Was that looking at the thing too rosily? Was he flattering himself?

But even to be pondering such questions was *human*, and that was the great thing. Like the liberals were always saying, hey, my skin might look different than yours, but *inside* I'm just like you. If pigs could laugh, he would have had a good chuckle at that. At the fucking irony. And maybe that was the most human thing of all.

As with his pig namesake, Hamlet, all this soliloquizing was a way of spinning his wheels before the action started. Diana was definitely taking her time, and Carl, crouched down behind some teaberry bushes at the far edge of Merle's property, had begun to wonder if he dared venture back to the cabin, when he was astonished to see his own Chevy bouncing toward the cabin on the gravel road. He felt a flash of possessive rage: *she* was in *his* car!

But (he realized when she got out of the car) she also had his shotgun. Or *a* shotgun (for his distance vision was not very keen as a pig). So, with an enemy armed and decidedly dangerous, Carl bided his time behind the bushes.

A light came on in the cabin window (it was getting to be twilight), and then Diana appeared in the doorway with Alan beside her, his arm slung over her shoulders for support. Very slowly they made their way to the Chevy. Alan was groaning, but Diana seemed intent on helping him.

Carl waited until she had helped Alan into the passenger seat of the car, and then made a low grunt. It didn't seem to register, so Carl raised the decibel level. This time she looked up. She had heard him, and now he let her see him—but only his hindside, for he feared her power to command his actions if their eyes should meet.

In her most commanding tone she shouted, "Stop!"

He did *not* stop.

And then he did—but of his own volition. Waiting, baiting the trap with the target of his ass.

After a longish silence he risked looking back at the cabin. She had retrieved the shotgun, as he'd expected, but she was not yet very close.

He headed for the path that would lead to Merle's body. There was one blast from the shotgun, and he felt the sting of pellets in his hindparts, but pigs do have thick skin. He knew she would follow where he led her—and felt a whoosh of triumph when she came upon the body and screamed.

She had seen what he had done to Merle, and that was a great satisfaction.

But as so often, success made him careless. When, not long later, he'd heard the Chevy drive off, he decided that a little celebration was in order and returned to the cabin. He remembered the food he'd kicked into the basement. The Hungry Man dinners, the frozen sunfish, all of which would be thawed now. Plus whatever treats had been wrapped in the foil, or was melting in the plastic tub. Alan wouldn't need those provisions now, and Carl was hungry.

The light in the basement had been left on, and Carl was careful on the steps. But he'd broken one tread himself, and Diana's and Alan's combined weight had seriously weakened two others. Both broke under Carl's weight.

No way would he get up those stairs again.

But the sunfish were a meal to die for.

56

It is commonly believed, wrongly, that Eden was lost by the sexual transgression of Adam and Eve, that the apple they ate was a euphemism for sex. In fact, they had often had sex before they fell from grace, but like animals, they didn't remember what they'd done. After their fall and exile from Eden, they remembered everything and regretted everything, for once we are aware that there is an ethical dimension to the universe, evil becomes intrinsic to our existence. We live by eating other living things, and all our heirs are born to follow us (if not precede us) to death. That is the meaning of original sin.

Alan had thought a great deal about original sin and related matters while he'd been chained in Merle's basement and was starving. A slow death fosters theological meditation, and Merle himself, for his own reasons, had often engaged Alan in discussions on such subjects. He had wanted to bring Alan to a state of complete despair, and they had both been very candid, Alan from a hope that candor might soften Merle's heart, and Merle? Merle had a cat's simple curiosity. He'd quizzed Alan endlessly about his peculiar upbringing as the son of a Lutheran minister who had sired Alan on his own daughter. When, he wondered, had Alan begun to guess? How sincere, Merle asked, had been the religious beliefs of Reverend Johnson? Was he consumed by guilt or inured to it?

These were matters of interest to Alan as well (though a torment to the spider hidden in his ear), but the more he thought about it, the less he understood. The matter, for instance, of his virginity: how had that protected him from Diana's magic? He had grown up cocooned in evil, lied to and hated by both his parents. Yet he seemed to have preserved some essential innocence. Merle himself remarked on the oddity of this. Alan hypothesized, in a Lutheran way, that perhaps it was a gift of God's grace, which is always inexplicable and unearned. Merle allowed as how that made sense; his own gifts were of the same sort.

Finally, neither of them was much changed by all their theological talk. Merle remained merciless and Alan suffered, though never entirely despaired, for he'd always known that somehow things would work out for the best. This was his closest-kept secret and, as well, a real embarrassment, for another way to put it was that he'd been chosen by God or Destiny or whatever as an exception to the general rule that Shit Happens. He always had believed in the Psalm he'd had to memorize so long ago: Yea, though I walk through the valley of the shadow of death, I will fear no evil.

Even now, sitting beside Diana in the car, heading he didn't know where, he feared no evil. Diana was as evil as they come, he knew that now. And he'd long ago realized that being in love with her had been a big mistake. But even so he wasn't afraid of her, and rationally he should have been. Maybe he was having a sugar high from all that ice cream.

The road was zipping by on fast-forward. He'd asked at first if they were going to the police, but Diana had got a cagey look and started explaining why that would not be a good idea. There was nothing to be afraid of, she insisted, because Merle was dead, she'd seen his body, the nightmare was over.

"You're upset," she said, "I can understand that. Anyone would be. But that's all over. The important thing is, we're together again."

She put her hand on the dirty denim of his jeans and squeezed. It hurt. Almost anything did.

Then she pulled over to the side of the road. He could tell she'd finally made up her mind what to do.

"I forgot," she said. "I have just the thing you need."

She opened the glove compartment and took out a bottle of Jack Daniel's.

"It isn't what you suppose," she told him.

"I didn't suppose anything," he protested.

"Have a sip. You'll feel better."

"No, thank you."

"Do you think it's poison?" she asked with a weird cheerfulness. "Look!" She opened the bottle, tilted it to her lips, and took a small swallow. Then she handed it to him.

"No, thank you," he said again, and turned the bottle upside down. It glugged itself empty onto the floor of the Chevy. Then he rolled the window down to get rid of the smell and the bottle.

"Alan! Good Lord! What are you *thinking*?"

He was thinking that she wanted to kill him but didn't have the courage. But he didn't say so, because it wouldn't have been polite. She was his wife, after all.

57

Jim alit on a branch of an apple tree completely exhausted. And starving. Eating had not been a major focus of his life at New Ravensburg, and he didn't give much thought to the process. But he had always got his three squares a day, and this crow had not.

This crow needed some food—and something a lot more substantial than stunted August apples and whatever worms might be found in them. He fluttered down to the ground and scouted about, but the few insects he could discover were no more satisfying than cocktail peanuts when what you need is meatballs and spaghetti.

Or, in the present case, some ripe carrion. And he could smell just that, not far off. He didn't like to let his crow instincts take the driver's seat, but he was hungry, and he really couldn't help it. He lifted off the shaggy lawn beneath the apple tree and, gaining some altitude, headed where his crow nature took him.

It proved a fool's errand, for the savory smell issued from the flue of a smokehouse that was visible beyond a hill at rooftop height on the other side of the house. And that smokehouse, and its very smoke, was the source of the miasma of evil he'd sensed as he'd zeroed in on the farmhouse.

But visible from the same high vantage Jim spied a vegetarian alternative to the curing tissues he smelled. Beyond the same rise of ground that hid the smokehouse was a pigsty, and by the sty a corn-crib, and in the crib, much browsed already, cobs and cobs of corn. Unhusking the corn to get at the kernels required skills the crow had learned well. Jim let his crow nature have its way.

The crow had its way more than Jim had quite intended. For the next thing he was aware of, beyond the sheer bingeing satisfaction of scarfing down the corn, was a woman's shrill voice.

"Kelly! Kelly, you get in here! At once! Do you hear me?"

It was, Jim knew, his enemy's voice, and he made himself stop pecking at the corn.

"Kelly!" the voice insisted. "I want you *in* this house!"

Jim's talons let loose from the wire hexagons they'd been grasping, and he rose, on wings still weary, to where he could see her, standing by an old Chevy, radiant with anger.

But even so, or for that reason, an enticing presence. A fucking babe. Jim did not often have an opportunity, and then only in movies or magazines, to see women of her sort. Women who had made themselves objects of desire. Women to die for.

Unthinkingly he emitted a *caw!* and she looked up. But the crow she saw circling up from behind the hill did not enlist her attention.

A lucky thing for Jim, perhaps, for he realized, with closer attention (and crows do have wonderfully acute vision), that she was cradling a shotgun at her shoulder. Just the way to say hello to a crow.

She let out one final, defeated summons—"Kelly! God damn you!"—and even as she did, Jim knew that the shotgun was meant for Kelly.

Perhaps Kelly knew that, too, for there was no sign of her.

The woman got into the car and drove off, and not long after, Jim, perched on the chimney of the farmhouse, had his first sight of the girl who'd refused to respond to the woman's call.

Though he'd seen small children from time to time in the prison's visiting room, he still felt a shock at seeing a living child. That had been the cruelest deprivation of his imprisonment, to live in a world in which there were no children, and so, no future.

He fell in love, at once, and wholly, as a dog might do. Or perhaps it was just the calories that were finally moving from his gut into the rest of his system. Love, hope, or just energy: whatever, he had it back again, and he could think thoughts that weren't just crow hunger and crow fear.

From his perch on the chimney he watched the child, Kelly. She seemed to be in a state of indecision. She walked to where the house's driveway connected to the asphalt of the road connecting to County Road B, and then a little way along that.

But then she turned back to the house and, lifting her head toward Jim (though probably, he realized, toward an upstairs window), she called out three times, each time more loudly, "Mommy!"

When there was no response, she circled round the house and began to climb the very apple tree that Jim had first alighted on. After she'd cleared the lower branches, Jim could not see her through the obscuring foliage. Also, he realized, it was getting dark. How much time had he let slip by in his corncrib feeding frenzy? He rose from his perch on the chimney and took a wide flight about the tree that Kelly was mounting.

On his second gyre he caught sight of her, perched, birdlike, on a little platform of timber three quarters of the way up the tree. A tree house. She could not have built it herself, and Jim was amazed to think that a girl, and such a small girl, could have made her way to it. But now that she was there, she was probably safe, if only she had the good sense to remain where she was.

Jim set down soundlessly on a branch, barely more than a twig, scarcely six feet above her. She had wrapped herself in a blanket, as though she meant to go to sleep.

He could feel the fear radiating from her little body. Indeed, he could *see* it, as you can see, in early autumn, the moisture lifting in distinct feathery shapes from the surface of a lake.

Nothing could have been more pitiable, a child so vulnerable, so helpless, and so brave.

And yet he had to do it. For her own sake, but also to do what must be done: he violated her innocence.

When he knew she was at the edge of sleep and her eyes, with the onset of dreams, had begun to quiver beneath closed eyelids, he took possession.

She yielded utterly, as he'd known she must.

Innocence has no defense against the pure of heart.

The crow, released from its bondage, flew off toward the woods.

58

They reached Navaho House later than she would have liked, because she'd taken a detour around the lake so as to avoid the spot where the police car had pulled her over. Wise criminals *avoid* the scenes of their crimes. Her mother and three of the residents were on the front porch, all of them bundled in shawls or sweaters, though the temperature must still be somewhere in the upper seventies.

"I'm just going to have a word with Mother," she told Alan, placing her hand on the filthy denim of his jeans as a token of her tender concern. "Then I'll check to be sure we can go up the back stairs without causing a flutter among all those old hens. I won't be away more than a couple minutes. Okay?"

He offered not so much as a sideways glance. He'd been like that the whole time they were in the car. It was infuriating. It had also given her time to frame a course of action.

"Okay?" She squeezed his thigh for emphasis.

He winced, and produced a murmur that might have been "Okay."

She hesitated as she opened the car door, reluctant to leave him by himself for even a little while. But what could he do, after all? Since his earlier act of symbolic rebellion, throwing the bottle from the car, Alan had lost most of his zip, and there'd never been that much. She wondered whether she'd even be able to get him up the back stairway to the bathroom. Perhaps she could get him cleaned up in the kitchen. But Louise was always in the kitchen, and it was Louise's attention she most wanted to avoid.

Diana took the flagstone path to the front of the house and approached to within hailing distance of the women sitting on the porch. "Mother? It's me."

"I figured it was," said Mrs. Turney. Diana could see the burning tip of her mother's cigarette trace a slow arc in the darkness. "Is Janet feeling better?"

"Oh, yes. Alan finally showed up. She was worried something had happened to him. We all were."

"The Johnson boy?" asked one of the ladies. Mrs. Gerhardi, by the sound of her voice. "Is he all right?"

"More or less, yes. But he must have got into some kind of trouble. He's in the car now. I thought I'd bring him in the back way and help him get cleaned up. Is Louise around?"

"Not tonight."

"She's at the hospital!" Mrs. Gerhardi announced portentously. The hospital had a special significance for all the residents, for it was so often the first stop on the way to the funeral home.

"Is she all right?" Diana tried to sound properly concerned.

"*She's* all right. It's her son, Jim: there was some kind of accident at the prison, and an ambulance took him off to Duluth. So she had to go up there and left me here to finish making the dinner."

"*I* did most of the cooking," said Mrs. Gerhardi. "It was tuna casserole."

"And real good, too," chipped in another woman. "First rate."

"There was seconds for everyone who wanted seconds," added the third woman. "And hot gingerbread for dessert."

"Yeah, we had ourselves a binge, all right," Mrs. Turney said. "But we still haven't washed those dishes."

"I'll tell you what," said Diana. "You ladies stay here on the porch and enjoy the breeze. I'll do the dishes. After I've helped Alan up to his room."

Mrs. Gerhardi chuckled. "He needs help getting up the stairs, does he? I think I know what *his* problem is."

The three residents chuckled in concert, and then Mrs. Turney said, "Actually, it's getting a little chilly out here. Maybe we should just turn in."

"Nonsense," said Diana. "It's the middle of August. But how about I brew up a pot of Mom's special cocoa and bring it out to you here on the porch? That should warm you up."

"Oh, don't go to any trouble over us," said Mrs. Turney, in a tone of tacit agreement.

"No trouble at all," said Diana, feeling a surge of new energy, for her plan was working without a hitch.

She remembered fat Mrs. Collier, back in tenth-grade English, declaiming a speech by Lady Macbeth: "Be bloody, bold, and res-olute, and you'll not fail." Or was it "Screw your courage to the stick-ing point"? Either way, the moral of the story was that Lady Macbeth had understood the situation and taken charge, while her husband was wimping out.

"Alan," she said, tapping on the window of the car. "Everything's okay. We can go in the house and get you cleaned up."

Alan let her help him out of the car and be his prop as he dragged his feet across the unmown lawn toward the back door of Navaho House. Diana kept trying to get him to move faster, for she felt exposed until they were in the house. The moon was a damned spot-light.

And the fluorescent light in the kitchen was even worse. Before she'd left Merle's cabin she'd wiped off the worst crud from Alan's face with a wet towel, but that had only exposed thick constellations of scabs and open sores and swollen insect bites, which now, in the kitchen's glare, made him look like some kind of leper. A good thing Louise Cottonwood wasn't here to be a witness.

"I think we should go straight upstairs," she told him.

But that was easier said than done. He had little strength left in his legs, and even with the weight he'd lost, he was too heavy for Diana to carry. At last, by propping him against the handrail (a mandate for every nursing home in the state and an expense Mrs. Turney bitterly resented) and lifting his legs from one tread to the next, she got him to the top of the stairs. But she almost despaired of getting him into the tub until she simply let him tumble backward into it.

She was relieved to see, once she'd managed to tug his clothes off, that Merle had inflicted no serious damage to his body beyond that done by the insects. She turned on the hot water, which at Navaho House was never more than lukewarm, and then went down to the kitchen to start the cocoa.

The ladies (she checked) were still on the porch, reminiscing about the tragic death of Mrs. Witz earlier that summer. Diana lingered with them only long enough to confer with her mother as to where in the pantry to look for the secret ingredients of her special cocoa. It was just where Diana remembered, at the back of the top shelf, in a jar masquerading as Shop 'n' Save marjoram. Does anyone *ever* use marjoram?

Mrs. Turney had long ago come to an understanding with Dr. Karbenkian that a ready supply of barbiturates was an absolute necessity for the operation of an adult residence such as Navaho House. No home remedy was more efficacious, and these particular pills had the special benefit of being undetectable to all but the most sensitive palate, especially when dissolved in hot cocoa. The slight aftertaste of cinnamon simply registered as that special touch. None of the residents had ever suspected. Anytime there had been a flutter in the hen coop, Mrs. Turney had brewed a pot of her special cocoa, and the flutter stilled.

While the kettle on the stove came to a boil, Diana went back up to the bathroom, where she found that Alan had had the presence of mind to turn off the water before it posed a threat of flooding to the bathroom floor.

She sat on the edge of the tub and spoke, in a soothing way, of how relieved she was, and how happy, to have found him basically safe and sound. How horrified she was at Merle's behavior. How lucky they were to still have each other.

Alan's response was no more than a nod, but he seemed content to soak in the tub indefinitely.

Back then to the ladies with the pot of cocoa, three empty mugs, and, for her mother, a fourth already full. "This one," she confided in a whisper, "isn't decaf." Mrs. Turney puckered her lips about her cigarette to show that she'd taken Diana's meaning: *her* cocoa hadn't been doctored.

The four of them chatted awhile, in a desultory way, and then one of the ladies yawned, and Diana yawned herself, and Mrs. Turney suggested that they all turn in. The ladies went up to their rooms with no further persuasion.

"Mother," said Diana when they were alone in the TV room, "before you go to bed, we have to talk."

"Sure. Just let me get my cigarettes."

While Mrs. Turney went out to the porch, Diana poured the last of the cocoa in the pot into her mother's mug. One for the road, so to speak.

"What's up? Did you and Alan get into a scrap?" Mrs. Turney asked, trailing cigarette smoke.

"No, no, nothing like that. It's Janet. I think she's pregnant."

Mrs. Turney thought about this for two deep inhales. "She can't be," she declared at last. "She hasn't been back from Mankato long enough. Besides, she looked *thinner* when I was there for that pork dinner of yours."

"Well, it may be it's just what she thinks. Anyway she won't come out of her room."

"Yeah, Kelly told me that on the phone. So why would she *think* she's pregnant if she's not?"

"Alan."

"I thought you were married to Alan," said Mrs. Turney, slurping down the last of the cocoa and then taking a ferocious drag on her cigarette.

"Maybe that's why he disappeared right after that dinner. He couldn't go on living with both of us in the same house."

"Well, it's your problem," said Mrs. Turney after some thought. She lit another cigarette from the one she was smoking and then set both of them down in the heaping ashtray on the end table beside her chair. "And her problem, and Alan's, too, I guess." She sighed. "I'm tired, Diana. This has been a hard day all round."

"Go up to bed then, Mom. I'll straighten away things down here. But don't go into the bathroom. Alan's still up there in the tub."

When she'd heard her mother trudge to the top of the stairs, Diana went to where she knew her mother kept her secret store of Christian Brothers brandy. She sloshed some on the shag carpet beside the chair her mother had been sitting in, and then some more on the chair's threadbare armrest.

Now?

No. First she checked to see that Alan was still in the tub. He was, and, even without benefit of the cocoa, snoozing.

Her mother (she checked) was already conked out in her bed, still dressed, except for her shoes.

Then Diana dealt with windows and doors. The bathroom window shut, its door open; the same in her mother's room. Fumes were the most important consideration. People usually didn't burn to death in these situations, they were asphyxiated.

She went through the rest of the house, making strategic adjustments and feeling a transcendental assurance that she was acting as an angel of mercy. All these women, even her mother, had simply been living in heaven's waiting room.

At the last minute she remembered the alarm system and went about the house removing the batteries from the smoke detectors. Their absence would only register as one more of Mrs. Turney's little economies.

When she was done, she looked up the back stairway, wondering if she should do a last inspection of Alan, slumped in the tub. But what would have been the point?

Their love had been, on the whole, an enriching experience. But it was over now.

Be bloody, bold, and resolute, she reminded herself.

The time had come.

But *both* the cigarettes her mother had left smoking in the ashtray had gone out, so it was not, finally, that easy. She had to light both cigarettes again. A vile taste, and a vile habit, but she squared her shoulders and did it.

She waited until both the shag rug and the fabric of the chair had caught fire, and then she sprinkled some more brandy at strategic points. The flames were knee-high when she left the room.

She couldn't stay longer. Someone might see the fire and report it.

"Good-bye, Alan," she called out from the bottom of the stairs. "I really do love you. So much! I can't tell you."

59

The tree house in which Kelly lay asleep, more profoundly asleep than ever before in her life, had been built in 1972 by her mother and two of her school friends, Sharon Ohr and Patti-Ann Witz. Janet never told anyone about it—especially not Diana. Janet was eight then, Diana fourteen, and already too heavy and too dignified to be climbing trees. Kelly had discovered it herself just last spring when she'd climbed far enough up the lower limbs of the tree to be able to see the two pieces of scrap plywood that formed the tree house's floor. Robins sometimes inherit their parents' nest in the same way, unaware of whose it had been or how it was built, just eager to get busy putting it back in shape.

As Kelly slept, Jim Cottonwood learned to work the strings that moved his little puppet. It was a more delicate task than commanding the actions of a crow. At first, as when waking after an accident, he only wiggled the fingers of one hand. Then he became more venturesome. He lifted both her arms to salute the rising moon where it was visible, intermittently, through the leaves above. The little girl's sleep was undisturbed. Indeed, it deepened, and she began to dream.

Jim's own state resembled dreaming in its way. He could see what was about him clearly, and move through that space confidently, but he could not be too purposeful, or the strings of the puppet might be snapped. He had to move about as one drives a familiar car along familiar roads.

The girl climbed down from the tree house deftly, for her feet knew each limb of the descent, her hands had memorized the way. When she reached the base of the tree, she knew at once where she was, for there before her, gleaming in the moonlight, was the witch's cottage she'd seen so often in the storybook that Aunty Di had given her on her fifth birthday, with its gingerbread siding and its frosted roof with icicles of white icing dripping from the eaves. The illustrator, Mary Clellan Hogarth, had won the Caldecott Medal for her version of *Hansel and Gretel*, and it was undeniably creepy. Several school libraries had removed the book from their shelves when parents complained that it had given their children nightmares, but this enhanced rather than impaired the book's commercial success. Now, in her dream, as Jim rode her body about like a bicycle, Kelly moved through the dark woods and candle-lit corridors of Mary Clellan Hogarth's imagination, a jungle gym of Jungian archetypes, an echo chamber of Sadean whispers. (It was not generally known that Hogarth, under the pseudonym Sylvan Plath, had brought out a pricey limited edition, much abridged, of de Sade's *Justine* and *Juliette*.) For anyone who ever looked at Hogarth's version of the tale, no other *Hansel and Gretel* would ever exist.

Jim's actions were as little of his own volition as Kelly's, for as Diana systematically went about Navaho House preparing its torching, Jim did the same, matching her actions with his own. As Diana was sprinkling the brandy on the carpet of the TV room, Jim doused the weathered siding and the wooden door of the smokehouse with the fire starter that was kept by the brick barbecue. (Kelly's fingers had known just where to reach, and knew where to find the Bic beside it.)

As Diana went about Navaho House opening and closing doors and windows, as one might adjust the vents of a woodstove, Jim poured what was left of the gasoline for the mower over the inner walls of the smokehouse.

The place reeked of the cured flesh of the slaughtered pigs, still hanging on hooks. Within the witch's kitchen there was a similar stench as the witch heated up the oven in preparation for roasting Hansel. Kelly loathed the smell, but like Gretel in the storybook, she made herself ignore it—and was not awakened from her dream.

And then, as Diana left Navaho House and began to drive back to the farm, Kelly and Jim waited, huddled behind the far side of the smokehouse, whose door stood ajar, letting out the reek of the meat to mask the scent of gasoline. In Kelly's dream, the witch, with her silvery hair and her spiky fingernails, fussed about in her shadowy kitchen, which was partly the kitchen of Navaho House and partly the one that Mary Clellan Hogarth had drawn.

In the far corner of the kitchen Hansel was dimly visible, in the cage in which he was being fattened, the shadow of a child, any child, all children. This was the picture that was so often missing from library copies of the book, the work sometimes of distressed parents, sometimes of mesmerized children, sometimes of dealers in rare prints.

And then, at last, there was the rattle of the Chevy as it approached the farmhouse, and the slam of the car door.

"Kelly!" Diana called out. "Are you still out here? It's *time* to come in the house."

"I'm here!" Jim replied. Not that loudly, but Kelly's voice carried through the night air, and Diana heard.

"Kelly! Into the house! Right now!"

"I can't!" her voice insisted, as Gretel had insisted that she could not put her head into the oven.

"You *can't*? Don't be ridiculous? Where *are* you?"

But her voice was nearer. She must have reached the top of the hill from which the smokehouse could be seen.

"I'm in here," Jim replied. "I can't get out."

"You can't get out?" Diana repeated with chill sarcasm. She was standing just outside the door of the smokehouse.

"*Why* is this door open? I've told you a hundred times, the door has to stay shut for the meat to cure."

Jim was silent, and in her dream Kelly acted quickly. When the witch had put her own head in the oven to show how it was done, Kelly gave her a quick shove from behind.

Jim was ready. The bent nail that was used in place of a padlock to keep the door shut slipped back in place. Within, Diana let out a cry of pain and protest.

Jim took up the Bic and held it at arm's length next to a small pile of gas-soaked kindling at the base of the smokehouse. Impossible to say which of them, Jim or Kelly, thumbed the lighter to life. The kindling caught at once, and Jim backed away as blue flames circled the base of the smokehouse.

Within her pyre, Diana was not alone.

Wes was with her again as she'd seen him last, hanging upside down, blood streaming across his face. They faced each other almost eye to eye, for she'd fallen to her knees as she entered.

"Please," she begged him. "Help me!"

When he only grinned in reply, she pushed herself to her feet, dislodging one of the curing hams. The flames were within the smokehouse now, licking at her clothes, singeing the silvery hair. She battered at the door, but it did not give way.

"None of us ever wants to die," Wes said calmly. The flames had no effect on him. "But this time I will save you. If you do what I say."

"Please!" she implored him as her clothes began to burn and her skin to blacken.

"Hug me," he told her.

Diana threw her arms about her father, and he wrapped her in his own, and with just a small tug of assistance she slid from her burning skin and entered a new life.

60

After a dutiful hourlong sit at the bedside of her son, Louise Cotton-wood realized that Gordon had been right and she'd been wrong. The trip to Duluth had been a waste of time. Jim did not seem about to return to his senses anytime soon. He lay there in the hospital bed like a corpse set out for display at Good Shepherd. It was sad, but it was also aggravating to hear Gordon Pillager saying he'd told her so.

"He's going to be okay, I promise you," Gordon went on when they were back in his pickup. "Right now he's still doing his shaman thing. But he knows where to head for when that's done. We just got to sit tight till he gets in touch."

"And I just have to wait till a crow comes and perches on the windowsill?"

"Believe it," he assured her.

In fact, she did believe it, though she was not about to give Gordon Pillager the satisfaction of saying so.

"He *looks* okay," said Gordon, taking a pack of his dreadful stogies from the inside pocket of his suitcoat.

"He looks dead," said Louise, "and I wish you wouldn't smoke one of those things in here. I live with a woman who never stops smoking, and the one good thing about this trip is not having to breathe her smoke."

"Right," said Gordon, and tucked the pack back in his pocket. "Hey, I got an idea. How about my treating you to a restaurant dinner? That could be the second good thing. You ever been to Red Lobster?"

"There is a houseful of women waiting for me to put them in their beds."

Gordon just ignored that. He knew that Louise had told her boss she might be gone the whole night. "You ever eaten lobster?"

"Never!" Louise declared virtuously.

She had, however, had a mad fling with Gordon Pillager thirty years ago when he'd had all his hair and most of his teeth and was the best-looking man on the rez. And that's what this invitation was all about, and probably the reason he'd driven her to Duluth after telling her it would be a wild-goose chase.

"I'm not saying let's stop at a motel," said Gordon, reading her mind. "I'm saying this is a good chance to find out about lobster. I don't know about you, but myself, I'm hungry."

"Oh, well," she agreed.

It was obvious that Gordon had been planning this all along, since he was wearing his suit, and at the hospital he'd behaved like what he was officially supposed to be, which was Jim's Spiritual Advisor. Anyhow, Louise never had had lobster, and she was curious to know what the fuss was about.

When they'd been led to their own private table in the biggest restaurant Louise had ever been in, Gordon excused himself and headed for the bathroom so he could put in his teeth. While he was gone, the waiter, a blond college boy who reminded her a lot of Alan, though not quite as heavy, brought a little basket to the table and explained that inside the napkin there was garlic bread.

Louise had made garlic bread herself, at the insistence of Mrs. Gerhardi. Mrs. Gerhardi was a nice lady, but she often complained about Louise's cooking. Even when Louise had made her the garlic bread there was no big thank you. Now Louise understood why. This wasn't regular bread. It didn't come in slices, and the restaurant used real butter, and maybe something besides ordinary garlic powder. It was unbelievably delicious.

When Gordon got back to the table, Louise apologized for eating all the garlic bread in the basket.

"You liked it, huh?" he said with a real grin. With his teeth in he looked almost the way he had thirty years ago.

She nodded, and looked down at the litter of crumbs on the tablecloth.

Gordon signaled for the waiter and ordered another basket of garlic bread and the lobster special for both of them, and to top it off, a whole bottle of white white, which the waiter brought to them lickety-split in a silver bucket that stood beside the table on its own pedestal like a flowerpot. It was like Sodom and Gomorrah.

Louise protested that she didn't drink wine.

"But *I* do," he'd bragged.

When it came, she wouldn't take a sip—at first. But Gordon guzzled it with such satisfaction, and the garlic bread had made her thirsty. So against her own principles she sampled the few tablespoons the waiter had poured into her fancy glass, and when he brought the lobster, he filled the empty glass all the way to the brim.

Gordon showed her how you had to break the shell of the lobster apart with a giant nutcracker. And then!

The first taste reminded Louise of trout that had gone off.

The second taste was like the garlic bread.

Each bite after that tasted like something else again, until she understood: this was lobster, and it was like nothing else, and no wonder people made a fuss.

At some point in the drive back to Navaho House, Louise realized that she must be drunk, because it was as though no time had gone by. She was still in love with Gordon Pillager. He was a good man, and there weren't that many. He was *still* a good man. Kind and generous, and if he didn't have much to say, neither did she.

"You're crying," he said as he hung a right on the main turnoff into town.

"No, I'm not."

"Jim will be all right," he assured her in his usual mumble. He'd taken his teeth out as soon as they left the restaurant and stuck them in the pocket of his suitcoat.

"I suppose he will," she agreed.

And then they came to Navaho House.

It was on fire. There were flames coming from the window of what, in a quick reckoning, she realized was Alan's room. She was out of the pickup almost before it had come to a stop, and headed straight for the ladies she could see on the front lawn.

"Have you called the fire department?" she yelled.

None of them could say they had, so she figured no one had done so. Maybe one of the neighbors might have, or, this late, maybe not. So she looked for Gordon, who was there beside her, and told him to phone for the fire department on the little phone he had in his pickup, or else to wake up the next-door neighbor, Mrs. Kusick, and use her phone.

When he'd gone off, Louise went into the house herself. It was full of smoke, but she crouched low and headed for the back staircase. The smoke was thicker in that direction, but that was the way to Mrs. Turney's room, and Mrs. Turney had not been among the ladies on the front lawn. There were flames in the TV room, but Louise got round them and up the stairs, holding her breath.

The door to the bathroom was open, and as she glanced in, she saw Alan Johnson, stark naked and coughing, on the floor beside the tub. She hauled him to his feet and, with a sideways glance at his equipment (which was nothing like Gordon's but better than John Cottonwood's, her only standards of comparison), she got him to wrap himself in towels that she'd flung into the half-full tub. He seemed as feeble as any of the old ladies, so she helped him down the stairs and pointed him to the back door.

When she tried to get up the stairs again, it was no longer possible. If Mrs. Turney was up there, it was too late.

But there was still the main staircase at the front of the house, and Louise was sure that she hadn't seen Mrs. Gerhardi among the ladies on the lawn. She was Louise's favorite among all the residents despite the way she bitched about her cooking. She'd been right about the garlic bread; maybe she'd been right about other things.

With her head wrapped in a towel doused in water from the kitchen sink, Louise got up the staircase (why wasn't the damned sprinkler system working?), and sure enough, there in her bedroom was Mrs. Gerhardi, conked out in bed. The door had been closed (until Louise opened it) and the window open, which had kept her from asphyxiation but had also let her go on sleeping.

Louise managed to get Mrs. Gerhardi out of bed and out of the room and down the hall to the head of the stairs, but then her luck ran out. Was it the fact that the fire had spread to the front of the house? Was it Mrs. Gerhardi's bad back and bum right ankle? Was it the wine at dinner? Whatever it was, they didn't make it down the stairs. Mrs. Gerhardi took a stumble at the head of the stairs, Louise tried to grab hold, and they went down together, Mrs. Gerhardi on top.

Mrs. Gerhardi had lost almost a hundred pounds since she'd come to Navaho House and had to get by on Louise's cooking, but she was still a large woman.

61

When the district attorney finally had talked to everyone concerned and sorted through the physical evidence, he decided, not without some misgivings, that there was no need for anyone to be arrested.

This is what he figured had happened:

Diana Turney and Merle Two Moons had begun to have an affair shortly after she'd moved into the Kellog farmhouse. She had also been having an affair with her brother-in-law, Carl (though he denied this, as one might expect). In any case, Merle, whether out of jealousy or acting in collusion with Diana, had abducted Carl and held him captive in the cellar of his shack in the woods, where he'd been discovered the day after the fires, and where there was evidence of his long suffering.

There was also the medical evidence: Carl had been castrated. This fact was withheld from the media, from a sense that he should not be subjected to more needless humiliation.

Diana Turney had seduced the Johnson boy months ago. Her motive had obviously been mercenary, for they had been married by a justice of the peace up in Brainerd without any hoopla, but just days after the wedding the lady had paid for a two-year-term joint-life with a hefty payoff.

At about the same time, the boy's grandfather, Martin Johnson, had committed suicide. That the man was almost certainly Alan's father did not concern the D.A.'s office, though the newspapers and TV couldn't leave that side of it alone. The reverend's disgrace may have speeded up the probate of the will in which he left his entire estate to Jim Cottonwood, the prisoner who'd served so many years because of Judy Johnson's perjury. Louise Cottonwood, shortly before her death, had sent Johnson's will to Bruce McGrath, her son's attorney, with a note explaining how she'd come to have it in her possession. Apparently Diana Turney had planted it among Alan's effects in Navaho House with the intention of making it seem

(a) that Alan had found and secreted the will to cheat Jim Cottonwood of his surprising bequest, and (b) that Alan might have been responsible for his mother's death.

Who *had* killed Judy Johnson, and why? From the violence done to her body, the district attorney supposed it had been Merle Two Moons, and that Merle was, in fact, a serial killer. For, under the big rock near which Merle's body had been found, the skeletal remains of Bonnie Poupillier were also discovered. Merle's guilt in this instance could only be supposition, for the body had decayed beyond the possibility of a meaningful autopsy. Bonnie's next of kin was duly informed, but Louis Poupillier was not in a position to do much about it, for he was serving time in the New Ravensburg prison on charges of manslaughter. He'd got drunk one night and shot his common-law wife. The district attorney had always supposed that Louis Poupillier might also have been responsible for his daughter's disappearance and presumed death, and who knows, perhaps he was. It did not seem worth pursuing. One way or another Poupillier was going to die in prison, and Merle Two Moons was already dead, sparing the county the expense of what would have been a very nasty trial.

How Merle had met his end was another puzzle, but the district attorney was certain that Diana Turney had been responsible for that public benefaction. Among her possible motives the most likely was a wish to be rid of an accomplice who might, if discovered, implicate her in Carl's and (perhaps) Judy Johnson's deaths.

And in how many others the district attorney did not want to speculate. For in the smokehouse in which she'd died, there were traces of *other* incinerated remains, which the forensic examiners had tentatively identified as human. Any more exact identification would have been impossible, and so this gruesome possibility was also withheld from the media. Merle was known to have assisted Diana in the slaughter of a number of pigs that had been raised in a sty on the property, and it might well have been the bones of these pigs that were found in the charred rubble of the smokehouse. Or, as the coroner suggested, six of one and half a dozen of the other. Sometimes it's best to let sleeping dogs lie. The county did not need the publicity of having been home to a team of Jeffrey Dahmers.

That left only Diana's own misdeeds to be accounted for. It was she, certainly, who'd set fire to Navaho House, in which her own mother and Louise Cottonwood and one of the residents, a Mrs. Gerhardi, had perished. That the death toll was limited to those three was chiefly due to the heroic efforts of Louise Cottonwood. Diana had clearly intended for her husband, Alan Johnson, to be among the victims of the blaze. Indeed, in view of that insurance policy, his death had probably been her main object.

And she could have succeeded in her whole enterprise, inheriting her husband's properties and a share of her mother's estate, plus the insurance on Navaho House, not to mention money her mother had tucked away. Nearly a million dollars, all told.

That accounted for everything but the question of how Diana Turney herself had died. It was clear that after setting fire to Navaho House she had driven back to the Kellog farm, and very soon after that had died, trapped inside the burning smokehouse.

Diana Turney, surely, had not set the fire in which she'd been immolated. Nor had it been an accident. The old wooden siding had been doused with lighter fluid and gasoline. The empty containers had been found only a few yards from the smokehouse. And the door to the structure had been secured, from the outside, with a bent, rusty nail that had been serving in place of a padlock for years. It didn't require a Sherlock Holmes to deduce that she, who'd murdered so many others, had finally been murdered herself.

But who could have done it? There were many who might have wanted to, but the likeliest candidates were all accounted for. Carl had been discovered, unconscious and half-starved, in the cellar of Merle's cabin late the same night. Diana's husband, Alan Johnson, had been left to die in Navaho House and was in an ambulance on the way to the hospital in St. Cloud at the time the volunteer firemen arrived at the Kellog farm, responding to the smokehouse fire. Diana's sister, Janet, was discovered by those same firemen, locked in her own bedroom, in a state of stupor and confusion, and the key to the bedroom was later found in the pocket of Diana's jeans.

That left only the most unlikely suspect, six-year-old Kelly Kellog. It was Kelly who'd reported that the smokehouse was on fire, having walked half a mile to the Kellogs' nearest neighbor to use the phone. The Kellogs' own telephone was later discovered in her brother-in-law's car, which Diana had driven earlier to Merle's cabin (there were clear tracks) and to Navaho House and, having set the fire there, back again to the farm. The district attorney had initially assumed that Diana herself must have taken the phone from the house to prevent its use while she was away.

But suppose that Kelly had put it there? Suppose the girl had killed Diana. An absurdity, on the face of it, but who else was there? She had motive, opportunity, and means.

She was also a very strange little girl. When he'd first questioned her, after the crew of the fire truck had reported Diana's death and he'd driven out to the farm, Kelly had seemed almost weirdly calm. Trauma, you might think. But not so traumatized that she'd been unable to answer most of his questions. And her answers seemed too good to be true. Too pat, as though she'd been rehearsed before he got there by a canny defense attorney: she knew nothing of where her aunt had driven off to in the late afternoon, or how her mother had come to be locked inside her room. Why had she climbed up to the tree house in the apple tree from which, she claimed, she'd seen the glow of the burning smokehouse? Because, she said, she liked it there.

He'd let it go at that, not wanting to seem an ogre, but the next day, when the pieces of the puzzle were beginning to fall together, Kelly was even cagier and less forthcoming.

"Where is my aunt?" she'd asked him. "Is she all right?"

"Didn't your mother tell you, Kelly?" he'd asked.

"Tell me what?"

"Your aunt Diana is dead. She was in the smokehouse when it burned."

"Oh, dear," she'd said, with no more reaction than if he'd told her the latest news from Serbia. "How terrible."

That was when the first suspicion began to form. But it was already too late. He knew he'd never be able to nail her.

And anyhow, even if sweet little Kelly *had* begun to follow in the footsteps of Diana Turney, hadn't the bitch deserved whatever she got? Kelly had been, in that respect, an instrument of justice.

The district attorney wasn't going to make a public spectacle of himself by bringing charges against a six-year-old girl.

Still, he couldn't resist one final shot, just to let her know he wasn't that dumb. "Kelly, tell me one thing. Did you set that fire?"

Her eyes avoided his for a moment, and then ventured one triumphant glance that said, so what: he knew, and she knew that he knew, and there was nothing he could do about it.

"Wasn't it an accident? That's what Mommy said."

And that's what went into the report, death by accidental means. Case closed.

62

"And you don't remember anything *at all* about that night?" Carl demanded of his daughter, whose answer this time was even less forthcoming.

Indeed, after a quick tremulous shake, she retaliated with "Mother says you had *amnesia* about the whole time you were away. And *she* can't remember what happened since Mankato. Can't *I* have amnesia, too?"

"Fair enough," Carl agreed. "Let me ask you this, then. When did you start calling your mother Mother?"

"Well, what *should* I call her?"

"You always used to call her Mommy."

"Aunt Diana said Mother is more respectful."

Carl just nodded. He could imagine Diana saying that to Kelly easy enough, but there was something in the way Kelly talked about it that unsettled him. None of them were the same as they'd been a year ago. Maybe he had the same effect on the kid and on Janet. There was so much weirdness that they'd agreed they wouldn't talk about, that it was like living in a Bluebeard's castle in which every room was off-limits to everyone but the person inside it.

And now there was this latest weirdness for which Kelly had no explanation to offer, except that Louise Cottonwood had asked Kelly the last time she'd visited Navaho House if she would come along with her the next time she visited her son. Louise was dead now, but an old Indian from the rez had come round to the farm and asked if her parents would allow Kelly to go to Mercy Hospital in Duluth with him. The guy said he was Jim's "spiritual advisor" and registered as such at the hospital, where Jim was still lying in a coma. He couldn't explain exactly what Kelly had to do with it, except that Louise had recognized some kind of special spiritual power in the girl.

The whole thing made Carl uneasy and Janet suspicious. Both of them wanted to get back to everyday life and forget about all things misty and mysterious. But Kelly kept on pestering. She assured them that all she was going to do was kneel down by Jim's hospital bed and pray for him alongside Gordon Pillager. Carl and Janet could be there too if they wanted.

At last, more from curiosity than from any belief in the power of Kelly's prayers, they drove to Duluth in Carl's Chevy and reconnoitered with Gordon in the hospital's chapel, where he was all decked out in beads and feathers. Carl had been meaning to insist on getting an explanation from Gordon then and there, but it's hard to get serious with someone who's dressed up with such bizarre fuss.

Janet stayed in the waiting room, leafing through a copy of *Minnesota Medicine*, and Carl tagged along to Jim's room after a nurse, a security officer, Gordon Pillager (already shaking a rattle and chanting), and his own daughter, who'd been equipped with a fringed buckskin shawl, a beaded headband, and her own rattle. If Carl had still been a pig, he could not have felt any sillier or more conspicuous bringing up the rear of such a procession.

In the hospital room the nurse helped Gordon get Jim's limp body fixed up with its own array of beads and feathers, and then Gordon and Kelly really got to work with the noisemakers and bird imitations and even the Lord's Prayer, which Kelly delivered in a loud, complaining whine, just as though she were at the Shop 'n' Save getting ready to have a conniption if she couldn't get just what she wanted. Then, at some signal Carl hadn't caught, there was complete silence. Gordon squatted down on his haunches and covered his head with his feathered arms, and Kelly placed her own hands over the mouth of the man in the bed.

The first thing Jim said, after his eyes had fluttered open, was "Carl Kellog! My God, whatever happened to you, man?"

Carl was too flabbergasted to reply. (In any case, it was a question he was not about to answer.) Evasively, he answered another question, one that Jim ought to have asked: "We're at Mercy Hospital in Duluth."

Whereupon, looking bewildered and dropping the medicine rattle onto the bedsheets, Kelly looked at her father and asked the question for which he'd just given an answer. "Daddy—where are we?"

First Gordon, then Jim, and at last even the security guard and the nurse started laughing.

Carl had finally caught on to what had been happening, but he couldn't pretend to be amused. Kelly had been under some kind of spell (as Carl had been himself for such a long time), and that spell had finally been broken.

Kelly looked about the room in wonderment until her eyes fixed on the mirror fastened to the door of the wardrobe. "I'm all dressed up like Pocahontas!"

"That's because you're a Wabasha Indian now," Gordon informed her. Then he let out a Wabasha whoop of celebration, which prompted the security guard to signal, by a wave of his hand, that the hospital had its limits on freedom of expression even with regard to religious ceremonies.

Kelly approached the mirror, entranced. "I am?" She looked over her shoulder to her father for confirmation. "Really?"

"If that's what you want, honey, sure. But you'll still live at home with your dad and mom." Carl looked at Gordon, who had risen to his feet. "Right, Mr. Pillager?"

"Oh, yes. She can come to the Wabasha powwows, but she'll live at home. Except on nights when she's an owl, and then she'll fly to the moon."

"I will?" Kelly marveled.

Carl nodded, with some of the dismay that any parent feels on realizing that a child will grow up and leave the nest. "If he says so, darling, yes, I guess you will."

63

State Highway Patrolman John Gerhardi would never know that the perp responsible for his grandmother's death in the Navaho House fire was the same woman who'd made his own life so miserable by turning him into a pig. It's not likely he would have mourned his grandmother's loss that keenly if he had known of it. Having declared to his siblings, once and for all, that he was not going to help with any part of the never-ending expense of keeping the old babe in a nursing home, he had stopped visiting her. He had his own family to raise, after all, and he'd been too young to know his grandmother before she was sent off to Navaho House. He probably would have gone to the funeral if he'd been invited, his wife would have insisted, and he might have kicked in something for a wreath, but his only feeling would have been that kind of bite-your-tongue resentment we feel toward those to whom we've done a serious injustice.

In his few years of work on the highway patrol, John Gerhardi had accomplished more than his share of serious and not-so-serious injustices. He liked giving people grief: unlucky motorists, his wife, Lorraine, the kids, or anyone else who happened to get in his way. Usually there had to be a pretext for his lashing out when he did: somebody'd fucked up, and John was just setting the balance right.

Now that he was a pig, he didn't need a pretext. He could be as mean as he liked, and who was going to know? He'd missed Nam, but he got the impression from some of his buddies' more candid reminiscences that that was what it had been like there. The only problem with being as mean as he liked now was that a feral pig, living on his own, doesn't get many opportunities. He had no drivers to harass, no children to bully, no friends to spar with, not even the proverbial dog to kick. He could snarl at smaller animals, but not pursue them; he could start deer, and snap at the few cows or sheep he came upon, but this was not grazing land. And he had to be wary of humans, even of children, for he knew he might be hunted down.

Already the leaves were turning, and soon enough the hunters would be out with their rifles and scopes. John himself, if he had not become a pig, would have been out there with them in his new orange camo fatigues from the Minnesota Waters and Woodlands mail-order catalogue.

And so when he came upon Diana in the private hidey-hole he'd dug for himself, John was not disposed toward a policy of coexistence and tolerance. This was his last chance to wreak havoc and have some fun. Even if the human remnant of his mind had not recognized her as the one responsible for his present problem, the pig component of his nature would have gone after her. Pigs don't like snakes.

The hidey-hole was under a ledge by a big rock at the edge of the swamp where the woods ended and bogland began. When John had first found it, the rock had been freshly swathed with yellow POLICE tape by way of marking the scene of a crime. The tape seemed unnecessary, for the spot attracted no other visitors than John himself.

As the days grew shorter and the rains set in, the space John had hollowed out under the rock ledge had a double benefit, for it kept off the rain from above and it formed a nice slurry of warming mud into which he could wedge himself for a night's sleep.

Diana's reasons for returning to the rock were more complicated than a simple need for warmth and shelter. Chief among them was John's presence, for he was the last evidence of her witchcraft. By a quirk of topography of the sort that blacks out TV and radio reception in some areas, John had remained unaffected when others under the enchantment of Diana's witchcraft and the mandragora had reverted to human form. Even those ectoplasmic anemones that had been the eruptions of Wes Turney's unquiet spirit had vanished from the smokehouse area of the Kellog farm, for Wes Turney had achieved the vengeance that he'd sought and was, at last, at peace.

So all the evil that had swollen recently to such prodigious dimensions had shrunk back to just this innocuous garden snake, slithering nervously about lawn and pasture, woodland and bog, her human nature abrading more with each passing day, and snake in the ascendant.

Yet when Diana came upon John Gerhardi, enough of the witch still survived in her makeup, enough of the human in his, that the encounter was not just one more episode from the world's endless miniseries of nature red in tooth and claw.

When John lunged at the snake that had so unwisely ventured into the shadowy warmth of his hole, and when he caught the luckless thing in his powerful jaws, there was still some ethical and human dimension to the encounter. It even appeared, for a little while, that Diana might enjoy some final, Pyrrhic victory, for even though John had done, and continued to do, irrevocable harm to her snake body, he had chomped down too far back from the head of the snake and its needle-sharp teeth. She got his right eye first. But John was an obstinate fellow. His own jaw remained clenched tight.

They died in that embrace. Only one of his eyes remained within range of her spasmodic jaws, and he found his way to the edge of the swamp, where bog gave way to quagmire. Her spirit, sensing his intention, begged to be released. She was more desperate than she had been in the flames of the smokehouse, for Wes had been with her then, and she'd known he had the power to save her. And so he had—for this.

John Gerhardi died quickly, but it takes a snake, even a badly wounded snake, a long time to drown. Indeed, some little shiver of sentience survived in the decaying tissues of the snake until the first firm freeze late in November. Then Diana Turney was gone, and even God Almighty could not have resurrected her.

64

On the night before he was to leave for the seminary, Alan Johnson came to dinner at the farmhouse, along with Jim Cottonwood. They had brought two bottles of French wine, but either it was spoiled or none of them knew enough about wine to appreciate its fine points.

After they'd toasted each other with the fancy glasses, Carl and Janet switched to beer, and Jim and Alan opted for Shop 'n' Save diet cola, the only soda in the icebox.

The food was no better than the wine. A strict vegan dinner is hard enough to cook for company at the best of times, and the Shop 'n' Save produce department was a pretty sorry sight at the end of November. The main course was baked acorn squash, with a side dish of lima beans, and another of brown rice, but without butter, without eggs or cheese or milk, the veggies were pretty dull and a real dessert out of the question. Even Jell-O, it turned out, is taboo for vegans. But no one complained, not even Kelly. In its constraint and blandness, the dinner reminded Alan of those his mother had cooked at the rectory.

"So," said Janet brightly, "how long does it take to become a minister?"

"Well, if I take a heavy load and do summer sessions, I can get the degree in five years."

"Well, I won't sell the church to anyone else till you're back here," Jim promised. "If it's the church you think you'll want."

"I don't suppose many of my father's parishioners will be left by then, and if there still is one or two, I don't figure I would be their first choice for a minister. People like to have ministers more their own age."

"Why do you *want* to be a minister?" Kelly asked in the voice she reserved for boring conversations with grown-ups. It was the question they'd all wanted to ask.

"I'm not sure I do want to, exactly. It's more like the wine we brought. It's something you're supposed to do. Once they're a certain age, people are supposed to get jobs, and I'm already older than that. Maybe it'll turn out it's the wrong idea. But I've got a head-start, kind of, since I did all the office work for my father."

"I thought Reverend Johnson was your grandfather," said Kelly.

"He was that, too," Alan agreed.

"And you, Mr. Cottonwood," Janet asked, using a hostess's prerogative to change the subject. "What are your plans for the future?"

"I don't know. A race car driver? A rock singer? Those were the leading ideas I had before I was put away. A few days ago I signed up at the unemployment office, and I'll find out what they can offer along those lines. But my lawyer says the settlement he's hammered out with the state will work out about the same as if I'd been a lottery winner. So that's my plan for a career, winning the lottery. How about you?"

She had had no intention of springing the news this evening. But once she had blurted it out—"I'm going to be a mother," adding, so there would be no confusion, "It will be a boy this time"—she felt a heaven of relief.

Jim Cottonwood was the first to break the ensuing silence with a quiet "Congratulations."

"I'm going to have a brother?" Kelly marveled.

Janet nodded. "Sometime in March."

"How long have you known?" Alan asked.

"Since just after Grandma Turney's funeral. But that didn't seem like the best time to make the announcement, everyone was in such a state. I'm sorry, Alan, I should have said something before this. Carl has been after me, but—" She sighed. "It's hard to be honest about *everything*."

Janet looked confidingly at Jim. "Which is what we all agreed we were going to try and do, Carl and me and Alan. We'd talked it over and agreed that all the problems people have come from their not being up-front about things."

"I'm the father?" Alan finally had the nerve to ask.

Carl nodded. "I'm pretty sure I'm not, and Janet says you're the only other candidate. But nowadays, with DNA testing, you don't have to settle for a good guess. You can nail it down, as you know from experience. I don't see any practical difficulties. Janet and I are looking forward to bringing up a boy, and we're well fixed for money, thanks to the insurance. And we hope you'll be a regular visitor."

"But I thought you said you wanted to move to Arizona?"

"To Scottsdale," Carl said, nodding. "As soon as we can sell this house. We've got it listed with three different agencies."

There was another silence, and then Kelly said, "Doesn't anyone want to know what *my* plans are?"

"Of course, sweetheart," said Janet, rising to clear the dishes. "What *are* your plans?"

"I want to be a teacher. Like Aunty Di."

Thomas M. Disch (1940–2008) was a best-selling and prolific American science fiction writer and poet. His books won several awards, including the Hugo Award for Best Nonfiction Book in 1999.

Elizabeth Hand lives in Maine and London. Her books include *Winterlong, Aestival Tide, Icarus Descending, Waking the Moon,* and *Generation Loss,* and her story collections are *Last Summer at Mars Hill, Bibliomancy,* and *Saffron and Brimstone: Strange Stories.*